OFF THE ALGO

A NOVEL

MICHAEL W. BARNES

Off-the-Algo.com
Twin Nickel Press

ISBN: 979-8-9864963-2-0

A warrior may worry and think before making any decision, but once he makes it, he goes his way, free from worries or thoughts; there will be a million other decisions still awaiting him. That's the warrior's way.

– *CARLOS CASTANEDA,*
A Separate Reality (1971)

I'm inclined to reserve all judgments. The abnormal mind is quick to detect and attach itself to this quality when it appears in a normal person. And so it came about that I was privy to the secret griefs of wild, unknown men. But my tolerance has a limit. A sense of the fundamental decencies is parceled out unequally at birth.

– *F. SCOTT FITZGERALD,*
The Great Gatsby (1925)

OFF THE ALGO
MENU OF CONTENTS

Epilogue | 446

Annex | 450

Endnotes | 465

Author's Note | 476

TWO WEEKS AGO

SYDNEY AND LOS ANGELES

Sydney.

THE TEXT ALARM awakened the Aussie just after midnight. He hit the snooze button and gently shook his girlfriend's shoulder to wake her. "There's a chase starting, love." He got out of bed, shuffled into the living room and powered his laptop out of its sleep mode.

His girlfriend, clad only in a thin robe, emerged from the bedroom and joined her boyfriend next to the computer screen. The smell of the prior evening's dinner still hung in the air. Two nearly empty bottles of wine rested on the sofa table. A peeper might guess that some emergency warning had just been received that was sufficiently alarming to justify their getting up in the middle of the night. "I'm going to cast it to the TV," he said.

The image from the computer screen flickered onto the large screen television, illuminating the dark room. It was a live event feed of a police vehicle chase. A watermark reading "CKS" was burnt into the video stream, which featured an older SUV speeding along a boulevard with flashing blue police car lights visible in the distance against a pre-dawn sky. The screen constantly repopulated updates in data windows which resembled a television broadcast of a horse race. Various bidding data streamed along the screen's margins.

"I'm bidding a green soldier," said the now wide-awake Aussie. "I get points just for the punting."

His girlfriend had also awakened, and this was not her first time watching this kind of spectacle. The Aussie typed in his hundred dollar bid amount while his girlfriend began her color commentary.

"Only ten seconds left to bid. Holy shit, it's up to twenty thousand dollars!" she said.

The screen image scrambled for a moment but came back with a sharper digital image seemingly feeding from a better camera. The point-of-view of this video feed was from above the speeding SUV, somewhat like a high-def video of a drone missile about to be fired upon a nest of terrorists.

The screen graphics revealed that a player with the moniker 'Urban Toreador' had placed the winning bid of forty thousand dollars in this pop-up worldwide cyberspace auction attended by thousands participating online. Urban Toreador's bid entitled them to a two-minute window to pilot an attack drone now circling above the rogue SUV. A timer embedded in the CKS screen frame was already counting down the time remaining before a runner-up bidder would take control if Urban Toreador failed to fire.

No one really knew what CKS meant, but a world of die-hard fans pretended to know the "real story." Fan chatrooms buzzed with backronym rumors that it meant "Chase Kill & Split," "Car Kill System," or "California Kamikaze Squad" among others.

There were several audio feeds on the CKS screen accessed via various buttons – the local police radio, the local television news stations, the microphone feed of the Urban Toreador bidder as he narrated his own hunt, and numerous live channels of group chat rooms organized by various fans. One window showed the rapidly increasing number of viewers as the live feed went viral across the globe.

South Central Los Angeles.

Rodrigo Nuñez figured that it would take less than a month for him to conquer the remaining turf in this particular Los Angeles gang war. The knuckles of his hands gripped the steering wheel and displayed his Mara Salvatrucha gang tattoos, more commonly known as MS-13. He felt pride, like he was flying his gang colors in a battle.

Rodrigo Nuñez was only 22, but had taken charge of his south Los Angeles faction of the MS-13 gang comprised mostly of young Latino males. Historically, the neighborhood blocks had been fought over by Crips and Bloods gang factions, but membership in Rodrigo's MS-13 gang was swelling. His current plan was to kill a few remaining local Crip leaders and take over their lucrative drug turf.

Rodrigo had street smarts and preferred to attack before dawn, which was exactly what he was currently doing. In two attacks during the past week, Rodrigo had ordered some of his younger MS-13 minions to raid the targeted houses with orders to "shoot all the men and ask questions later." Two of his young recruits had died in that week's attacks, but Rodrigo had successfully taken down three top Crip gang leaders. Messy, perhaps, but to Rodrigo sacrificing a few pawns was a necessity now and then.

Rodrigo never did the shootings himself. His M.O. was to remain blocks away from the immediate vicinity of the raid thereby eliminating the chances of being arrested at a crime scene. After an attack, his recruits had to find their way to a rendezvous point blocks away from the shooting. Safe from the responding police squads, Rodrigo would then escort the young gang recruits away in a getaway vehicle fresh from their kill. Rodrigo's gunners – still high on adrenaline - could engage any rival Crips or Bloods gang members who might be in pursuit. His squad leaders also had orders from Rodrigo to shoot any minion who might get seriously wounded and be unable to escape the cops – Rodrigo didn't want small fry witnesses ratting him out. Best of all, Rodrigo knew that he was holding a sort of get-out-of-jail-free pass. He knew that the Los Angeles Police rules forbade the cops from pursuing a high-speed car on surface streets. If any police car began to chase him, he could simply accelerate to 90 mph, and the chase would end. To Rodrigo, the choice was simple: If a cop was on your tail, speed fast and you go free.

And now, just after his juniors had completed another shootout raid, three of his young guerilla fighters had arrived at the rendezvous point and jumped into his getaway SUV which he had stolen from a towing yard the night before. As he drove east on a surface street as the sky was showing first light, a police car passed him and did an abrupt U-turn and turned on its lights and siren. Whatever had caused the cop to suspect that Rodrigo's SUV was worth stopping, Rodrigo was not going to chance it. He accelerated hard swerving in and out of the few cars carrying night workers coming off their graveyard shifts. He was quickly traveling at freeway speed on the surface street. The police car stayed in pursuit for about half a minute, long enough to call in the fleeing vehicle's location and direction, but then it fell back, as the officers were unwilling to violate LAPD's prohibition against high speed pursuits on neighborhood streets.

Rodrigo continued speeding until he lost sight of the police car and slowed as he turned a hard left onto South Central Avenue. Rodrigo figured he had five to ten minutes to escape before a police helicopter might arrive. That was more than enough time. The 105 freeway interchange and overpass were just a few minutes ahead, which was an ideal place to ditch the SUV and scatter away along with his passengers as planned.

After a few minutes of driving, Rodrigo could see the freeway overpass on the horizon. Far off behind him in the rearview mirror he could see the flashing blue lights of a couple of police cruisers. His three passengers were still giddy with adrenaline and excitement from the night's events, and their voices mixed with the beat of the music on the car stereo. "¡Órale! No hay bronca, guey," said Rodrigo to no one in particular.

Rodrigo was in control, and he realized that he had won again. It had been a good week, he thought. Within days, the Crips' territory would belong to him. He was almost there.

Momentarily lost in his victory thoughts, Rodrigo did not initially see the drone as it circled over him.

Sydney.

Despite the hour, the Aussie and his girlfriend closely watched the technique of the winning bidder in the CKS shoot. Whoever this 'Urban Toreador' bidder was, they didn't go straight for the instant kill. Instead, Urban Toreador showed off a bit during the two-minute time window by standing off in a circling maneuver above the speeding vehicle, like a sniper repeatedly centering the crosshairs of a gun scope onto a target. Then, with about half a minute of their allotted time remaining, Urban Toreador banked the drone and dove in a straight course directly towards the SUV target. Urban Toreador was aligning their shot. The CKS screen showed the 100-meter range to target, and it was closing quickly. Contact was now only a matter of seconds.

The drone was approaching the SUV at a 45-degree angle from the vehicle's front right side. The Urban Toreador bidder nudged the drone's nose downward, dropping it to treetop level. Suddenly, like an approaching train, the

SUV target was now just 50 meters away. The on-screen targeting grid flashed a green "on trajectory" message, and then the screen image vibrated as Urban Toreador fired the drone's taser lead wire at the moving vehicle.

The Aussie and his girlfriend were engrossed as the screen showed an orange tracer directly hit the front grill of Rodrigo's SUV. Mesmerized, neither noticed that the girlfriend's silk robe had slipped off her shoulders leaving her almost naked as she was transfixed on the screen.

A pop-up gauge on the CKS screen showed that 52,320 volts, at over 200 amps, had just been delivered into the getaway vehicle.

The girlfriend softly noted in amazement, "Bloody Christ, he just rammed into that lorry," as if everything else that had just transpired on screen was somehow normal.

South Central Los Angeles.

Rodrigo first noticed the drone when it turned and headed straight towards his windshield. This was not the random fluttering of some airborne trash. As the drone quickly closed upon Rodrigo's getaway car, he was momentarily confused. Before his brain could process anything further, there was a brusque popping sound followed by the car's stereo speakers falling silent. The entire car shimmied, as if the car had just bent a wheel rim in a giant pothole. The SUV's control panel went dark.

The car engine died, and Rodrigo and his three passengers lurched forward as if he had braked hard. The SUV yawed to the left and the front left wheel bounced on and off the cement road median. He tried to steer to the right to get his faltering car off the street, but the steering was mushy. Rodrigo sideswiped a delivery van in the lane next to him, and the impact punched his car right back into his lane as his disabled car rolled to a stop. Rodrigo desperately tried turning the key to restart the engine, but there was no sound. The car was dead, and panic set in with his passengers. With the car stereo silent, the faint sirens of the police cruisers grew louder. Only a few cars dotted the intersection a block ahead, as the morning rush hour traffic was still an hour away.

The three gang recruits in the car with Rodrigo were now breathing hard in a full adrenaline-fueled panic. One of the shooters started pounding on the window of the SUV. A moment later, the smell of feces filled the air, as one of them shit his pants. Rodrigo tried to roll down his own window, but the switch was dead. Everything in the car was dead.

The soft whopping sound of an approaching television news helicopter could be heard faintly. The video feed from the television copter appeared in a new window on the CKS site. A police helicopter would undoubtedly arrive shortly. The blue flashing lights of the police cruisers drew closer from behind, now just a few blocks away. Rodrigo and his gang assassins were trapped inside a stolen car, in full panic knowing that the police would be surrounding them imminently.

Rodrigo reacted in a flash. He didn't care about his three gangbangers. His best chance to save his own skin was for everyone to flee on foot. Rodrigo could escape while the cops focused on the other three. He yelled, "Go, go, go," and the three gangbangers opened their doors and ran. Rodrigo paused for a few seconds, and then jumped out and ran across the median, trying to find a seam between the few cars on the road. A short distance away, two police cars drew near. The news traffic helicopter was now hovering overhead and a police copter had just arrived. Two backup police units were just blocks away.

Rodrigo's escape was a complete bust. In less than two minutes, guided by instructions from the police helicopter above, the police had found, tasered and handcuffed Rodrigo and all three of his shooters.

In their panic, Rodrigo's gang had all left their weapons in the abandoned vehicle.

Once the chase ended, a CKS operator took control of the drone and piloted it silently away from the scene back towards its hidden garage. The CKS feed switched its main display away from the drone's camera to a televised feed from the news helicopter. A global audience continued to watch the live takedown and arrest of Rodrigo and his gang.

Almost 30,000 bidders from across the globe had wagered for the privilege of tasing Rodrigo's getaway car while a worldwide audience of 100,000 viewers watched. Within a day, over 10 million global viewers would watch the highlight video, after yet another round of publicity was provided by talk show hosts and social media influencers lampooning the urban hunt.

Los Angeles Mayor Paul Gonzales called a press conference to denounce this "grotesque spectacle." He declared a $10,000 bounty for information leading to the arrest and conviction of the CKS drone perpetrators. Later, at a private meeting with his key staff, the Mayor issued an ultimatum: "This is war. If these drone vigilantes are not arrested, I will fire every one of you, and you will never work in government again. Go!"

Two days later, a law firm petitioned the court to allow Rodrigo to be permitted to host a daily podcast from the county jail while awaiting trial. Rodrigo's social media account already had garnered tens of thousands of followers. Two television networks hastily announced development projects for reality shows called "Drone Bounty Hunters" and "Tasers Over Sunset."

FREEWAY AMBER ALERT

THE LOCAL TV news station's afternoon anchor heard the direction in his earpiece as he narrated the helicopter footage of a speeding vehicle on a Los Angeles freeway. "We're cutting over to our Spanish-language sister station Radio KMMC in Anaheim, 890 on your AM dial," said the reporter. "We have with us a Martina Garcia, who is the mother of the girl in the vehicle that we've been covering here the last half-hour. Ms. Garcia, can you describe what you are going through right now?" asked the anchor, hoping for an emotional display to punctuate the all-too-common car chase being broadcast by his station.

The DJ at Radio KMMC translated the question for Ms. Garcia who spoke rapidly in Spanish. Her emotional anguish was manifest in her rapid-fire exclamations, which were instantaneously translated and captioned into English on the television screen. "Where is the little airplane, the drone, to stop these monsters? I pray to the Virgin and to Jesus, bring my baby back to me… Salva a este niño, Dios. Te lo ruego por favor!"

The Amber Alert car getaway chase had been broadcasting on CKS for over five minutes, and now had over 10,000 viewers and increasing by hundreds every few seconds. Two viewers were sharing a terminal watching the spectacle. The well-dressed man looked over the shoulder of his 12-year-old son, both transfixed by the car chase image on the screen of the PC in the son's bedroom. The room was typical of a pre-teenager, but from the décor it was obvious that this was a wealthy family. In fact, they were successful second-generation immigrants from Mexico running retail financing businesses for immigrants. "OK, you can bid $25,000. This is for your birthday. And son… don't miss," said the father, almost sternly. The boy placed the winning bid on the CKS portal, and with excitement took control of the CKS drone. For a minute, he piloted the CKS drone towards the speeding car barreling along on the freeway. The Amber Alert activation of the local emergency broadcast channels portended that this was a kidnapping of a minor.

As the son piloted the drone into shooting position, the TV channel continued with the histrionic lamentations of the mother of the abducted girl. The CKS feed included the image and sound of the television station's broadcast and its audio, and it trailed the TV audio by almost a full second.

The aural effect caused the wailing woman's voice to echo, almost as if the repetition was for dramatic emphasis.

Then the son took the taser shot. His shot hit the getaway vehicle, and it lurched and then slowed as its engine died. Several thousand "thumbs up" approvals registered on the CKS screen. The young shooter was ecstatic, and his father had a look of pride on his face. "Best birthday present, ever!" he said to his dad, as he continued to enjoy the upvotes from the CKS audience for his kill shot.

In less than a minute, police cars surrounded the disabled car and the drama ended.

The mother of the kidnapped child continued narrating the TV feed in hysterical Spanish. It was pure pandemonium. As the mother realized that the getaway car with her child had been stopped, she exclaimed – all captioned in English on the TV feed - "Jesus and the Virgin have answered, they sent the blessed little airplanes, they saved my baby!"

"That pretty much summarizes the situation here," intoned the TV news anchor. "A heroic rescue by the mysterious good-guy drone force."

ON THE PALESTINIAN BORDER

Colonel Majedah Simon of the Israeli Defense Force stared at the monitor. A team of eight IDF soldiers was in place, plus one sniper and two spotters. They were in a rundown

Palestinian residential area three miles outside of Israeli territory. They had solid fresh intelligence that the interior courtyard of a building had been used to launch as many as six rockets into Israel, part of the daily harassment of the intifada campaign to terrorize Israeli civilians. Worse, the intelligence indicated that there was a veritable bomb factory in the basement of the building, and that a top-floor flat was being used as a targeting range spotter for the rocket crews.

The monitor streamed high qualify real-time video from an Israeli drone. The rocket launch pad building was lit up with several infrared lasers by the spotters, and Israeli missiles could destroy the target within thirty seconds of the order being given.

As the drone came about, the interior courtyard of the building came into better view. At first obscured by a shadow, in a moment the image clarified, revealing a three-meter-high rocket sitting on a primitive wire launch pad — an inviting target verified by high-definition video. As the drone image streamed in, there was no indication of anyone attending the rocket.

"Hold fire," said Majedah. "Repeat, hold fire."

After a moment, a voice said, "Copy that, Team K7 holding fire."

"Sergeant, are you seeing anything from your position?" asked Colonel Simon over the radio to the IDF squad commander on the ground. Her crisp military intonation left no doubt as to who was in charge.

"Nothing unusual, Colonel," replied Ben Lincoln, the squad sergeant.

"Street traffic?" asked Majedah.

"The street is pretty quiet from our vantage, Colonel. Empty," radioed the squad leader.

Majedah paused a moment, and a frown appeared on her forehead, which then spread to her entire face. Majedah's aide, Rebecca Biton, worked long hours with her boss, and was well attuned with situational awareness in these settings. Rebecca could see the evolving expression on Majedah's face. Perhaps Rebecca was the only person in the room other than Majedah to understand that the chemistry in the room had just changed.

"Hold in position," commanded Majedah.

Lieutenant Colonel Majedah Simon was excited but concerned. The intelligence was solid, and the drone's video image was compelling. With the spotting team in place, the rocket launch site and arms factory could be taken out. It would be a successful mission, and a proud victory for her team.

But the rocket sitting unattended on the launcher was just too inviting. If the Israeli guided missile didn't perfectly hit its target, the entire five-story building might collapse, killing or maiming anyone inside. If all the casualties were militia members launching deadly rockets into civilian areas of Israel, so be it. But what if they weren't militia? What if this was just another apartment building filled with Palestinian civilians?

Why were there no militia men attending to the rocket? And why was there no automobile traffic outside? Had the area been ordered cleared?

Two possibilities sprang to Majedah's mind and were causing the intense look on her face. If the missile hit and took down the building, how many civilians would be killed? And if instead she ordered her team to enter the building, what would they find?

A brief memory flashed in Majedah's mind, the same memory that often visited her in high stress situations, when she sensed something was not quite right. She had learned to consciously push it aside. The haunting memory was of herself as a kid when her school in Beirut was on spring holiday. Her mother had just dropped Majedah off at a friend's apartment, which was a few blocks from the American Embassy where her mom worked part-time. As Majedah waited for her friend to answer the door, she saw a van race down the street and then crash through the outer gate of the US embassy. The van exploded moments later. Majedah ran down the street, but she could not see her mother's car, which had just turned into the embassy parking structure and was partially shielded from the blast by a low concrete wall. Nonetheless, her mom's car was flipped over and slammed onto another wall, and her mother was badly injured by the blast. The memory triggered the gamut of emotions in Majedah, including anger at the poor security preparation at the outer gate.

Majedah's distraction lasted only for a few seconds, and as she shook the memory away, her focus sharpened, and she made a battlefield decision. "Sergeant, get your team out of there, immediately. Repeat, abort mission, immediately, back to base. Hostile engagement imminent. Assume small arms and possibly grenades the moment your retreat is detected. Take all precautions but move with deliberate speed. Move it, now!" she commanded. If there was uncertainty in her mind, there was none in her command.

"Copy that, Colonel. You want everyone out?" Ben asked, to confirm her orders for the spotters and the sniper.

"Everyone out, now!" said Majedah.

"Copy that, we're bugging out," said the sergeant.

"Air support will be available in a few minutes at the rendezvous," Majedah added.

Majedah turned to the two uniformed officers also looking at the terminal. "Get those '64s in there, immediately," she ordered. "Fully armed for suppressing fire."

Three armored Humvee trucks approached the rendezvous point a few blocks from the targeted building, arriving from different streets. The extraction exercise had been practiced scores of times to the annoyance of the Israeli soldiers. As the team members emerged from the cover of the buildings to move to the rendezvous point, a fusillade of small arms fire began, coming from two adjacent buildings. Yet because of their training, including under simulated fire, the soldiers' movements were efficient and without error. They quickly moved several blocks to the awaiting Humvees. A few bullets ricocheted off the vehicles, but they were – for the moment - effectively out of range. That relative safety would evaporate in a fraction of a minute unless the Humvees exited without delay.

As the drone sent images of the Humvees beginning to speed away, one of the officers sitting next to Majedah advised, "The 64s are in range and have the target."

"Begin firing. Immediately. One salvo, and then get them out of there after ten seconds," she said.

The officer relayed the order, and moments later a hail of thirty-millimeter bullets shot from the machine guns on the two Israeli Air Force AH-64 helicopters, better known as Apache attack helicopters, began to slam into the adjacent buildings from where the AK-47 weapon fire was coming. The helicopters' machine guns were deafening, firing ten rounds per second, each round packed with enough energy to splinter a heavy wooden door. The effect was immediate. The windows and facades of the targeted cement buildings began to melt like beach sand hit by a wave. The militants' small arms fire ceased immediately, and on command just ten seconds later, the two AH-64s turned and escorted the three Humvees as they carried the squad several miles back to Israel.

Four Iranian-backed militiamen lay dead and another five were wounded. But another forty militia men remained safely ensconced within the interior of two adjacent buildings. Majedah Simon's suspicions had been correct. It had been a trap, designed either to capture or kill the Israeli squad. Had Majedah used a missile to attack the rocket launch site, per usual procedure, her team would have quickly attempted a visual on-site confirmation that the munitions and rockets had been destroyed. They would have been surrounded and attacked by four dozen soldiers. And if had Colonel Simon had instead ordered her team to enter the building to confirm the absence of civilians prior to launching the attack, the outcome would have been the same.

What five minutes earlier had looked like a surefire successful mission had been, in reality, a deadly ambush. And it had almost worked. To the eleven team members who had spent two days infiltrating three miles into hostile territory, undetected, it was an inexplicable failure. But that evening, their families, girlfriends and boyfriends would be oblivious to the disaster that had been averted and to the fact that their loved ones had been in a hot war zone just a few miles across the border.

When the Apache leader radioed that the Humvees had crossed back into Israeli territory, Majedah radioed to the team, "Let's reconvene at 9 am. Lieutenant Abrams, can you take charge of the intake of the team back at their base, please."

"Yes, ma'am," replied Abrams.

As Majedah turned to leave the room, her aide Rebecca strode out with her. Once in the hallway, Rebecca spoke up. "Colonel Simon… you look exhausted. May I order a car to take you home?" she asked.

"Thank you, Rebecca, that won't be necessary," Majedah replied.

Rebecca continued, "Well, may I drive you home, then. I… I think that was a little more intense than an ordinary day. I…."

Majedah stopped. She felt a chill in several parts of her body – it was the perspiration now cooling her skin as she emerged from the humid situation room. She realized that Rebecca was correct that it had been a very intense situation, and driving home herself was a bad idea, with post-traumatic stress being a risk.

"Thank you, Rebecca. That's an astute observation. Yes, you can drive me home. I'd appreciate that. I'll make my follow-up calls from home."

The truth was, Majedah only partially appreciated how traumatizing the episode had been. She was trained to override emotion and stress - almost too well. Her young aide often had to transition the colonel out of the battlefield mindset.

A MAYOR'S HISSY FIT IN LOS ANGELES

Vera Cruz, the Chief of Staff for Los Angeles Mayor Paul Gonzales, had just summoned the mayor's key personnel to her office. The local TV chyron and its website screamed, "Heroic Rescue by Mystery Drone." The AP and Univision newswires carried the same headline.

The mayor was not going to be happy.

Ten minutes later, after the mayor had been briefed, he spoke to the group in a measured tone, his fury barely contained. "I want the bounty raised to $100,000. I want the support of the governor's office. I want the feds to give me an open line to their tech rooms, so we can track and catch these criminal - 'vigilantes.'" Gonzales spit the word as if it were a forbidden curse word. He continued, "They are not heroes, and these drones are not holy. Jesus Christ does not sanction them. And the Amber Alert system will not be used by outlaws, by criminals, to make themselves into heroes. And they will not – I repeat, not – defy or defeat my administration."

After a dramatic pause, he continued, "We meet back here at 6 pm today. I want a full plan of attack in place, with details.

And cancel your dinner plans. Go!" The meeting ended, except for his chief of staff, Vera Cruz, who stayed behind.

"Vera, silo what I'm about to say away from anyone else. Get ahold of our best insider at Homeland Security. We need their resources. Maybe some kind of sting to catch these drone people. DHS and ICE runs these all the time. If DHS or ICE wants us to play nicely with all their demands for cooperation and information sharing, then they're going to help me – us – with this drone problem. But DHS needs to do this quietly. We're in campaign season. I need to score this victory, not the DHS. If it looks like I needed DHS to solve this, I look weak."

"Understood," said Vera. "Let me dig into that."

Within a few days, the publicity team of Los Angeles Mayor Paul Gonzales had staged a "command center" for the press. Almost a dozen computer terminals with glowing screens were arranged on several desks, and the walls were adorned with the mayor's official emblem with his name prominently displayed. It gave the impression that Mayor Gonzales was in control of the situation. It was classic stage-crafting, likely intended to become the footage for a campaign commercial.

A number of friendly journalists were assembled for a "deep background" briefing on the public dangers posed by the outlaw drones, all courtesy of the mayor's office. Gonzales' aide Vera Cruz highlighted the talking points with the journalists using PowerPoints and other visuals pulled up on the various computer terminals in the room. Unbeknownst to the journalists, a bureaucrat at the regional DHS offices had arranged a few of their technicians to manage the feeds going into those terminals in the war room.

At the end of the background briefing, Paul Gonzales entered the room right on cue. "It's great to see you all here. I'm glad that Vera was able to give you an inside look at this great danger facing our community, and how I'm – we're – working to protect hardworking residents of Los Angeles," he said.

After some more blather, one journalist floated a soft-ball question to Gonzales. "Your Honor, with all this advanced technology you've assembled, will you be able to track these drones back to their source, and put an end to this drone invasion?"

Used to being served easy questions, the mayor had become too confident that everyone would follow a script. He turned to his aide Vera and asked, "Vera, can you open up the comms with our guys?" by which he meant the DHS techs who were operating the screens on display. Vera showed her concern over that idea and paused enough of a beat that Gonzales should have known to catch himself. But he didn't, and Vera disengaged the mute button with the DHS team.

"Guys – and ladies – great job," said Gonzales. "A question from one of the fine journalists here – can you give a quick overview of how we'll track and trace the criminals running these drones?" Vera sensed it had been a mistake to accede to Gonzales' request for an open connection, and she was quickly proven correct.

The voice of the unnamed DHS technician came

through the computer terminal. He was used to providing factual analyst reports without the politician's double-speak. "They use an encrypted distributed network broadcast. Like if the old Napster was streaming a live concert. All the viewers form a peer-to-peer broadcast network. The broadcast alternates itself every few seconds among all the nodes, and it's mil-spec encrypted."

Mayor Gonzales followed up, "Thanks, and for our viewers, what does all that mean in plain English?"

The voice paused a second, and then replied, "It can't be traced. These guys are too good. The very best."

Even though the assembled journalists were all somewhat friendly to the mayor, the moment was just too juicy. The gossip started immediately, and by the end of the day, several insider media blogs had published stories about the "secret admission" by the mayor's tech office: "Secret Drone Squad Is the Very Best" and "Vigilante Drones Are Too Good to Be Caught." The *Los Angeles Times* ran with the story – and headline – the next morning.

It was a public relations disaster for the mayor – a debacle of his own making.

PRESENT DAY

PREDATORS BALL IN NEW ORLEANS

SEVERAL DECADES AGO, John Gabriel had adopted the city of New Orleans as a second home. As the years passed, he spent more and more time there. This Drone Convention, though, was a new thing.

In the 1700s, New Orleans was a mélange of French, Spanish, German and British settlers, and of course slaves. New Orleans had been the third largest city in the United States, but the Civil War changed the course of the city's future. It later garnered the nickname of the "Big Easy" on account of its relatively lax moral code, which resulted in it becoming one of the great "business convention" locations on Earth, typically hosting a hundred or so each year.

This week's big convention had been inaugurated

only three years earlier. It had grown so fast and become so popular that convention industry insiders referred to it – somewhat enviously – as a circus. Officially called the "Aerospace Industries Specialty Verticals Convention," or "AISVC," the event had somewhat flown under the radar its first two years, until a blogger with a video drone posted online his footage - shot through a hotel window - of a state senator and a Lockheed lobbyist wearing camouflage loincloths and holding toy bows and arrows, playing a version of strip pin-the-tail-on-the-donkey with three "ladies of the evening" who worked the local convention bar scene.

"Predators Ball at Drone Convention!" screamed the triple entendre on a popular social media site. Old timers appreciated the long-forgotten reference to an annual junk bond financier's convention in the 1980's. Middle-aged folks recognized the reference to the name of one model of modern military drones, the Predator. The average social media reader simply liked the name "Drone Convention." Overnight, tens of millions of people worldwide gained some vague knowledge that there was an annual Drone Convention in New Orleans…and that it was, well, not all business. Thus, the stage was set for the third year of AISVC, aka The Predators Ball, aka The Drone Convention, being held at the sprawling World Trade Convention Center alongside the Mississippi River in New Orleans, Louisiana.

Pavilion after pavilion of the third Predators Ball was packed with anyone who was, or wanted to be, somebody in the "drone" business. Drones themselves were barely one generation old. Since the 1960's, hobbyists had flown housecat-sized model airplanes with whining engines running on "glow fuel"- a high octane mix of methanol and nitromethane. In the 1980's, hand-sized toy helicopters had become a staple Christmas gift, typically not surviving longer than three hours after the box was opened. In 2002, the US military began using a first generation of surveillance and weaponized winged drones during the Afghanistan War. A decade later, a convergence of model airplanes, small helicopter drones, video cameras and cell phones had begun in earnest, with an ever-increasing number of models available on Amazon and numerous other outlets. In short, the whizzing model airplane had married high-tech helicopter drones. The Drone Convention was like a huge wedding reception with various tribes and branches of the family gathering in one place.

For the week of the Drone Convention, New Orleans was a boom town in the fast-changing drone gold rush. Designers, manufacturers, financiers, buyers, sellers, servicers, regulators, venture capitalists, civil aviators, hobbyists, professionals, reporters, call girls, and a bunch of merely curious or geek-addicted locals flocked to the Drone Convention. Anything remotely related to drones, civilian aircraft, video technology or the like, could be found among the sprawling pavilions. Old-time aerospace giants such as Boeing and Lockheed had their sales teams on the floor. But it was the scores – even hundreds - of start-ups scattered about the pavilions that created the boom town, wild-west feeling. Most of the start-up entrepreneurs on the convention floor had not even been born when the American space program was landing astronauts on the Moon in the late 60's and early 70's.

The bureaucrats were in attendance, too. The FAA, the

CAB, Homeland Security, TSA, ICE, the Louisiana Governor's Office of Technology, the Congressional Technology Caucus, all the military branches, and even the FBI, United Nations, and the European Union – all had booths at the Space Convention.

This was the third Drone Convention that John Gabriel was attending. With the popularity of the convention skyrocketing, he had decided to take a very low-key approach this year. He intentionally blended into the convention crowds as he roamed the pavilions that housed everything from start-up drone companies and small operators to multinational aerospace contractors, hawking their high-end military and civilian drones. Many of the convention companies were small, one-to-three-person startups. Some were selling various drone control software. One company built drone hangars. Several others specialized in lighting arrays. Others sold various tools and utilities that could be used with drones – pick up arms, drop lines, and the like. There was a unifying theme, albeit unstated. Everyone at the convention viewed drones as a growth industry. John chuckled when he looked at the convention program and saw the number of regulatory agencies in attendance – the FAA, CAB, DHS, the Congressional Technology Caucus, even the FBI, among others. Even though drones combined parts made by the aircraft and rocket industries, they did not yet have their own legal designation with the FAA, and the turf battles over who would regulate drones were just heating up.

Many people attended business conventions to get noticed. John had the exact opposite goal. He'd purposely dressed down, in jeans and a muted blue and gray sports coat on top of a black T-shirt. Although he was six feet tall with an athlete's build, it was difficult to identify his age. Maybe early forty-something, or a well-maintained fifty-something? His sandy brown hair was covered by a dark gray baseball cap with the fleur de lys logo of the local professional football team – ubiquitous in New Orleans.

Blending in like a chameleon, John was attending the Drone Convention today to observe and learn. He was effectively on a reconnaissance mission, taking in as much information as possible, walking the pavilion floors, incognito, as a free agent, beholden to no one. John wore his "general public" credential badge as a tip-off to the salesmen that he wasn't a likely prospect as a buyer. This perfectly suited John Gabriel, allowing him uninterrupted flow through the countless booths in the scores of aisles in the many pavilions.

Raised in northern California and a lawyer by training, Gabriel had done his half-dozen- year stint at a big law firm early in his career – where you get twenty years' experience compressed into just a few years on account of the sheer number of hours toiled. A bit burnt out, he had stepped out of private practice to teach business and law school courses in "Business Law in Emerging Industries."

He eventually held a visiting adjunct professor title at universities in California, Texas, and New Orleans, meaning he could pick when and where he'd settle down for three months to teach a class or two. Entrepreneurial types tended to take his courses, and when several of his former students had joined start-up ventures, they often turned to him for some seasoned advice. John received founders' stock in some of those companies as part of his fee.

Two of the companies later launched successful initial public offerings of their stock and John made a very nice chunk of money. Just as importantly, success begat more opportunity, and thus more start-ups sought him out to sit on their boards of directors, and the process of stock sales continued. Venture funds began to seek his input, hoping to gain his insight into "the next big thing" being planned in someone's garage. John was acutely aware that he had been lucky with his timing, although he had worked hard and taken some risks in leaving the big law firm so young.

Having made a lot of money, John had gone on sabbatical, but one university realized that having some loose affiliation with him was beneficial to their recruitment of students who were interested in technology. John had thereupon transitioned to adjunct professor emeritus. He had no specific obligation to the school other than to show up once a year and sit on a panel or shake hands with donors. He was a sort of "friend with benefits" to the university.

In addition to his public face with the university, John was an investor in several start-up companies similar to those at the Drone Convention. John didn't chase publicity like so many of his colleagues who were desperate to appear on the newest issue of some venture capital or entrepreneur magazine. Nor was he a recluse. An observer might suggest that John had time to waste, dallying about with his various companies, hobbies and charitable work – perhaps because he did not have a wife and family. But that observation would miss the point. No observer would understand how John's seemingly disparate activities were connected.

In fact, John Gabriel had on his own volition developed himself into an undercover private operative. But he didn't work for any government or special interest. His objectives and missions were of his own choosing, unknown and undetected by those close and distant. But his existence as an outsider – under the radar and hidden from anyone's algorithm – was about to be challenged.

John approached a small booth manned by two slightly unkempt guys and a sunburned woman in their mid-twenties. She put down her cup of whatever coffee concoction she was drinking, as if emerging from what was probably the lingering fog of a hangover, and said to John, "Hi, welcome to Gumdrop Technologies."

"What a great name," John responded quietly. "Apollo 9, right?" With that, both guys in the booth turned their heads and started paying attention.

"Actually, yes. Not many people recognize that," replied the sunburned woman.

John looked at the product display piece hanging in the booth. It looked like a long surfboard with a coupling attached at the midpoint. "Apollo 9 didn't need an airfoil for Gumdrop to release Spider when orbiting the Moon," John remarked. "This looks interesting."

Her two wingmen, who in another setting could have been guitarist and bass player to her lead singer, stepped forward.

"I'm Samantha," she said. "Let me introduce Rand and Philip."

John nodded to all three but didn't give his name. Instead, he asked, "So the wing carries the drone to the target?"

Rand eagerly replied, "Yes sir. Our airfoil is like the original command module named Gumdrop. It travels to the desired area to release a surgical helicopter drone, just like Gumdrop deposited the lunar module to the moon's surface."

John was fascinated. "And the airfoil remains in the area and can retrieve the drone when before it runs out of juice?"

"Exactly," chimed in Philip, the other member of the team.

"What's your total aloft time capability?" asked John.

"We're in beta right now and have it at two hours. With our planned solar battery on the wing, our operational model will be about six hours," said Rand.

John wasted no time. "Are you looking for investors?"

Rand wasted no time in replying, "Yes, and…"

"Let's meet privately this week. You guys are on the right track," said John.

Three minutes later, after gathering the private contact information of the Gumdrop founders, John was back into scouting mode. As he roamed the pavilions of the Drone Convention, his cellphone rang. It was his assistant, Luke Mandeville. "Hi Luke," answered John. The din of the convention floor necessitated that he speak a bit more loudly than he otherwise would.

Luke jumped right into business. "No emergencies,

things are running pretty smoothly, I just have a couple of items to run by you."

"This is a good time, let's roll through them," said John. "Hey, before I forget, stop by Pavilion 6, there's an outfit called Gumdrop Tech, make sure you invite them to the Lead Cap party. Two guys and their marketing gal."

"Will do," said Luke. "Number one item, there was a bit of a ruckus in Los Angeles this morning. The CKS site was running a routine chase auction, but it turned out to be a kidnapping and the car was on an Amber Alert. The local media love the story and are referring to it as a heroic rescue by a drone. The mayor is sorta stuck, but he made some comment about interference with an official investigation, which endangered a student."

"Yeah, blah blah blah," replied John. "Jesus, the mayor is such a douchebag. Anyway, did the drone make it back to the landing port undetected?"

"It returned just fine, no tracking. We'll keep it iced for a week before we retrieve it. Anyway, we had over 150,000 live viewers, and almost 40,000 bidders," reported Luke.

"Can you ask the tech team – actually, ask Nick directly, I want his eyes on this - to go through the anti-infiltration protocols again. Let's make sure we screen out any potential nut job shooters who might be looking to do something stupid or dangerous," said John. "Hey Luke, there's a lot of background noise here, let me call you back a little later to go through the other items."

As he hung up, John realized that it would not be long before his assistant Luke would need staff. Luke had worked for John for several years, but John had actually met Luke almost two decades ago. Luke was a native New Orleanian, born in the Seventh Ward, otherwise called a ghetto. Back then, John had happened across nine-year-old Luke at a gas station. Luke was on a bike, tagging along with some older boys who were buying gas for their all-terrain vehicles, which were popular as rebel street rods. The New Orleans cops generally ignored the unlicensed ATVs driven by pre-teens and teens alike, as they had far worse crime to combat.

All those years ago, John had struck up a conversation with Luke and his three ATV pals. Luke had been noticeably younger than his pre-teen friends. John had asked them if they wanted to make some money with their ATVs that weekend doing some "plant bombing," which was really just a cool phrase for shovel work and gardening in vacant lots. Luke and one of his friends seemed interested, and that weekend, the friend actually showed up back at the filling station at the appointed hour. So too did Luke's mother, Cassandra Mandeville, along with Luke.

John had been caught off-guard and felt like a dumbass. It hadn't really occurred to him that a parent of a pre-teen kid might have some concern when the kid claimed he needed to go somewhere because some white guy had offered him money. Cassandra Mandeville was then a late-twenties single mom. She sported a blouse with the name of Luke's school, and Luke wore his school T-shirt. John, on the other hand, was dressed in the clothing of a manual laborer, and was driving a pickup truck. In short, he wasn't making a confidence-building impression on an already skeptical mother. Cassandra asked John a few questions as to what the work entailed, where it would take place, what was the pay, and tellingly – why didn't John just hire a few guys at the labor exchange parking lot half a mile away?

The last question made John realize how sketchy his labor proposition might seem to a concerned parent. "You know what, you have a point," John said. "There are some good guys at the labor exchange, but also a lot who aren't. I have a suggestion. Maybe I can also hire you today to supervise the boys and see what you think. Maybe it's work that is better suited for labor exchange guys. You'll probably have a better perspective on that than me because you're a parent." He then explained to her that Luke and his friend's job would be to shuttle several hundred tree saplings in one gallon nursery pots from several flatbed trucks across some narrow levies to a swamp restoration site that John was running. The ATV would be very helpful for that.

Cassandra was no dummy. "So, is there some opportunity for this to be a regular gig?" she asked.

"Yes. It's called the Bayou Benefactor Foundation, and we do this several times a month, so, yes, there's some opportunity," replied John.

"I'll take you up on your offer to be a supervisor today," replied Cassandra. "Mind you, just today to see what's going on."

After a couple more questions, including asking to see John's driver's license and insurance, she was satisfied. She followed John to the job site fifteen minutes away, with the boys riding in the back of John's truck along with the ATV. After about an hour at the site, she assessed that everything was on the up-and-up. She approached John during a break.

"I think I've 'supervised' enough here, Mr. John. Will you bring them back to the gas station when they are through?"

"Better than that, I'm happy to drop them off at your home if you'd prefer. And we can exchange numbers and I can text you in advance when we're closing up and heading home," he offered.

"OK, that would be great. And please, Mr. John, one other thing. Don't let Luke know that you are doing that. It's hard enough being an over-protective single helicopter mom, and it's probably tough for Luke, with his older friend, that his momma had to chaperone him out here today. So maybe let's keep the text reports to momma on the down-low for the rest of the day, so he can regain a little of that pride he mighta lost," she said.

John was duly impressed at the insight Cassandra had into a boy's psyche.

"Yes, ma'am, I'll be very discreet," said John, and they exchanged numbers. And so had begun an unusual set of relationships.

Thereafter, John had provided the tree planting and related odds jobs here and there for young Luke and a shifting group of neighborhood boys, but Luke always showed up, goaded on by Cassandra.

There were weekend days when Luke was John's shadow. Over time, it developed into a de facto mentoring situation. John soon realized that young Luke was a fast learner with a sharp mind. Over a decade later, Luke had successfully graduated college with a double major in civil engineering and history, with strong guidance from his mother Cassandra and some inspiration from John. Upon graduation, Luke's summer jobs with John easily morphed into his management of a nationwide tree-planting program that John had founded, based partly on the success of the weekend tree-bombing outings in the bayou outside of New Orleans.

A SPACE COWBOY'S PANEL

While John Gabriel continued to roam the floor in the start-ups pavilion of the Drone Convention, Wayne Palmer greeted visitors at his company's main booth in the aerospace manufacturers pavilion. Wayne was the CEO of the aerospace company General Space Ltd.

As a small group of men approached the General Space booth, Wayne's assistant, Maggie Needham, handed Wayne a briefing card. He studied it for a few seconds, quickly memorizing the names of the members of the approaching Brazilian Space Agency team. Wayne advanced toward the group, pretending to recognize its director.

"Senor Silva, what a pleasure to see you and your group here," said Wayne, with his hand outstretched. Their smiles matching their national pride, the Brazilians appreciated being recognized by Wayne Palmer. After all, there were thousands of attendees at the Predators Ball. "I've been wanting to show you personally the payload-on-demand features of our new quarterly orbital launches. It might be of interest to your national telecom companies as they upgrade," said Wayne. "Also, I'd like to show you the features of our new generation of sea-borne recovery pads, which would be a good fit with the Falcoa reusable rocket development program you announced last month. Brazil is well-served by your forward-thinking focus on your nation's own telecommunications satellites, particularly when guarding against the rising threats from hostile forces. That foresight may be the deciding factor that determines which nations remain free and prosperous in the future."

Wayne didn't miss a beat and laid it on thick. Minutes later, the four members of the Brazilian contingent were all smiles as Wayne and his key sales executives dazzled them. In that moment, Antonio Silva, the Director of the Brazilian Space Agency, was the most important space executive in the world. And the other members of the Brazilian contingent were all witness to it - courtesy of the force of nature named Wayne Palmer. And with that, General Space was in the running to supply a major satellite project in South America.

Wayne Palmer was larger than life - a Texas-sized persona but packaged differently than similar cowboys of prior generations. Unlike the Texas oil titans of the 1950s -1980s with their bulging bellies augmented by daily feasts of prime rib and scotch whiskey, Wayne was more in the mold of a tech titan of Silicon Valley. If Steven Jobs of Apple had been a lanky athlete who promoted space trucks instead of personal computers, he would have been Wayne Palmer's identical twin. Palmer stood six feet two inches and sported a close-cropped hair cut – tall enough to command attention, but not so tall as to cause everyone to ask whether he had played basketball. Although he was a Texan, he didn't wear a cowboy hat. He didn't need to. His booming voice and laugh matched his outsized presence in a room. Yet if he dropped his voice to a whisper, he garnered even more attention, as if the listener expected to learn some hidden secret of the universe.

As a young man, Wayne had been with the Marine Reconnaissance Battalion before being recruited into the Special Activities Division of the Central Intelligence Agency. Assigned to the Air Branch, Wayne took a special interest in the fast-changing aviation and space platforms. Now in his late fifties, he was firmly civilian and operated in the aerospace and space technology sectors. His competitors might snipe that Wayne's company was in the money-raising business, rather than the space business. While it was true that investors poured funds into Palmer's General Space Ltd., it was equally true that General Space was one of the leading space vehicle companies in the world. Its regular rocket launches were live streamed on social media, with multiple high-def cameras on board giving millions of viewers the thrill of a ride into space.

General Space launched rockets and put satellites in space. Initially, its clients were mostly telecommunications companies and governments. But unlike the CEOs of the traditional aerospace contractors, which had for several generations formed part of the military-industrial complex, Wayne Palmer had a knack for entrepreneurship and timing. In the past decade, government entities such as NASA had withdrawn from the nuts and bolts of the satellite business, leaving private companies like General Space Ltd. to fill the vacuum. And as the distinction between space rockets and aerospace planes became murkier as technology advanced,

General Space was also a leader in the growing fields of hypersonic and unmanned aircraft. These large drones – mostly used for military purposes - intersected with the smaller drone machines that looked like toy helicopters and delivered internet orders or made beautiful real estate videos. As such, General Space was one of the dominant players at the Drone Convention.

General Space Ltd. had attracted its share of opponents. Existing aerospace contractors that had reaped fortunes in the American space program and the Cold War defense buildup, were burdened by decades of union work rules, pension costs and bureaucratic red tape, rendering them unable to compete in the modern landscape of nimble tech startups. Wayne's company's success to date was in no small part because he had navigated the political waters and capital markets so well. But that had become more challenging. The new federal Transparency Act was threatening to impose an overwhelming level of regulation on Wayne's young business and was empowering his opponents to attack his company with red tape in the coming year when new regulations were set to go into effect. Wayne was no fan of the Transparency Act. It would strip General Space of the very nimbleness that defined its success.

With politics and publicity in mind, Wayne had made sure General Space was a key sponsor of the Drone Convention. It had booths in several different pavilions and was hosting several panels, one of which was an industry-regulatory panel discussion, entitled "Kitty Hawk, the Sea of Tranquility and Post Office Delivery-by-Robot: Drones and Government Oversight." It was the kind of title only a lawyer or a bureaucrat could love. But given the size of this year's Predators Ball, the panel discussion would be well-attended, including by the press looking for an angle for the news feed.

Just a few blocks from the World Trade Convention Center, Jill Serrano exited a taxi at her New Orleans hotel. She had just arrived from Washington DC. If you included her two-inch heels, she stood five feet nine inches tall and she wore her brown hair in a professional neck-length cut. Her classic skirt and jacket combination exuded just the right amount of professional standing as well as style consciousness. Jill attracted a few glances even though she was understated. She didn't need to make a spectacle of herself with loud colors, teenager fashions or dyed blonde hair.

Jill was attending the Drone Convention as a panelist on the General Space "Kitty Hawk" panel, appearing as the Department of Homeland Security's representative. Her DHS business card read, "DHS Liaison to FAA for Experimental Aircraft Certification Coordination." What she actually did was to serve as an assuring public face for the many government bureaucracies who were busy infighting over drone regulation and competing for the Congressional dollars that would be allocated to the winners.

Jill was a mid-level government bureaucrat, and a competent one. Although some might disregard her as merely being a government bureaucrat, Jill was adept like a chameleon, able to pivot as the circumstances demanded. She was comfortable mingling with the gamut of old-guard corporate suits, to start-up entrepreneurs, venture capital sharks and the usual stable of politicians and their entourages. Her job had worked well for Jill – the steady pay and benefits of a government post in a technical field had allowed her to be a great mother to her son after her marriage ended in divorce.

Standing in the hotel lobby, Jill finished a cellphone call with her son before checking in. He was facing midterms and needed a little coaching, which she was happy to provide. After listening to her anxious son, Jill said, "I think that's a good idea, Jamie. And just write down a list of the three things you think you need to work on the most, and then write two sentences describing each a little more. That exercise will move you forward in the right direction," Jill coached. "I'll call you back in an hour to see how you're doing. You're gonna be just fine."

Jill had a few hours to spare before her panel presentation, so she decided to head over to the convention floor early to have a look around and visit one of the General Space booths, which was a key sponsor of her panel. She registered at the convention desk and was issued an official looking credential with her name and affiliation, and with an orange bar on top to identify her as a presenter. It also had a small gold eagle in the corner identifying her as a "government official," a fair warning for tipsy private sector attendees.

Jill was raised in Texas, with a father who held technical and engineering jobs in the aerospace industry as it waxed and waned with the government funding behind each project. Because her father had to move to wherever the work was, her family never remained in any one city long enough for Jill to develop the long-term friendships and hobbies that most other girls enjoyed. Jill's interests were strongly influenced by her father, and she finished college with a mechanical engineering degree.

There weren't many women in that field, but Jill had held her own, acquiring the knowledge, skills, and experience to help government leaders establish rules for experimental aircraft, including drones, which were increasingly impacting people's lives. The news media exacerbated matters, not only with tabloid stories about peeping toms using drone-mounted cameras to spy through windows, but also labor market stories about drones replacing local deliverymen, and dystopian portraits of a surveillance state empowered by the constant eye-in-the-sky of fleets of police drones. And recently Jill's agencies had been inundated with news stories about the mysterious network of worldwide gamers bidding on a dark web platform that piloted drones to zap criminal getaway cars on Los Angeles freeways. It seemed that the Los Angeles mayor had Jill's office on speed dial, lodging multiple weekly complaints that the federal government "must do something," even though the problem was largely caused by the mayor's increasingly histrionic public clown-act for local television stations.

As Jill moved through the convention pavilions, she was surprised at the number of businesses represented at the convention. It truly was a booming industry. The sights, sounds and smells were as varied as those in a Moroccan souk. There was a robust background din, as hundreds of conversations and general bustle mixed to form a sonic blanket. She couldn't help wondering whether there was a place for her in the private sector.

Jill came upon the main exhibit booth of General Space, and she saw the nametag of Maggie Needham, with whom she had briefly dealt regarding her invitation to participate in the upcoming panel. Jill introduced herself, and Maggie in turn introduced her to her boss, Wayne Palmer, who thanked her for agreeing to participate on the "Kitty Hawk" panel.

"It's a bit of a man's game, isn't it, all this space and drone stuff?" Wayne asked Jill. Jill had spent most of her life around male engineers and military men and had long ago programmed herself never to take offense at how professional questions might be worded. She was hard to trigger, and she felt that women horribly disadvantaged themselves by falling prey to victimhood mentalities.

"That makes it easy to stand out, don't you think?" replied Jill. "And my guess is that Ms. Needham here might be a 'key man' keeping General Space together," she playfully added, nodding to Maggie.

Wayne smiled. "Did you two just conspire to cost me a bigger year-end bonus?" He immediately liked this quick-tongued panelist named Jill, despite the government bureaucrat star on her nametag. "And bonuses aside, I truly appreciate your coming here and helping out on this panel," Wayne said with sincerity. He turned to Maggie. "Could you give my private number and email to Ms. Serrano, so that she can cut through to me if she ever needs anything?"

"Absolutely, Mr. Palmer," said Maggie. Jill realized that she seemed to have just been rewarded with something

– access to Wayne - that Maggie spent all her waking hours trying to juggle.

"It's Wayne, please. So, Ms. Serrano," began Wayne…

"It's Jill," interrupted Jill.

Wayne paused a beat, and continued, "Jill, I must meet another group shortly. I hope the panel goes well, and I may swing by if things slow down here. Thanks again for coming." He shook her hand and exited. Professional, to the point but not too abrupt. He was a guy getting things done. Maggie then chatted with Jill and gave her Wayne's contact information.

"Does he do that with everyone?" Jill asked.

"What, give out his private contact information to someone he just met?" said Maggie. There was a slight, knowing pause. "Nope, apparently you cracked the code," said Maggie. "And quite quickly."

"Well, I won't abuse it," promised Jill. Maggie gave Jill an appreciative smile.

"I'll see you at the panel room in fifteen minutes," said Maggie. "I'll do a quick briefing there for you and the other panelists."

Jill made her way to the sign-in table near the large conference hall where the Kitty Hawk panel was scheduled to convene. Several of the other panelists were milling about, their orange-barred name tags identifying them. A few minutes later, Maggie arrived and greeted the panelists, and did some last-minute coordination with several General Space employees who were helping her run the panel.

Jill introduced herself to the other panelists. One was Percy Lacksman, a thirty-something aide to Senator Bob

Baxter, who was the current Chairman of the Commerce, Science and Transportation Committee, which was the designated Senate committee for handling various governmental aviation and space policies. The committee was a big-time lobbyist target, given its power over the big aerospace contractors and multi-billion-dollar contract oversight. Jill noticed that Lacksman wore a power tie with a matching pocket handkerchief.

Another was Jessie Wales, a young attorney with a big Washington DC law and lobbying firm. Jessie had brought his styling game, expertly meshing it with his big law firm's button-down establishment reputation. His slightly long hair and four-day stubble were all the fashion rage with young professionals.

Lindsey Zevon, a thirty-something senior vice president with General Space, was also a panelist. Zevon seemed to Jill to be a junior version of Palmer – a confident cowboy inside a burgeoning corporate organization.

The moderator of the panel was Kyle Duke, a technology writer for the *Wall Street Journal*. Kyle was the only participant other than Jill who was not wearing a tie, and he had what might have been called a goatee a generation ago. His blue button-down shirt was tucked in under his sport coat, but one got the sense that tucked-in shirts were an irregular occurrence in Kyle's daily life.

After Maggie had gone through some basics with the panelists, she turned them over to Kyle Duke for some specific panel preparation from the moderator's viewpoint. The video cameras and microphones were all queued to record the session, and a smattering of tech, aviation and general business journalists milled about, both seated and standing at the back of the room. Scores of eager attendees filed through the doors and took their seats, and the Kitty Hawk panelists moved toward the stage at the front of the room.

One of the Kitty Hawk panelists, Percy Lacksman, was no stranger to making up talking points to augment his career moves up the bureaucratic ladder. Percy was adept at operating in the vast apparatus of politically appointed personnel doing the bidding of their bosses, their sponsors, and their own careers. Percy wasn't shy about letting people know that his current position was the result of his superior talents, and that as Senator Baxter's aide, he was at the center of a fast growing "Transparency Compliance" regulatory sector of bureaucracies under the recently passed Transparency Act. "Aviation and Aerospace Transparency Compliance" was a euphemism for regulation of private aircraft and spacecraft manufacturing.

Percy Lacksman reveled in that feeling of power. After half a dozen years as a bureaucrat in state government, he had recently joined Senator Baxter's staff after being quietly "suggested" to Senator Baxter by the Clean Air Global Initiative lobby.

A HENCHWOMAN WITH A BENEFACTOR

Not everyone viewed Percy Lacksman's conceit as a negative trait. Properly managed, it could be useful, which was precisely why Ilene Meinhoff had taken an interest in Lacksman. Percy was the perfect cross between a useful idiot and a preening fall guy. A patsy.

Ilene Meinhoff might charitably be described as a fixer, a cleaner or a handler. Others would more accurately categorize her as a shady operator, a henchwoman and a nasty piece of work. And indeed she did work, for a billionaire named Seymour Gacy. Unbeknownst to Percy Lacksman, Ilene had pulled a few hidden levers to get Percy his current job with Senator Baxter's committee.

Ilene had the look of an aging hippie, no longer with youthful vitality but rather late middle-aged bitterness. Although she was Caucasian, she maintained her frizzy "afro" hair decades after sensible women had abandoned it, as if to signal her bitterness that the glorious worldwide collectivist revolution had not happened, angry that the Soviet Union had turned out to be such an embarrassing disappointment for radicals, consigned to the junk heap of history's failed totalitarian regimes.

Ilene had attained tenure at an early age at the University of California at Berkeley in the late 1970s as the first wave of radicals began to take posts in colleges. She and other faculty had successfully gotten the administration to abolish the grading curve, under the guise that a grading curve was merely a continuation of the subjugation of historically disadvantaged groups who instead needed a safe nurturing classroom – that is, the kind provided by her seminars on radical political thought – and that safe space meant that she was free to give all of her students an "A" if she so chose.

This racket had worked well for Ilene, until it didn't. A Berkeley fraternity boy learned from a girlfriend that Meinhoff's seminar course was a guaranteed "A", so long as one spouted radical anger on the written exams. The frat boy took the class, got an "A," and told his housemates. Ilene's course soon became sought out by the most unlikely of students – privileged frat boys.

At some point, the exact genesis of which never became clear, Meinhoff began accepting $500 cash payments from the frat members who didn't want to bother attending class or even submitting required essays. When one of these ghost students entered rehab two weeks after he paid the $500, his angry parents sought answers for their son's fall from grace, and among other unsavory details of their son's failed collegiate experience they uncovered Meinhoff's scam and the dozen or so frat brothers who had been run through her payoff system. Although tenured, Meinhoff was fired after a nasty but short battle with the Berkeley administration.

Seymour Gacy, a rising financial mogul, had tracked Ilene Meinhoff and her journey through public humili-ation, from the initial sympathetic stories in the radical communist Bay Area press to the full scandal reported by the *San Francisco Chronicle*. Over time, the man emotion-ally bonded with Ilene's predicament, and decided that with her assistance, he would do the important, hard work of tearing down the evil systems of the world. Seymour Gacy had quietly hired Ilene as an advisor to some of the radical front groups that he was funding. A few years later, when the public had moved on to the next outrage, Meinhoff took on a more active role in Gacy's operations. Energetic, bitter, and willing to buy fully into radical ideology despite the obvious personal issues involved, Ilene became the manager of the various corrupt and crony networks that Gacy maintained. She was a hammer of influence and graft, all at the direction of Seymour Gacy.

THE REVOLUTION WILL NOT BE EMAILED

Seymour Gacy's study was filled with caged birds. Exotics from around the world. One of the Caique birds squawked in its cage, as a nearby pair of Senegal parrots engaged in a minor cage spat. "Stop it you two," said Seymour, and the birds fell silent. A resident of Nevis and St. Kitts, a Caribbean tax haven, but Dutch by birth, Seymour M. Gacy spent most of his time in the tony financial capitals of the West: New York, London, Berlin, Paris, and Los Angeles. He was six feet tall, and his tanned face and half-bald head were like those of any number of wealthy European aristocratic types. But his gray eyes had a piercing quality that was vaguely threatening.

Seymour Gacy viewed himself as a brilliant, creative

man, much smarter than any world leader or Fortune 500 CEO. In reality, he was a fucked-up megalomaniac billionaire who more or less personified evil.

Seymour's coffee service had been laid out just so by one of his servants. Seymour was very particular, even precious, about the protocols his staff used when serving him. But Seymour was used to having his way. Not only was he a trust fund billionaire, or as some would call him, "a member of the lucky sperm club," he had enjoyed great success himself speculating in commodities' markets, thereby quadrupling the fortune his father had made in arms dealing and a contraband import/export business.

Seymour relished the campaigns he carried out through his worldwide political machine. As he issued his commands to his people, Seymour thought of himself as a secret freedom fighter. Seymour had just finished reviewing a stack of reports prepared by his operatives. The reports were gleaned from reams of reports now routinely filed by multinational corporations in accordance with the Transparency Act's requirements to disclose the terms of their contracts with the U.S. government, as well as the negotiations for those contracts. In an effort to establish a new secret police force within the government, Gacy had placed his chosen people on the all-powerful bureaucracy known as the Transparency Council, and in some cases the members were not only unaware that Gacy had put them there, but that he had handpicked many of their key staff. Gacy had a legion of loyal spies who routinely accessed the confidential data dumps, including all military and CIA "black-ops" contracts, searching for information that was useful to him.

One of the reports in front of Gacy referenced a technology company being engaged to provide money transfer tracing services for wire transfers out of Iran and Syria to Germany. The US would then share this information with the German police. These money transfers were known to be used by jihadist syndicates to deliver monies to their suicide bombers and soldiers in Western Europe. Seymour copied that section of the report and sent it to one of his staffers in Berlin on an encrypted email that read: "Leak this to the *New Dawn Today* reporter. Make sure it makes headlines. Hint that it's an excuse to stop medical monies for infant care. Kill the program."

Another report concerned an advertising campaign from a creative agency for a federal/state pilot program to advertise the availability of private school vouchers for the upcoming school year. Using his encrypted communications platform, Seymour forwarded the report section to one of his dozens of domestic operatives. "Get a protest group to the agency president's house. Stress there are fascist elements and racist overtones in the advertising," read Seymour's encrypted order.

Another report referenced a university's application for federal matching funds for its campus speaker series. Seymour forwarded the paragraph to yet another operative. "Target the next trustee meeting. Demand an end to Jewish speakers on campus. Claim that it is hate speech," read Seymour's directive.

The construction contracts were especially interesting to Seymour. One report described a parking lot paving contract at a hospital in Cairo, involving an affiliate of an American construction company. Fourteen Americans would be on site for a couple of weeks. Seymour forwarded the section, again using the encrypted email system. "Get this to MB, easy to target or hostage this crew," read Seymour's directive. "And run it through Awakened Dawn Foundation, give Rachid the full read-in," he ended. Awakened Dawn was one of Seymour's non-profit organizations through which he steered millions of dollars, supposedly to support humanitarian efforts. MB was the Muslim Brotherhood, a radical jihadist group operating in Egypt. Seymour subscribed to Stalin's quip that, "to make an omelet, a few eggs need to be broken."

Seymour viewed himself as a brilliant man deserving to be the master of the world. It was difficult to reconcile that with the fact that he'd built his fortune on inherited wealth and rampant fraud. Facing such cognitive dissonance, Seymour's brain had constructed the belief that he was not the evil actor; rather, the world economic order itself was evil and had to be destroyed. To him, his bad actions - like those of other heroic figures – were not bad, but rather were for the greater good. He had merely transgressed against an irredeemably corrupt and evil system, which made him a virtuous hero, not a criminal. By this mental delusion, he cleared his conscience. And so, with Ilene's assistance, he would do the hard and important work of tearing that evil system down. Whatever that meant.

Seymour had assembled a hidden influence and control mechanism over much of the federal bureaucracy under a law called the Transparency Act. Undetected, it was Seymour Gacy's power platform. He was pleased with how quickly it was hobbling the United States. Private contractors – from the pillars of the military-industrial complex to small, specialized forensic accountants and CIA mercenaries – could be targeted by foreign operatives, and military-technology espionage was facilitated. His two key objectives, and thus a 24/7 concern of Ilene Meinhoff, were to keep U.S. President Howard Jackson in support of the Transparency Act, in accordance with the promises that Jackson had made to Gacy when he had accepted Gacy's illegal ten-million-dollar donation to his fledgling presidential campaign. And equally as important as a fail-safe, to make sure there were never 67 votes in the Senate to override Jackson's guaranteed veto of any repeal of the Transparency Act. But with a vague understanding spreading among the American people that the act went too far in involving the government in private business affairs, the Transparency Act was becoming politically unpopular. With about 65 senators now opposed to the Transparency Act, Ilene had her hands full threatening and extorting a diminishing pool of senators.

Years earlier, Gacy had appreciated Ilene Meinhoff's troubled predicament as he witnessed it play out in the news. Perhaps it was his innate recognition that Ilene, like Seymour, had a similar strong subconscious drive to reconcile reality with an egotistic self-image. Now, from the Drone Convention, Ilene was speaking with Seymour Gacy about that very task. Gacy listened intently to Ilene's efficient delivery of her report. "Nine million dollars. Half of that will be in direct monies, disbursed to the three campaigns. The other half will be in opposition ad buys, directly against their opponents. These three are locked up. I know it's expensive, but their votes are solid. I know for certain," said Ilene, referring to her continuing efforts to keep a few senators from withdrawing their support of the Transparency Act.

"Excellent. Go ahead and draw the funds as needed," replied Seymour Gacy.

THE HENCHWOMAN IN ACTION

Shortly after her call with her boss, Ilene Meinhoff sat by herself in one of the Drone Convention lounges, waiting for her next meeting. The compressor of a soft drink cooler a few yards away was emitting a rattling hiss. Oddly, the annoying noise made her more comfortable. She was here to do dirty work, and a dirty work soundtrack was just fine with her. She had set up a meeting with Tim Hollings, the chief of staff for Senator Chuck Bloom, who sat on the Senate Subcommittee on Aviation Operations, Safety, and Security. That gave the staffer the excuse he needed to take a business trip to New Orleans with his wife, courtesy of the Subcommittee's travel budget. Little did he know that his cushy junket trip to New Orleans was about to involve some very hard ball play.

Hollings' boss, Senator Bloom of Indiana, was up for re-election, and Ilene had learned that Bloom was being offered significant campaign support from various trade groups that were opposed to new regulations that Seymour

Gacy had engineered to be promulgated under the Transparency Act. There were already enough votes in the House of Representatives to override an expected veto by President Jackson of any repeal or amendment to the Transparency Act, but in the Senate, any override of a veto would require 67 of 100 votes. The pro-repeal forces appeared to already have 65 votes, and they needed Senator Bloom to get closer to the magic 67 number.

Tim Hollings approached Ilene and said, "Hello, Ilene, glad to see you." Of course, he was not telling the truth.

Ilene squeezed her cheeks upwards and raised the sides of her mouth, like a mime trying to fake a smile. It was unclear whether she knew how horribly fake her attempted smile came off, or whether she cared. Ilene dove right in as Tim sat down across the small table from her. "I'll get straight to the point, Mr. Hollings. It's this simple. We have two security tapes. One, we have the bimbo herself on the video, telling the whole fucking story. And two, we also have the nanny cam tape that she made. Senator Bloom likes garter belts - who knew? We have the Senator's private credit card statements detailing the entire affair – hotels, jewelry, restaurants, Bloomingdales. And we have his girlfriend's bank records – all of them - showing that she received several hundred thousand dollars of campaign funds for 'campaign services.'

"And we have two other nails in the coffin that I'm not even going to tell you about. If we release all of these, every couple of days for a few weeks, Bloom's campaign is over. So is his marriage. And the wife will get custody of the kids. He might even go to jail – look what happened to John Edwards for the same thing. We know all of this, and now you know.

"Now, even though he has a relatively safe seat, we know the Senator needs money to win re-election," continued Ilene. "Half a million to scare off any primary opponents, and two million for the general election will suffice. But we'll provide you with twice that - four million dollars. It's the deal of the century. And the catch is simple: The Senator will never, ever move or vote against the Transparency Act. Period. Otherwise, we release it all. Jail, divorce, kids gone, all of it. So, make the choice. As the saying goes, 'Plata o plomo, 'Tim?" Ilene enjoyed using the lingo of narco-gangsters who often bribed people with the choice of silver or lead – that is, choose the silver or choose the bullet.

Other than his initial greeting, Tim hadn't said a word. He detested Ilene, and now he feared her. "How do we know that you wouldn't…," began Tim.

"You don't have any assurances. We're buying Bloom. He obeys or he burns. And we're giving him four million bucks. End of negotiation. So, stop the baby talk," cooed Ilene. "If I don't hear from you by 6 pm, then he'll burn. Tell the good Senator to take the money, Tim." With that, Ilene stood up.

"I'll – I'll – we'll get back to you by the end of the day," replied Tim.

The loud clanging of the nearby soda machine stopped. "Six p.m., and not a second later," said Ilene as she walked away.

Seymour Gacy now owned Senator Bloom. No one at the convention noticed the raw extortion that had just occurred in plain sight.

A MESSAGE FROM BERMUDA

At the Drone Convention, John Gabriel walked over to the pavilion where a panel on drone regulation was scheduled to take place. He'd read that it being moderated by a journalist named Kyle Duke. He liked Duke's columns in the *Wall Street Journal* and thought that Kyle's moderation would make the session worthwhile. On his way there, his cellphone rang. The caller ID on his phone indicated it was Kirk Woodbury, a friend and business colleague in Bermuda.

"Hey there, Kirk, how are you? I haven't heard from you for a while. How's the Devil Island treating you?" said John.

"Oh, it's all quite good, you know. So long as we avoid another Fabian, we're happy," Kirk said, referring to a legendary hurricane that had badly damaged Bermuda.

"I can relate; I'm in New Orleans right now and we still feel the same way about Katrina." They small-talked for a bit, and then Kirk asked, "Hey, I want to know if I can refer someone to you. They're good people, my colleagues and I have known them for a while, and they are very discreet, probably the most discreet folks I know. I can vouch for them on that, but sometimes I just keep my mouth shut, you know, no matter how good they are."

"I appreciate that, Kirk. So, what are they calling about?" asked John.

"They made an inquiry to my close associate here this morning about, uh, you know, how the heck that whole

Somali piracy thing was brought under control. They inquired very much off-the-record. I was surprised they called us at all. They hedged their question about 5 different ways, so I'm not sure if it was just a fishing expedition. Or maybe there is some kind of insider knowledge at play, I dunno. But they said they thought we might have some insight, however tangential. Again, I can vouch for this person, there's a level of trust there, but I played it very vague and non-committal. I provided zero information. They don't know whether our group or I have any information. The only thing that was relayed by my group back to the caller was that we would get back to them after we reviewed their request," said Kirk as he finished describing the odd inquiry they had received.

John didn't hesitate, which was a testament to his trust in Kirk. "Sure, so long as you can absolutely vouch for them. As much as anyone, you understand how we kept that off of everyone's algorithm. Right now isn't a good time, but maybe in a few hours?"

"OK, great. And just for protection, I will have my assistant forward their call through my office number, so when you see a call from my number in a few hours, it will be them dialing you. They'll be calling you completely blind, so you can have anyone answer the call — they won't know anything about you, your location or even your gender. I'll tell them they must make their pitch to whoever answers the phone, from square one," said Kirk.

"OK. I'll turn my voice mail off. Be sure to tell them to call back if there's no answer after five rings. And, you don't have any idea what they want?" asked John.

"I know who they are, but I'll let them divulge themselves to you. Other than that, the only thing I know is what I just told you," replied Kirk.

"OK, pal," said John. "Thanks for keeping me under cover on this one, whatever it is. I'll take the call, and then you and I can reconnect. Nice hearing from you," said John.

"Thanks, John, and I look forward to your next trip here," said Kirk.

THE KITTY HAWK PANEL

As he ended his peculiar call with Kirk Woodbury, John Gabriel took a seat along with a couple hundred other audience members at the Kitty Hawk seminar. At the front of the conference room, he saw the reporter Kyle Duke sitting with the panelists. As John scanned the program materials, he was startled to read that Jill Serrano was one of the panelists. He looked up at the dais and sure enough, there she was - sitting just seventy-five feet away from him among the otherwise all-male panel. That alone made her stand out.

A sociologist could conduct a fascinating study by sampling a dozen audience members as to their first impression of Jill. The reactions would run the gamut from "professional," "confident," "next door neighbor" and "real," to "poised," "attractive" and "could have been a model in another life." But John's reaction was not that of some stranger upon whom Jill was making a first impression.

John had known her by her maiden name, Jill Seneca, and he only vaguely recalled her married name, Serrano, from a wedding announcement he had received years ago.

"Jesus H. Christ, what a coincidence," he thought, more as a self-narration of his feeling a shot of adrenaline rush through him. It was a bona fide nervousness, something he rarely experienced anymore. John oddly wondered if he had observed proper social protocol by acknowledging that long-ago wedding announcement with a gift, or at least a card. Then he caught himself – what kind of immediate reaction was that, wondering if he'd sent a card years ago? John then recalled the timing - he had received Jill's wedding announcement a few months after his own wife had died. Whatever the combination of emotions and excuses, John now realized he had likely just ignored Jill's announcement, and thus they had lost contact when Jill was getting married and he had just become a widower.

As John's mind raced to piece together the timeline from those lost years, Kyle Duke introduced the panelists, including Jill Serrano. After the mundane five minutes of introductions of the panelists, Jill gave a short presentation. Having had hours of informal conversations with Jill years ago, it was a bit surreal for John to be re-introduced to Jill as she said, "The blueprint of our federal, state and local governmental systems really did not envision air travel, much less pilotless drone travel, or radio wave networking across many states. So, it's no wonder that the regulation of the fast-moving drone industry is chaotic." Her concise, intriguing presentation ended a few minutes later with, "And if to illustrate all of this, just last week in Chicago, we all saw the competing TV stations' news helicopters, where one used a drone based with a frequency jammer to block the feeds of the others covering that downtown explosion. As you've read, the Chicago police, the Illinois attorney general, Homeland Security, the FAA, the FCC and the FBI have all opened their own investigations. Who will make the rules for that kind of situation?" asked Jill. "And who will enforce them? And let's not forget the continuing situation in L.A. where police chases have been turned into an internet high-bidder game show. I hope my points here are well taken," Jill concluded.

The panelist Lindsey Zevon was then asked to comment, and he lit up the discussion when he insisted that the example of a public explosion and consequent police action was misleading. "A far more relevant situation is whether the First, Fourth and Fifth Amendments permit federal government regulation of neighborhood drones delivering pizza and packages to your front door. Isn't the Post Office the only constitutional federal entity that could do that? And the half million employees of the Post Office might have a viewpoint on how this should be handled," insisted Zevon. This commenced a robust debate free-for-all among the panelists, with the attorney-panelist Jessie Wales noting wryly that he loved these issues because they were a "guaranteed jobs program for Washington lawyers for a decade."

The moderator, Kyle Duke, then focused the discussion by asking, "Does our experience with the regulation of domestic airlines, international flights and even space satellites, provide a useful template for drone regulation?" The panelists all chimed in. "Hard-working Americans deserve more than this chaos! And we need to consider all the stakeholders, including the half million hard-working postal workers whose jobs may be put at risk by these schemes," insisted Lacksman. Jill Serrano remained somewhat muted, almost recoiling at the pretentious manner of Percy Lacksman, who simply repeated what other panelists had said along with a few additional meaningless sound-bite generalities. It was all a typical convention panel, serving mostly as a means to network with others.

Despite the theatrics provided by the panelists Zevon, Lacksman and Wales, two people in the audience couldn't help focusing on Jill Serrano. One was John Gabriel, and the other was Ilene Meinhoff, who was sitting near the back of the room wearing oversized glasses and dressed in muted colors as if to avoid attention.

Ilene left the conference room just as Kyle Duke began wrapping up by asking if there were any questions from the audience. Ilene pulled out her cellphone, speed dialed, and after a pause said, "Hi, I've found a candidate for that Section D placement…Yes, I think within a few weeks, or a month at most. Yes, on first impression she fits the profile perfectly…. I'll need a week or so to investigate it further."

"OK then let's move forward. Send over a profile," replied Seymour Gacy.

"I will," said Ilene, and she hung up and strolled off to the next pavilion.

Back in the conference room as the Q&A session continued, a media assistant to the Los Angeles mayor, pretending to be an ordinary audience member with no agenda, posed a provocative question to Jill Serrano:

"Ms. Serrano, what exactly is the federal government doing to stop this rogue drone fleet that is terrorizing motorists on the Los Angeles freeways, despite the bold leadership of Los Angeles Mayor Paul Gonzales in his efforts to combat the menace?" It was a question only a political hack would ask. Within a few hours, it had backfired spectacularly as a mocking autotuned rendition of her question had gone viral on social media, further humiliating the Los Angeles mayor.

Already unnerved at seeing Jill Serrano after so many years, the pointed question about the Los Angeles drones unsettled John even further.

THE LOS ANGELES DRONE FLEET

John's connection with drones had started as a brief notion almost a half-decade ago, born of frustration and annoyance. What had eventually resulted was a hidden fleet of small drones, remotely piloted by gamers worldwide in an occasional live-fire game targeting actual criminal get-away cars marauding the Los Angeles freeways.

The idea was born when John had been stuck in traffic for hours and missed most of a ball game. The hours-long traffic delay was on account of the police shutting down a Los Angeles freeway because they were pursuing a speeding get-away car – seemingly a weekly event. "Cops and bad guys" chases on the vast grid of Los Angeles freeways and streets sometimes lasted for hours over many square miles.

Police procedure was to shut many miles of streets to prevent the high-speed cars from endangering more residents. Inevitably, traffic became frozen across large areas for a half day or longer. As John had sat in traffic, his mind had come up with fanciful solutions to the traffic messes, ranging from helicopter air cranes to robot truck barriers. But one of John's simple ideas had stuck with him: Why not use simple model airplane-type drones to snipe and disable the speeding cars with an electro-magnetic pulse? In other words, use a taser to fry the car's electrical system, thereby shutting down the car? The chase would end, avoiding hours of traffic shut-downs and hundreds of thousands of hours of delay and destruction of people's daily life. It was unacceptable to John that the city just seemed to accept the terrorism-like episodes as the new normal.

"Why is tasing them a bad idea, precisely?" was the question John repeatedly asked himself. No disabling answers came. The concept was too easy, too obvious, thought John. But after a little technical research, he had confirmed that it could be, really, that easy.

John's resulting idea was to mount a taser unit – similar to those used by police – onto a winged hobby drone, incorporated with a remote control and a high-definition camera. The pilot could thus divebomb the taser drone toward a car like a torpedo bomber approaching a large ship. The drone could fire the taser comprised of two small magnetic taser tips tethered to the drone by a thin wire. Like a lightning rod, the taser heads only needed to touch the car body for an instant, thereby allowing a massive static shock to disable the speeding vehicle's electrical system and shut down the engine along with the entire car.

John's tinkering proceeded once he enlisted his buddy Nick de Stijl, an aerospace and computer guy, to create a few prototypes. John tested them out on a couple of rental cars, and it worked. Then he tried it with Nick driving on the Pomona freeway outside of East L.A., and it worked again. A further revelation came to John when he stopped by his assistant Luke's apartment and found him playing video games with a few friends: The point-of-view from the high-definition camera on the drone was almost indistinguishable from the screen of a video game. Luke and his friends were hooked on the games, which were increasingly online, and the young men (along with some women) were part of a worldwide club of gamers. That was how John got the idea to merge his taser-shooting drones with remote gamers.

The next steps involved developing an alert system which notified him when a police car chase started up and garaging a bunch of drones around Los Angeles where the chases tended to happen. The real leap was in taking the rather basic technology and incorporating it with the dark web internet platforms, plus the technology of live auction sites and the blockchain trading exchanges.

The digital gamer world now knew the secretive drone live-action shooter game as "CKS" and speculated in chat rooms as to the meaning of the CKS acronym. Only John, Nick, and – recently, Luke - knew what CKS actually meant: "Civilians' Kill Switch."

It didn't escape John's notice that the five million CKS members were a form of citizen soldier crowdsourcing. Like a military guard-in-waiting, if the need arose, the entire group could rise like the Maquis, the French underground resistance in World War II. Although most of the rank-and-file police supported CKS for helping them make the city safer, it irked John that the politicians who decried CKS never once mentioned that it had massively eliminated traffic shutdowns and saved lives. So as John watched the Kitty Hawk panel, he realized just how advanced his own CKS drone system had become. Here they all were, sitting in front of him – the ecosystem of regulators, lawyers, politicians and journalists — all declaring John's creation to be some kind of scourge. Yet none of them had any idea who was behind it.

A LOAF OF TERROR

Pachid was excited about his first day of work. When he was younger, he had hung around his uncle's bakery in Gaza City, sometimes sweeping the dusty sidewalk out front. But today, his shirt bore the name of his employer – Crescent Fresh. He was early for his first day as a delivery man for the bakery. His new friend Labib had insisted on helping Pachid arrive on time and had picked him up and driven him on his morning's deliveries.

Labib pulled up to the delicatessen, and Pachid lugged the two satchels of bread loaves through the front door of the deli, which was already filled with customers seeking the best goods when they were first delivered. The deli did a brisk business, given its prime location on a block where three separate Palestinian Authority government offices were located. It was filled with wives and servants of mid-ranking bureaucrats and politicians attending to their errands right after seeing their children off to school.

As Pachid entered, the harried deli owner quickly looked up at Pachid and remarked, "You're early today. Filling in for Aref?" as he waved his hand to Pachid, giving him directions. No matter - with a shop full of waiting customers, the owner was happy with an early delivery.

Pachid knew that he wasn't gifted at talking. But his friend Labib had reminded him several times that Aref was ill today and that he should let the shop know that. Pachid dutifully told the owner, "Aref is sick today."

"Here, put them here," said the owner. He pointed to the countertop, and Pachid's smile grew as his first-day nervousness began to subside into pride of a job well done. The crowd of customers stepped aside so that Pachid could set down his packages, although they were all eyeing the fresh loaves to spot the one they hoped to claim as their own. As he set the packages on the counter, Pachid felt a sense of accomplishment. He had learned so fast the past week. It was nice to be accepted and have new friends.

The deli owner positioned one of the packages of loaves on the counter and ripped off some of the brown baking paper wrapping. Outside in the truck, Pachid's friend, Labib, had been watching as Pachid made his first delivery. Labib pulled away as he saw the deli owner pick up one of the bread loaves, and punched a three-number code on this cell phone keypad. The signal was sent, and a moment later the explosive charges inside four of the bread loaves exploded in unison. The deli's large storefront glass panes blasted out across the sidewalk. The front door was torn from its frame and molded itself onto a car parked in front of the shop, which itself was blown back into the middle of the street. Flames and smoke followed. Screams from the sidewalk and adjoining stores rang out. But no sound came from the demolished deli, now just a burning room on a concrete frame.

Before detonating the bombs, Labib had counted the number of people in the deli, and his total was fairly accurate. Pachid and eight others in the shop were instantly killed, and six others were critically injured, including the owner's wife and daughter working in the back of the shop. Labib snapped a few pictures from a safe vantage point down the street, and then drove away. He would upload the pictures and his body count estimate in a few minutes to his principal, Nadim Rachid.

A PECULIAR SCHOOL FOR BOYS

Nadim Rachid's security detail had secured the building before he entered. One of his loyal commanders, Dhuli Hassan, oversaw the six dozen young men living there. The school was named the Zaydi Benevolence Home, and among its financial sponsors was the Awakened Dawn

Foundation, one of billionaire Seymour Gacy's humanitarian charity fronts.

Dhuli moved toward Nadim to greet him and dropped his head in a show of subservience. "Welcome to your loyal quarters," said Dhuli. "It is an honor to have you here. Praise God."

"Your hospitality is exceeded only by your value to God and our work. We shall prevail over the infidels because of you and great warriors like you," said Nadim, heaping praise on Dhuli.

Nadim Badr Rachid was a bipolar radical Islamist son of a wealthy Saudi prince. Like Osama bin Laden in the previous generation, Nadim Rachid's radical views were the result of bad brain chemistry and an environment so full of contradiction that even a chemically balanced person would struggle to maintain sanity. Rachid had come to view modernization as evil. He knew that as the planet prospered in times of peace, the rising standards of living created demand and expectation in the Arab world for more Western-style things, like universal education and abolition of slavery, and western-style open society and culture, particularly for women.

In other words, peace led to prosperity which led to increased demand for secular reform, freedom and equal rights. But such reforms threatened Rachid. In Rachid's head, peace meant the exit from the Dark Ages culture over which the royal house presided. Peace thus meant failure because of the loss of power in the culture. And simply put, to Rachid war was the opposite of peace, and thus war was the most viable way to arrest the process of peace and its secular reform. In Rachid's logic, war preserved the status quo, and radical Islam was spreading fast under the status quo. Therefore, war was good, as constant war and chaos meant the advance of Islam and a caliphate. Rachid may have been bi-polar, but he worked in logical steps. And a dark curtain was falling on vast areas of the globe.

Dhuli Hassan had several skills that were invaluable to Nadim Rachid. Primarily, Dhuli was adept at identifying a certain type of poor street kid in Palestine, Cairo and Riyadh: simple-minded or outright mentally retarded, but generally able-bodied young males. Dhuli had an almost instinctive knack of knowing what to look for in the faces and the mannerisms of the hundreds of poor young men hanging out near the public squares and markets of the large urban centers of the Middle East.

With an offer of a cigarette, or perhaps just sharing a bite from a food vendor, Dhuli was adept at identifying and then screening the young men. On a typical evening of recruiting, he'd screen a dozen or more and end up selecting three or four to be "hired." When they showed up for the job Dhuli had offered at his facility, they were assigned basic labor chores along with the other men. They were fed and soon offered a place to sleep. It only took a few days before they were fully recruited as employees and wards at Dhuli Hassan's institution.

It could take a year or more to groom the psychology of a voluntary suicide bomber, and the attrition and failure rates were high. So Nadim and Dhuli had created a far more efficient factory for producing bombers. They were unknowing patsies. Trained in basic manual labor, and now part of perhaps the only organization that had ever accepted them as members, the wards were ready for action within a few weeks or months. They would first be dispatched in small crews to basic cleaning and unskilled labor jobs, hauling garbage or clearing debris. They would then be given an overnight assignment, perhaps in a neighboring town, with a small crew.

As such, the larger group at Dhuli's institution became accustomed to its members leaving the facility, first for a few days at a time, and then for longer when being transferred to an important work project in another town. The group of mentally challenged men did not understand that they were being graduated into bombing missions or other suicide/fodder actions.

In the past two weeks, a few of Dhuli's crew had been sent into Istanbul. Each of the three members wore a uniform and believed that the fire extinguishers they were carrying aboard the cruise ship were to be exchanged for extinguishers in the ship's restaurant that needed to be replaced. Proudly wearing their service uniforms, they had no idea they were delivering improvised explosives to the target. Two of the three bombs detonated, killing all three of Dhuli's wards, but also killing 15 tourists and injuring another 30.

In another instance that week, one of Dhuli Hassan's trainees had been taught to make deliveries on his motor scooter. All dressed up in his messenger uniform, he was blissfully unaware that the explosion that killed him was caused by a bomb in the package he had just carried into the office building lobby. It also killed several people in the reception area and terrorized the entire community.

Nadim Rachid and Dhuli ate and discussed how the recruiting was proceeding. Dhuli expressed some worry that he had picked most of the low hanging fruit in the cities from which he had been recruiting. Nadim Rachid instructed his minion to branch out to new cities, as needed, to keep the supply of naïve soldiers coming forth. Dhuli promised that he would, and Nadim promised the financial resources that Dhuli would need.

Nadim cautioned Dhuli to pay special attention to severing any ties between the recruits and their families. It was through such family contacts that investigators might trace things back to Dhuli. He also cautioned against allowing television and internet access for the wards, as they might recognize the name of a suspect in a media report.

With Nadim's approval and monies, Dhuli had outfitted several video-game rooms, designed to keep the young men busy with selected off-line games, as well as sports broadcasts.

Nadim Rachid was pleased. This was so much more efficient than training ideological bombers, he thought. In a single year, they would be responsible for almost 100 attacks. Rachid was at the top of his game.

COINCIDENCE AT THE PREDATORS BALL

As the Kitty Hawk panel at the Predators Ball finished, people milled about asking questions of the panelists, exchanging business cards, and promising to email with this and that. Each of the panelists around the dais had a small line of people wishing to chat directly, as was typical with convention seminars.

John hung back in his seat and answered a few emails. After about five minutes, the post-panel crowd had dissipated. He walked up to the dais and stood behind a technology blogger who was finishing a monologue posing as a question, directed to Jill Serrano, about the importance of women in the drone business considering male hegemonic superstructures and such things. Jill was nodding and listening, and then she thanked the monologist for his insightful comments. As the blogger moved away, John stepped up to Jill.

"That's a hard act to follow," he quipped.

There was a moment of hesitation as Jill's mental processing completed its operation, and then she said, "John? John Gabriel?" A smile with a little energy coupled with a slight 'what on Earth are you doing here?' look overtook her face. "Oh my God, what a surprise seeing you here!" were the words that came out, and they executed a half-hug, a bit awkwardly given the place and circumstances, but the awkwardness quickly abated. They both had genuine smiles on their faces.

"I'm sorry I didn't know that you were on this panel. Otherwise, I would have reached out to you instead of surprising you," said John.

"This is a surprise. A good one, for sure. But a surprise," said Jill, as she looked at three people milling about waiting to speak with her.

"You do what you're here to do. I'm around through the end of the convention. Give me a call, let's catch a drink after you've finished up your official activities," said John. He pulled out a business card and wrote his cell number on it.

"I will," replied Jill. She looked at the people waiting behind John, and added, "Give me an hour or two?"

"Great," said John, "We'll talk in a bit."

As John stepped back, another conventioneer stepped up and started asking Jill a detailed question about a proposed Code of Federal Regulation rule and its comment period. Poor Jill, thought John. Their brief re-encounter had been a bit awkward but genuine, and the handful of eager spectators had eased the situation by forcing them to be brief and professional. He looked forward to Jill texting or calling. He was a little less anxious about a possible botched wedding present.

John continued to roam the convention pavilions. At a booth presenting a high-definition drone-mounted camera and video featuring wireless image transmission, John saw the Kitty Hawk moderator Kyle Duke, and he struck up a conversation. John asked Kyle some insightful questions about some of his recent *Wall Street Journal* columns. Kyle gave John a little unpublished backstory on a few of them.

When they had finished, John said, "Nice speaking with you, and please keep up the great work, you have at least one devoted reader." He reached into his coat pocket. "Hey, the wine broker Tom Gallier is showing some killer wine vintages at a private tasting tomorrow. I scored a few extra passes," said John, fibbing a bit. He handed Kyle a pass. "Here, consider this my annual squaring up of my subscription account, because your paper clearly doesn't charge me enough for your great columns."

"Oh, thanks very much. I don't ever write about it, but I'm a bit of a wine snob, and the paper's wine writer mentioned that I should try to score an invite. I've asked around and no one really knew how to get one," said Kyle. "Hey, really, Mr. Gabriel, this is very kind of you. I'll be there."

"Please, it's John. My pleasure. See you there," said John.

John had described the reception as being hosted by Tom Gallier, which was not entirely true. In fact, John and Tom Gallier had worked out quite a little arrangement. John was able to obscure the fact that he was the organizer of the power gathering that was disguised as a wine event. Even the event's name was bait to super wine geeks: Lead Head. Few people other than oenophiles knew that prior to 1990, the corks in wine bottles were covered by a poisonous soft lead alloy cap.

John's reception co-host, a successful wine broker named Tom Gallier, had rolodex of worldwide clients that would be the envy of any Davos event planner. His casual access to a world of influential people rivaled that of a national president. Curated from Tom's and John's rolodexes and wish lists, the invite list for the party was coveted all over New

Orleans, as well as the Predators Ball. John's assistant Luke oversaw the invitation list for the Lead Head event.

John's phone chirped, signaling a text had been received. It was from an unknown number and said, "Jill here, stuck with some folks, how about we meet @ 6:30 at the Carousel Bar at the Monteleone Hotel?"

John texted back immediately, "Yes, perfect, C U there!"

He ducked into a quieter area of the pavilion and called Luke. As it turned out, John and Luke were standing in the same pavilion, a mere 50 meters apart. "I'm at booth 55M, c'mon over and let's stroll while we go over things," said John. Luke joined him moments later, and they went through some miscellaneous agenda items, speaking in shorthand.

"Has the insurance for the shelterbelt corps program been fixed?" John asked.

"Yes, we got it approved yesterday, except anyone under age 21 will have to fill out a special form," replied Luke.

"Great. Are the end-of-summer concert tickets all lined up for the kids?" asked John.

"I'm still working on the Colorado Rockies' group sales for everyone; it's a little more difficult since they've had a good season, but it will happen. The concert tickets won't be a problem," said Luke.

"Good work. I hope the new hybrid of Juniper tree is worth the effort." John was referring to the nationwide tree planting program which John had delegated to Luke to manage. It built and repaired shelterbelts of trees, bushes and grasses in the semi-dry Great Plains. It was a modern-day Civilian Conservation Corps, but this one employed underprivileged kids on summer break. This was one of John's quirky ideas by which he quietly tried to make the world better in small ways.

"Is Lead Head all set to go?" asked John. "I've got a few additional names that I'll text to you; I gave them hard copy invitations. Be sure to forward me the updated guest list, so I can make sure no one was left off. And make sure the last-minute invitations get delivered. You've got the music covered, right?" asked John.

Luke hesitated, looking a little put out by the suggestion that he might have failed, but then offered, "Uh, yeah, I've got that covered."

"C'mon, who'd you get?" goaded John. He knew that Luke spent a lot of his spare time immersed in various music scenes and he wasn't really worried about whether Luke could find live music. Rather, he wanted to make sure there wouldn't be a DJ playing gangster rap to a group of executives, geeks and financiers at a wine tasting.

"A north African ambient guitar group just finished recording here in town, and they're gonna jam for a couple of hours…maybe with some friends," said Luke.

"Some friends, huh? How many Grammys might these 'friends' have won?" John asked.

"Well, a few. Some brass would really be a whole new angle to their Blue Man guitar thing," said Luke.

"And I supposed you've arranged for that brass," asked John, already knowing the answer. "I'm sure it would be a great scoop for a music writer to cover, except there's no press allowed."

"Well," said Luke, "I was gonna ask you if it was OK if I gave a couple of press passes.…"

"Might I guess that she's beautiful?" said John.

The few second pause revealed Luke's bewilderment at how John could have guessed his plans. "Well, actually it's my friend's girlfriend and she's the music and culture editor for…"

"Use your best judgment," said John. "Just no pictures of any guests, and no guest names or specific venue location given, but she can write about the food, wine and music to her heart's content. And she must mention Lead Head - twice. Tell her that's the quid pro quo."

"Two admits, two mentions. Got it, done," replied Luke.

"Anything else?" asked John.

"Just little stuff. It looks like the travel agent has arranged all the European lodging for the architectural student interns in all six cities," reported Luke, referring to another internship program organized by John, whereby students spent a summer as a docent, tour guide and general gofer for various churches in major European tourist cities, when crowds were large and local workers desired high-season vacation time off.

"How many are in the program this summer?" asked John.

"It looks like about 125. We had a few issues with the new administration in Rome, but it's all set now with no problems," Luke reported.

"Great," said John, "sounds like you are right in the thick of it."

They paused as they approached a booth called "Reboot Cowboys." It was a ragtag group of geek hobbyists. One guy in the booth was wearing a badly tied necktie, another a striped shirt. John took one look at the printed sign and had a hunch that they were the tech team involved with what had become known as the 'ICE-3' satellite. It was a research satellite officially named International Cometary Explorer, launched in the pre-Reagan era by NASA and the European Space Administration. The satellite had been abandoned decades ago when its mission ended, but in 2014 a group of space hobbyists began communicating with ICE-3 with a radio transmitter, and they used social media crowdsourcing to re-assemble the long-lost ICE-3 operating instructions. There was a spike in publicity for a year, but a few months later the ICE-3 satellite's signal reportedly went dead and ICE-3 dropped out of the news.

"You're the ICE-3 guys, aren't you?" John asked the techie with the tie. Another guy in the booth heard John's question, turned, and approached John.

"We were," said Jimmy Bedford. He was a late thirties-something guy who looked part engineer and part weekend fantasy baseball league enthusiast, complete with a plaid shirt.

"I read about you guys," said John, with the sort of deep admiration that a teenaged boy would display when meeting the lead singer of a rock band. They introduced themselves and made small talk. After an enthusiastic discussion about the ICE spacecraft and the excitement of the summer of its brief rebirth, John said, "Well, I'm sorry ICE went silent on you. That's too bad."

Jimmy Bedford adjusted his glasses, looked down at some brochures on the table as he straightened them into a neat pile, and after a pause said, "Yeah, we were all disappointed to lose it."

One never really expects to hear a fire alarm, but to John it was as if a fire alarm had sounded. As a young lawyer, John had undergone some training at a law firm seminar in detecting when a witness was not telling the truth. Years later, as a teacher, John had fielded excuses from students as to why homework wasn't turned in, or that a student had purportedly overslept an exam, etc. Truth and fiction are usually mixed. But John had become attuned to key telltale signs of when someone was either lying or seriously shading the truth.

And just now, when responding to John's statement, Jimmy Bedford had averted his eyes, touched his face, fidgeted with the pile of paper and paused before responding. Any single one of those actions was an indicator of discomfort on the part of the speaker, which often meant he was lying, or at least telling a half-truth. But a rapid succession of four such signs was an unmistakable "tell." John knew there was much, much more to the ICE-3 story.

"Listen, Jimmy, I have to run. Can I get your card?" John asked.

Jimmy fumbled a bit more, grabbed a slightly folded business card out of his laptop bag, and said, "Let me write in the correct email." Like old eight-track tape players, physical business cards weren't the big deal that they'd once been. In a few years, a college kid might have no reference point when watching the brilliant business card-envy scene from the film "American Psycho," in which a group of young New York attorneys and bankers engage in a collective one-upmanship and implicit status ranking over the particular lithographic details of their business cards.

Luke was engaged in a conversation with a young woman at the booth next to the Reboot Cowboys. She had the look of a business-development executive for a tech start-up. Not wanting to interfere with Luke's discussion, John began to walk away and said to Luke, "I'll catch you later."

Luke was momentarily torn between staying with his boss - which was his job— and talking with the undeniably good-looking woman with whom he had successfully struck up a conversation. But then he realized that John had already made the decision for him. "Okay, John, I'll be along in a minute," said Luke. He then turned back to his new friend.

"How did you get involved in all of this?" Luke asked, using an innocuous line. Regardless of current fashion trends, Luke couldn't decide whether her hard-rimmed eyeglasses really suited her intelligent brown eyes.

"I find it quite exciting. The industry, I mean. A convention like this is like a dream. To be quite honest, it's the reason I took all those damned STEM courses and got a minor in programming. It brought my grade point down, for sure. But that's the currency of the realm," the young lady said.

"That's an interesting way to look at it; the currency of the realm," Luke replied.

"You know, if you don't have a tiger mom or a quantum physicist as a father, it's not exactly easy to pull a 4.3 in engineering. You know, Larry Summers got fired for saying that, in so many words, even though it's true. So, you do what you need to do. I'm a marketing assistant for Tygar Engineering. We're based in Minneapolis. That's not what I'll be doing in ten years, but right now I'm the best at my work at my level," she said.

"I'm Luke, by the way," said Luke.

"Janine," she replied. "Glad to meet you. What about you?"

The question caught Luke somewhat off guard; he wasn't often asked about his work. He made a note-to-self that the informality of his position as John's assistant needed to change, immediately. Like in the next ten seconds. So, Luke proceeded to change it himself.

"I'm… a vice president at a technology investment company," he said.

"Cool, what do you guys invest in mostly?" Janine asked.

Luke felt a bit flummoxed. "Actually, I'm the owner's executive assistant. I handle most of his NGO stuff, but he's getting more and more into aeronautics and drone tech. That's why we're here."

"Hey, it's all about where you'll be in five years, not five minutes," Janine quipped.

Luke felt an immediate liking for Janine.

"One of the things I've been doing is event management for a private VIP function tomorrow," Luke said. "It sorta blew up into a thing, and it's been a time-suck making it happen again this year."

"What is it?" Janine asked.

"A wine tasting with some big wigs. It's sorta hush hush and all that."

"Are you talking about - Lead Head?" Janine asked, with a hopeful inquisitive look on her face.

Suddenly Luke felt like the most powerful guy in the room. "Yep, you've heard of it?"

"Holy shit, my boss is all over my ass – I mean, really riding me – I mean, is highly desirous of getting into that event," Janine said. "He's heard about it and he's obsessed because, well, he's a middle-aged wine geek, so you can imagine what my text messages from him have looked like the past two days."

"OK, so give me his name and what the company does, and make it seem super-legit," Luke said. "Is he alone or are there others?"

"Just him and the CTO," Janine replied.

"OK, I'll put down both their names." Then Luke's tone changed a notch. "Janine, can I give him a plus-one, so you can come? Or I can also put you on the list, so you're not tethered to him? I've lined up some great musicians and there will likely be a great jam session after the event."

"You're not kidding, right? This sounds great, I'll definitely come. And thanks, Luke, I think you just made my Christmas bonus," she said. "My boss will be so stoked. You don't understand."

Luke knew the event was a hot ticket, but Janine had just schooled him on how hot it really was, especially among this tech group. Luke and Janine exchanged numbers and information, and Luke said he'd text her to follow up. He was excited that he might have a quasi "date" for the party.

A few minutes later, Luke caught up with John. "I assume you obtained her contact information, for important professional follow-ups?" asked John. For a second, Luke was caught off guard until John chuckled and then changed the subject. "I liked that guy, Jimmy, at the Reboot Cowboys booth, but there's a whole lot more to that old satellite story. Did you see him melt down when I asked him about it?"

Luke confessed that he hadn't been paying much attention to Jimmy.

"Yeah, I know that," chided John. "She was a good-looking techie, that's for sure." John was having a little good-natured fun with Luke, and it was even more fun that Luke had been completely distracted, and now didn't quite know how to respond.

"Here, I'll text you his info and later I'll bring you up to speed with what happened," said John. He took a cellphone picture of Jimmy's card and then recorded a quick message as he texted it to Luke, "ICE-3 guy, find out what really happened to that satellite."

"I'll do some digging," promised Luke.

"Good, and make sure Lead Head is all squared away. And Luke – try to stay out of trouble with all these beautiful tech ladies – tomorrow is a big day."

John had scant idea how prophetic his words would become.

A FUNERAL IN MOSCOW — SIX MONTHS AGO

THE COLOR GUARD at the Federal Military Memorial Cemetery stood at attention, as a quartet played "You Feel a Victim," a typical funeral hymn. A fellow officer of retired Colonel Pavel Gurin was being laid to rest. The deceased, Yuri Belov, had served alongside Pavel in the Soviet rocket corps for several decades.

Other than the government personnel administering the service, no one besides wheelchair-bound Pavel Gurin and his stepson Lieutenant Taras Shimko attended Belov's funeral.

As the quartet finished its tribute, Pavel looked skyward and saw a Russian oligarch's private jet climbing into the sky. He motioned to his stepson to lean in. "It's over, isn't it?

The Soviet Union that I knew, it's gone and it's not coming back, is it?" asked Pavel rhetorically, as a deep cough caused pain in his chest. "There's not even enough of us left to attend our friends' funerals. It's all gone."

Pavel Gurin had witnessed both the highs and lows of the twentieth-century Soviet Union. His career had started in the late 1950's when he was recruited as a young missile technician in the 43rd Rocket Army, which worked closely with the OKB-1, the original Soviet aerospace department. Through the decades Pavel had advanced on account of his technical prowess, rather than any family or political connections. By 1980 he had been named the chief technical officer of the Soviet Strategic Missile Corps.

"There's something I need to give to you," Pavel said to his stepson. "I want to do it as soon as we get back home." Now long retired and in declining health, Pavel lived in an assisted living facility on the outskirts of Moscow.

Gurin wished that he could have passed along to his stepson a better legacy. Had the Soviet program not been dismantled, Shimko could have been one of its leaders, perhaps even a lead cosmonaut. Instead, Shimko was a technician in a now far smaller Russian space program.

An hour later, Pavel asked Taras to retrieve a folder from a bookshelf in his small room. With a sigh, Pavel opened the folder on his lap. "In my life, I've been part of some very good projects. Achievements we can be proud of. I've also been part of some questionable projects. In difficult times, it happens. All we can really hope for is to be able to maximize the good that we do and minimize the bad. At least that's what I've told myself all these years...."

"I've been so proud of you, Taras. But I told you a lie that I need to rectify. And in doing so, I want you to have the opportunity to be a patriot. To do your part for the Rodina."

"What is it, Father? I don't understand what you are saying," said Taras.

Sitting in the small room of the nursing home after the funeral, Pavel took a deep breath and straightened his posture as well as he could manage. He wanted to emphasize the importance of what he was about to say. He said, "It concerns the nuclear-tipped satellite we called Firebird."

Sensing Pavel's seriousness, Taras Shimko listened intently to his stepfather, the once-great rocket engineer Pavel Gurin.

"Do you remember that nuclear-armed MIRV satellite I told you about years ago, how I had decayed its orbit to burn it up during an accelerated re-entry?" Pavel asked. "Taras, that story was not true. I didn't burn it up. I left it there, hoping that one day I could present it to a responsible government and bring pride and honor to our family. But that is not how things worked out for Russia, or me, or you. Worse, the MIRV may soon be discovered with the new software programs that Putin and the FSB have been employing. I fear the worst if the FSB gets control of that bird."

"Are you sure you are feeling well, Father? I can't believe what you are saying. You told me it was destroyed. You and Gorbachev prevented the West from taking advantage of our misfortune during the unrest. You are a hero, Father."

"No. You are not hearing me, Taras. Listen to an old

man – your old man. I'll tell you what really happened in the Soviet Union in its last decade before it disintegrated. Because it is crucially relevant to what I will ask you to do today. Some of this you already know, but there is so much that you – that no one, really – knows."

Pavel then recounted, with new details, some of what Taras already knew. Following the death of Soviet Premier Leonid Brezhnev in 1982, Yuri Andropov, the chief of the Soviet secret police, assumed power in the wake of a dangerous and fast-changing geopolitical world that commenced with the January 1981 inauguration of American President Ronald Reagan.[1] In March of 1983, Reagan unilaterally changed the strategic game board of the Cold War by announcing his "Star Wars" defense initiative, the gist of which was the American intention to develop a weapons system that could shoot down Soviet intercontinental nuclear missiles in mid-flight.

The hard liners in the Politburo, including Andropov, felt compelled to react. Publicly, Andropov assured the world that the Soviet Union was unilaterally giving up any space-based nuclear weapon programs. Privately, however, Andropov did the opposite, even though the Soviet intercontinental ballistic missile program was already doomed in the decrepit Soviet planned economy.

To counteract Reagan's plan, Andropov revived an old 1960's Soviet plan for an orbital nuclear weapon. Andropov secretly launched the Soviet nuclear-armed satellite in the fall of 1983, its existence known only to a small group of Kremlin insiders, including Andropov's defense minister, his KGB chief and a small secret team of technical officers.

The satellite was dubbed the "Firebird," after an old Russian folk story of a mythical bird. Pavel Gurin had been one of the few technical officers working in the inner circle of the Firebird project.

But the Soviet Union began to devolve the moment Firebird was put into orbit, and Andropov himself died of kidney failure just a few months after Firebird was launched. Various Kremlin insiders were killed or imprisoned in the soft coups and Politburo intrigue which followed. Andropov's defense chief - one of the few who knew of Firebird – received a bullet in the head just two months later, although the Soviet propaganda outlet Pravda reported his demise as being caused by pneumonia.

The Firebird nuclear satellite had indeed managed to rise, but its destiny would soon be that of an orphan. With Andropov and his close cronies either dead or exiled to Siberia,[2] the internal power struggle at the Kremlin[3] resulted in the appointment of a short-term new Soviet leader, Konstantin Chernenko, who was dead just a year after taking office. The reformer Mikhail Gorbachev became the General Secretary of the Soviet Union in 1985, despite pockets of hardliner opposition inside the Kremlin.

Those hardliners, including an Andropov crony KGB chief who was the only remaining Politburo member who knew of Firebird, were fired by Gorbachev in 1988. The Berlin Wall fell just a year later, and throughout 1990, the Soviet Bloc of states in Eastern Europe and Asia broke away from Soviet control. By 1991, the constituent Soviet republics declared their independence from the USSR.

In the face of the economic and political collapse of

the Soviet Union, by the summer of 1991 Mikhail Gorbachev had lost the support of almost every key faction in the Kremlin, and a military coup d'état was staged by the key Kremlin hardliners, who announced that Gorbachev was "on vacation." But for reasons still debated, the coup attempt failed, as a few key military detachments refused to fire upon Soviet citizens who set up defensive barricades in Moscow. As the attempted coup unraveled, the Soviet Union descended into barely controlled chaos.

Pavel Gurin had felt dejected as he watched the August 1991 coup unfold. But despite that, he realized that he was one of the very few "leaders" who were not part of the coup. He was trained to act when the situation warranted. Realizing that civil war might break out at any time in the power vacuum, Gurin asked himself, "Who could – and would – step up and defend the Soviet Union at this critical time?"

It was an easy choice for the still-patriotic Gurin. He arranged an emergency meeting with Gorbachev, who brought a few loyal Politburo allies. Recognizing that a second coup attempt might be made, Gorbachev excluded the KGB from their meeting, a political act that would have meant certain death anytime in the previous 70 years.

Gorbachev had just dissolved the Central Committee[4], and any new secret "committee" he might form would now bear the taint of treason and coup d'état. Gorbachev wryly noted to Gurin and the small group that they were the "Non-Committee," and the ironic name stuck.

Drawing from existing KGB, Politburo and military files, the Non-Committee hastily assembled an inventory of Soviet nuclear weapons, launch codes and the like, and began taking emergency procedures to lock down control of those weapons, most urgently to remove the known cronies of the coup leaders from any position of control over the Soviet state's nuclear weapons. Gurin's technical prowess made him indispensable to the Non-Committee, and he oversaw much of the lock-down.

Gurin was surprised that there were no Politburo files on Andropov's long-hidden Firebird Plan. Gurin then realized that the Firebird program itself was a forgotten ghost, a pet project of KGB chief Andropov, and any Kremlin member who might possibly have known about it was now dead or imprisoned. Firebird had been conducted as a special operation under Andropov, rather than under military command and control. Even the KGB's main files, and the index of which was sometimes accessible to the right Politburo member, were bereft of any mention of Firebird.

The lack of any Firebird files was a red flag to Gurin. He realized that the nuclear satellite was either forgotten (which seemed impossible), or known to just a tiny faction inside the Kremlin. Those would likely include a KGB faction and some of the coup plotters. They had proven themselves unfaithful and dangerous, yet they might be in control of the Firebird launch codes. And there was no fail safe. Although Soviet intercontinental nuclear missiles generally had various levels of double and triple authorizations required to launch, the paranoid Andropov had designed the Firebird system with single launch authority.

Gurin paused in his recounting of past events and

looked at his stepson. "I was alarmed when I realized during the Soviet disintegration that it was possible that Firebird had become a rogue KGB nuclear satellite. That was when I had to make a damned-if-you-do, damned-if-you-don't decision: I deleted the real Firebird files from the Non-Committee's database and cloaked the Firebird satellite, so that Firebird would be unavailable to any faction in the impending civil war in Soviet Russia."

Gurin explained that to achieve the disappearing-act of the nuclear satellite, he had retrieved his own Firebird files and codes from his classified safe. But after a few initial failures, Gurin found one platform within the Soviet satellite controls that accepted his old Firebird log-in credentials. Once logged in, the dashboard indicated that the Firebird satellite had responded, by pinging back. Gurin just stared at the terminal. There it was – an orbital platform with ten nuclear weapons aboard, and a dashboard control panel now sitting on his screen. In addition to the various satellite telemetry controls, there were ominous "targeting modules" on the screen. Firebird was intact, and possibly up for grabs during the chaos following the attempted Soviet coup. He decided upon a plan that he would enact the next day.

The next evening, when the room was clear during the dinner break for the rag-tag team assisting the Non-Committee, Gurin logged in and worked as fast as he could. His cloaking plan for Firebird was fourfold.

First, Gurin switched the satellite's telecommunications to a different frequency. This could prevent others from finding Firebird on its old channel.

Second, Gurin changed the password controlling the satellite.

Third, Gurin activated the retro rockets on the Firebird, moving it 10 miles higher in orbit, and 20 miles wide of its original orbital path. If a reconnaissance or retrieval satellite was ever to show up at the old orbital path of Firebird, it would find nothing.

Finally, Gurin created and inserted a dummy Firebird file into the Non-Committee's collected files, falsely showing that Firebird had been destroyed by a space junk collision. Gurin also saved a back-up of his work on a private drive. He was the only person who knew the truth – that Firebird was still active and in orbit.

Gurin had previously told his stepson Pavel that he had destroyed the Firebird satellite by degrading its orbital path so that it burnt up during re-entry. However, Gurin had rejected that plan in 1991 as being too risky. Plunging ten nuclear weapons from space into the Earth's atmosphere, unannounced, as the Soviet nuclear super-power was dis-integrating, had just experienced an armed coup and was teetering on the brink of civil war, was a bad idea. The world might – justifiably – panic. The Americans might believe that a first strike had been launched by Soviet hardliners and quickly decide to retaliate. The re-entry of Firebird could have triggered a pre-emptive or retaliatory nuclear strike by the US or other power, even if in error. And the prospect that the Soviet Union had placed nuclear weapons into orbit would forever taint the country and its leaders.

Pavel shook his head as he finished telling Taras his story. "That was the best I could do under the circumstances.

I tried to shield Mother Russia and the world from the evils of a rogue Firebird satellite – at least temporarily. I thought perhaps at some future point when a responsible Russian government was in place, I would be able to disclose Firebird to a proper Russian authority. But the oligarchs, along with Putin and his cronies, destroyed that dream." said Gurin. "Not just for me, but for all of Russia."

"Father, you've kept the satellite's existence a secret for several decades, based solely on that hope?" asked Taras.

"Yes," said Gurin. "It's been several years since I contacted the Firebird. I used the computer of my retired colleagues to check in on the satellite. But with the deaths of so many of them, those opportunities became harder to call upon. I realize my focus was wrong. Now, Firebird must be destroyed. With digital technology so advanced, and with several thousand other satellites in orbit now, Firebird is too easy to discover. It's not a matter of 'if' but 'when.' Putin and his cronies already have the new software technology to enable them to search and reconstruct the old files of the KGB and the Non-Committee to locate assets and weapons which Putin says were 'national treasures' of Russia squandered by outside agents and traitors – traitors like me and Gorbachev."

Gurin continued, "I need your help. I need your promise, son. Russia needs your help. There are ten active nuclear warheads on that satellite. What might these people do with it? God help us all."

"What – what do you want me to do?" asked Taras.

"I will give you the file with the Firebird access codes. I need you to destroy Firebird, once and for all. Perhaps introduce a virus to its circuits. Degrade its orbit and burn it up. Anything, or everything, just destroy it to keep it away from these people. Do not underestimate their ruthlessness when they learn of it – if they haven't already. You must think it through. Please, son. I can only redeem the sins of my hubris by imploring you to help Russia."

There was another pause.

"Yes, Father. Of course, I will do it."

Gurin sighed in relief. "Thank you, son. I love you. As I loved your mother."

IN DOHA, QATAR

The elderly Pavel Gurin passed away a few days after Taras Shimko had made his promise to destroy the Firebird satellite. But in the weeks after his father passed, Shimko's resolve faltered. He began to feel ashamed of the decline of the once-mighty Soviet space program he worked for, and the cronyism and theft that were obviously playing out daily in Putin's Russia.

Taras Shimko had watched the Russian oligarchs get rich without regard for morality or honor. And with the loss of his stepfather, Taras' last real connection to a proud legacy was broken, and bitterness and blame set in. Taras began to question why his own stepfather had never become an oligarch. And he began to assign blame for the fall of Russian honor. Why had Pavel Gurin failed to become rich, when hundreds of others had succeeded and now ran the country? Had Pavel Gurin been weak, and had that kind of weakness doomed the Soviet Union?

Taras knew that his stepfather had helped him get admitted into the prestigious Russian space program, but Shimko couldn't help feeling that he had been wronged – by someone. It wasn't his fault that the Soviet Union had unraveled, decimating its space program and military rocketry programs. Taras felt that his own future had been stolen from him. His distress soon led him to conclude that his stepfather had not been thinking clearly when he had extracted Taras' promise to destroy Firebird. Had Pavel Gurin analyzed the situation clearly and with the same sharp mental faculties he'd used to advance the Soviet space program, he clearly would not have wanted his own sins to burden Taras. Pavel Gurin would have wanted Taras Shimko to act like an oligarch and use Firebird as a means to assure his own success. And for Taras, success meant leaving Russia and living the luxurious life of an oligarch.

Soon after, Taras decided on a plan. He would sell Firebird to the highest bidder. Taras developed a list of potential buyers for his rogue satellite. Confident that there were ample potential buyers, he understood that he needed to avoid detection by any of the Western intelligence agencies as well as Russia's Federal Security Service. He arranged to be assigned to the trade delegation visiting a large international arms market, the annual SOFEX event held in Jordan. It wasn't particularly difficult to spot the outright frauds, poseurs and likely Western intelligence agents. He was surprised, however, by the level of acceptance by nearly everyone that much of the arms business was illegal or gray-market. Taras decided that bona fide buyers would work through one or two levels of intermediaries, and he chose to make vague inquiries with those who were geopolitical analysts on various Al Jazeera[5] news programs. Taras reasoned that some of these analysts used that medium as a marketing device – almost an infomercial for their various endeavors.

A few meetings had resulted, typically commencing with a general discussion about the massive export of weapons out of the Soviet Union after its collapse. Taras carefully hinted of his potential connection with someone who controlled a dozen missing thermo-nuclear devices of Soviet origin. A few weeks later, Taras had taken a third meeting with one such intermediary. Afterward, he had felt he had broken through to the middle ranks of arms buyers and their agents. The next day, he was notified that an additional meeting had been set in Doha, Qatar[6] which would be attended by a high-level agent for various jihadist organizations.

Taras was now en route to that meeting, and he leaned back in the seat of the jet and closed his eyes, gratified that he was taking a big step toward becoming an oligarch.

The next morning, he took a taxi from his modest hotel to the famed Ritz Carlton in Doha and waited in the hotel lounge until he received a text providing a room number. He went to the room, and his knock on the door was answered by a man dressed in a Western business suit. The man briefly explained the security protocol. As directed, they then went to the freight elevator, and Taras was asked to don ear buds and a blackout hood, which he did. The iPod music was Eastern European speed metal – the kind used to break terrorists in captivity. The elevator moved from floor to floor, with the door opening a few times, all of which made it impossible to know on which floor of the hotel they had arrived. At last, the elevator stopped, and another man began to speak with Shimko's escort.

With his hood still on, Taras was escorted into the hallway, and after various spins and turns designed to prevent Taras from tracking directions, they came to a halt, and a hotel door opened. Taras was led inside and then his ear buds and hood were removed. He was standing in a hotel suite.

Taras went through another security search, including a scan for devices. When it was done, he was asked to prepare his presentation. Taras booted his laptop and then waited for several minutes. A bearded Arab man entered, wearing a western business suit, large eyeglasses and a keffiyeh head-dress. It occurred to Taras that he could never identify the man in a line-up; his features were effectively camouflaged by his wardrobe.

"Thank you for coming, Mr. Shimko," said the man in British English. "I am Mr. Abdullah. I have been fully briefed. We are intrigued by you and your presence. We are eager to learn of what it is that you propose," he continued. "I ask that we adhere to the formalities of a short presentation. Of course, this meeting is confidential. We will assume that you have adequate devices to ensure that we keep it so. And you are to rest assured that we also have the means in place to ensure that you, also, maintain the strict confidentiality of this meeting."

Taras realized he had just been threatened with consequences if he leaked any information about the meeting. Rather than being frightened, he felt a rush of adrenaline. This guy was serious.

Taras replied, "Thank you Mr. Abdullah. I will get right to the presentation, which is best made with my laptop slides." Shimko turned the laptop to face Abdullah and started the PowerPoint presentation. It lasted a mere five minutes, and identified enough details to entice a buyer, but also left out enough so that the laptop was useless to anyone trying to steal the Firebird nuclear array.

Taras concluded, "In short, Mr. Abdullah, I offer membership into the nuclear arms club of nations, along with the military delivery system to make it real. The price is $500 million dollars." It was a polished and professional presentation by Taras.

Mr. Abdullah was a smooth operator too, but his interest was palpable. His immediate concern was not with the price, but with Shimko's authenticity.

"Mr. Shimko, I will relay your message to certain persons. Whether such a system does exist and whether you indeed have control of it would require some due diligence. I presume that you have contemplated this type of scrutiny - rigorous scrutiny?" asked Abdullah.

"We have no illusions that anyone is going to part with half a billion dollars on my personal assurances," replied Taras. Again, Taras was polished and effective.

Abdullah paused and placed his hands together as he

thought. Whether for show, or because he really was deeply thinking, didn't matter – the effect was that one could hear a pin drop. Taras wisely remained as silent as the Sphinx.

"Is that the 'royal we'?" asked Abdullah.

Taras didn't miss a beat. "You will of course learn much in your rigorous diligence," he replied.

Abdullah remained silent for ten seconds. He had a background file on Shimko, which identified him as the stepson of the recently deceased Soviet rocket engineer Pavel Gurin. That explained how Shimko might have information about - or even control of - the Firebird. But it might also be a con game or an intelligence agency sting operation. Abdullah cocked his head and said, "Thank you Mr. Shimko. We will be in touch with you if there is any interest. My colleagues will escort you out." Abdullah rose, and without shaking hands he exited into an adjoining room.

The two men who had brought Taras to the room appeared, and one explained that they were going follow the same security protocol. Taras once again donned the hood and the earphones, and after some hall walking and a roller coaster elevator ride, he was let off in the lobby.

"Thank you, Mr. Shimko" said the escort, and Taras exited the elevator.

NEW ORLEANS - A CAROUSEL GATHERING

As HE HAD arranged with Jill Serrano earlier in the day, at 6:30 John arrived at the bar in the grand old Monteleone Hotel in the French Quarter of New Orleans. Jill was already seated at the hotel's Carousel revolving bar – a tourist favorite. She rose as John approached. "What a small world," she said, as she gave John a single-sided cheek kiss. She was grinning broadly. John was glad they had broken the ice a few hours earlier.

"It's a huge world, but it got very small today," said John, "And if I recall correctly, you used to work at a winery, so I think the protocol is that you suggest a wine."

"Oh, come on, you're confusing me with one of the bottle girls from the convention! But I did notice that there is a Chateau Palmer white by the glass. Someone pulled some strings to get that. Shall we?" said Jill.

"Absolutely," replied John.

They began catching up and explained what they had been doing since they'd lost touch a couple of decades ago. Yes, Jill had gotten married, and was now divorced. She insisted that John had sent a wedding gift but faltered a bit when he asked what color the vase had been. "Okay, we're both guilty – you forgot, and I lied," Jill said. They shared some more catching-up details; Jill had a son entering his teen years. She spoke about her job with DHS and how she had fallen into it, and how it was a perfect gig for a divorced mother raising a kid. She had moved to Washington, D.C.

The wine disappeared quickly. "I really do remember that you had a job at a winery, way back when?" asked John. "Didn't you send a Christmas card taken in a barrel room? God that was a long time ago."

Jill laughed. "It wasn't that long ago – well I guess it was. Yes, I remember that card, and yes, I did, I helped a couple of guys who were building their first winery. All kinds of gravity fed pipes and tanks. Their venture didn't last long, but it wasn't the fault of the facility. They both went on to other wine gigs," recalled Jill. "Far more successful wine gigs, I might add."

"I think I'm going to need at least an hour's worth of details on that, so shall we just keep ordering by the glass?" asked John.

"No, I think we're allowed a whole bottle. And an adult table. How about some food to go with it?" asked Jill.

"An excellent idea. Shall we stay here or hit someplace less…touristy?" asked John.

"Ah, talking like a local already? That's good! Okay, do you wanna pick? I can check an app to see who has a table available now," offered Jill.

"Let's walk up the street. A local place called Freddy's. It's probably not on Yelp. And he's got a real wine list," said John. "But since you are the former wine pro, I'll let you be the official judge of that."

"Wow, I was just kidding about the knowledge of a local. How do you know of that place?" asked Jill.

"I live here on and off, mostly in the spring and fall. I have a complicated relationship with geography, but I do live here."

Jill smiled, realizing she knew scant details about John Gabriel's life. "I won't call you Ignatius J. Reilly, so long as Freddy's isn't a hot dog cart," quipped Jill.

John smiled back. He had forgotten that Jill had a quick wit and had read some literature.

As John and Jill departed to walk over to Freddy's, John's phone rang. It was Kirk Woodbury's Bermuda number. John hesitated and then hit "ignore call."

"Need to take it?" asked Jill, recognizing that on "convention time," business calls could run to any hour.

"Nope," replied John. "They'll call back." He was enjoying his reunion with Jill and was glad he had told Kirk to have the caller try him back if there was no answer.

A light warm rain began to fall, and John and Jill clung to the narrow sidewalk to stay protected by the many balconies and awnings that accented the streets of the historic

Vieux Carre of New Orleans. Small rickshaw bikes passed by as the peddlers scrambled to deliver their passengers to their destinations before the rainstorm became stronger. The loud sounds of the Bourbon Street music clubs a block away were barely audible.

As they bobbed and weaved to dry areas of the sidewalk, Jill glanced up at a small balcony above a corner liquor store across the street. A man took a long drag off some kind of pipe as he pushed two young women back through the balcony door into an apartment. Were they friends moving inside because of the rain? Or something else? Something seemed off to Jill. She made a mental note of the liquor store's address.

DINNER AT FREDDY'S

From the street, Freddy's was nothing more than an unmarked doorway in a small alley several blocks off the tourist routes in the French Quarter. As he and Jill approached the wrought-iron-framed front door, marked only by a blue light bulb under an awning, John said, "We're here." Jill stepped through the doorway into Freddy's, gaining an entirely different view of New Orleans.

The place was small, a bar and a lounge area with leather club chairs. Stacks of books – real books, not movie-set books – lined the walls, as did small-framed paintings. Less than 20 tables were dotted around the room. It was difficult to gauge the size of the room because of the darkness, except each table was lit from above with a focused beam of soft light. The high ceiling faded to black in some places. A low hanging ceiling over the center bar made it an inviting spot when one first walked through the door.

The owner was a crusty but charming old southerner straight out of a Ken Burns documentary. Freddy Quibonne (pronounced, 'Key-Bone-Ay') could write a book, "How to Not Make Money with a Bar Restaurant in a Tourist Town," but he didn't care. Freddy's was more of a tasting room mausoleum to something or someone. There was rumored to be a huge wine cellar adjoining the restaurant in a forgotten chamber, but Freddy would never publicly talk about it. There was no wine list, per se, other than talking to Freddy and navigating his mood.

The food prices at Freddy's were outrageous – most dinner entrees were listed at $75 to $200 – because Freddy didn't like tourists and wanted to scare them away. But there was an unwritten rule for the local's discount. Here, the discount was more like 50%, or whatever Freddy decided – if you were a "regular," and more importantly, if Freddy liked you or at least tolerated you. It kept Freddy's off the mobile apps used by tourists. Google Maps did purport to show a location pin for Freddy's, but at a wrong address three blocks away. One of Freddy's regulars who was a marketing executive had executed the misdirection, with Freddy's blessing.

A dozen small speakers were perched high up in the

ceiling. A steady stream of obscure and classic jazz filled the room. Someone very particular knew what they were doing.

Knowing a bit about jazz from playing clarinet in the school band, Jill immediately noticed that "So What?" by jazz trumpeter Miles Davis was playing over the stereo system. She turned around to John with a genuine smile and said, "It's my new favorite place and I've only been here for ten seconds."

John gave her the "yeah, I know" look, and then turned as Freddy approached them. To John, Freddy's was one of the perfect spots on Earth.

"Hiya, Mr. Freddy, how've you been?" John said as Freddy extended his hand to him.

"Real good, Mr. John. Can't complain, can't complain. C'mon in. Bring your friend, she's welcome too." Freddy did a double take on Jill. "She's real welcome. And so is your mother, young lady, bring her by anytime, anytime." Freddy was just the kind of guy who could pull off that kind of comment and appear charming while doing it. "I've got two tables left, or you can sit at the bar."

"We'll grab whatever table you recommend, Mr. Freddy," said John.

"Well, that's just nice and easy then. This way, right this way," Freddy said. That's how Freddy worked best; keep the immaterial requests to a minimum.

After sitting down, a formal introduction of Jill and Freddy followed, and Jill was treated to a lounge act like none other in the world – "The Freddy and John Show."

"Whaddaya thinking today, Mr. John?" asked Freddy.

"Well, Mr. Freddy, it's a nice low ambient temperature

outside tonight, a little bit of rain started. A cool room temperature, and the sun has dipped down so it will drop a bit further. I think the rain will stop in a bit, and the humidity will drop back to moderate, but a chill might roll in. And of course, with your choice of *Kind of Blue*[7] as the music tonight, I'm thinking we can do a couple of stops. Medium bodied, perfect age, Old World unless you've got something up your sleeve," recited John, as if some form of language between Clint Eastwood and his bartender.

"Next up, it'll be Mr. Davis helping out Mr. Malle on the way to the gallows," said Freddy.[8] "Just a figure of speech, of course. Although you never know, you never know. And I think I've got just the thing you want, Mr. John, just the thing," replied Freddy, as he left the table. Of course, he had just the thing; Freddy always had just the thing, if you were a friend of Freddy, that is.

"Did you just order dinner or was that a weather forecast?" asked Jill.

"Yes and no. Freddy is a wine hoarder, but also is sorta like 'Rain Man.'[9] I like different wines in different situations, usually based upon the ambient and environmental factors. Along with the music. So, I give Freddy a few of those environmental criteria that I think are relevant now. Spitting out those impressions is somewhat of an emotional response. And Freddy's Rain-Man antennae seem to connect with that, and he runs with it. God knows what the microprocessor in his head does with it. But Freddy's choice is always a fantastic surprise," explained John. "Except it scares me that it's not always a surprise."

"But you don't know what you're eating yet," noted Jill.

"Of course, I do. I'll be eating whatever goes with the wine Freddy brings," said John.

Jill thought that through. "Okay, I get it. And I did say that you got to pick." After a moment, Jill added, "I'm getting some flashbacks, John Gabriel. I forgot those witty little rejoinders of yours. It's been a few decades. You can tell me about the gallows thing later, though."

"I think Freddy was referring to the soundtrack that's up next, but I'm not quite sure about that one, to be honest," said John.

Freddy came back and presented a bottle of red Bordeaux, a 1995 Gruaud Larose. The label was badly stained. "Flood wine," said Freddy.

"Flood wine? What is flood wine?" asked Jill.

"Flood wine," Freddy repeated. "Insurers paid it off. A whole warehouse was supposed to end up at the parish dump, but a cousin of one of my associates just couldn't let that happen. Not gonna happen, nope." Freddy then made a disapproving "tsk" noise, implying that no rational person would allow good wine to be dumped, and Freddy then gave a few details on how his cousin's salvage operations had worked. The flood, of course, was the devastating 2005 Hurricane Katrina. "The good prophet John Hiatt says never trash a perfectly good guitar, and I would add, never trash a perfectly good Bordeaux, never, ever,'" Freddy said as he grinned.

The wine was poured; it was perfect. "Cheers! What a great surprise!" John said in a toast to Jill.

"Cheers back, and I got a front row seat to this secret

show somewhere in the back alleys of New Orleans. I think that's a real insider's privilege," said Jill.

"So…how did you end up on that panel today?" asked John. "You're a long way from the nation's capital."

Jill recounted her engineering career trail over the past twenty years, and how it had led to her sitting on today's "Kitty Hawk" panel. After her winery adventure in Sonoma County, she'd moved to San Francisco. She explained that as the various civilian, military and commercial airports in the San Francisco Bay area began to coordinate their operations more closely with the advent of the digital age and underwent massive construction projects, she had taken a job with the FAA, which was then assuming new roles among the various airport authorities.

Jill gave up the FAA for motherhood, but her marriage ended soon after the birth of her son, and she returned to work, joining the legions of working single mothers in America. Jill had kept her married surname Serrano. And while she admitted that with her auburn hair and light freckles, she wasn't exactly the textbook picture of a Hispanic-surnamed woman, as a single working mom with an engineering degree, a Spanish surname and governmental tenure, her resume would always be in demand. She didn't think of herself as a corporate go-getter, but nor was she a nine-to-five lackey.

John also brought Jill up to date. After law school, he had done his stint as an associate at a big law firm and had had his own "starter marriage." He squirmed a bit when he deflected the conversation from the subject of his marriage, saying, "We didn't make it to the second anniversary." He quickly continued, explaining that unmarried with no kids, in his early thirties, he'd left the firm and become an adjunct professor of law. Technically, John didn't lie to Jill when he left out the part about his marriage ending because his wife died, but it certainly was not a high-water mark of transparency.

John was a bit reserved in that he didn't want to divulge too much to Jill. He wasn't sure why; perhaps he didn't want to be seen as complaining or bragging to her. They had known each other for a relatively short time a long time ago. He described a few of his investment projects and hobbies. Perhaps because of her engineering background, Jill had more than a casual interest in hearing about some of them. They prattled on, back and forth, for a couple of hours.

At some point during their conversation, a waiter took a food order, which of course was in conjunction with a second bottle brought over by Freddy. "Why not compare the 1995 Bordeaux with a 1995 Napa?" he asked. "It's so fashionable to 'dis the Mondavi Reserve, poor Robert rest his soul, but as far as I'm concerned, that's great because it keeps it affordable. Yeah, I said it, affordable! Fools!" declared Freddy, as he opened a bottle of 1995 Robert Mondavi Cabernet Sauvignon Reserve. It was sublime. And the ritual opening and decanting was accompanied by Freddy's story about Robert Mondavi himself coming to the restaurant with the governor, who of course later went to prison, as Freddy recounted. The Freddy Show just kept giving.

The flowing wine had loosened up John and Jill. Like

any corporate or government executive, Jill certainly had the ability to avoid saying anything substantive, but with a decades-old friend and a healthy blood alcohol level, those normal inhibitions were lessened. John was similarly enjoying a heady buzz.

"So, did you ever get to meet Mondavi when you worked in Sonoma?" John asked. Jill recounted an evening when indeed she had seen Mondavi and his dining entourage at the French Laundry Restaurant in Napa. John hung on every detail.

Talk then drifted to some of the characters at the Predators Ball. They exchanged a little gossip about various business items, and then Jill asked, "Wait a minute, I forgot to ask you, why are you here at the convention in the first place?"

John rolled into an answer. "I invested with a few start-ups, and sometimes there were other venture capital funds that also invested. The partners of those funds are a bit egotistical and are intrigued that a mere mortal who isn't with a big-named fund – me - can also spot a good deal. So now and then they call me and pick my brain for free, but I pick theirs back. So, I guess this is a scouting trip of sorts, so I have something to talk about."

John realized that what he had just told Jill was only about twenty percent correct, and he silently scolded himself; he was falling into a pattern of telling half-truths to Jill. So, with only the slightest of slurring, which helped mitigate his fibbing, he added, "One of those technology projects helped our people overseas. There weren't any government solutions available, and we helped make the impossible happen, quietly and privately, a little bit Leonardo da Vinci style."

As if to punctuate that, John's phone rang again. He glanced at it and after a short pause he pushed the 'decline call' button on his phone, as he'd done earlier in the evening.

Jill looked at her watch; it was past 11 pm. She quipped, "Okay, even convention time has its limits, da Vinci or Michelangelo."

"Sometimes patriots in foreign time zones are indistinguishable from zealots," John said, feigning annoyance at the call, almost under his breath.

"Well, that means that you can sleep in. Unfortunately, I must be smiling and representing our fine Department of Homeland Security in its territorial pissing match with the FAA at a breakfast seminar starting at 8 am, and I'm already dreading the mini-hangover that's got a reserved front-row seat right next to the danish tray," Jill said.

"I get it, you're turning into a pumpkin," said John. "Truth be told, I probably need to return a couple of calls. But this has been great. More than great."

Freddy called two cabs after the bill was paid. As Jill and John left the restaurant, John promised, "Just to prove that I am not a lightweight, I will make every effort to drop by the end of your breakfast seminar tomorrow, just to show support."

"Deal. But no pictures and no autographs," said Jill.

"I agree," said John. They exchanged a long warm hug.

Jill said, "I can't tell you how much I have enjoyed this. Every bit of it."

She was a bit tipsy, and so was John. He had an odd

flashback from decades ago, when every fiber of his body and brain had been focused on figuring out how to kiss her, consequences be damned. As they stood there, he realized he was experiencing an equivalent uneasiness now. He was about to make a clever quip, but it would have extended the evening another three hours.

"Can we please do this again? I mean, above and beyond my solemn pledge to stop by for coffee and donuts tomorrow?" John asked.

"The answer is, hell yes," said Jill.

They hugged again. John then gave her a kiss on her cheek – not the short European kiss, but a slightly longer, "damn it is good to see you again" kiss.

He opened the taxi door for Jill, and she was off. John waved as her taxi departed. It had been a great reunion, even though they hadn't discussed the circumstances under which they had known each other decades ago.

He pulled out his wallet, grabbed a five-dollar bill, and handed it to the other taxi driver. "Thanks, but I won't be needing you."

In the cab, Jill realized she was tipsy. She was thinking what a good evening it had been. As she glanced out of the window of the taxi, she saw a liquor store which reminded her of the mental note she had made while walking to Freddy's. She pulled her phone from her purse and wrote herself a to-do note: "Give a discreet call to Nancy at DHS – possible trafficking apartment, top floor balcony above the liquor store at 774. Check street name. A block from Freddy's. The real Freddy's, not the fake address." Her thoughts then shifted back to more pleasant matters – the evening's reunion of sorts.

FREDDY'S REDUX

John then went back into Freddy's and grabbed a seat at the bar. The diners had mostly departed, so Freddy moved over to the bar. "Something go wrong, Mr. John? That was one good lookin' lady. Yes, on that. Ms. Jill, wasn't that her name? I thought you'd be tied up through breakfast, if you don't mind my saying so."

"How about a nightcap, Freddy. Got anything worth the pounding head I'll get from it?" asked John.

"Matter of fact, I have just the thing. Just it." Freddy grabbed a bottle from below the bar. "Birthday party was in here last night, six of them or so, some guy kept talking on about how he loved his cigars and port. So, he wanted a bottle of the best port in the house. Now, damn I'm not giving some stranger the best bottle. Even if it was his birthday. But he's a good fellow. A good one. So I sold him a good bottle. Not the best bottle, but a real good bottle. Or something like that." Freddy grabbed two wine glasses and poured a glass for John and one for himself. Freddy kept a bar towel over the bottle, hiding its label. "Take a guess, John."

They clinked glasses, and both sipped. John inhaled deeply. "It's got age, a medium body. A great finish. A bit feminine, so not Fonseca or Taylor's. I'll say Graham's. 1970 Graham's."

"You are good with your ports, Mr. John," said Freddy. He pulled the towel off the bottle. It was 1966 Graham's vintage port.

"Graham's it is! Pretty close on the vintage, Freddy, thanks. I can't remember the last time I had a 1966," said John.

Then the combination of alcohol, plus the renewed memories of a teenaged summer with Jill, plus the southern comfort of sitting with Freddy at his bar, shifted John into high speed. "This bottle sat in the winery for two and a half years before it was shipped out. So, someone bought it in 1969.

"You know, Freddy, the late sixties were sorta fucked up in America, but it was also an incredible time. I know there was Vietnam and the hippie generation and the civil rights movement. But here's what gets me, Freddy. In July of 1969, we walked on the moon. This was after a decade-long space race. That race was a winner-take-all Olympics, with only one gold medal just for the winner. And the United States won. And that month, every kid in every Third World country wanted to emulate the Americans. They wanted to be an American. They wanted our system, our freedoms, our economy. So did the kids in the Soviet Bloc. Hell, most adults, too.

"But Freddy… you know what I'm asking. Did we blow it? We just walked away from it. And instead, we announced 'joint ventures' with the Soviets. As if it had been a tie. Basically, just telling the world, 'never mind, we're the same, you can be totalitarian communist or a western liberal, no difference. We're gonna share rockets together.'"

"Bring it, Mr. John," goaded Freddy, nodding his head. "That '66 port is really speaking to ya, isn't it, Mr. John," said Freddy. "I mean it's speaking to ya, and you got an even bigger story you mean to tell it right back."

"I mean, Freddy, what the fuck is a joint venture? I don't remember the Pittsburgh Steelers announcing any joint venture with the Saints. I don't remember Tom Dempsey announcing his 63-yard field goal was gonna be shared, so it was now a joint venture of two kicks of 32 yards each. So anyway, we called this joint venture "Apollo-Soyuz." Who decided that? Like having our name first was supposed to make it all right? A joint venture?"

They sat in silence for a minute. Freddy knew to let John roll when he wanted to roll.

"So, in Russia, did they call it Soyuz-Apollo? They didn't even do that, Freddy. They called it 'Soyuz 19.' Jesus, they didn't even bother giving a nod to the winner. We were just erased - airbrushed out of the photograph, as if it had never happened.

"You know what we did right before Apollo-Soyuz? We sent up a space station. Skylab. We knew it was broken, but we sent it up anyway. It came crashing down a couple years later.

"Like all those 1970s movies about fucking disasters. Sinking ships. Burning buildings. Killer bees. Was the new generation realizing they sucked compared to their parents? So, they just walked away, abandoned space and made movies about how everything they did was doomed?"

"Mr. John, remind me to pour you the 1938 madeira one of these nights," joked Freddy. It took a few seconds for John to catch the reference, and then they both broke out laughing.

"That's your best work, right there," said John as he tried to check his laughter.

"C'mon, bring some more," encouraged Freddy.

"But why do nations, why do people just walk away?" continued John.

"Even worse…After winning? 'Hey, never mind, thanks for dying in our wars, we were just kidding.' We were the shining city on the hill, Freddy. Why did we turn off the lights for the billions of people whose hope was for our shining city?" muttered John.

Freddy chuckled. "John, by my watch, you're only a minute shy of your own record for ranting. A damned good rant, though. I can make a copy of it from the security camera, if you want. It was that good. Real good."

John drank his port. Freddy poured him a bit more.

"Did you go off like this with that pretty brunette, Ms. Jill? Is that why your date ended so early? I'm not sure there were any Soviet rockets at that table tonight. Or did she just get you all worked up? Maybe so, so maybe we need to call this one the Brunette Rant. It's one for the books, yep," said Freddy. They both savored a few more sips, and Freddy asked, "All this rocket talk makes some sense, Mr. John, but did something go wrong with her? I would have bet twenty dollars that she'd be making breakfast with you in a few hours."

"Believe it or not, Freddy, she was my high school

girlfriend, for a few weeks. Haven't seen her for, gosh, decades," said John. "Ran into her by coincidence at the convention today."

"Well, you musta had a helluva new girlfriend to have gotten rid of her," said Freddy. "Oops, I mean…maybe that's not how it went down. But excuse me for saying, it looked to me like if you wanted to couple up with her, she wasn't going to be objecting too hard."

"It's a bit complicated, so…I thought I'd buy myself a time-out to give it some thought. The last time I had any contact with her was around the time my wife died. And seeing her triggered some old…memories, I guess," said John.

"Hell, Freddy, I'll have hundreds of kids out on the prairie this summer at tree-planting camp. And before she died, my wife worked with a non-profit environmental group involved in trees and things. Connection? My dad died in a submarine accident, so I hate pirates but love deep ocean treasure hunting. Related? You think maybe a shrink would say I have some issues to sort out? Well those are just coincidences compared to my short time with my old girlfriend Jill. I have no idea but suddenly today the whole closet door got opened, full of old stuffed toys of teenaged psychology. I'd make a good subject for an article in a psychology magazine… if those still existed," said John. "So I needed a little pause tonight, a little speed bump. A beautiful old girlfriend dropping in was a little unsettling."

There was a pause. "Lemme know if I can help," said Freddy. And then after a jazz-timed beat, "But I already told you, she was one fine looking lady and you weren't looking like you were in any hurry to get rid of her. Now I gotta go crack the whip to get this place cleaned up. I've served up an ocean tonight, I gotta make sure no one drowns in the tide. See you next time, John." Freddy gave John a little touch slap on the shoulder.

"Thanks again, Freddy." John left a fifty in the well as Freddy headed back to the kitchen.

The rain had stopped and John grabbed a tourist rickshaw bike ride and was back at his place in a few minutes. He was woozy and a bit tired, but strangely energized by his dinner with Jill. His house in New Orleans was a two-story brick building on Governor Nichols Street, overlooking a small park in the French Quarter. The house had a red-brick exterior, and the interior walls included floor-to-ceiling red brick fireplaces, a vestige from the ante-bellum era. The doors were high and had transoms to encourage air flow. In the days before electricity and air conditioning, architects had to use clever design to deal with the climate.

The floors were original oak hardwood. One-hundred-fifty years of use and varnish had left them with a majestic glow. Wooden millwork, much of it cypress and cedar, accented the rooms. The lighting was impeccable – there were no glaring lights anywhere. Subdued and indirect lighting was fused with some spot lighting on notable features and artwork.

The house décor included a bit of 'steampunk,' as evidenced by the twenty-first century design standards, consisting of old wood, metal and leather items that were refashioned into furniture or lighting. But there were also antiques and relics of the past, many of which were part of the house's original design and others that John had acquired himself.

He chugged a bottle of water, thinking about what Freddy had said about Jill. Was she there for the taking? Did John want that? Why had he begged off on putting the moves on an old girlfriend? He decided the night wasn't yet over. He opened an old bottle of vintage port from an obscure port producer– the 1985 Burmester – and cut a chunk of blue cheese to go with it. His earlier rant to Freddy had been quirky, but he was going deeper.

He moved into his front room where there was a large window overlooking the street, which was largely deserted at this hour. He sat in the big leather chair situated there, perfect for reading or contemplation, and a couple of antique combination safes served as end tables. 'Mantiques,' as John called them. On top of one of them sat an old manual typewriter that had belonged to his father. The other was an old combination safe from a submarine, a gift from a friend a few years earlier, with a jar of various old copper and silver coins.

Different people felt comfortable around different things. Years ago, John had realized that old combination safes were what put him into a calm zone. Perhaps it was because the inner workings of a safe combination, like the movement of an old watch, could be looked at and contemplated for hours.

The last thing John needed was more alcohol, but it didn't matter. Some personal revelations were quivering on the horizon, and he was strapping into his favorite chair with comfort booze as an incoming wave set assembled itself on the breakwaters of his brain. He struggled to recall the details of the last time he'd seen Jill Serrano – then, Jill Seneca. Once he remembered a few details, the rest sprang forth.

A NIGHTCAP WITH AN OLD MEMORY

John recalled the time - it was the summer after John and Jill's senior year of high school. Jill's family had moved to town a few months earlier, near the end of senior year. Jill joined his graduating class in the closing weeks of the school year, making her part outsider but also the new kid who everyone else was checking out. After graduation, as the summer wore on, kids were variously preparing for college, jobs or trade school.

John recalled that Jill and a couple of her new acquaintances ended up at a pizza parlor hangout with John and some of his friends. He and Jill had ended up in the same booth. Both would be heading off to college at the end of the summer. Whether John's attraction to Jill was something special, or just the natural function of his seventeen-year-old hormones being in proximity to Jill's eighteen-year-old hormones, wasn't quite clear.

In those days, the ritual was that a guy asked a girl out on a date. So, John had awkwardly asked Jill out on a date, which had proceeded in a perfectly normal manner. The hormones were raging by the time of their second date, which also proceeded perfectly well. Around midnight, they had begun to hold hands and even kissed a bit. They were headed back to Jill's house, and John was desperately hoping they'd end up on the couch in the darkened living room, and Jill wasn't really indicating that she had any objection to that. Were her parents still awake?

But the extended family living in Jill's house included her mother's no-good brother, James Eaton, Jr. In and out of drug rehab, he was a loser who in effect was an adult problem ward of Jill's family.

As John and Jill went to grab a midnight bite in her kitchen, the creepy uncle, drugged out and in a violent mood, entered. John had no idea who the big man was, but he began spewing sexual suggestions at Jill and threats at John.

The situation devolved in mere seconds when James Eaton picked up a large carving knife . He began swinging it, and although he was drugged, he was strong and knew how to wield a knife because he had served in the Army. Eaton lunged at John, slashing him with the knife. It was only a superficial cut to the scalp, just above the ear, but copious amounts of blood poured forth.

Rather than slowing down the assault, the blood seemed to incite Uncle James to further violence, this time against Jill. Blurting out obscenities, he drew the knife as he turned to her in a madman's rage. Seeing his own blood all over himself, John had an immediate surge of adrenaline, and he lunged forward to tackle Eaton to prevent the imminent attack on Jill.

John slammed into Uncle James, but the larger man was only knocked down on his knees while John tumbled to the floor. But as Uncle James was down to his knee, the five seconds' delay had bought Jill enough time for her to grab a large frying pan from the stove top. As Uncle James came back to his feet, Jill slammed the heavy iron skillet into his face. It was almost like an old Warner Bros. cartoon, except that it was real. Uncle James went down and as he fell the knife pierced his abdomen.

A half-minute after Uncle James had started the drug-fueled attack, it was over. He lay semi-conscious on the floor, moaning and bleeding profusely from his nose, temple and gut. John had risen to his feet after his partial tackle of Uncle James, with blood streaming down the side of his head from the shallow gash in his scalp. Jill had dropped the frying pan and was standing over the scene, shock rapidly overwhelming her.

Perhaps it was the effect of panic chemicals in John's bloodstream that continued to stave off shock, if only momentarily. John may have been young, but he quickly processed that his not-yet-girlfriend Jill had just seriously wounded an attacker in a bloody knife fight, in self-defense. John moved to the telephone on the kitchen wall to call for an ambulance, and he realized he also needed to call the police.

Jill was partly in shock, and she just stared at John, not really able to process things. She whimpered, "It's my uncle. He's crazy. Oh shit, oh shit…"

"Fuck," blurted John. And whether it was chivalry, bravado, embarrassment for not disabling the uncle, or just smart thinking in an emergency, John kicked into action. In a strained, stress-wracked voice that sounded like a command shouted in a foxhole, John said, "You just turned eighteen. I'm only seventeen, a juvie. The story is, I hit him, not you, just go with it, just go with it."

John dialed zero, excitedly asked for an ambulance and the police. Moments later, when he was connected to the police, he blurted out, "I just hit a crazy guy, he tried to kill us in the kitchen, he has a knife, he is bleeding really bad, you need to send the cops and an ambulance. I'm bleeding, too."

The police dispatcher tried to calm John and asked the basic questions - what is the address, etc. John was able to get Jill focused enough to repeat her address. John then repeated it to the dispatcher, "He attacked me and Jill with a big knife. He cut me, I'm bleeding. I hit him hard with a frying pan. He's out cold. He's whacked out on some kind of drugs. I think I killed him."

After John hung up, Jill was now kneeling, still in mild shock and fighting nausea. Blood was everywhere, on the floor and all over John's ear, neck and shirt. It had happened too fast.

John picked up the frying pan, rubbed it a few times as if to wipe away fingerprints, and in the process covered it in his own blood. He then kneeled next to Jill, showed her the bloody frying pan, and said, "It's done. I told the cops the story, that I hit him. The skillet has my prints and blood on it. He attacked me; I've got a gash on my head. I picked up the skillet and hit him. He fell. It's done now, you have to stick with that. I'm only 17, I can't get in trouble."

The wailing sirens awoke Jill's parents, who came upon the scene in the kitchen in shocked disbelief as the police and ambulance arrived. The paramedics staved the bleeding of Uncle James and rushed him to the hospital. Later after his head was bandaged, John reconfirmed to the cops the story he'd told the police dispatcher. The assistant detective on duty that night – it was high vacation season – did not delve into details with Jill. He told her what John had said, and she agreed that John's version was what she had witnessed. It was mercifully easy. Jill's parents had no details to offer.

When Uncle James came out of intensive care a few days later, he was booked on a variety of felony charges, including attempted murder.

As a matter of law and policy, juvenile names, particularly those of victims, were not released to the press. The local news reported only that a domestic battery had occurred, but since Uncle James's surname did not match that of the Seneca family, the connection to Jill was never made, and with school being out of session, the normal high school rumor mill was disengaged.

John was not charged, as he'd clearly acted in self-defense against the attack of a junked-up felon. Nor was there any sensational criminal trial at which John or Jill would have to testify, as Uncle James ended up pleading guilty to a laundry list of charges and was sent off to prison. Within a few decades, all the courthouse, police and emergency services personnel involved in the criminal case had long retired. No media reports at the time mentioned either Jill's or John's name, and there remained no institutional record that could ever reconstruct the violent events of that pre-digital-age summer.

Only John and Jill, if they concentrated hard, had any knowledge of the events of that horrific night. The tragedy took place just two weeks before they left for college. The days following the incident were awkward, and hard enough for an adult to deal with, much less for a teenaged boy and a new girl in town. Jill and John never did get to make out on a couch together.

After they went off to their respective colleges, Jill's family moved again, and John and Jill wrote to each other a few times, and exchanged a few awkward calls at holiday break. But soon they had immersed themselves in new lives at college and moved on to other places, romances and jobs. The trauma and the calendar had aborted their youthful fling just minutes before it had started.

Coming out of his reverie about that long-ago horrific night, John felt a twinge of guilt about Jill. Maybe he was bad news for Jill, and he should just stay away. Or, was John inventing excuses to avoid an inevitable clash with his high-school girlfriend who was now a sort of drone cop and might consider him a drone outlaw? His thoughts segued back to his dinner with Jill. He hadn't told her what he was doing with his life. He'd given her incomplete, cryptic answers – not actual lies, but certainly misleading by omission.

He laughed as he imagined himself as a bronco rider, trying to look like he was in control, maintaining a casual conversation with a pretty woman as the rodeo gate opened and the bronco underneath him broke away and dragged him into a wild shivering dance.

That image wasn't too far from the truth.

A STRANGER CALLS FROM BERMUDA

On the other side of the world, as the sun's rays struck the picture window of her dining room, Majedah Simon picked up a stack of papers off her table. She had just finished making a number of calls from home, trying to navigate the various time zones around the world. She gazed out the window to her backyard where she had planned to spend a few hours that day. That was a typical way to begin the weekend, and that was her plan, anyway, until events interrupted. She had not been able to connect an important call that Kirk Woodbury in Bermuda had arranged for her. She resigned herself to trying a few hours later, as half the world was sleeping now, and she had no idea to whom or where her call was being forwarded.

Four hours later, Majedah again dialed the phone number.

Halfway around the world, just an hour after the sun rose in New Orleans, John was awakened by his vibrating phone. He had fallen asleep in his big comfortable chair. His slightly swollen sinuses were a bit painful, but he saw that the call was from Kirk Woodbury's Bermuda phone number. Groggy, and before he had the sense to ignore it, he answered the call. "Yeah," was all he said. Such was the nature of a hangover.

"Hello, sir," said a female voice, "I am calling you at the request of a mutual friend. I am afraid I do not know your name, and I am connected with you through our mutual friend's office. May I be so forward as to provide you with a dial-in number, which will make for an encrypted call connection? It would be much better if we spoke that way. I can do the formal introductions on that call; I won't take more than five minutes of your time." The caller did not identify herself.

Based upon his respect for Kirk Woodbury, John agreed. "Yes, but first please call me back in twenty minutes. It's early here and I need caffeine." He hung up. He had bought himself a few minutes to use the bathroom and brew some coffee.

It was mid-day across the globe, and over the past day Majedah Simon had made several dozen calls to a number of reliable acquaintances looking for a possible lead to her current task. It was a fishing expedition, but nonetheless it was necessary to seek information through diverse sources. Now she had twenty minutes. Should she try to squeeze in another call first?

Majedah noticed that Beethoven's "Moonlight Sonata" had just started playing on her stereo's playlist, and that it would conclude just before she needed to make the follow up call. She decided to take a break from her calls. She gazed out the window at her modest enclosed backyard. A center path split the yard into two parts and led to a small table set against the back wall and a tiny pool and fountain. From her vantage point, the left side of the yard was a beautifully maintained garden, similar in quality to those that appeared in local gardening magazines. Well-tended exotics and local plants dotted this half of the garden, which was loaded with grasses, flowers, and some miniature shrubs, palms and fruit trees. It stood in stark contrast to the right side of her yard, which would charitably be called a feral weed patch, comprised of a beguilingly random mixture of annuals and perennials, grasses, flowers, weeds and the like. It resembled a random but fertile field off an inaccessible highway on-ramp. It was as if Majedah's yard was tended by two different minds – one an attentive gardener, the other an absentee owner of an empty building. Yet as she regarded her back yard, the dichotomy brought great comfort to her.

A breeze caused a window curtain to flutter, and for a split second the breeze caused the sound of Moonlight Sonata to oscillate. Unexpectedly, the fluctuation triggered a long-lost memory. As the recollection flashed, Majedah was back to when she was a young woman just completing her military training. It was just minutes after sunset, and she was perched on the small balcony of her tenth-floor apartment in Beirut. The cityscape was scarred by various battles of the country's on-and-off-again civil war, and just two miles away the various factions had drawn to a stalemate, but they continued sporadic small-arms firing. An informal understanding – more of a *modus operandi* – was that each faction would cease fire at half past sunset. There was an end-of-day din of motorcycles, trucks and cars below, as the city's residents scrambled to get home before darkness fell. The cacophony was punctuated by occasional deep but muffled booms of military shelling miles away in the hill country east of Beirut, the last of the day before the informal daily cessation of war.

The memory which Majedah recalled was of her looking out upon the city, and she had focused on an open window in an apartment house half a block away, noticing its curtains moving in the evening breeze. In her head, the din of the city simply disappeared, as if the volume knob had been turned down to near silence. Like a gifted sonarman aboard a submarine, Majedah discerned and then focused on the faint, intermittent sound of a Beethoven sonata coming from inside that distant apartment.

Her trainers and supervisors had also taken note, in many contexts, of Majedah's extraordinary ability to discern signal from noise – particularly, in recognizing meaningful signal amidst cascading chaos. Chaos, as during a live-fire battle.

Her thoughts pivoted her back to the afternoon sun currently flooding her backyard, sharply highlighting all the plant life as well as the butterflies and birds that flitted about. Majedah smiled at her creation. Chaos and order. Both sides of the garden. They were perfect. The Moonlight Sonata continued to fill her living room.

Back in New Orleans, John had finished half a cup of coffee and splashed his slightly puffy, hung-over face with water. His phone rang again, precisely twenty minutes after he had hung up on his mystery caller. "Hello," he said, sounding only slightly more alert and courteous than he had earlier.

"Hello," the female voice said, "I'm calling back as you requested. May I give you that secure dial-up number so that we may have a five-minute call? Of course, you may anonymize your outgoing number if you'd like, or use any other encryption method that makes you comfortable," she continued in a voice that was authoritative without being off-putting. The scenario was a bit bizarre, but because of Kirk's referral, John was willing to go along at least for five minutes.

"Sure," replied John. "What is that number?" The caller gave him the number, and John hung up and then redialed the call number after anonymizing his line by first dialing *67. The line rang twice, and the caller picked up.

"Thank you for calling back," she said. There was an ever so slight delay in the feed, but it was not long enough to interrupt the conversation. The caller began her pitch. "Sir, I work closely with some persons with an interest in peace in the Middle East. We are on a secure line, but I am nonetheless limited in what I may say, and I certainly do not want to put you in any uncomfortable situation. So, let me introduce myself with what I know, and what I am seeking.

"Back in 2009, one of my projects was to track some anomalies in the Arabian Sea and the Gulf of Aden. Specifically, there were numerous Somali-based pirate boats in action, but that piracy scourge was quite effectively decimated by unidentified vectors. Such a development was of interest to my…" - the voice paused – "colleagues. We had deduced a plausible scenario of what might have been occurring, but then it abruptly ceased when an American submarine became involved."

The voice continued, "That's ancient history. Forward to today, we now have a situation facing us, and our – my - educated guess back then has caused us to reach out to some contacts in Bermuda, including our mutual friend in Bermuda. This current situation is a delicate one, similar in some respects to the Somali piracy situation back then. The government forces that one would expect to handle this developing scenario are not able to address it."

The caller had a mild British accent, but with a dialect that John could not place. She continued, "And sir, if I may say so, because I was personally involved in monitoring the Somali piracy matter, I was somewhat perplexed by how the operator of that mission was able to pull it off, for months, virtually undetected and without leaving any footprint. A textbook ghost operation – so completely dark that no government or intelligence service anywhere had any connection to it or even knowledge of it. Our curiosity caused us to ultimately gain access to one of the instrumentalities – a balloon array - that we suspected was involved, and it confirmed our suspicion that there was no government actor involved.

"That led us to hypothesize that commercial interests were behind it – harkening back to colonial days. We stopped the inquiry when the operation seemed to have terminated when the Americans raised a fuss about a potential act of war against one of their submarines.

"But because of a current and time-sensitive situation, our mutual friend suggested that I make this call to you. And hence this call," the woman said. "I'd like to enquire if I am speaking to an appropriate person regarding that former matter. And thank you for engaging with me," the woman said.

John was caught a bit off guard, and he paused for a second, realizing that speaking to an unknown stranger on the telephone was not the way to maintain security.

"Ma'am, I'm afraid I'm not quite following everything here. Can you elaborate a bit?" he asked, buying himself a little time for the coffee to kick in and his head to clear a bit more.

The caller seemed to welcome the fact that John didn't simply hang up. "Certainly. My group – we – surmised back then that maritime insurance interests were somehow involved in clearing the shipping lanes of the pirate fleets, but we never learned any details other than assuming that aerial-based bombardment was involved, based upon our recovery of one such potential array. I might add, as a personal observation, it was a tactical stroke of genius, which probably explains why I remember it to this day. And it – what is the phrase? — it certainly 'got a lot of peoples' panties into a bunch,'" the caller said.

"I've told our Bermuda insurance friends that we'd like to learn more about whatever these actors did. I can state it more bluntly: Whatever team was involved back then, could be vital to resolving a similar situation we face right now. Peace is at stake. And like that piracy operation in the Arabian Sea, we need it to remain an enigma – completely off the books. Whatever that team did to keep their operation so dark, it remains, again, textbook. Hence our inquiry to ascertain if the non-governmental group involved in that operation might be available for current work."

The caller paused, and then added, "I am acutely aware of the oddity of this inquiry, including my not even knowing the name of the person I am speaking with or whether you are drinking coffee or tea."

John also paused. The caller's voice had an almost

hypnotic effect on him. It wasn't just the accent and slightly authoritative but rich tone. It was also that this caller knew too much – way, way too much. He realized that he must have been slurping his coffee a bit – he tended to do that when he was nursing a hangover, and anyone might have guessed what that sound was.

But John's friend Kirk Woodbury had assured him that he had not divulged anything to the caller. So John quickly realized that the caller's knowledge came from a source other than the reinsurer group. That limited the potentials to a very small handful. Which meant that the caller was probably affiliated with a state-sponsored intelligence community. In short, she was a spy.

John had some obvious questions, but he knew the value of asking a few more warm-ups, if for no other reason than to help clear his head. "How did your organization conclude that the insurance interests were connected to the Arabian Sea situation?" asked John.

"Sir, that's a fair question about our sources and methods. What I can divulge is that I do not believe in Batman or Superman. They're fiction. When some significant operation plays, it's not because of heroes or good Samaritans. We focus on the actor who directly benefits. Simply put, motive. Ruling out state- or multi-state actors, that left two obvious candidates with motive: The shipping companies and their insurers. But since the pirate ransoms were generally being paid by insurers and the costs impacted a small but powerful group of maritime insurers, we ascertained a high likelihood that the maritime insurers were the primary actors involved," the caller responded.

"And why did you rule out governments?" asked John.

There was a pause, and the voice continued, "That's another fair question about our methods and sources. Certain governments are the typical actors. Certainly so under Bretton Woods. But with the piracy countermeasures, there was no nation state that was sponsoring such piracy. Somalia was a broken state at the time. There was no embassy or UN office to complain to. Governments typically pair their military operations with diplomacy. Since no diplomacy was possible, we discounted that possibility of government sponsorship," she continued.

John realized that whoever she was, she was damned good at her job, and he was now enjoying this conversation. "But wouldn't it have been extremely easy for a government to take covert action against the pirates? They would seem to be a discrete and easy target to attack," John asked.

There was a pause at the other end. "It certainly was possible. But a fear of blowback is always a strong inhibitor, particularly so when there is no diplomacy channel operating alongside a military action," the caller offered. "The pirates were associated with various Muslim sectarian interests and warlords. The regional press could have reported any such operations as yet another attack against the Muslim community writ large. It could present a strong jihadist recruiting tool in the area, or elsewhere. The emotional appeal of defending against an attack on kinfolk is strong. Simply put, there was limited upside for a government, and a lot of downside, and no government counterparty to dampen that downside," she said. "Think 'Black Hawk Down.' "

John recognized that he wanted to continue with almost irrelevant questions, if only to hear the caller talk about something that he had kept confidential for years. To know that another person had been tracking his actions was a bit exhilarating. John had to check himself; talking to this voice put him into uncharted territory. And his safety and his freedom were at issue. After all, in the eyes of many, perhaps he had killed a bunch of people without sanction by any country. That was called mass murder.

John decided to buy a little more time to analyze the situation, and to shift the risk to the caller. After all, he was not obliged to provide anything to her.

He asked, "Thank you for your overview. Let me ask, on whose behalf is this inquiry being made, exactly?" It was time for her to show him a few of her cards.

There was a pause. "Officially, I cannot reveal that," the caller replied.

John paused again, and then said, "Yes, I understand, but despite your mesmerizing accent and facility in referencing American comic book heroes, you realize that this call will shortly be coming to a close?"

The caller paused, as if John's request was in complete violation of protocol. But that was the nature of this fishing expedition. "Sir, may we reconvene this call on a more secure line? That might permit me a little more latitude in our discussion," the caller asked.

"Yes, so long as it's not a collect call," John quipped. He realized he was being a bit flippant, but on the other hand, he had not hung up.

"I hate to ask this – you have been so helpful – can you

indulge me with twenty minutes' time to arrange for that more secure line?" asked his caller.

"Sure, and I need to refresh my mug of coffee – or maybe my tea," John said.

"Let me give you a telephone number, which will go live in twenty minutes." The caller then gave him an 855-toll free number, which he wrote down. "Thank you, sir, and we'll speak in twenty. But do note that because of the enhanced encryption on that line, my voice might be unrecognizable to you."

"Okay, but I have one more requirement. Before you go, tell me this. What is your name, real or otherwise?" asked John. "And please, not 'Tiffany' or 'Crystal,' those are already reserved for strippers, and I don't think that's how you earn your paycheck."

Another pause, then, "You may call me Majedah."

"Is that your first name or last?" John asked, but the line clicked dead as he spoke.

The unfolding of the call and the circumstances which led to it were too extraordinary for any rational person to comprehend, much less believe. Had John attempted to confide any of it to Mr. Freddy, or his old girlfriend Jill, their first and continuing reactions would have been that John Gabriel was suffering an acute mental episode involving vivid fabulations.

Yet it was not only true, but it had just been encapsulated by the mysterious phone calls with 'Majedah.' As the click of the line registered with him, a flash flood of memories rushed in, like a wall of water cascading down a dry canyon.

John's current situation was indecipherable to any observer without the benefit of knowing the secret world that he had gradually constructed over the prior decade.

BERMUDA AND PLACES RELATED — 2000-2008

For John Gabriel, it began in Bermuda. A few years after the millennial celebration of 2000, he had visited Bermuda[10] along with a crowd of attorneys to attend a routine continuing legal education law conference/junket, and he happened to catch a half-hour seminar about the Bermuda reinsurance industry. It struck John as an odd place for such a powerful arm of the world financing industry to be located. He learned that after World War II insurance companies had been drawn there because English was the predominant language and its legal and accounting systems were closely parallel to those in the United States.

John had struck up a conversation with one of the

insurance executives presenting at the panel, Kirk Woodbury, and the topic (naturally) turned to libations, and specifically the wine cellar at the conference resort. Both John and Kirk Woodbury were wine fans, and a few hours later they met up in the hotel's swanky lounge to examine the wine list.

John and Kirk had swapped stories about how they got interested in wine, including what they held in their wine refrigerators. Referencing the bottle of 1989 Bordeaux wine they were drinking, Kirk then recounted to John the unusual story of how the administrators for the bankrupt Lloyd's of London syndicates had ended up having to dispose of so much wine in the 1990's, and how Woodbury had as a matter of business research, done a bit of study on Bordeaux wine and had become hooked. Kirk promised to introduce John to a wine broker he dealt with, an American expat named Thomas Gallier, who had been living in Paris for some years, and John recorded his contact information before it might be forgotten in a fog of wine.

When it came time for a second bottle, John, feeling like he was hearing the war stories of a lifetime, decided to buy a stellar bottle. He asked Woodbury a few questions about vintages, etc., and chose a 1982 Cheval Blanc. They poured the wine, let it breathe, and marveled at how a bottle of decaying fruit juice could smell and taste so good.

Sufficiently lubricated, Gabriel asked Woodbury, "So Kirk, what's the real story of why all these insurance companies are in Bermuda? Why are you and so many other professionals here? I just don't get it."

"Pretty simple," replied Kirk. "All the relative benefits,

efficiencies and the like that we tout and that were included in my presentation are fine and dandy. But that's not why tens of billions of dollars are parked here."

"What is it, then?" John asked.

"This island is a fortress with a moat," replied Kirk. "Legally, that is. Wars for treasure are no longer limited to physical armies on battlefields trying to storm the castle's inner keep. Wars are fought in the courts of law and public opinion, and in financial centers. It's law fare, not warfare. It's the wanna-haves versus the currently-haves. And here in Bermuda, we are one of the safest vaults for the currently-haves. Everything else is just detail.

"You see," Kirk continued, "insurance companies are sitting ducks. 'Disfavored' is the polite term. They are increasingly viewed as the faceless 'currently-haves,' especially by juries. So, the insurance companies that advertise on television, they are just pawns, the expendable foot soldiers. They are the front men for the real money, the keepers of large policies, for hundreds of millions of dollars, and large pools made up of conglomerates. They are called "re-insurers." A better term would be "the deepest pockets" or "where the buck finally stops." And the money backing those policies – the vast pools of capital – a lot of it resides here. These are the real 'currently-haves.' And they are the golden goose that everyone around the globe wants to slay."

"So, explain your reference to a fortress with a moat," asked John.

"Easy. Our courts and treaties do not allow any outsider to sue us here. We are, by design, exempt from the direct grasp of United States courts and juries. You wanna come grab our money? Then come to our courts and try. But to do that, you must have a Bermuda law license. Good luck getting that. It's our bat, our ball and our field, so we make the rules. Plus it's in our courts, not yours.

"That's why you have to fly here to speak to us. We simply won't do business outside of our island. Inside our protected walls, behind our moat. What that means is that money is safe here, away from the silver-tongued lawyers enthralling low-information jurors about how 'someone must pay' for some outrage 'in order to send a message.' Blah blah blah. And that's the real reason why there are so many bankers, lawyers and insurance executives here. We man the vault. And it's an incredibly secure vault."

John gave that some thought for a moment. He raised his wine glass in a toast. "Here's to the modern lords of the castle's keep, and to the knights who protect the vault!"

Kirk raised his glass and replied, "Now you know." After a pause, he added, "But there's more to it than that. Let's head over to a wine bar down the street and I'll explain. Tonight's when some good local jazz players show up and just jam," said Kirk. "Believe it or not, there's a pianist who is quite good, apparently he's in town fixing up the old organ at the Cathedral of the Holy Trinity."

"Your island, your rules," said John, and off they went to the bar.

By the time they arrived, Kirk had finished up his deep dive explanation about the Bermuda financial history. As they entered, Kirk said, "Let me introduce you to the pianist. His name is Frank Clicquot. That wine broker I mentioned, Tom Gallier, introduced me to him. And someday when you have half a day to kill, ask Frank to explain his world to you."

"Something tells me I'm not gonna believe it," said John.

"I'm not going to spoil it," said Kirk, and they sat down at a table.

THE PIRATES OF ADEN

Over the ensuing years, John returned to Bermuda many times. After he'd earned some money with the start-up stocks, he set up his own so-called captive Bermuda insurance company, which was an ideal device within which to structure some of his financial and charitable affairs.

On one of his visits, Kirk Woodbury casually mentioned the mounting problem of the Somali piracy scourge. Groups of pirates, often affiliated with local warlords, used Somali harbors to stage raids on nearby shipping lanes. The Gulf of Aden lay to the south of the Red Sea, along the chaotic northern coast of Somalia, and as such was a bottleneck of world shipping. The warlord-controlled feudalism of Somalia, combined with the busy waters of the Gulf of Aden, were fertile breeding grounds for piracy and terrorism.

As Kirk detailed, by the end of 2008, pirate raids by Somali gangs were out of control. Hundreds of ships had been attacked. Ransoms were demanded, crews were slain, boats were burned, shipments delayed. Some maritime insurers faced losing vast amounts on multi-year reinsurance contracts. If the raids and losses did not stop, insurers faced several more years of massive losses, possibly even bankruptcy. The world's shipping industry was descending into chaos, and the worldwide economic melt-down which began in 2008 diverted the world's attention from the far-off waters on the coast of Somalia. The American Navy would not be coming to rescue anytime soon.

John was fascinated by the problem that Kirk described. It was a perfect confluence of law, politics, war, business, and risk. He peppered Kirk with questions about the piracy situation and asked why the insurers could not just do X, or Y or Z. Kirk explained why some obvious mitigations would not work. It was impossible for the insurers to use weapons or military assets to address the problem. First, the insurers didn't have a military. Second, and ironically, insurers did not allow mercenary action or warfare under their contracts with each other. Finally, as a matter of international law, merchant ships could not be armed, at least not if they wished to enter and depart other ports.

John pondered the dilemma at a waterside table at Hamilton Harbour in Bermuda, including all the reasons preventing the merchant vessels from using weapons against the pirates. Frigatebirds – sometimes called man-o-war birds – lazily circled high above the harbor, their three-pound bodies floating almost effortlessly thanks to their eight feet of wingspan. Below the frigatebirds were flocks of seagulls and other birds working the harbor for scraps. Occasionally a squadron of pelicans would arrive and, when a school of fish revealed itself, the dive-bombing would begin.

Perhaps it was the ornamental anchors on display in the harbor, or the suggestive name of the yacht *Flechette* anchored just a stone's throw from John's seat at the harbor restaurant, or the second glass of lunch wine. But John's "eureka" moment did arrive, as his thoughts lined up in succession as he studied nature's aerial circus play out over the harbor. What if a combination of the capabilities of the long-range frigate bird and those of the dive bomber pelican could be arrayed against the pirate boats? The frigatebirds rarely flapped their wings, they just soared. And then John's associative creativity made the connection.

A few years earlier, he had invested in a rudimentary orbital balloon venture of some of his former students, which basically used balloons to haul payloads to high altitudes. That start-up company's prospectus included the potential commercial use for balloon-lifted payloads as "kinetic bombardment systems." In a prior paradigm, World War I pilots had dumped iron 'flechette' bombs onto enemy positions. Vietnam-era war armorers experimented with similar weapons ideas. These were largely lost down the memory hole of history, with only an occasional Pentagon whitepaper to contemplate tungsten girders weighing a ton or more being dropped from low space orbit at supersonic speed to serve as a "bunker buster" against hardened missile silos.

John wondered if some modified kinetic bombardment could be a way to address the Somali piracy issue. The pelicans he was watching certainly were not dropping tungsten girders into missile silos. But pirate skiffs were relatively small, and their thin hulls were vulnerable - quite fragile, really. A 50-caliber bullet - like an old-fashioned fist-size flechette bomblet - could pierce clean through both sides of a pirate ship. Even a common soldier's armor-piercing cartridge, like the standard NATO-issued 5.56 green tip cartridge, might suffice to disable a pirate vessel. All that was needed to be done was to poke a couple of holes in a pirate boat, and the pirates' mission would come to an abrupt halt as their boat flooded with water.

Thus, it occurred to John that a projectile the size and configuration of a common lawn dart, travelling fast enough, might suffice. And the weapon didn't need to be accurate, like a rifle. Why not use a bundle of small flechette darts, carried aloft by the equivalent of the frigatebird, and then aim them in dive-bomb fashion like the pelican attacking a school of fish? They could be low-tech, cheap, and not susceptible to telemetry jamming by pirates or governments. Like the floating frigate bird, they would not need to be positioned aloft indefinitely, but rather for just a day or two, given the huge number of pirate attacks.

And the balloon-based bombing platforms didn't need to be in orbit, but rather just "up there" high enough so that targeting could be done, and for the bomblets to have enough altitude so that they would accelerate while in free fall to the required speed to do the job. Weather balloons seemed like the perfect vehicle.

And so, John Gabriel's first operation as a mercenary began over two glasses of white burgundy wine while sitting next to the Bermuda harbor watching seabirds.

TO KILL OR NOT TO KILL

John had realized that he was getting sucked into the puzzle aspects of the pirate problem, as if it were merely a technical problem. But this one also presented a moral problem. Some introspection was called for, and introspection was best done with a great bottle. Back at his hotel that evening, John ordered a special bottle of 1985 Lynch Bages Bordeaux and sat on his balcony overlooking the harbor. For John, choosing an old wine was a key device for critical thinking. Older wines have flaws, even if tiny. And the act of continually analyzing the aroma, body and finish of an old wine for features as well as flaws, was an ideal mental state for critical thinking. That is, analyzing over and over, searching for flaws and appreciating structure.

Ideally, John's anti-piracy plan would simply disable every pirate boat and make sure the would-be pirates would have good paying jobs with benefits waiting for them, loading cargo back at their port town. But that wasn't the real world. John's dilemma was his inability to come up with a solution that did not kill pirates. So, John confronted the question: Could he kill pirates?

John wrestled with the essence of what a Somali pirate leader or crew actually did. They took up arms, drove a boat for 100 miles into the gulf or ocean, forced their way onto an unarmed ship under threat of violence, commandeered the ship and crew at gunpoint, and threatened to kill hostages if they weren't paid a ransom. They were not poor, innocent fishermen caught trolling for fish in the wrong area or failing to carry the proper license. Those were mere infractions attributable to ignorance or poverty. These pirates were something else – they acted with malice. Called "mens rea," or "evil mind" in legal and philosophical literature,[11] it was different from mere "malum prohibitum," or an act which happens to be prohibited for expediency, and not because it is inherently wrongful.

But how could John be so sure that pirates knew they were morally wrong? He used the mind game of putting himself in their place, stripping out cultural and educational differences. Would a man who was being paid one hundred times a normal wage to take weapons onto a boat and threaten to kill the sailors inherently know that what he was doing was wrong – morally wrong? John easily concluded any man would know; to him, it was a no-brainer. And with that realization, John decided that he could kill pirates.

PUTTING THE BAND TOGETHER

After sorting through the moral questions, John did some technical thinking, and after running some basic numbers and sketching out a few configurations, he called an old college friend, Milo Patton, with whom he had maintained contact over the years. Milo Patton had been a rugby-playing baller who had whole-heartedly joined the military after college. John knew that he had supposedly retired, but John suspected – despite his friend's vague and wishy-washy denials– that Milo had left for more lucrative "private" work. Milo was more Blackwater than Company-man.[12]

After catching up on the past year, John asked Milo if they could have a cone-of-silence discussion.

John and Milo had never discussed anything like the Somali piracy matter, and John prefaced it by saying that he wasn't punking Milo, and that he was going to speak elliptically because he flatly didn't know if telephone calls really were being scanned by NSA algorithms searching for key words. John laid out the basics of his fast-developing plan to hunt Somali pirate boats, using non-specific wording, which made him sound like a foreigner with only a 200-word vocabulary trying to explain something technical.

After a few minutes, Milo interrupted him and said, "Look, John, I can tell you're serious about discussing this, either because it is very real, or someone has a machete at your head and is making you speak in code like bad eastern European cable TV reruns. I'm in Vegas right now and, frankly, I'm bored. What say you use some of those millions of frequent flyer miles you've undoubtedly accumulated and fly here tomorrow, and we have a proper meeting, under a proper cone of silence?"

John thought about that for a moment, and about four light bulbs went off in his head simultaneously. "Let me book my flight and we'll meet tomorrow," replied John.

"Remember way back, when you used to roll one joint so that it looked just like a cigarette, and you'd put it into a pack of cigarettes and then just gallivant your ass anywhere you wanted?" Milo asked. "You called it, 'Hiding in plain sight.'"

"I was kinda hoping those exploits had disappeared into a pre-digital memory hole," replied John. "Doesn't the slate wipe clean every seven years?"

"We were lucky. There was a memory hole, and stuff just went right down that drain…assuming you weren't dumb enough to let people take pictures. Not anymore, not in the digital age. So, remember that 'cone of silence' on this kinda stuff means remembering that everything is 'in plain sight,' as you used to call it…times a hundred," intoned Milo. "Or a thousand."

John understood that his friend was telling him, "The NSA records everything, you dumbass, so speak cryptically."

"Got it," said John. "I'll see you tomorrow."

When John met with Milo, he detailed his thoughts. John's call to Milo was well-timed as his old friend had recently divorced and completed some business projects. The opportunity for some unusual stimulation in a far-off locale was irresistible to Milo. He focused on the feasibility of John's concepts considering the military, political and logistics factors involved. "Y'know, this is a pretty crazy idea, John. But I think it could work. I stress, 'could work,' not 'will work.' Maybe," said Milo.

"I take that as a strong reassurance," said John.

After their meeting and a night on the town in Las Vegas, John called another of his acquaintances, Nick de Stijl, who had been a student of John's a decade ago. Since then, Nick had split his time between mechanical engineering work for start-ups and working on a few business matters with John. Nick had mentioned to John several times over the years that he'd love first dibs on any project John wanted to pursue.

Part nerd and part mild-mannered linebacker, Nick had a demeanor of controlled competence. He was even keeled and difficult to rattle except when he was watching his favorite professional football teams play. He had a penchant for following a few of the worst teams in the NFL, year after year. But his loyalty was repaid when those ugly ducklings inevitably had their Cinderella seasons – even if the wait could be excruciatingly embarrassing.

After John presented the concept, Nick asked to think it over and meet up the next day. John took that as an encouraging sign. After asking for more details, including how they would make money, Nick said, "I think this might be perfect for Scott and Brian," referring to the Nick's old classmates Scott Canto and Brian Dietz, who were founders of Sounding Engineering, a commercial high-altitude balloon company, with whom Nick and John had worked. If one didn't know better, one would mistake Scott and Brian for a radio disc jockey team. Now in their twenties, Scott was tall and gregarious, the pitch guy for the company, and Brian was more the technical side, but with a biting wit. Frequently, Scott was the straight man to Brian's zingers. But they worked well as a team and had become experts on balloon-launched platforms.

That night, Scott and Brian - until that morning just two entrepreneurs living in Florida - were on a plane to participate in a "white board" transformation of their fledgling company into a private air force.

Michael W. Barnes

BERMUDA AND THE SCIENCE OF SINKING

Seventy-two hours later, John's burgeoning team included Nick, Scott and Brian, and had on paper a working aerial bombardment program to combat the Somali pirates. John also realized that he had pretty much hired his mercenary friend – Milo Patton – to help him. Now they were all mercenaries.

John's plan to solve the insurers' Somali piracy problem using kinetic bombardment was at its most basic level an updated version of the sixteenth-century tactic of dropping a basket of rocks from a balloon onto an enemy. John's task was to be able to hit a pirate vessel *en route* to an attack. For that, he needed about fifteen minutes of lead time.

Gabriel called Kirk Woodbury in Bermuda and asked about the insurers' and reinsurers' real-time access to client radio and communications systems. He also arranged with Kirk Woodbury to set up a meeting in Bermuda whereby John could propose a solution to the insurers' risks on the piracy problem. He didn't tell Kirk anything about the plan – that would remain a secret, but he asked Kirk whether the insurers might pay a bounty of twenty-five percent of the amount by which John could cut the insurers' losses over a six-month period. If the losses didn't abate, then no fee would be payable.

"How will you achieve that, John? Are you going to get the UN to intercede?" Kirk half- joked.

"Well, if I did and it saves your guys $500 million, wouldn't that be worth the $125 million?" asked John.

"Of course, it would," said Kirk.

"So, let's structure it as a call right for retrocession on the excess layer of the pro forma loss. I have a captive Bermuda reinsurance company, you might remember," offered John.

"Ah, you're a fast study, John. Look, since you are not a rated company, it would have to be a small amount, written as a facultative retrocession under the limits, capped at ten percent of the risk pool, for a limited time period," said Kirk, delving into technical insurance structures. He was somewhat proud that he had sufficiently educated Gabriel as to the rules that they could be having such a technical discussion.

"Let me ask around. Now, there will be some questions, but, well, the insurers really don't want to know details, just results," said Kirk.

"Let's just keep it vague and say it has to do with working with the local authorities to step up their anti-piracy actions on shore, including security measures out of Mombasa," said John. "But I will need to have complete real-time access to the insureds' manifests and radio communications."

"Sounds like a total bullshit answer, but that's the kind of answer people like," said Kirk. "As to the radio communications let me kick it around and get back to you."

After a couple of days spent making calls to some key reinsurers, Kirk Woodbury called John with an update. "There's some interest here, John. I think your fee would be closer to ten to fifteen percent than twenty-five percent, but we quibble. Perhaps you should come visit Bermuda, say, this Friday?"

"I'll book my flight."

A few days later, John was in Bermuda, moving in and out of a variety of small conference rooms. Kirk Woodbury introduced John to the various insurance executives involved. By the next week, an official "Facultative Retrocession" agreement had been hammered out. It was signed between John's local Bermuda reinsurance company and a syndicate of five Bermuda-based maritime reinsurers, and the local notary public affixed the proper seals and stamps to make it official.

After John had signed his retrocession agreement, he and Kirk Woodbury decided to have a closing dinner celebration at the Ironmen, a fabled restaurant with an exceptional wine list.

Their reservation wasn't for ninety minutes, so as they walked from John's hotel to the restaurant, Kirk offered to show John the island's best wine merchant and its cellar which reportedly dated back to colonial times. John was impressed by the merchant and the ancient brick cellar 30 feet below ground. As they left the wine store, they walked by a store on the block – Bermuda Mantiques. The store was an homage to the history of Bermuda and its maritime past and had a whole wing that incorporated the theme of ships, shipwrecks, and the lore of the Bermuda Triangle. The shop's owner had some quasi-military artifacts to accompany the items, including interesting metal pieces from various vessels that had traversed or wrecked in the Triangle. There were several maritime safes on display, typically from the captain's berth. There was also a dual-di-aled safe. John asked the shop owner what type of safe it was, and was told it was from a submarine.

John fiddled with the combination dials and then said to Kirk, "You know, I have this weird hobby. I'm good with safes. Old safes, the ones that were purely mechanical."

"Yeah, it's sorta hard not to love a good safe," said Kirk. "Like we discussed, our modern island was built on that concept."

"I've read about these, but I've never actually seen one. A submarine safe, I mean. My father was a submariner. He was one of the unlucky ones; his boat went down before I was old enough to know what his actual job was," said John.

"Well, I'm sorry to hear that, John. I'm sure he was a good man. Was his boat taken out in combat?" asked Kirk. "That would make you a helluva lot older than you look, if your dad was in the Big One."

"Officially, it was an accident. But I don't know, really. Cold War governments didn't provide details when a vessel was lost. I guess it was hard enough for the government when so many of our space rockets were blowing up on the launch pad, in full view of everyone. It was just a different time. So, I'm not sure how or why the submarine went down," said John. "I've read all kinds of stories that there were months of hot submarine wars going on during the so-called Cold War."

"What was the name of his ship, if I may ask?" inquired Kirk.

"The *Crescent*. The *USS Crescent*," replied John.

"Oh, gosh yes," said Kirk. "Of course, I know of the

Crescent. I'm a middle-aged male living and working in the Bermuda Triangle. I can chapter and verse you on that boat," said Kirk. "I'm on the Board of the Bermuda Maritime Museum."

"Well, then you and I are going to have a lot to talk about," said John.

It had been a transformative week for John. Such was the nature of these things.

AN ISLAND IN A SEA OF CHAOS

While John finished matters in Bermuda, his team made their way to the Seychelles Islands, an independent nation in the Western Indian Ocean. The islands are located about 700 miles southeast of Somalia with favorable south/south-easterly winds. Each man traveled separately under plans formulated by Milo Patton. As with a pub crawl treasure hunt, they each had a list of provisions to collect and tasks to accomplish along the way. Sometimes, when dealing with merchants and middlemen, team members explained their urgent and immediate need for unusual items by claiming an upcoming visit by a rock star or the need for props for a Hollywood film. Milo could not control the gossip in such areas, but with such fanciful but plausible cover stories, he knew that the story would be mangled beyond recognition after it had been repeated more than twice.

In short, John was hiding his fabrication plans in plain sight.

As soon as John arrived in the Seychelles Islands, the team got to work putting theory into practice. During the first few weeks they tested their balloon-based kinetic bombardment system by launching test balloons several hundred miles upwind of the active piracy areas off the Somalia coast. Once aloft at an altitude of about 120,000 feet, a balloon array and its bomblets had an effective target area of about 8,000 square miles, which is a circle with a diameter of 200 miles. John's team practiced at keeping one, and sometimes two, balloon arrays aloft over hundreds of square miles of ocean. John's team was tapped into the insurance companies' communications and navigation links of the ships in the area.

A mayday transmission about a pirate attack would typically include precise directions of the ship and the vector of the attacking pirate boat. As soon as a mayday signal was monitored, John's crew would quickly determine whether they had a balloon array aloft within 100 miles of the attack. If they did, they would activate the balloon array's systems to quickly position and release a winged bundle of attack darts to intercept the pirate boat.

The balloons themselves were ordinary helium weather and hobbyist balloons, available widely worldwide. Several hundred darts were carried as the attack weapon, bound together in a thin metal fuselage which roughly resembled a trash can with wings. Each glider featured two big fins on the back and two small fins near the nose, making the contraption aerodynamic. When released from a weather balloon array, a tethered glider cluster could glide to a target a hundred miles away, far beyond the area just directly below the balloon.

A radio transmitter on the balloon array synced with John's crew and permitted John to crudely steer the cluster by GPS data toward the distressed ship, much like a falling parachutist can vector himself toward a target area by using fins, airfoils or the newest "bat wing" arrays.

Gabriel's team had become adept at piloting the arrays. They figured out the sweet spot – that releasing the dart bombs from the glider at 5,000 feet instead of 20,000 feet, increased accuracy, even if each dart packed less punch because it hadn't accelerated with a 4-mile drop. But even at such lower bombing altitude, a pirate boat would sink when hit by a single flechette dart.

Once John and his crew released an array to pursue an attack boat, within minutes the pirate vessel would experience the wrath of an unseen, angry and unforgiving god.

THE SPORT OF SINKING

In their makeshift command center in Seychelles, Milo and Nick sat next to each other, each man having several computer screens in front of him. John had his own screens, and they were actively working a targeting operation. A Liberian-flagged cargo ship, *Esposito*, in the Gulf of Aden about 100 miles off the northern Somalian coast had radioed a mayday several minutes earlier. Shortly thereafter, John's team had calculated that their balloon array was only 50 miles away, and John had ordered its dart cluster to be released. The bomb cluster assembly was now dive gliding at 200 mph toward the mayday signal. The *Esposito* had subsequently sent several updated distress calls, including the coordinates and vector of the attacking pirate boat. John and his team were constantly updating their targeting analysis.

"The *Esposito* is moving at 20 knots, and the attacker is closing at about 28 knots from the south at 210 degrees," said Nick. "The bad guys are about three clicks out, and they'll overtake her in about 19 minutes. We lose our safety buffer in about 12 minutes," he continued, referring to the point where the pirate boat would be too close to the *Esposito* for them to risk shot-gunning hundreds of steel darts on the area. Even though a large ship like the *Esposito* was in no risk of being sunk by John's darts, they could cause explosions or kill crew. Like a surgeon who didn't want to kill patients, John didn't want his darts to hit the big boats he was protecting.

Each man had a refreshing screen video from a high-definition digital video camera mounted on the fuselage of the dart cluster, with the signal transmitted by encrypted radiowave. Once the sole province of spy agencies, these cameras were now sold at sporting goods stores for a few hundred dollars.

"We're about 30 seconds away," said Milo. "There's a small skiff moving south through the target area. Probably a fishing boat."

"Let's tweak this a bit to avoid that fisherman, hold off an additional 10 more seconds, and drop lower to tighten the cluster," said John. "It's still at 8500 feet – hold that and then take it into a sharper dive and release around 5000 feet when you're on target," said John.

Both Milo and Nick had become adept at piloting and bombing. Their MO was to bring a cluster glider within a few miles of a target area, piloting the glider to drop its nose like a WWII Pacific dive bomber in a literal dive-bombing against a pirate ship.

Now, the video feed on the screens Milo, Nick and John were watching clearly showed the white wake of the pirate boat, highlighted sharply against the blue ocean water. The small fishing skiff had moved out of the target area and off the bottom of the screen. The area was now devoid of any craft other than the marauders on the pirate boat closing fast upon the *Esposito*.

"OK, we're almost at five, I'm gonna shed the skin," said Nick, as he engaged a key on his keyboard. A second window now began to transmit video from another high-def camera ejected from the fuselage and positioned over the attack area by a small parachute. "Bombs away," said Nick, almost under his breath.

With the push of a button, a radio signal sent by Gabriel's team released the bolts holding the glider's fuselage in place. The glider's fuselage ripped away like the BBs from a shotgun blast emerging from the girdle of the shotgun barrel. Several hundred individual darts were now in a screaming free fall, accelerating towards a speed of 500 mph or more. The video feed provided John's team with a bird's-eye view of the attack.

About 15 seconds after the cluster shed its skin releasing the individual darts, the dart bomblets began slamming into the target area. A few of the darts broke the sound barrier in the final few seconds before hitting the water, emitting sonic booms that sounded like a shotgun blast. To a pirate, there was no worse soundtrack to the final minute of life.

John and his team stared at their monitors. The video image showed hundreds of white water bursts, as if a large machine gun was spraying bullets into the water.

"It's like a video game, isn't it?" said John. "We're hundreds of miles away, watching the action unfold on a screen a few inches wide."

"It's a lot worse than a video game for the bad guys on that pirate boat," said Milo. The video that John's team watched from a mile high viewpoint belied a very different reality at the water's surface.

GULF OF ADEN, OFF THE NORTHERN COAST SOMALIA

The boat didn't have a name. About thirty feet long, it looked like any number of small fishing boats working out of its Third World harbor. The sun had not yet risen, but there were signs of life all over the small marina. The water was tranquil, but gulls squawked and fought over breakfast morsels. Deep gurgling sounds of submerged boat engines mixed with the slightly acrid smell of diesel fumes and the dank odor of day-old dead fish.

The boat's captain, Tawfeeq, did not know the full names of most of the boat's crewmembers. His right-hand man, Amad, had recruited them a few days ago from the slums of Bosaso, a city on the northern coast of Somalia. Tawfeeq piloted his boat due north out of the harbor, into the Gulf of Aden, with eight souls aboard. Unlike the two dozen other fishing boats heading to sea, his boat had no fishing nets. Instead, the storage boxes held AK47 rifles, knives, boarding ladders and duct tape. Tawfeeq and his pirate crew were hunting a cargo ship, its crew, and the ransom they could demand.

Merchant ships were never armed, so Tawfeeq's mission wasn't a particularly risky adventure. The crew had been easily hired, since Tawfeeq was paying the mercenary rate which was ten times the going rate for deckhand work on a fishing trawler working the local waters.

Of his eight-man crew, only Amad had previously participated in a raid. Tawfeeq compensated for his own lack of experience by projecting himself as a strong, fierce captain. He had participated in a few other raids as a crew member, but the past two weeks were his first outings as a pirate captain. He had bought the skiff and had also obtained the week's maritime shipping schedule with a bribe to a crime syndicate operating out of Mombasa, Kenya, where ships registered their manifests. It simplified Tawfeeq's identification of targets. He knew that five suitable cargo ships would be passing through his hunting grounds that morning.

An hour after sunrise, one of Tawfeeq's crew spotted a cargo ship's bridge on the horizon. Tawfeeq ordered his boatman to speed up. After twenty-five minutes the prey was in full view. It was the *Esposito*, one of the ships listed on the manifest. Aboard the *Esposito*, the captain spotted Tawfeeq's incoming boat and radioed a general mayday. But the *Esposito* captain knew it was useless. No navy would be coming to the rescue.

Tawfeeq's boat was closing fast; it would catch up to the *Esposito* in about ten minutes. Tawfeeq moved to the bow, surveying the horizon to make sure there were no other pirate boats in the area. Scaling and boarding the unarmed *Esposito* would be relatively easy, but a fight with another pirate vessel could be deadly. With the two outboard motors roaring and the humid salty wind racing by, he felt proud as well as exhilarated. He was the captain of his boat and the admiral of his own navy.

And then the sea erupted. For a second, Tawfeeq thought that a school of fish was jumping into the air all around his boat, rising in a perfect vertical formation, cre-ating small geysers as they shot out of the water. But then there were two loud crashes which sent horrible vibrations through his trawler, as if his boat was skimming across the top of a coral reef. Off-balance, Tawfeeq stepped back from the bow, and as he turned himself around toward the stern the boat shuddered with a thunderous thud.

Tawfeeq couldn't comprehend the scene before him. The white noise of the wind and the boat motors was replaced by abrasive clanking and shuddering throughout the hull. One of his crew had simply disintegrated, as if a grenade had exploded inside his chest and blasted his bloody remains down upon the deck.

Seawater poured into the boat, washing away the

massive blood puddle that had been a pirate just a few seconds earlier. Three waterspouts gushed up from the hull like open fire hydrants on a summer street. The boat's forward momentum collapsed.

Excitement and anticipation were replaced by adrenaline and panic. As Tawfeeq's brain tried to sort out the sensory overload in front of him, a final loud thud like a wrecking ball hitting a brick wall overwhelmed the boat, and the rear five feet of the stern fell into the water, like a faltering iceberg breaking into pieces.

The remains of the fast-sinking boat listed to port. Then with a loud pop, the hull cracked down the middle. Two of the crew tumbled into the sea where two others were already thrashing about frantically. Amad was panicked, still in what remained of the destroyed boat, up to his waist in bloody red water. He looked at Tawfeeq as if Tawfeeq could and should somehow fix things. As the boat further disintegrated, they both tumbled into the sea.

It had all happened so fast that Tawfeeq was frozen despite the adrenaline. In less than ten seconds, the rear third of the boat with the heavy engines was already underwater plummeting downward to the seabed. The remainder of the boat was in partially submerged pieces, bobbing on top of the waves. Tawfeeq and what remained of his crew thrashed about in the briny water, trying to cling to the flotsam. Reddish-brown blood clouds stained the otherwise blue water.

"What the fuck just happened?" thought Tawfeeq's racing mind.

Tawfeeq began to call out panicked orders. But no

sooner had he started his roll call than one of the crew let out a bloodcurdling scream as a shark tore away half of his thigh. Within moments, the shark frenzy grew as other pirates screamed in horror. Tawfeeq tried to turn to swat at a shark he felt against his shoulder, but neither his arm nor his head would pivot. He tried again to turn and push, but to no avail. He was fighting against the reality that the muscles and tissue connecting his head and shoulder to his body had been largely severed by the thrusting bite of a large shark.

Then in Tawfeeq's brain, the panicked screaming subsided as if someone were turning down the volume knob on a stereo. Tawfeeq's field of vision rapidly collapsed as if he were peering through a hazy pipe in front of him. It wasn't a real-time image; it was the vestige from a few seconds earlier, retained by his brain as it shut down. Tawfeeq, decapitated, was dead, and with a zap the vestigial picture and sound ceased. A minute later, none of his crew remained of this Earth to tell their story. All souls aboard the unnamed trawler were gone. Two miles away, the *Esposito* sailed on. It sent a radio signal cancelling its earlier mayday, and the captain noted in his log that the attacking pirate boat had simply disappeared from sight and radar.

The *Esposito's* crew thanked their various gods.

The fate of Tawfeeq's boat was like scores of other pirate craft attacked by John's team. The mass and the speed of the darts were lethal to any life form and devastating to any substance in their path. They pierced a ship and its hull, and occasionally a gas tank or other hard object, sometimes resulting in a fireball explosion. If not immediately broken into pieces if hit by several darts, a pirate boat would otherwise take on water and capsize in a minute. Even if the pirate boat crew managed to radio a mayday distress signal to its mothership, typically 50 or 100 miles away, the speed of the destruction ensured that no detail of the event could ever be broadcast.

The hundreds of other darts hitting the water created the semblance of Old-Faithful geysers which rose 15 to 30 stories high – as if the ocean itself was shooting up at the sky. Any crew member who was alert not only felt the vibration of the dart hitting the boat and heard the sonic booms, but also saw and heard the hiss and rush of hundreds of miniature geysers blowing up from the ocean at the same time. For a poor ignorant pirate, it was indistinguishable from the vengeance of an angry sea god.

A rare survivor who clung to flotsam returned to shore recounting a story of evil spirits and magic. In reality, they had no idea what had hit them or what had sunk their boat given the invisibility and speed of the darts.

Stories began to circulate in the maritime community about dozens of pirate ships just disappearing ten or fifteen minutes after the first mayday calls were broadcast by big cargo vessels. The stories filtered up to intelligence sources and their governments, along with the incredible tales exchanged among the warlords' tribes from the few survivors who made it back to shore. The intelligence community was baffled by the reports as there were no radar indications of any ordnance or interdictions by ships or airplanes. Indeed, by design Gabriel's darts were too small and fast, and radar coverage in the area was too spotty for radar to capture the low-tech darts. The balloons themselves were effectively radar-invisible.

Defense ministers and intelligence agencies began quietly inquiring as to which country or military was behind the pirate boat disappearances, with the key suspects being, of course, the US, the UK, Russia, Israel, China and somewhat ironically, Iran. It was a lose-lose situation for these powers. Their denials were not believed and thereby the trust they had with allies was damaged. That they also came off as being clueless or powerless was politically troubling.

As John and his team carried out their mission, the maritime insurers' losses and their payout of ransom money suddenly slowed and dropped to almost zero. The possible shutdown of oceanic shipping around the Horn of Africa was reversed in less than ninety days. Hundreds of millions of dollars were saved – that is, it was not disbursed from banks in Bermuda to warlords in Somalia. John and his team were earning a fifteen percent bounty on those savings under his "Facultative Retrocession."

HITTING A SUBMARINE

John Gabriel's Somali anti-piracy operation had stopped over 75 pirate attacks over about five months. As a direct result, Somalia piracy was in a precipitous collapse as was the available "navy" of boats being used for piracy. The dwindling number of available pirate vessels caused pirates to begin hijacking the boats of other pirates. This sectarian battle among pirate clans made it more difficult to assemble and keep a pirate crew and boat operational. Asymmetrically, John and his rag-tag band were defeating a veritable pirate navy using weather balloons and metal darts.

John's mission continued smoothly until all hell broke loose, not just in the waters off the coast of Somalia but on the international stage. The uproar was not caused by boat or balloon. The problem sprang from what lay 100 feet beneath a disintegrated pirate boat.

The captain of the *USS Donovan*, an American Los Angeles-class submarine on routine patrols, was alarmed by the sudden burst of hundreds of sonic pings. Unknown to him, those sounds were caused by the barrage of hundreds of John's supersonic metal spears hitting the water 100 feet above the sub. To the astute captain in the middle of a drill, these seemed like nothing short of an attack. The captain called the *Donovan* to full battle-ready alert. Ten seconds later, several dozen metallic thud sounds occurred, as submerged darts falling to the bottom of the sea clinked against the skin of the sub. Shortly thereafter, every U.S. military craft in the Arabian Sea and western Indian Ocean elevated its status to tactical alert. Defcon.

Within an hour, the siren call initiated by the *Donovan* was cancelled when it became known that a pirate ship had exploded and sunk directly over the submarine. The military alert was stood down, but unless delicately handled, propaganda would state that an American submarine had used a Somali boat full of Muslim fishermen for target practice. The truth didn't matter. Such is the nature of such things. It could have become an unwelcome diplomatic flashpoint.

The Pentagon quickly alerted every Western intelligence service that, whatever the hell was behind the disappearance of the Somali pirates in the past months, it had now resulted in a perceived attack upon a US warship. "This must stop immediately, or it will be deemed an act of war against the United States," was the gist of the Pentagon's unsubtle message.

Meanwhile, the Mossad, the Israeli intelligence agency, had been delighted that someone else was doing the kind of dirty work that it normally had to undertake when others were too timid to act. But the Mossad had also become a bit alarmed, worried that one of its hostile neighbors had acquired some new capability that could be turned against Israel.

The Mossad's analysts had narrowed the likely actors to a short list, and one of those potential actors was "the maritime insurers." The Mossad analysis had just begun when the *Donovan* incident occurred. When the Mossad and the Israeli Defense Forces received the Pentagon's "This Stops Now" threat, the Mossad chiefs made a few calls to its short list, including to a few key insurance executives in Bermuda, passing along the American warning "as a courtesy to our friends in the maritime industries." The Mossad's message soon reached Kirk Woodbury, who was known to a select few in Bermuda insurance circles as the intermediary who had arranged the retrocession among the reinsurers and John Gabriel. Within a few hours, Kirk notified John with an encrypted short message: "Stop immediately all maritime opps."

Later when Kirk and John were able to speak, Kirk put it into context. "Sounds like that American sub just called the game, don't you think?" said Kirk.

"Well, I sure as hell am not planning any trips to Somalia right now, and if I had any family members there, I'd have them out on the next flight."

"Good thinking," agreed Woodbury. "Listen, swing by Bermuda soon. I've got some bottles for you to try. And hurry, they won't be here very long."

"Sounds like a solid plan, Kirk. I'll send you my dates, and I'll see you soon." And with that, John Gabriel's Somali anti-pirate mercenary exploits drew to an immediate halt. Seventy-six thwarted pirate attacks, no losses of friendlies, and – at least currently – the operation had remained completely hidden.

Although the reinsurers had not followed the details of John Gabriel's mission, they considered him a genius. The numbers didn't lie. The Somalia piracy scourge had ended. John was an effective fixer – the reinsurers didn't need further details. And their payments of an eight–figure "fixer" fee to an obscure Bermuda-based reinsurer was a bargain. It – John's anti-pirate operation – had undoubtedly spared the lives of some crew, prevented the hostage-taking of hundreds of crew members and rescued the insurers from the piracy scourge. In the process, it had also saved an entire portion of the planet from a devastating halt in commerce which - quite literally - may have prevented starvation, factional wars and death. Those saved lives would never be reflected on any year-end balance sheet. But the insurers' continued solvency was reflected there, and to those in the know, John's bargain was the bargain of the decade.

John took away a lot of know-how from the anti-pirate mission, and it also inspired much thinking on his part. Two things John concluded for sure: That there would be table-pounding pontifications of gamma-males at hipster coffee shops who would scornfully view him as nothing more than a blood-money mercenary doing the dirty work for modern Western colonialists; and, that their pontifications could not be completely dismissed. There was a point to be made, but too often it was just the misguided words of useful idiots who too often convinced good people to do nothing in the face of horror.

But John also knew that he could never stop listening to what the table pounders might say. There could come a time when the gamma male crowd was right – that a "just cause" was just an excuse to become the secret police. That is, a Stasi can be born of good intentions.

John and his team divvied up the tasks to wind down the anti-pirate operation office in the Seychelles. There was little to clean up, but in any event John decided it was appropriate to host a formal end-of-action meeting with the team. In three days, Milo, Nick and the balloon engineers Scott and Brian were scheduled to join him in Paris.

REWARD AND CONTEMPLATION AT 33,000 FEET

John flew ahead to Paris on his own, allowing him time to gather his thoughts. His flight connected through the Emirates, so he decided to fly first class from Abu Dhabi to Paris.

When the stewardess handed John the in-flight menu and a separate in-flight wine list, he was a bit perplexed.

"Which one are you serving on this flight?" he asked, as he nodded towards the wine list. He felt a momentary tinge of guilt speaking English, and not even trying to use a few words of a local language.

"All of them, of course," replied the flight attendant, in impeccable British English. It was impossible to discern any mocking in her attitude by the smile on her face. Whether John was the first to ever ask that question, or the thousandth, was her secret.

John looked at the wine list again, and quickly counted. "I'm sorry. Did you say that you are pouring all eleven of these wines…on this flight?" he asked, just for reassurance.

"Yes, of course, plus two others that we're serving in coach," she with the professional assurance one might give to someone inquiring whether the air on board contained oxygen.

"In that case, I'll need a few minutes to review the list. Thank you so much," said John.

"My pleasure. I'll come back in a moment," said the stewardess. "And I can assist you if you have any inquiries – the list can be daunting."

The thoughts came to John's mind as she walked away: "Had he ever heard a stewardess use the word 'daunting?' Why on Earth does this service not exist in America? Was she wearing a ring?" There was something beguiling about a woman – or any person – who could effortlessly discuss, order and taste wine. Even more so if they knew when Even more so if they know when to pour a bad glass down the drain. John chuckled to himself and focused on the wine list. "Choose the wine first, and the food will naturally follow," was his motto.

And choose he did. John worked his way through a few small pours of South American chardonnay, French Chablis, a New Zealand sauvignon blanc, and finally a French white Chateauneuf du Pape, or CDP for short. It was the last white, from southern France, which gave John the clue that someone was just showing off or playing favorites with the list. CDP white wines were rare and they were rarely exported to America.

When the stewardess returned, John asked, "Ma'am, I am deeply appreciative that there's a Chateauneuf blanc on this list. May I ask, how did it end up there?"

Bullseye! The ultra-professional demeanor of the stewardess cracked for a split second. John detected a slight blush on her face and a slightly different, almost conspiratorial, smile. Perhaps it was only his perception that had changed. Ethanol at high altitude can have its effects.

"It is the Queen's favorite," she replied, in a slightly hushed tone, as if it were a state secret. "We always carry at least two vintages, just in case."

Whether intended or not by her, John inferred in her reply a long treatise. Those two sentences could yield an hour's worth of lively conversation in another group exploring any number of meanings about The Emirates, their politics, economy and culture, and the world writ large.

When it came time to order dinner, John chose a hearty red Bordeaux, but it didn't really matter. Being served a Pauillac at 33,000 feet by an exotic stewardess speaking English as a fourth language was reward enough.

The pampered treatment in the first-class cabin of the Emirates airline allowed John Gabriel's thoughts to drift from the just-ended operation. How had he ended up devising and running an anti-pirate black-op? What building blocks from his youth had enabled him to even attempt it? His mind reverted to his pre-teen years, even before he had met Jill Seneca. He recalled having pulled a prank in the night sky. John discerned a connection, even if was merely a faint trace.

In his memory, the nightly television newscasts included stories that an American space satellite, "Skylab," was in orbital decay and was going to crash to Earth in an uncontrolled fiery reentry from space. Occurring at a time when the country was already beset by an oil embargo, a recession, and inflation, one could not help but draw the conclusion that America's best days were behind her. The nation's damned spacecraft couldn't even remain in orbit.

On the lighter side, "Skylab parties" were a staple of college social calendars, complete with large targets drawn on a lawn and kegs of beer flowing.

Youngster John Gabriel decided to play a prank. He mounted a few primitive pinwheels on a board, with the whole contraption to be lifted by a couple of big black helium balloons he'd bought from the Edmunds Scientific mail-order catalog. Several roman candle fireworks were attached to each of the pinwheels on the board. An hour after dusk, Gabriel launched the balloon array half a mile upwind from the local college campus where students were hosting yet another Skylab party. John used several minutes of dynamite fuse – a staple of model rocketry – which burned slowly, just as portrayed in motion pictures.

John's balloon array rose invisibly in the night sky and drifted over the college campus. After a few minutes the first of several roman candle fireworks ignited. A dazzling display of sparks and fireballs filled the sky. The collegiate kegger partiers went wild. Dozens of town residents called the police to report that they had just witnessed the re-entry and burn-up of the Skylab spacecraft.

A local television channel ran some grainy footage captured on a home video camera. It scared some gullible people and over the ensuing few days, national news organizations ran the local station's footage. Like supposed blurry photos of a UFO, Bigfoot or the Loch Ness Monster, the footage was a hit. Even though Skylab had crashed nowhere in the area, people were convinced that they had personally witnessed Skylab's fall.

As John thought back upon his Skylab prank, he realized that the stunt had earned him the begrudging admiration of a few of his classmates. He also realized that unlike his harmless Skylab prank, his pirate eradication project was a felony in any number of countries, and that the only thing keeping his team from being viewed as a group of international mass murderers was…not getting caught.

John had kept his Skylab prank a secret for only a couple of days, which had been adequate back then. Now, however, it was imperative that they keep the whole Somali episode quiet – forever. He would use the upcoming after-mission celebration in Paris to impress that upon his small crew. Perhaps they would invent a detailed cover story that each member could tell– a fishing trip, or a scuba venture or a ship-wreck retrieval – and embellish over the years without falling prey to the need to disclose the story of what they had really done.

John also thought about how important the "psy op" aspect had been to the success of the anti-pirate operation. There was no way a rag-tag band with weather balloons and darts could defeat a veritable pirate navy. But they had done exactly that. John wanted to learn from the operation and separated their psy op success into several factors.

One factor was that he had parlayed upon the unknown to create fear. Second, John enhanced fear of the unknown with existing culture and religion, by using voodoo, gris gris, pagan rites and the memes of Islamic and Christian sects, each version goading its adherents to attribute the pirate disappearances to an angry god. A rumor campaign spread the fear that a swift death from an angry god awaited anyone who became a pirate. Keeping the identity of the attacker secret helped foment these beliefs, suspicions and resulting chaos.

Also, John had targeted the risk-reward equation for small capitalists who were enabling piracy – the boat owners. For a boat owner, renting the boat to a pirate suddenly meant the boat might be destroyed. Boat owners stopped providing their boats to pirates. Fewer boats meant fewer pirate raids.

John realized that psychological aspects of the pirate mission had been equally as effective as the physical destruction of the pirate boats. Or more. John wondered if this was true in all operations. And, what if they were ten times more effective? As he gazed out his window at the Red Sea below, he began to appreciate the asymmetric effect of such missions and their impact on the public psyche. It was like playing God. No wonder it appealed to so many psychopaths.

GATHERINGS IN PARIS

As John's crew was assembling in Paris for the pirate operation after-action meet-up, John had accepted Kirk Woodbury's offer to introduce him to Thomas Gallier, a wine merchant based in Paris. Gallier's office was quite unique – it was a boat moored along one of the many small canals connecting to the Seine River. There were thousands of these wharf boats, although Paris had somehow never garnered the reputation as a city of canals to the extent that Venice, Amsterdam or St. Petersburg had.

The exterior of Gallier's boat gave no clues as to what lay inside. This was in accordance with the reigning design trend among the boat owners and lessees. It made them less obvious as targets for thieves who frequented the waterfronts after hours.

A small wooden plaque above the galley doorway simply read, *Rabelo Gallier*. John knocked on the door of the boat which was set slightly ajar, and Thomas Gallier greeted him. "You must be Mr. John Gabriel. I'm glad you found my peculiar little bureau." Tom Gallier was well dressed in a country-club-casual sort of way, or what used to be called laid-back preppy. He wore his slightly graying hair a bit longer than most men his age would do.

"Yes I am, and please, it's John. I'm not even sure I recognize my last name, if it's preceded by 'Mr.' And thank you, Mr. Gallier. I'm glad you could make time to meet with me," said John.

"Please, it's Thomas or Tom, your choice," his host replied.

The exchanging of formal names, followed by a grant of permission to use first names or nicknames, might come off as stuffy or old-fashioned to a new generation. But like a dialect in speech, or a hand signal exchanged among gang members, or a knowing acknowledgement of a piece of art on a wall, in fact it was far more substantive. The ease with which someone handled such exchanges revealed much about their background and psychographic makeup. Such tribal signals had been exchanged for hundreds of years, sometimes knowingly, other times unknowingly.

"And let me introduce Frank Clicquot, who I mentioned to you on the phone," said Tom.

"Hello again, Mr. Clicquot," said John. "We met briefly at a jazz club in Bermuda. I was with my friend Kirk Woodbury. And this is where I would normally insert some attempt at humor based upon the exciting prospects of social interaction among the insurance actuaries of the island of Bermuda," said John. They all were grinning, the way one does when hearing a new comic and liking the first few warm-up jokes.

"Nice to see you again, John," said Frank.

"Kirk told me that there was a longer story that I would need to extract from you, best done with some wine. My guess is that it has something to do with jazz, champagne or insurance," said John.

Tom interjected, "Good guess, John. There is only a small degree of separation between Frank, music and the champagne trade. In some ways, Frank and I are in similar businesses, although I just realized that now as I was thinking about how to introduce him. Frank is one of Europe's foremost pipe organ restorers."

"Pipe organ restorer? Like in churches? OK, I'll bite. How are the wine and organ-fixing businesses the same?" asked John.

Frank the organ repairman looked at Tom Gallier the wine broker and said, "Well, Tom, since you just invented that one, I'll let you explain it."

"You mean I have to make this up without any help?" said Tom. "OK, fine, I will. So…. I've got customers all over the world, wanting me to locate old round containers that were made in old stone buildings. They are convinced that they contain magic powers which grow more powerful as they age. Wine, that is. And Frank here, he has customers all over the world wanting him to come to them to repair ancient round containers in old stone buildings that also hold magic power. Music, that is," said Tom. "Frank's cylinders are hundreds of years old. Mine, maybe a few decades old. But we're different in that, in my business, once the old ones are drunk up, they're gone. For Frank, though, they're not gone once they play music. It's his job to fix up the old ones, give them a refill," said Tom, somewhat pleased that his improvisational routine had not ended in disaster.

"That's pretty good, Tom," said Frank. "I should put you on the spot more often. I might use it on my website."

"Are there enough organs to keep you busy?" asked John.

Frank gave him a good-natured look that suggested, "You're kidding, right," but instead he said, "Oh, yes, and more so every month. Apparently, the old guys who do what I do are dying off. So, it seems more and more work finds its way to me. It surprises even me, and I thought I had gotten to a point that I wasn't capable of being surprised anymore."

John picked up on that wording by Frank, that he "wasn't capable of being surprised anymore," which matched what Kirk Woodbury had hinted to John. John made a mental note to follow up on that. He had started a European student exchange program a decade ago and was intrigued by the architecture and infrastructure of old European churches. "Well, I will definitely pay closer attention to the next set of trackers that I come across," said John.

"I'm hiring, if you'd care to make that a full-time commitment," quipped Frank. "It was cutting-edge tech work … 500 years ago. I guess things wax and wane."

"OK, enough about pipe work. Let me give you guys a quick tour of the boat," said Thomas.

John couldn't help but marvel at the boat-turned-office. It had some discrete trappings of a place to effect commerce – there were several telephones, a few discreetly placed monitors, and several flat surfaces where documents or wine bottles and glasses could be placed. But the office was not cluttered, and there were no stacks or cases of wines set about, as was common with most wine brokerage offices. Clearly, this boat was Tom's domain; it was not the province of shipping clerks.

The boat had two main parlors plus a kitchen. One parlor was old world style, with wooden panels and rarefied classic art with gallery-style lighting. Mantique artifacts and beaux arts lay about, as in an old school men's club. There was nothing dainty about anything.

The second room gave more of a nod to modernity. One panel of several modern art paintings could be raised 90 degrees to reveal a large modern TV screen underneath. The galley had modern compact appliances, and the ceiling featured a large skylight that opened to the deck.

After a quick tour, Thomas opened a refrigerator and

pulled out a bottle of white burgundy wine – fancy speak for French chardonnay - and three glasses. "It's pretty nice outside, so let's head out on the deck and enjoy the weather," Tom suggested.

They sat on cushioned chairs. "I'm a little guilty of excessively tricking out my man cave, I think. At least that's what my ex-wife claimed," Thomas said, as he punched a couple of buttons on a small box mounted near his seat. Eight wooden slots on the deck, each about 4 feet long by 10 inches wide and arranged in an octagon around them, folded back like an automatic roof on a convertible car. Then, a stack of long clear acrylic panels arose from each hole, unfolding upward like a complicated multi-part car window being rolled up with the touch of a switch. Both John and Frank were fixated, watching the panels rise. In half a minute, the little deck sitting area was surrounded by a four-feet high fence comprised of eight see-through acrylic panels. As the panels completed their synchronized-swimming sort of formation, a flock of three ducks glided over the deck and splashed into the canal, with a few muted quacks as they landed.

"Are the birds controlled by that button, too?" joked John.

"No, but there is a little tent awning I can put up, on a circus pole right in the middle here, if it rains," said Thomas, evincing both pride and a little bit of bourgeois embarrassment. "This will sound all first-worldly, but Paris tends to get a bit breezy and cold in the evening, and I finally just hacked around the problem," he said. "I can also run an electric current through the panels, which polarize in one direction and make the panels opaque from the outside. No one can see in."

As Tom finished, a small drop of pigeon poop landed on the deck next to him, a missive from one of the flock of tens of thousands in Paris. "Like I said that awning can be useful," quipped Tom. "Perfect protection against bird poop, and the prying eyes of Parisian tourists, at the flick of a switch."

John did notice that the acrylic walls more or less ensconced them in a draft-free cocoon right on the deck of a boat moored in the Canal St. Martin, as the city of Paris went about its frenetic gestures just fifty meters away up the steep canal wall.

"We had a phrase for this that I learned in law school," said John.

"Really? What was it?" replied Tom, eagerly.

"It was, 'Holy fucking shit this is cool,'" quipped John.

All three of them laughed and sipped. Whether Thomas did this daily, or this was a special event in the history of this specific man cave, John didn't know. But the spot had been designed for this, and they were doing it.

"If you think this is cool, wait until Frank tells you about some of the man caves he's seen," said Tom.

"How on Earth did you end up here, doing this?" John asked. "Your dialect is Midwestern United States. That's a long way from the bywaters of the Second Arrondissement."

Thomas didn't give away any confidences to John or Frank, but he did give an overview of how he had arrived where he was today. He explained that he had not been born into the highfalutin world of international wine brokering. When he graduated from St. Olaf College in the early 1980's, jobs were scarce, and he landed a job in a suburb outside Paris coordinating travel study groups from America. Then he took a clerk post with World Wine Brokers in Paris. Even though he didn't know much of anything about wine, his willingness to work the graveyard shift landed him the clerk position.

Many US merchant buyers, notoriously penny pinching, waited until 5 pm, or even 11 pm local time, to place cheap calls to Paris. Tom's job was to take the incoming orders. Customer preferences were kept on paper ledgers, with the customers' prior years' orders. Thomas was expected to pull the customer ledger before calling the customer back, to compare current orders he was taking against prior orders, which helped verify preferences, shipping addresses and payment information.

It was during these late-night clerking sessions that the newbie clerk first spotted an anomaly: Some American buyers were doubling or tripling the size of their previous orders.

On one call, Gallier took the opportunity to ask the buyer why he was buying so much more wine this year. "Because of the rating that the Wine Advocate newsletter gave to the 1982 vintage last week. Robert Parker says it's the vintage of the century," replied the customer.

The next day, Gallier asked his boss if he had ever heard of The Wine Advocate or Robert Parker. "Isn't he the South African doctor with the wine store in Johannesburg?" replied his boss. Gallier may have been young, but he was getting a quick study in arbitrage and inside information. If his boss – a major European wine broker - didn't yet know about this "inside information," how would anyone else? Perhaps only someone with access to the prior orders on the ledger cards that Gallier had sitting next to him.

That evening, Gallier made a decision. He borrowed every penny he could, and drained his own savings account of what was supposed to be future tuition money. He persuaded his French girlfriend to chip in from her trust fund. Cash on hand, Thomas Gallier placed deposits on advance orders for scores of cases of 1982 Bordeaux, a year prior to their release. The rest of the money – which he didn't have – would not be due for a year, upon delivery. Gallier had in effect made a leveraged commodity bet.

A mere six months later, the "futures" market for 1982 Bordeaux had doubled, based upon emerging critical consensus for the vintage. Gallier's investment had increased twenty-fold in value. Gallier decided that he liked the wine business. And international business dealings…and the 1980s. In the early 90's, he opened his own wine brokerage – Thomas Gallier Wines. The 1990 Gulf War had caused a worldwide bust as the 1989 Bordeaux futures were being offered to the world, which provided Thomas with another wine buying opportunity.[13]

At the same time, the supposedly deep pockets of the world's reinsurance pool, including "Lloyd's of London," were crippled by asbestos claims and other policies. The famous Lloyd's of London went bust.[14] Hundreds of Lloyd's guarantors, called "names," faced catastrophic capital calls, and they scrambled to raise cash by selling off assets. Elite families of England and Europe were forced to make wrenching decisions about what to sell - the family home, jewels, art treasures or the wine cellar? Often, the Lloyd's investor "names" raised quick cash by dumping thousands of cases of fine wine onto the world wine auction and broker markets. Prices slumped. The world was awash with Bordeaux, and prices were ravaged by war, recession and huge new vintages coming to market.

Some of those bankrupt Lloyd's names lost their wine holdings to bankruptcy proceedings, and thousands of cases in bonded storage were turned over to various UK bankruptcy administrators.

For a small fee, Gallier had provided price appraisals to those insolvency administrators. Gallier was the messenger delivering the bad news. Inevitably, Thomas was asked whether he could find buyers – any buyers, at any price - for thousands and thousands of cases of various vintages of Bordeaux, as well as vintage port and French Burgundy. Buyers were scarce, but Gallier was able to locate some who made bona fide purchases albeit at steep discounts. Seeing those low prices, and optimistic that the world would always be thirsty, Gallier decided to roll the dice again. He risked most of his bankroll to purchase the wine inventory that was being dumped onto the markets in the early 1990's. He was often the only bidder.

Before closing out positions, the bankruptcy admin-istrator typically sought the approval of one of the chief creditor groups in the Lloyds' bankruptcy, which were a group of reinsurers based in Bermuda. Kirk Woodbury had been assigned the task of approving such sales. Kirk Woodbury had called Gallier directly about Gallier's offer to buy thousands of cases now controlled by the UK administrators. Woodbury intentionally stretched out the "negotiations" with Gallier for a month, because they were the most interesting phone calls that the wine-lover Woodbury got to make. And with Woodbury's blessing, as a matter of "due diligence," Gallier made sure that five "audit sample" cases made their way to Woodbury at his Bermuda offices.

The world wine markets rebounded sharply a few years later, and Gallier had done it again. He now had the capital and the worldwide contacts that made him a leading global wine broker. Instead of the century of time it took other firms to build a worldwide wine brokerage, Tom Gallier had built his business in a mere decade.

Thomas turned to Frank Clicquot and said, "So that's my enthralling story of the past few decades in the wine business. Do you think John can process a story about several centuries in the church organ business?"

John, again feeling the liberty of ethanol plus being on a mini-vacation, couldn't help himself, and asked Frank, "So your last name, Clicquot – is it the same one as on the famous champagne house, 'Clicquot'?"

Frank paused a moment, took a sip, and said, "Actually, yes. Another branch of the family. My great-great grandfather was the cousin of the Widow Clicquot's father-in-law, who started the champagne house. My given name is actually Francois Clicquot."

John was dumbstruck for a moment. It was like asking someone named Ford if they were related to Henry Ford, and getting a "yes" answer. He jumped right in. "Okay

I'm confused. What does a bottle from the family of the Grand Dame Rose have to do with fixing old organs?" he asked. Frank took note of John's particular reference to one of the best but rarest champagnes on Earth – Grand Dame Rose – virtually unknown to 99% of humanity. Clicquot, like Volkswagen, is a popular consumer brand. But comparatively few know that Volkswagen owns Bentley, Porsche, and Lamborghini. Similarly, few would know the specialized holdings of the house of Clicquot.

"It's an old story. Predates the Revolution," deadpanned Frank, who then described the seven-generation, centuries-old connection between his branch of the famous organ-building Clicquot family, and the champagne house "Clicquot." Tom already knew the story, but Frank genuinely appreciated retelling it to those who could appreciate it.

John asked an almost joking question of Frank, having no idea of the color and depth which would be revealed in the response. "This may be naïve, but which clientele is more interesting – the organ clients or the champagne clients?"

A smile came to Frank's face. "I didn't understand why my ancestors stayed with this line of business, until it started happening to me," said Frank. "Let me give you a sampling." And then Frank began to tell a story.

Frank recounted how he had been called in by the Chinese 'government' on an emergency basis. The subject was a grand two-story pipe organ which had originally been imported into Shanghai in the early 1800's for the Anglican Cathedral of the Trinity. It was moved to various locations within Shanghai over the decades, and when Mao Zedong and the Chinese communists seized control of China in 1949, several millions of people were executed - including most landlords - and their properties confiscated. This particular organ was commandeered by Mao loyalists and presented to Mao as a gift, who installed the instrument in a party hall near one of his private residences. It disappeared in the chaos of the ensuing decades as genocide raged throughout China in its "Cultural Revolution."

Like many valuable artifacts which disappear in purges, family members stole it. One of Mao's many grandsons, Mao Zhisui, a powerful general in the Chinese Army, came to possess the organ and built a wing on his villa to house it. Mao may have been long gone, but if there were 40 people who ruled China, the grandson Zhisui was in that group. Several of Zhisui's children played the great piece, but several of the key mechanisms had recently failed and needed repair. Frank Clicquot was summoned.

Frank was met at the Shanghai Pudong airport by a coterie of General Zhisui's staff, who whisked Frank off to his hotel and an hour later directly to Mao Zhisui's home. Wise to the exertions and even extortions that might be involved, Frank had fully cleared his Chinese visit in advance with the French Ministry of Foreign Affairs, as well as the U.S. State Department, and had arranged for one of his college classmates and a friend to play a part. They had dressed in ostentatiously Western apparel and were waiting in the hotel lobby to greet him as he was departing with the general's staff. Frank's friends referenced their dinner plans with Frank later that day at the residence of the French chargé d'affaires, and Frank loudly confirmed for everyone to hear that "General Zhisui" would have him back by then, for sure. It was a clunky piece of spy craft, but effective. Any option of not returning Frank to the company of the French ambassador had just been nixed. Failure would become an international incident.

Frank arrived at the site and after he inspected the organ, he inquired as to when he would be speaking with the general. Zhisui's staff indicated that General Zhisui wasn't available. Frank had been through this dance before, in many countries and cultures. As had his ancestors.

"Well, why don't you take me back to my hotel, I'll catch tonight's flight back to Paris after my dinner with the charges d'affairs. I may be able to return in three months, if the general is available then," said Frank, matter-of-factly, as he zipped closed his well-worn leather bag of hand tools.

The general's aide quickly withdrew from the room. A few minutes later, General Zhisui entered. Undoubtedly fully briefed that Frank was expected at the French embassy in a few hours and that he would be departing if the general was not present, General Zhisui had no choice but to employ charm. After all, it was imperative that his children continued their organ lessons, and his wife had been insufferable for weeks with the organ in disrepair.

The conversation proceeded quickly, and Frank even employed a few choice Chinese phrases. His expert eye discerned some decorative Chinese calligraphy on the organ console. Knowing that Chairman Mao had famously admired calligraphy and even invented a popular style of the lettering, Frank asked Zhisui, "Is that your grandfather's calligraphy? It's beautiful."

Zhisui wasn't expecting that, and the stoicism on his face broke with the swelling of pride. Here was this Westerner, summoned to fix this priceless spoil of the decades of civil and external wars, standing in his home – and the first thing he mentioned was his grandfather Mao's exquisite artwork. Zhisui, in his best broken yet excited English, dropped all eminence pretense and began to tell the story. His interpreter, waiting in the wings, stepped in and assisted with the translation. Zhisui spoke excitedly for 20 minutes. The discussion ensued for another hour, much of it by Zhisui proudly telling both his family history and the known history of the organ. Frank provided some details about the style of organ which Zhisui did not know, and Zhisui hung on every word. A few times, Zhisui had his interpreter ask for clarification, so that every detail could be included in meticulous notes without error.

Frank Clicquot then realized that, from that moment onward, there would be no one running interference between General Zhisui and Frank. In effect, he had Zhisui's direct line. In the future, the general would personally take Frank's call, and extend him any favors inside China that Frank might one day need.

Frank was now hooked up at the highest levels of China. Because he could fix an organ.

With a bit of drama, Frank finished his recounting of the story by noting that as he had boarded his outbound flight the next evening, the airline seat included an anniversary brochure decorated with the flags of the many countries to which the airline flew. Frank counted the number of flags and reckoned that he was on a first-name, direct-call basis with the leaders of at least as many countries as depicted on the airline's flashy brochure.

"And that, John, is the best way I can answer whether I get to meet interesting people in my line of work," said Frank.

Later, Frank excused himself from Tom's boat in order to attend a dinner engagement, and John and Thomas headed off to dinner at Marie-Helene's, a small bistro in the Marais district about six blocks from Tom's office. Thomas was a regular there, and among its clientele, he was the only person allowed to "BYOB." Thomas knew there was an underground well-stocked cellar dating back over two centuries. The lore was that Thomas Jefferson had frequented the cellar during his years in Paris.

Thomas Gallier told John he was going to show off a little bit. By the end of their dinner, they had polished off three bottles. Gabriel was enthusiastic about picking Gallier's brain regarding the Bordeaux wine trade, and they spent almost an hour discussing the pricing anomalies pertaining to these specific bottles, versus their more famous competitors. This later melded into a discussion of perceived valuations of antiques and relics, and after Gallier made a specific literary reference, they discovered that they had both been fans of author Philip K. Dick and his themes of alternative histories juxtaposed against the market for real antiques versus counterfeits.

Thomas gave John an overview of the clients for the high-end Bordeaux and Burgundy wines. Gallier explained to John that when he first started his brokerage, he had studiously maintained his ledger of the buyers that he had arranged for Lloyd's, and Gallier's rolodex was now the Who's Who of the international elites.

Gallier confided to John that all his business really needed was a good phone, a good computer and a call answering service. And, of course, his rolodex ledger.

"Hasn't it all changed with the internet?" John asked. Tom paused and then gave a considered explanation. Sure, there were internet sites and newcomers to the wine business. But the real value was information that wasn't public. "Google's algorithm is pretty good, but the most valuable information isn't there," noted Tom. And possessing that information led to getting more of it. Gallier gave John a few examples of events which he had been asked to outfit over the past few years.

Thomas told John that he could always call him to pick his brain on wine matters, if and when John might need a particular introduction into a particular echelon in a particular part of the world – the echelons which had always been on Thomas' ledger of buyers, and which seemed to keep increasing as the world's wealth increased.

John took him up on the offer, on the spot. "Actually, I could use a hookup, the day after tomorrow. I'm hosting four business associates here in town, in what you'd call a closing dinner, a celebration of a job well done. I'd love a private room, or rooms, club style, where we could raid a restaurant's cave and more of less hold court for hours on end," said John.

"I've got a couple of those, and I've got one here in the Fourth," referring to the Fourth Arrondissement section of Paris. "It would be perfect if your guys are here in town for the first time," said Thomas. "But maybe not for the wives," he intoned.

"Not an issue here," said John. "This will be an obnoxious display of ingrained patriarchal hegemonic ritualism," mocked John. "Or something like that." Thomas promised to call and book the spot the next morning for John.

The dinner prattle between John and Thomas, alternately referencing market dynamics for luxury goods and whether the Harrison Ford voiceover in the original *Blade Runner* film was a good thing or not, would have bored most people silly, as some sort of aging yuppie nerd talk. But the boys had made a night of it.

John realized that the Somali pirate mission after-action celebration in Paris was going to be epic.

Two days later, in a private room in a tony restaurant on a side street in central Paris, John's crew began to arrive at an address they had each been given. The sign outside gave no indication that any food and beverage were served inside. The street-facing window was dressed with faded old fabric samples and dated signs; the camouflage was that of a tiny family-run fabric store that likely was managed by an elderly immigrant lady who also darned socks and boiled ox bones and root vegetables in the small kitchen. No hipster would have any interest in the place.

As team members approached the front door, checking their phones to verify that they were at the correct address, the door opened a crack and a waiter called out, "In here, Monsieur, your party is waiting for you." Each of John's crew was led through the hidden entrance, and once through the ante-chamber was confronted with a classic old Parisian bar about 30 feet long, milled from old wood and fully stocked as if it were 1890. About 15 other people were there, each in their own small groups. This was not a pick-up bar at an airport.

Once John's college buddy Milo Patton, the engineer Nick de Stijl and the balloon entrepreneurs Scott Canto and Brian Dietz had all arrived, each expressing incredulousness as to "what is this place?," the group of five retreated to a private room on the top floor of the building. It had a small balcony with double doors that opened onto the street three stories below, and two other windows were opened, allowing the faint sounds of several cafes and restaurants on the block to waft in and out.

John had prepared some review items to run though – a classic "after-action" assessment — and the session got underway in a slightly formal style. The room was organized like a club room or men's study with overstuffed club chairs, side tables and footstools. Wait staff in formal attire entered every 10 minutes and replenished anything needed.

John spoke earnestly about the need for absolute confidentiality in accordance with his thoughts on his flight a few days earlier. Everyone needed a cover story, strong enough to withstand all scrutiny. He explained that part of the reason for tonight's festivities was to give everyone something to talk about in the future, besides what their actual mission had been. After that, and another hour spent following the agenda and discussing the good and bad points of the Somali anti-pirate mission, a sommelier entered with a bottle of 1961 Latour Bordeaux and a 1982 Petrus Bordeaux.

"Okay, men, that's the end of our formal session. Let the informal session begin," announced John. The entire team looked a bit confused. "Those brown leather books next to you are the wine and liquor vault list. Please, this is your chance. Order what you want. And if you order Cutty and 7, you're fired," John said. Now the assembled men began to understand what John meant about having something to talk about.

Ten minutes later, the entire team had in front of them the wine or liquor of their dreams. John began with the first toast. "Men, to a job well done, and to those who deserved to be with us here today, and to those who will undoubtedly join these sessions in the future."

Each of the five men then simultaneously began hooting and hollering in unison, like a band of wolves. It was a good thing they were in a secluded room. To anyone on the street below, it was just another raucous dance party up on the top floor of a Parisian apartment.

For the next three and a half hours, the real after-action session unfolded. The hours were filled with toasts, chidings, shared worries, reliving the good moments, bad jokes, good jokes, a few dirty stories and some speculation as to what had happened at the Pentagon when the *Donovan* had radioed that it was under attack. So too flowed the wine, liquor, steaks and cigars.

At some point, a cadre of foot masseurs from a local massage parlor entered the room. "You guys can do neck and shoulders if you're squeamish about your feet," John taunted. "But in twenty minutes, there will be more toasts!"

"More toasts!" echoed Milo.

Everyone earned their coming hangovers 100 times over. Each of the men finally left in the wee hours, and each had a name and number written on his arm of a pre-paid paramedic service that would visit them in the morning upon their command to administer an IV drip of hydration, vitamins and general anti-hangover therapy.

So it was with resounding success that John Gabriel wrapped up his Somali piracy operation in 2009. A core team had been assembled.

MORNING ROUTINES AT THE NEW ORLEANS DRONE CONVENTION

As John poured another coffee and prepared to make a return call to the mysterious "Majedah" caller, a different telephone call from New Orleans had just begun. Jill Serrano was finishing her call with her teenaged son, Jamie. She was already at the Drone convention pavilion a few minutes early before her breakfast meeting where she was delivering a routine presentation for the DHS in front of scores of attendees.

"I know you want one, Jamie, but you'll be going off to college in a few years and you won't be able to take a dog with you. It's just not something you can do right now," Jill reasoned. He was between classes, and Jill was checking in before her day began. "I've got nothing against pit bulls, either." She listened as Jamie continued to plead his case. "Jamie, every puppy is irresistible. And I'm sure it's a great breeder and that the litter will be full of champions. I'll tell you what. You and I will get up early on Saturday and we'll head over to the two rescue places over on Williams Street. We'll take a look at all the dogs and puppies there, and we can see what their volunteering schedule looks like. I'm sure there are a bunch of times during the week when they could use an enthusiastic helper to walk the dogs and clean up and bathe them and all the other stuff. And I'm sure they'll have some pit bulls," Jill said. "And then we'll reconsider this after you've gotten some face time with the different breeds."

She listened for a minute while her son tried to explain why having a new puppy was somehow different than having a part-time volunteer job with a local shelter. But like most teenagers, he had taken Jill's bait too quickly, and his reasoning was all over the place. It became apparent to both of them that Jamie's overwhelming desire for a pit bull was a momentary obsession, perhaps because other kids had been talking about pit bulls. And Jamie agreed to the Saturday morning visit to the shelter after Jill told him some of the girls at East High School volunteered there.

As Jill hung up, it dawned on her that she really should write some of this down. How many parents had to negotiate their kid out of a pit bull? She saw the phone notification of her note-to-self that she had made the night before. She pulled up a digital map of the French Quarter and figured out the name of the street she and John had walked down to get to Freddy's. She dialed the number of her friend Nancy Chandler at the Department of Homeland Security.

"How's the convention going?" Nancy asked.

"Truth be told, I'm a little fuzzy-headed this morning. Remind me that scheduling 8 a.m. presentations is not the "pro move" in a convention town like New Orleans. I had dinner with an old friend last night. Unexpectedly ran into him at the convention. Lots of old memories," said Jill. "So, Nancy, really quick before I space it, I saw something last night, I'll text you the address. Second floor apartment above a liquor store. Something wasn't right. Fifty-fifty that there's some human trafficking being run out of there. There are a dozen strip clubs within a few blocks, so you know the linkage. I don't have anything more, but could you just see if there's anything obvious that pops up? I saw two girls on a balcony with one creepy guy. It just seemed — off," said Jill.

"Got it. Text me the address and I'll look into it. And thanks, Jill. I don't know how you do it, but you have great intuition. That nail salon you flagged in Virginia Beach ended up being the hub of an entire trafficking ring. The agents don't know it came from you, but they are appreciative," said Nancy. "You make me look good."

"No, thank you. Listen, if I didn't pass along these things, I might as well just quit the Department, right? Anyway, I've gotta jump, my little pony show starts in five minutes!" said Jill.

The chances of John Gabriel dropping by Jill's morning presentation at the Drone Convention were diminishing quickly. John dialed the new number the caller named

'Majedah' had given him, again using *67 to shield his number. "Hello, sir, thank you for dialing back in, this is Majedah. And thank you for speaking with me under these circumstances." The caller put a slight emphasis on the name Majedah, which covered a millisecond pause that had occurred beforehand. But because of what John assumed was voice encryption software, the voice that he heard was no longer that of a female with a slight British accent, but a neutral, slightly computerized voice, like the voice command on a smart phone. The new voice was a complete buzz-kill to John.

"Now I'm really confused. You sound like 'Siri.' Anyway, is Majedah your first name, or last?" he asked.

There was another pause. "My first." "My name is Majedah Simon." She omitted her rank, which was Colonel.

"Thank you for that," said John. "Ms. Simon, does my voice sound as annoying to you as yours does to me on this new line?"

"Probably not, because I've gotten used to it. With the appropriate level of dual encryption as we are using now, the millisecond delay really does bollix up the intonation and pauses. After a bit of experience, to compensate there is a tendency to focus on words and phraseology in your speech pattern, rather than intonation. For example, my normal reply to your comment might be that, 'as far as my organization has discerned, the name Majedah is not yet popular among exotic pole dancers in your country – which I assume to be American because of your voice pattern and diction - so, accordingly, it is on my approved list of names to give you.' But if I am intruding into any areas of sensitivity concerning the name of any part-time personal trainers you may employ, we can certainly pick another name for me to use," said Colonel Majedah Simon, in the annoying computerized voice packages which were being double-wrapped in state-of-the-art encryption.

John immediately understood that this was humor, and he liked the humor, delivered right as another dose of caffeine was hitting the high center of his brain. It mitigated the impersonal sound of the scrambled voice. And it dawned on him that the caller was now playing the game right back, giving a little to get a little. And warming him back up. If her job involved telephone calls, this Majedah Simon was good at whatever she did, he thought.

"In any event," she said, "we are on a more secure line now. I can speak more frankly, albeit the sound of my voice may prove to be more annoying and may discourage you from speaking openly."

John was of course not aware that Majedah Simon was an Israeli Mossad agent whose public identity was that of an IDF Colonel. Nor did he have any idea of her unusual background. She was one of the few non-Jewish officers in the Mossad. She was a Lebanese Druze-Christian by birth.[15] Her father was a Protestant Christian, and her mother was a Druze polytheist. Now in her forties, she had continued her various training regimes for almost two decades, and as a result had the physique of a thirty-something professional athlete.

"I am pleased to meet you, Ms. Simon. For this call, you can call me John. And now that you know that, you know more than anyone else on the planet about the

Arabian Sea operations, other than the few people who were" - John caught himself – "probably… there." John knew that he was bragging a little at the expense of acting like a professional. And that this Majedah had goaded him into it. But his statement was tantamount to him admitting not only that he knew about the Somali affair, but that he was integral to it.

"Okay, John, I believe I understand what you are saying," she said.

"So now that I have given you that chunk of information, can you tell me who you are, and more about the situation you are facing?" asked John. "The shorter, to-the-point version is probably best." "Some unforeseen developments of the past twelve hours have not left me at my lucid best," said John.

"I am calling you unofficially, even though I normally act under the auspices of the Israeli Defense Forces and the State of Israel." Earlier, John had suspected the caller was a spy. He now assumed that he was correct, regardless of what specific governmental agency name was on the payroll check.

Majedah continued, "Frankly, as you might know from the news of the past year, diplomatic relations between the US and Israel are quite strained at the moment. And in reality, as you can imagine, it is much worse than portrayed in the media. My government simply does not trust your government with certain sensitive information. The concern is that certain information shared with sectors of the US intelligence or military will be leaked, likely through the diplomatic corps. It is a terrible situation."

"Why is that so?" asked John.

"I cannot give any operational details, but it involves both issues arising from the American Transparency Act, as well as some personal trust issues between our leaderships. Exacerbating that, again as you know from public reports, is America's policy not to engage against ISIS, because to do so would conflict with its official position not to put any boots-on-the-ground in ISIS matters.

"Now, my country has nonetheless sought to put a spotlight on the ISIS problem, and that creates certain operational problems for us."

"Okay, but why are you calling me?" asked John. "I'm a loyal American and certainly I am not a representative of the American government."

"I'm calling because of the Somalia operation. Our IDF is in a dilemma. We have a situation that requires immediate military action against elements of ISIS, but Israel cannot be seen to attack ISIS, or the United States will be put into the untenable position of having to publicly oppose us – its ally - and any operation we may undertake. Because if Israel acts, the US may feel that it has been painted into a corner. But since the US will not undertake the strike itself, the game theory of it all is that the US may be forced to take steps to render it impossible for Israel to defend itself. It is like Alice-In-Wonderland. Up is down, and down is up," Majedah explained.

"Okay. First and foremost, I won't commit treason or sedition. I'm a loyal American and that is not for sale. With that understanding, what is your immediate situation that correlates to someone who knows how to take out Somali pirates?" asked John.

It was another fair question. Majedah now had to make a further leap of faith, or else this "John" would likely end the conversation. While she did not know the Bermuda executive Kirk Woodbury very well, she knew that the anti-piracy operation had been carried out brilliantly and completely confidentially. Majedah reasoned that the people responsible for that operation must be professional, capable and trustworthy. Success and discretion speak strongly.

Yet all she knew about the man with whom she was talking was that he had told her his name was "John." If she could confirm that John was the brains behind the Somalia operation, her confidentiality concerns would be satisfied. Logically, anyway.

She replied, "Whose inquiry is that, exactly?"

John smiled a bit at that. "You know, Ms. Majedah Simon, I did not wake up this morning expecting a call like this. And I certainly didn't regulate the amount of wine at the table last night in hopes of doing well on an early morning pop quiz. A voluntary one, at that. So, well, it's my inquiry," said John. It was a slightly less harsh way of saying, "enough of the games, please."

Majedah responded, "I am in a poor position, here, Mr. John or whatever your real name is. All I know about you or, rather, what I assume from your dialect, time zone and diction is that you are an American male, between the ages of 40 and 60, likely with a post graduate degree, and yes, the speech analysis algorithm that my colleagues here are running did detect a slight sinus inflammation, likely caused by drinking alcohol within the past few hours. I also know with reasonable confidence that you are not overweight, you do not wear dentures, you don't smoke, you are not under the influence of amphetamines, you do not have a pacemaker and you are not taking hormone supplements. If you are on blood pressure medication, it is a low dose. And you - well, your voice pattern, at least – has exhibited very little stress in this call, and it also is comprised of an amalgam of regional dialects which suggests you have lived in various parts of your country and that you studied at least one romance language. The absence of any detectable rising inflection in your pattern suggests that you do not have children. On a personal note, I thank you for not subjecting me to that annoying upspeaking that seems to have infected the younger generations of your country.

"So, I am revealing to you, Mr. John Anonymous, that we are very, very interested in learning from you, and other than what I – no, actually, what a software program – has concluded based upon your voice patterns, I know nothing about you other than you are using the most common American name, John. So, my questions are to determine how closely you may have been connected with the operations off the Somali coast a decade ago. Of course, I do not expect you to divulge any information that conflicts with standard operating procedures of non-governmental groups. As our venture capitalists would phrase it, I'm asking you to 'lift the skirt'," said Majedah.

John was immediately struck by how effectively the phrase, 'lift the skirt' had just been used. Was she flirting with him? Or was this just standard-issue interrogation technique?

"So, to that end, John, sir, as a matter of prudent due diligence on our part, can you describe anything about the delivery vehicle that we might have recovered from the waters around Somalia?" asked Majedah.

John said, without hesitation, "The platform used was an untethered balloon array. The balloon was a typical weather balloon. Three different brands were used, so I am not sure which specific brand you might have recovered. The latching and fitting hardware was brass, available at any maritime supply store, untraceable. The platform was a kinetic bombardment delivery system. Flechettes, they used to be called. Did you recover one of them?"

There was a pause. Majedah was surprised at the frankness of the answer. "Yes, we have one in our possession, and forensics on three others."

"Steel-jacketed tip, with a partial three-inch interior steel or iron core, with a lead alloy comprising the jacket of the head and the tail. The alloy varied from foundry to foundry," offered John.

Again, there was a pause. "Can you hold a second, John." There was silence for thirty seconds, as Majedah conferred offline with an associate.

"I'm afraid my question was not sufficiently rigorous for my ... security colleague ... standing here with me, as the makeup of the device would fit a standard profile and might not require actual operational knowledge...."

"They were bundled like a fascio, in a winged fuselage, which was shed a quarter minute before impact," John said.

"Could you excuse me again," said Majedah.

"Yes, but my security team, or my movie watching experiences, or both, have taught me that if you don't come back on the line in thirty seconds, then I'll have to disconnect," said John. His patience was growing a bit short, and he also wanted to practice telling lies to foil Ms. Simon's lie-detector algorithm.

"Be right back," the annoying version of Majedah's voice said. In just under thirty seconds, she – the voice - was back on the line. "The fuselage makes sense. We had not discerned that. Again, I must be frank with you, there is a certain split in my camp. On the one hand, there is a fascination among my group with the unconventional - and in fact superior - thinking and design involved in these devices used against the Somalis. On the other hand, these types of weapons got classified as IEDs, and various analysts have trouble overcoming institutional prejudice against that somewhat negative characterization. IEDs don't play well here," said Majedah. "In plain English, for which you seem to have a gift, there is a bit of envy, or even jealousy, involved. But labeling an IED as being clever or brilliant doesn't enhance one's career in my … among people I know. So please appreciate that there is no mechanical engineering award to be given here. Even if one was deserved," said Majedah. John's inexperience with the absence of intonation from the voice encryption software continued to frustrate him.

"And I am acutely aware that sometimes we – my group - think we have a monopoly on clever. We clearly don't. That I am making this call should give you assurances that we realize that," said Majedah.

"Thank you for your kind words," said John, with a bit of smartass tossed in. "We call that a backhanded compliment here."

"And thank you, John. If we had some coffee and bagels, this could be a breakfast meeting, I guess, and I promise that I would have the courtesy not to ask that you divulge the details of your earlier dinner and drinking companion, other than to say I am grateful that things didn't progress past dinner because this call might have been pre-empted by – more pressing matters that would have kept you from answering your telephone."

"That was a masterful mouthful, Ms. Simon," said John. "I did wake up alone."

"Your personal loss last evening is my country's gain," Majedah said.

Jesus, John thought. This Majedah raised the art of interrogation and flirting to Olympian levels. He reminded himself that he was not dazzling her with hung-over brilliance and witty banter. She was well-trained at interrogation, and she needed something from him. But his aching head did feel better.

John continued, "I think you have had some practice at this phone line thing, Ms. Simon. I'm not sure how I will feel later today about your wishing ill on my personal life, but…for your information, it was a business dinner only. Mostly. Probably," said John.

"Well, let me see if I can one-up whatever you discussed at dinner," Majedah Simon replied. "We are on a very secure line, and I appreciate that you or your associates have appeared to have maintained the Somali project as one of the blackest-of-black operations in recent memory. That is impressive and confidence inspiring. So, let me give you some information, on a need-to-know basis. Because I am going to ask you for something at the end of this call."

EXPLAINING THE LOST AIRCRAFT

Majedah then gave John an overview that astounded him. She explained in very general terms that America had, for years, used Israeli operatives to recover or destroy missiles, jets and other sensitive ordnance that were lost or captured by hostile forces in the Middle East and elsewhere. Perversely, Majedah explained, the US military had in the past lost a few jets, and it had asked the Mossad to "handle the problem" when the US could not.

Similarly, Majedah revealed, there was a quid-pro-quo understanding that if Israeli defense and intelligence forces were to lose a critical asset outside of the Middle East, the U.S. would be available to help out. For example, perhaps Israel might need a US drone missile to destroy a compromised Israeli safehouse in Asia before it could fall into enemy hands.

It was an efficient little eco-system, explained Majedah, but it had started to fall apart in the past year due to the deteriorated political relations between the countries, and because Israel could not get assurances from America that its national security communications were exempt from America's Transparency Act. Israel didn't like the idea of a politicized American committee reviewing its security communications.

Then Majedah moved to the immediate problem. "ISIS has taken over some territory that had been controlled by the Kurds. The US was providing some support to the Kurds. Of course, that was never made public. Not officially, anyway. But ISIS recently captured several Kurdish supply depots. One of those depots was a small airbase. There were three US-supplied training jets there. One of the American training jets was destroyed as the Kurds withdrew," said Majedah. "But two of the American-made jets are now in the hands of ISIS. As well as some tanks and other armaments. The news reports about ISIS capturing a couple of Humvees – it's so much worse than that."

"That's fascinating. But what does that have to do with stopping pirates?" asked John, his hangover now acting up a bit.

"My group has been unofficially advised by the Americans that the two jets have been captured. But the official American stance is that since no American jets were ever there, then nothing has been captured. And worse, that the U.S. cannot and will not risk doing anything to get the jets back, because the news of any such American action might drag the U.S. into a bigger skirmish with ISIS. It is so sensitive, that our information on the captured jets came to us through unsanctioned channels," explained Majedah.

"Why do you care, though?" asked John. "If America wants to leave a couple of old jets with ISIS, why is that your problem? And again, what does it have to do with pirate boats in Somalia?" John had just upped his game from being the witty hung-over pirate guy, to a demanding intel officer annoyed at receiving an incomplete report.

There was a pause. Majedah had only given John a piece of the story. What Majedah had withheld from John was the highly-guarded secret that the contractors to the United States Defense Department had for decades installed kill switches in US fighter planes sold to allies like Israel. This was done purely to protect the American aerospace industry. If one errant American-made jet in the hands of an allied air force was used to attack the US or its facilities, the practice of selling jets to allies would come to a halt. The American aerospace contractor industry would be nationalized in one day, and its executives would be served to the wolves, perhaps even with criminal charges.

Majedah – and the Mossad – knew that the kill switch allowed the aerospace contractors to effectively disable any American plane that might fall into enemy hands. Specifically, by activating the kill switch, the plane's key systems would quickly fail for what seemed like a lack of ordinary maintenance. It was the equivalent of the "stop engine now" warning light coming on in one's car.

The aerospace contractor of the two captured jets had through backchannels notified the Mossad a few days ago that, in fact, their secret kill switches had been disabled. The Mossad had concluded that Iran, still furious after its nuclear weapons program was thwarted by the Stuxnet virus launched by US and Israeli agents, had in response developed a sort of turbo version of a virus-scan for all software programs. Iran was supporting ISIS and had likely used its new virus scanning software on the captured jets and discovered the kill switch program. In any event, the contractor's back door kill switches were no longer operable.

The truth was, such a kill switch was the principal way the IDF had in the past neutralized any captured American aircraft. The U.S. would advise Israel of the lost aircraft, assuming that an Israeli black operation would be used to take out the jet. In fact, the Mossad would often contact the aerospace contractor who had made the jet, and the kill switch would be activated by the contractor. The next time the jet was powered on, its systems would begin to degrade, and within minutes it would not be flight worthy. The IDF would have ample options to destroy the unflyable stolen jet, essentially a hunk of useless metal, in due course. But that trick was not available now – Iran had disabled the kill switch.

There was another matter that Majedah had not disclosed to John: The new Transparency Act regulations – on paper at least – would make the arrangements between the aerospace contractors and the Mossad, and those between the American government and Israel – subject to disclosure to the new Transparency Council. Any requests that Israel take action against ISIS on behalf of the US could be leaked through moles on the Transparency Council. That meant that Israel might be accused of an unprovoked direct military attack on ISIS.

So, the situation was that the US had lost two jets – albeit training jets lacking sophisticated weapons systems – and America could not admit it or retrieve the jets. The aerospace contractor's secret backdoor kill switch system had been removed. And anything that Israel might do could become public via the Transparency Act regulations, to both America's and Israel's detriment. It was a stalemate in a crisis.

Further, in this informational black hole, a Mossad colleague of Majedah's had quietly reached out to Wayne Palmer of General Space Ltd. with whom he had a good relationship. He had described the area in Northern Iran where a secret emergency backup beacon from the stolen jets had originated and asked if Palmer could reposition the imaging schedule on one of his company's satellites to take some fresh, high-definition pictures of the coordinates… within a day. This too was a state secret.

"We have some additional unsettling information," Majedah told John. "I can only share a small portion with you." Majedah then proceeded to disclose somewhat haltingly, as her colleagues were clearly analyzing – in real time – what she could and could not say. She told John that the Mossad believed ISIS was planning an imminent attack on Israel - an actual armed attack on its territory. The Mossad had analyzed the coming attack under three possible scenarios.

Majedah explained that the first scenario was that ISIS would attack a high-value target in Tel Aviv. The Mossad was not overly concerned about this, and did not need any assistance with this potential threat. It would be a suicide mission that would fail. But as Majedah gave John the brief overview of this first scenario, her mind momentarily flashed to another time and place.

In her flashback to decades earlier, Majedah was a just a girl sitting in a civilian conference room with her parents, being informed by a uniformed Lebanese military officer that her brother was dead. He had been on a school camping trip in Southern Lebanon, near the small town of Markaba. Majedah's brother had been killed by two PLO militants making an incursion that night across the Lebanese border into northern Israel. The officer had explained to Majedah and her parents that her brother and some others had apparently stumbled across the Intifada attack[16] as it was commencing. She recalled the Lebanese officer referring to the deaths as a freakish occurrence, that the Lebanese "had not been overly concerned about guarding against" this sort of attack.

The words, "not overly concerned," which she had just said herself, had triggered the memory. Realizing that her mind was drifting, she used her professional training to push the thoughts from her head and concentrate on the matter at hand.

Majedah described to John the second possible scenario, which was that ISIS might mount an attack on Israel as a means to capture or kidnap either IDF or US forces.

"But my call concerns a third potential scenario. There is a connection to those old anti-pirate operations," said Majedah. The Mossad was concerned that an attack on Israel might be part of a diversionary operation in which the US jets were used in some manner to inflame the already boiling political tensions. Majedah was vague, and John responded, "I'm not quite following. No one would believe that the US was attacking Israel, if ISIS uses the captured American jets to attack Israel," said John.

"We're still assessing the possibilities. Perhaps the

jihadists would claim to have shot them down and threaten to burn captured US airmen alive – even if the airmen are not real. Or that the American jets were shot down over their own territory, and they call for direct retaliatory attacks against American airbases or against Israel. These may sound unconventional, but we are dealing with a very unconventional enemy here, we just don't have certainty. The 'Arab street' is easily triggered by the flimsiest of propaganda.

"But the combination of American warplanes in jihadists' hands, with credible information of a pending attack on Israel, presents an imminent and existential risk to us. And under that scenario, the jets need to be destroyed, without delay," said Majedah.

"OK, I think I am beginning to appreciate the situation," said John. "These jets, what are they and where are they?" asked John.

"They are F-16s, one of the workhorses of the American Air Force. They are special stripped-down training models. Defanged, so to speak, of many current avionics and weapons systems. They've got two F-16 jets, four tanks, 20 missiles, and a few armored vehicles.

"Wow. How do you know where the F-16s are?" asked John.

Majedah paused again. There was just too much classified information that could not be divulged.

"I cannot tell you that, but we know," she replied, unable to reveal that Israel had access to a secondary homing beacon burst that was activated when the jet's avionics were turned on.

"What I can tell you is that, for now, the jets are beyond Israeli jet and bomber range. US refueling support would be needed, which is impossible. And in any event, politically Israel cannot simply attack the country where the jets are situated. It's not June 1981 anymore.[17] We don't know how long the jets will remain there, or when the suspected attack on Israel might happen," she said, "But we don't think it will be long. Hence our urgency."

In fact, the Mossad anticipated that within days the jets would likely be moved under camouflage. Although the IDF might learn of their location within an hour of their engines being fired up, that would be too late if an attack were underway. In addition, the IDF did not have a large enough drone force capable of accurately tracking the jets. The risk of the IDF failing was high enough that it was arranging for alternative plans; hence the call to John Gabriel.

"Do you have recent photos of the site where the planes are stored?" asked John.

"We'll receive a fresh set within the hour. I believe we could share them with you real time," she said.

"Okay. Let's take a break? I need to think this over. I also need a shower and a couple of aspirin. In the meantime, can you get me those photos, and we can reconvene in an hour?"

Majedah agreed, and her aide provided John with a new phone number and a secure URL address.

YASSIN HAS A PLAN

It had been a busy week for Salah Yassin. He was attending to his usual administration of the various details of rocket launches from apartment complexes in the Gaza Strip and the West Bank against residential compounds in Israel. The Bahaa and M-75 rockets were his typical armament. They were unguided dumb rockets, but the technology was improving every year. There would be a time in the near future, Salah hoped, when he would be able to program his rockets to hit specific buildings. Then his terror campaign against the Jews would rapidly bring down the state of Israel.

Yassin didn't intrinsically hate Jews. Rather, he loved power. And in the putrid landscape of anti-Semitism in the Middle East, having power by necessity meant being anti-Jew. Rabidly so. And by having power one received money. So, Yassin's anti-Semitism was more of a professional affectation. It was his direct link to power and money.

In Yassin's case, his group was currently receiving funding from Iran, which had landed a billion-dollar payoff in its recent nuclear disarmament negotiations with the U.S. In addition, Yassin's staff all held various educational titles with a charity that had been established by the radical financier Seymour Gacy.

The week was busy enough, and Yassin had the previous week been presented the opportunity to work with the cache of American weapons captured when several groups of jihadists had broken through some lines in northern Iraq and overrun some Kurdish territory. Several tanks as well as two American F-16 trainer jets had been captured. Yassin enthusiastically stepped up to exploit the windfall.

Yassin had been successful in arranging funding to the groups in order to secure possession of the jets and prepare them for their mission. The operation would be simple, yet it required complete secrecy. According to his blueprint, there would first be an attack by jihadist forces against an Israeli border post, using his huge cache of rockets. That would be followed by a concentrated mortar and rocket attack against a few Israeli settlements within striking distance. With any luck, there would be enough Israeli civilian deaths to warrant global media attention. Even the world press – which normally turned a blind eye to rocket attacks against Israel – would take notice. In addition to the rocket attacks, Yassin's militants would flood the tunnels beneath Israel's security wall and kill and kidnap as many people as possible before their inevitable repulsion by the Jewish forces, which were a mere arm of the imperialist West.

Following these attacks, the world would plead for Israel to use restraint. And that's where Yassin's plan was brilliant. The stolen American jets would be staged in southern Syria, using a local road as a takeoff runway. The jets – newly painted with Israeli Air Force insignia - would take off to the west, over the Mediterranean Sea, then head south toward Israel, and then eastward at high altitude to cross into Israeli airspace. Israeli fighter interceptors would be scrambled but would be unable to reach the disguised

F-16s before they had left Israeli airspace, turning southeast toward Mecca. With some select leaks to compliant media, the story would be that there had been a massive Israeli aircraft mobilization, with perhaps a dozen Israeli jets in the air. In this fog of war, the so-called Arab Street would be riveted by Al-Jazeera network reports that these Israeli jets had served as escort aircraft defending the two Israeli attack jets as they screamed southeastward. To the Arab world, this was a clear-cut story of the Israeli air force offensively attacking Islam.

Under Yassin's plan, the media would warn for an hour that the Israeli jets appeared to be heading into Saudi Arabia, and perhaps Mecca. Propaganda would then be uploaded to social media, purporting to reveal an apparent Israeli retaliation for the rocket attack on its border post and settlements.

The decoyed Israeli F-16 jets would likely be shot down by Saudi anti-aircraft gunners during their final bombing run toward the Kaaba shrine near the Great Mosque in Mecca. Video footage of this supposed Israeli attack on the most holy and sacred Islamic place on Earth would be repeated endlessly on Arabic television throughout the Middle East. Millions would be convinced that they had witnessed Israel launching an unprovoked attack on Mecca. Social media would call jihadists to arms. Western and Israeli denials would be dismissed by a radicalized Arab Street. Every radical imam would declare that full and complete jihad was now at hand.

No Middle East regime would be able to contain the demands to attack Israel. War would be inevitable.

It was a bold "false flag" deception.

Salah Yassin was sure that he would rightfully join the top tier of power brokers in the region. There would be no ceiling constraining his power.

DECOYS AND THE FALSE FLAG

Shortly after John Gabriel and Majedah Simon ended their call, a digital file with 20 reconnaissance photos was delivered into a secure cloud server to which John had access via the password provided by Majedah. Unbeknownst to John, Wayne Palmer had provided the satellite images to the Mossad. The satellite images revealed a hastily established military base, with the American jets and other armaments partially hidden under camouflage nets. Several improvised lean-tos, a hangar, some support vehicles and aviation fuel barrels dotted the immediate area. John studied the images closely. In several of the photos, he noticed the pile of construction debris among the various trucks and buildings, which was a sign of a recently built camp. Discarded crates and boxes from the incoming supplies were stacked in one area. John noticed something odd about the debris pile. He cross-checked several of the satellite images taken from different angles and found a clear image.

Sitting in the garbage pile was what appeared to be Israeli Air Force insignia stencils of various sizes attached to several boards. John thought for a minute and harkened back to what Majedah had told him about an imminent attack by ISIS, and the worries that the F-16s could be used as part of a diversionary attack.

"Why would ISIS want Israeli insignia on the jet?" John pondered. "Could that help the planes gain access to Israeli airspace?"

And then the light bulb went off in his head. Israel had scores of American-made F-16s in its air force. These captured American F-16 jets were being marked to look like Israeli planes.

John focused on the likely target audience of American planes with Israeli insignia. Disguised – even if poorly disguised - as Israeli jets purchased from America, they could be flown against a target pretending to be an Israeli attack. It was a classic false-flag scenario. And it corresponded almost perfectly with the Mossad's third scenario – their worst case.

John thought it through a bit more dynamically. In response to an initial direct attack by ISIS or other jihadists against Israel, what member of the so-called Arab Street would doubt that Israel would retaliate, for example by sending a couple of Israeli F-16 jets to counterstrike? And even better if the fake Israeli jets were shot down. It was a version of jihadist suicide bombers, similar to the hundreds of fanatical Japanese kamikaze bombers of WWII. But these suicide-mission pilots would be dressed as Israeli pilots, flying in American jets outfitted to look like Israeli Air Force jets, attacking an ISIS or Arab target.

It didn't matter that Israel would know the attack was fake. That is true of all false flag deceptions. Israel and the

West were not the intended audience. The audience was millions of Muslims watching their televisions and video channels.

Perhaps the target could be the Burj Khalifa tower in Dubai. Perhaps an Arab defense ministry. Or a Palestinian missile battery, especially since the jihadists intentionally placed them among civilians to maximize civilian deaths in the case of any Israeli attack. John realized that it could be any target recognized and revered by the so-called Arab Street. And with a perceived direct counterattack by Israel on an iconic Muslim target using an American-built F-16 jet, the war spirit in the Muslim world would boil over. No moderate regime in Jordan, Saudi Arabia or Egypt could resist; their Arab Street would erupt, which would all be in accordance with the jihadists' objectives.

Such an attack could enable and legitimize ISIS as the special forces' military wing of all the Middle East Muslim countries. The modern caliphate would immediately come back into existence, because it would now be a de facto joint military authority for the Middle East – a sort of belligerent NATO. No action by ISIS could be disavowed by any Islamic nation-state. It would be a bloodless hostile takeover of the various militaries by the most fanatical of the militants. Brilliant, if it were the plan.

Israel should be worried.

John quickly showered and ate as he tested and retested the analysis. Shortly thereafter he was back on a secure connection with Majedah Simon, but instead of being audio-only, this time it was via an encrypted video tele-conference. John could not help being curious as to what

Majedah Simon would look like. She had flirted with him a bit – or interrogated him – and if she tuned out to be a 300-lb. wart hog, John realized that he would be disappointed. For a moment, he realized how effective her interrogation techniques were. After all, John had given her what she sought, and he did so fairly quickly. "Maybe to protect myself, I should envision her as an obese interrogator in black net stockings," John thought. "Well, maybe not," his inner voice continued.

Once John had logged onto the secure video call, his active imagination was not disappointed. There was a big technical difference – this was clearly a 5G bandwidth for a high-definition call. Their voices were normalized although there was still a small delay as the encryption software integrated their conversation.

Majedah Simon appeared on the screen as a middle-aged blonde, with large glasses and her hair pulled back. On the video link, it was unclear to John if Majedah's hair color was natural or if her glasses were actually needed. They may have been mere props to partially disguise her face. It occurred to John that it would be difficult for him to pick her out of a routine line-up. But one cannot disguise attractive basic facial features, and Majedah was not only attractive, she carried herself with a certain air of a woman who didn't care whether or not she was attractive.

As they started the video conference, John shared his analysis with Majedah, specifically calling out several of the satellite images which revealed the debris pile with Israeli Air Force insignia stencils. Majedah said she needed a moment, and the video feed went to blank for half a minute. It occurred to John that Majedah's analysts were receiving this information for the first time. They had missed this detail.

When the video feed returned, Majedah said, "John, our analysts had not yet discerned what you are seeing. Perhaps they will come to concur with your observation, but for now, let's assume you are correct in your interpretation of the reconnaissance photos."

Majedah's realization that John had just out-analyzed her Mossad team was sobering, and it would have been embarrassing if John was affiliated with another intelligence agency. She needed this man's help with a situation that might quickly become an existential moment for her country. With that in mind, Majedah made a snap decision, like a star football quarterback calling an audible in the waning seconds of an important football game.

After a moment, Majedah removed her glasses – it was a bit dramatic, but not without impact – and looked directly into the screen camera to John.

He immediately noticed that her eyes were green, or at least she had on green contact lenses. Apparently, the glasses had indeed been a partial disguise. But her eyes, whatever their real color, were intelligent and penetrating.

Majedah asked, "Mr. John, whose last name I do not know, is this something you and your team could help us address in the coming few days?"

John paused and folded his hands as he thought. It was as if he was developing a plan, right then and there. But because of his prior Somali mission, during the last intermission between phone calls he had already sketched in his head a rudimentary outline of a plan.

"Ms. Simon, to respond to that, I have a several important questions. First, are you able to obtain for me 10 grams of spent plutonium from your nuclear program? It doesn't need to be enriched. For use against these rogue jets, that is," John asked. Israel's nuclear weapons program was the most widely known secret in the world, yet it remained classified.

The sound on Majedah's feed went silent for a few seconds, and John then saw Majedah look aside, engage in a few sentences of conversation with an off-camera colleague, and then return. But before she ended her muted side dialogue, it appeared to John she had barked an order to a subordinate. The sound came back on Majedah's feed, and she said, "Short answer, it can be arranged." Unbeknownst to John, Colonel Majedah Simon had just pulled rank on whomever else was in the room.

"Okay. My second question: Do you have access to the team with real-time control of the targeting avionics of the IDF's jets' missiles?"

The momentary expression on Majedah Simon conveyed, 'Oh for fuck's sake!' but she remained silent for a beat. This was a difficult request. The Mossad did not control those military personnel; special protocols would have to be accessed, and those protocols left traces. The purpose here was to avoid any linkage of the operation to the State of Israel.

John recognized her agonizing – he sensed that she wanted to say yes, but she knew there might be either security or operational issues. John decided to rephrase his question to remove the political sensitivities.

"Let me rephrase that. If IDF jets are running routine training operations within the borders of Israel, would you be able to arrange comms with the personnel who oversee the technical targeting parameters of armaments on those IDF jets?" It was a bit of lawyer-talk, but John did genuinely want to assist this Ms. Simon with her obviously delicate classified information quandary.

Her video feed sound went silent for ten seconds, and she nodded her head as she apparently was listening to her off-camera colleagues. Moments later, she turned to John, and the audio came back on. "Yes, we – I – under those limited operational circumstances, I would have communications access to those personnel," she replied. John couldn't tell if that was more of a wishful promise, or a factual answer.

"OK. Finally, is your organization still receiving the daily American satellite sweep images of any radioactive plumes?" asked John. He had asked a question for which any response would be highly classified. It was both a checkmate question, yet an ultimate verification of John's credibility.

American radioactivity satellite sweeps had been a daily occurrence since the fall of the Soviet Union, born of worry that rogue Soviet nuclear weapons or fissionable materials might be stolen or traded. Daily and sometimes twice-daily satellite sweeps had continued over the so-called "rogue crescent," comprised of the Islamic world from North Africa through the Middle East and into Pakistan, as well as the breakaway republics of the USSR, also often just called the "-stans" which was polite code for the southern Islamic portion of the former Soviet Union.

As a matter of routine, but highly classified, these images were shared with various NATO and other Five-Eyes defense ministries. Despite the recent chill in human diplomacy, the Israeli Defense Force, and by extension the Mossad, received these images daily. John's awareness of this arrangement, and his referencing it, was highly irregular under ordinary classified intelligence protocols. If Majedah provided a response, in effect she would be leaking state secrets and classified data without authorization. But John's question demonstrated that he had a knowledgeable plan and solution under exigent circumstances, normally confined to battlefield necessities. And clearly, without a response, John would decline the engagement. For Majedah, it was a difficult situation to balance.

Majedah looked off-camera as her microphone muted and she spoke a few words to some colleague, and then she looked back to John as her microphone re-engaged. The tone of her response suggested that the video would be critically, and perhaps harshly, reviewed. "John – sir - under chapter 19 and other authorities, I'm accepting your analysis of the stencils as an indication of the commencement of an imminent attack against the assets I represent, and I have determined that the area around the F-16 aircraft is an active zone of operation. Under the situational rules of engagement, I believe that I am authorized to make certain limited hypothetical disclosures to you in furtherance of exigent battlefield necessities. Solely within such limitations, if I were to respond to your question, hypothetically, the answer would be affirmative," she said.

In other words, "yes," but Majedah was clearly going to be second-guessed by everyone if anything went wrong, and she needed both the exigent circumstances on the record, and to provide her superiors with cover. That is, plausible deniability for them to disavow her decision, to declare her to have gone rogue.

John paused a few seconds to let the obvious stress abate.

"Then Ms. Simon, I believe I can help you and your colleagues, and we could do so right away." And taking a cue from her and her flourish of removing her glasses, he looked into the camera and said, "For right now, my name is John Smith, and I have several team members who will need to sign on."

Majedah could appreciate the tradecraft for this "John" to use the most common American name as an alias. She would have to accept that for now and face the consequences if her superiors second-guessed her decision. Black operations teams typically didn't do that. A technical assessment by the Mossad might be that these were serious security blunders by Majedah in her divulging her name to an unsanctioned and unknown operative. But she had sought him out, not vice versa. And this was an existential and immediate crisis. And despite the professional envy of some quarters, she held in high regard the fact that John and his team had previously run their anti-pirate operation for months, all while avoiding detection by the combined military and clandestine services of the entire world.

Majedah was focused on that. After all, she herself

had just called an audible with her offer to engage John's team. He was, technically, a third-party mercenary, outside of the ordinary military chain of command, without any clearances or sanction, and a resident of a foreign country. She would be responsible for John's actions, and have to answer for any problems, regardless of the success or failure of the operation. If things went wrong, perhaps she could be court-martialed. And, she had leaked classified information with a justification that could be attacked in hindsight.

She recognized that this "John Smith" operative certainly was unusual. He had shown her that he played a game in multiple dimensions, outside of normal groupthink, and his analysis of the satellite images had been best of breed. Beyond best, actually.

"What would your terms be, for you and your team?" she asked.

"A half million dollars per day. That covers the whole team. A two-million dollar advance. Additionally, all expenses, which would include the costs of an after-action gathering with an extravagant budget."

Majedah had authority to approve up to five-million dollars under exigent circumstances. She decided this wasn't the time to negotiate to save a few hundred grand. "I – we – look forward to working with you, Mr. John Smith," replied Majedah. "And your team. We can have a private jet waiting for you later today."

"I'll need a couple of hours or days to collect all of my folks," John said. "And to convince them to participate."

A few minutes later, the video call was over.

An avalanche of thoughts began to consume John's

brain. He visibly shook his head, and said out loud, "Immediate steps. Luke. Lead Head. Dammit, that breakfast thing." John then went into action. He texted Jill Serrano. "Head foggy. Hope the breakfast meeting went well, will see you soon, I have to leave town on business. But do come by the Lead Head event. Dammit. -John."

Next, he texted Luke. "Gonna be a busy day. Call me ASAP, big audible to discuss."

Another text went to Tom Gallier. "Lead Head is all ready, Luke will handle. I have to leave town, emergency situation that will trump any story of Frank Clicquot. Details later. Dammit. -John."

John and Luke spoke a few minutes later. "Well, we've got a fast-moving set of changes today. Bottom line, you're going to have to handle the Lead Head reception this evening by yourself. I have to leave town in a few hours. And you'll need to fly out tomorrow to join me, so behave yourself with that fine lady you met," said John. He almost sounded like a parent issuing pre-prom date instructions.

"Where to?" asked Luke.

"That's a good question. I don't precisely know yet, but it will be several time zones east of London. A long flight, or two," said John. "A couple of colleagues who you have not met will be involved."

"That sounds intriguing," replied Luke.

"It's intriguing enough that we can't discuss it on the telephone," said John. "Remember the whole story about chasing shipwrecks? Use that story tonight to explain my absence. Add something about a new wreck off Bermuda, and that we just learned that some competitive team was trying to beat us to the site. Just make it reasonable so I can run with it if someone asks me about it. And remember to tell me what the cover story is that you dream up!" John said. "And come swing by the house in an hour, just let yourself in, and we can go through a quick to-do list."

LUKE JOINS THE TEAM

An hour later, Luke arrived at John's house, which smelled of coffee and bacon. He had been in and out of the house for years. He had learned the provenance of many of the art pieces and other curiosities that John had collected. As he headed for the kitchen, he passed a display case containing one of his favorite items, a unique trio of artifacts, supposedly the only known example in the world. John had inherited the assembly from his father, and it had likely stoked his interest in metal, wood and leather antiques. One piece of the artifact was a thin book-sized undulating concave collar, almost like a tiny saddle. It consisted of layers of thick leather. The exterior side had an iron overlay. The matching piece was the headpiece of a blacksmith's snip, which looked like the head of a primitive bolt cutter. The two snipping blades were made of crucible steel. The artifact was like a primitive 18th-century bolt cutter. Strong steel – hard enough to cut through iron – was rare and expensive and had to be custom smithed in Europe. The third piece was a blacksmith tong.

The artifact trio was used to remove a slave collar[18] in the ante-Bellum American south. The artifact was, in its day, a terrorist's kit. Mere possession of it by a non-master was punishable by death.

Luke had known John for almost two decades, since he was a young boy. As Luke walked through John's house, a foggy memory of his youth ran through his mind.

About a year after Luke and his some of his friends had started doing chores for John on weekends, his mother, Cassandra, had invited John to attend a barbeque that was loosely organized by a couple of the local churches in the Treme area of New Orleans. Cassandra had told Luke that his attendance was mandatory - no excuses. It had been a hot summer afternoon. At some point, the heat, exhaustion, and the commotion of the day got the better of Cassandra, and she passed out.

Luke recollected that as John was attending to his mother, he told Luke to escort the paramedics over to his mother when they arrived. The words – almost commands – now flashed back in his mind. "Luke, come over here," John had said. He'd grabbed Luke's hand and pulled him over to the paramedic tending to his mom. "This is Mrs. Mandeville's son, Luke. Luke, I want you to help the paramedics here with any questions they might have."

Luke recalled that he'd been reluctant to answer. John had coaxed him a bit, and repeated some of Luke's answers in a firmer, louder voice. And Luke recalled, after he'd answered a few of the paramedic's questions, John no longer needed to repeat or rephrase his answers. His own voice had grown stronger, more confident, as he began to mimic the way John responded. It was battlefield coaching for Luke.

A few minutes later, Cassandra had improved, and the medics didn't think a trip to the hospital was necessary. John drove Luke and his mother home. Fifteen minutes later Cassandra was lying on her living room couch, and the calls started coming in from her friends at the barbeque, inquiring after her. Luke was there with her over the next several hours, as her friends stopped by to check on her.

Luke recalled that John had put him in charge. "Luke, do you think you've got a good handle on things here, and everything the medics talked about?" John had asked. "People are going to want to know details, and you were right there so you are the only one who can provide them with details. You'll have to do it a bunch of times, with each call, but it's important. Can you do that?" asked John, again giving Luke some spot coaching.

Luke replied that he did and could. John soon made his exit, allowing Luke to dutifully assume his role as the person in charge of the situation, and over the next few hours Luke not only recounted to Cassandra what had happened, but also to the various friends and neighbors who stopped by or called.

With each retelling that day to a dozen friends and neighbors, Luke matured a notch. By the end of the day, Luke had become an integral part of the story. Now, years later, the details of his mother's health emergency flooded back to Luke. Today appeared to be a different sort of emergency, but it had awakened that old memory.

"C'mon into the kitchen," shouted John.

"You look like you had quite a night," said Luke, taking the cup of coffee John handed him.

"I did. And that was just a short dinner date and some wine. It was nothing compared to this morning, or at least the last ninety minutes," said John. "You don't look so fresh yourself. A little after-party or two last night?

Luke paused a moment, not quite sure how much to reveal, and simply replied, "Yep, something like that."

Good for him, thought John. Don't kiss and tell.

John continued. "So, I was hoping to have a long discussion with you soon. But now, I've got an emergency on my hands, so I have to accelerate things and just bring you up to speed. 'Reading you in,' as the saying goes.

"Do you remember all that fuss about the Somali pirates hijacking cargo ships? Tom Hanks made a movie about it a decade ago," said John.

"Sure, I remember it. And I saw the movie, of course," said Luke.

"Well, I got involved with some colleagues who needed to provide protection to those cargo ships. So, I put together a team that protected those ships and those shipping lanes. We did it for about half a year," said John.

"I… I remember when you were gone for half a year, you were very cryptic about things. I had no idea what you were doing," said Luke.

"And Luke, there is a common ending about what happens to the bad guys in commando operations," intoned John. "Pretty much cliché in every show or movie,"

There was a slight pause, punctuating the somewhat surreal situation that Luke had not anticipated as his logic lined up the obvious answer with his emotion of realizing the ramifications of the obvious answer.

"They don't make it," said Luke.

"They get killed," replied John. After a beat, he added, "They get killed by people who kill them. That's reality."

There was another pause as John let his revelation sink in. Then he continued, "What we did was secret, and we cloaked our activities so well that intelligence agencies didn't know, either. And now it seems, some folks need that same kind of absolute blackout for a similar situation. And it's an emergency playing out over the next week or so, nothing long term. I'm still learning the details, and I'm jumping on a plane in a few hours.

"This is the time to open the door and invite you in to that world. I should have revealed this to you earlier, given you time to think it over, to do the pros and cons. But sometimes life just doesn't provide all of that convenient runway. So, after you finish handling tonight's Lead Head, you can stay and follow up the convention leads, and all of the projects you're running. Or you can ship out to come join the team I'm reassembling on site. Halfway across the world. You'll be the junior guy on the squad, basically a go-fer. You probably won't understand jack about what's going on.

"And Luke, this one is a good test-the-waters. There are no plans to leave any dead bad guys at the scene. But you never know, things can always go FUBAR. If you do this and decide it's not for you, that would be okay. Eyes wide open," said John, almost as if reading from a risk disclosure warning.

"And, Luke, a couple more things that come to mind.

One, there's personal danger involved. Bad guys aren't the only ones who can die or get hurt. A lot more danger than you spraining an ankle carrying tree saplings," John said, referencing Luke's work as a boy. "You can get off the bus now, if you want. Second, if you choose to come along, you'll be involved in a life-and-death situation and see things that cannot ever be discussed with anyone. Not with girlfriends or a wife, and for chrissakes no bragging at the gym or in the bar.

"And third, if you're in, I also want you to think about telling Cassandra," said John. "Years ago, I promised your mom that I'd look out for you. I've kept that promise, but if you come along on this, you're in a new stage. Something she didn't sign up for when she let me into your life."

Luke paused for a few seconds. His mind raced, but in a measured, excited way. "Thanks, John. There's no question, I'm in. And if I had any questions about joining in, I'd raise them right now," said Luke. "And yes, I will give Mom the heads-up. For a lot of reasons."

"I agree. And I think it should come from you, not me. Welcome aboard," John said, extending his hand. It was a bit odd, but Luke shook his hand. John then laughed and gave him a hearty bear hug. "Take a deep breath, then, because the next week or two of your life are going to be like no others. So, I've gotta run, keep your phone close, and I'll give you as much on-the-job briefing as I can. Focus on the Lead Head wine thing today. And right after, I'll have you pivot into this new project with 100% focus. That includes a really good story you're going to tell that undoubtedly pretty woman that you left an hour ago to come meet me here?" quizzed John.

"Not telling her nothing," replied Luke.

"Exactly right," said John.

LEAD HEAD BOOKENDS THE DRONE CONVENTION

As the day's formal Drone Conference activities drew to a close, the informal receptions, dinners and schmoozing began their last evening in earnest. These events ranged from forgettable plastic serving platters with rubberized chicken and gooey dim sum with cheap well liquor poured by bored wait staff to more elaborate and intimate affairs. This would be the second year of the "Lead Head" event. John had quietly started it at the previous year's convention, and had invited his friend, the wine merchant Tom Gallier, to co-host it as a very private after-hours affair, with a select group of about 100 people, including several of the culinary elite of the New Orleans restaurant industry and a few key sommeliers from the best joints in town. The chefs and sommeliers of New Orleans were world class, so in the first Lead Head, John and Tom knew the wines would have to be stunning. And if the culinary elite of New Orleans were impressed, Lead Head would become an event of legend – a highly sought-after invitation.

Both the 1982 and 1989 Bordeaux vintages had changed Tom Gallier's life when he'd bet everything he had on them, and thus John had thought it a good reason to arrange for a number of giant bottles of the best 1982 and 1989 Bordeaux wines to be poured at the first Lead Head at last year's Drone Convention. That event had established Lead Head as being a "must have" ticket.

And this year, Lead Head indeed did return. It was still a private party at the conclusion of the Predators Ball, but a few of the convention sponsors had caught wind that a ticket to the event defined the cool crowd and was a coveted item. The problem was there were no obvious strings to pull or calls to make to get an invitation. Money didn't buy a ticket.

The reception was being held the second-floor rooms of an old-school restaurant, Marnie's, in the heart of the French Quarter, complete with a private staircase entry, a wraparound balcony overlooking Jackson Square, and several opulent sitting parlors for semi-private conversations. And, of course, the place had a resident ghost.

With John having unexpectedly left town, Luke met up with Tom Gallier ninety minutes before the start time to finalize any last-minute details, and to make sure that John's absence would not cause any problems. John and Tom had invited a few key people to stop by a half-hour early, including John's old friend Mike Shepard, a retired military man whose unassuming manner masked a deep intelligence and a quick wit. There would be a special 'pre-bottle' for the crew.

Some of the 200 invited guests had arrived a bit early,

not wanting to risk that any truly great bottles might get emptied early in the affair. They were queued outside Marnie's by five plain-clothed security guards, two of whom were fast-rising female professional MMA fighters and two others were giant football linemen from the local college teams. A couple of fans recognized them as such, which only added to the sense that this was a must-have ticket for a clandestine speakeasy event.

Tom had pulled some incredible Bordeaux bottles from his inventory for the party, mostly from the 2000 and 2009 vintages. There was a lot of other fantastic wine being poured, too, and truly knowledgeable guests recognized the cornucopia. Lead Head living up to its reputation.

Luke alerted Tom and Mike Shepard to the names of a few guests that John had wanted Tom to personally meet, including Wayne Palmer and Lindsey Zevon of General Space, Kyle Duke of the WSJ, and several key executives from Boeing, Lockheed and Virgin Galactic. Louisiana's two senators were also guests, and Luke had enjoyed the several-weeks-long game of not allowing them a "+1" guest until just a few days before the event. Luke was in charge of securing the name and contact information of all "+1" guests.

The few lucky folks who had unexpectedly received last minute Lead Head invitations directly from Luke or John on the convention floor, including the newspaperman Kyle Duke, the Gumdrop tech team, the ICE-3 guys and Janine and her bosses, circulated around the room with the excited look of lottery winners. There was a richness to the room's atmosphere, not because it was a power room, but rather because one sensed that it was a power room and that one somehow had been selected to be admitted to the room. Hence, it was impossible to identify exactly who the powerful people were supposed to be other than a few obvious candidates. Even so, Wayne Palmer might go unnoticed standing next to a random techie who might grace the cover of next month's Wired magazine. An attractive woman commanding a circle of listeners may be a Silicon Valley hedge fund manager, or a veteran convention hostess. It was anyone's game and anyone's guess.

About half an hour into the Lead Head event, Luke Mandeville met Wayne Palmer and a couple of his key executives. John had especially wanted to meet Wayne, and Luke dutifully tried to explain his boss John's absence as due to an unexpected departure to Bermuda in connection with a hundred-year-old sunken boat. Luke had planted the story earlier that John Gabriel had discreetly located the shipwreck earlier in the year, but had kept the find secret to avoid scavengers hitting the dive first. Luke gave some additional details to Wayne, that a competing South African crew was preparing to visit the wreck first in order to try to claim it under the "first finder" rules of the Law of the Sea. According to Luke's story, John was on an emergency trip to beat the South African team to the wreck site.

"So, as I understand it, John Gabriel is missing a drone and aerospace convention to go dive hundreds of feet below the ocean halfway across the world, and leaves all this juice to be promiscuously pawed by this unsavory crowd?" bellowed Palmer. He was pleasantly benefitting from several glasses of great Bordeaux, slightly skeptical of Luke's story yet savvy enough not to openly dispute it. But Wayne also felt a little bit of admiration for this John Gabriel, who he had not yet met. "The important question is, can I get his portion of that '09 Pontet Canet?" It was standard wine geek/convention cocktail humor, to be sure.

John had asked Luke to personally make several introductions among various guests, and Luke was busy attending to those tasks. As he ushered Tom Gallier and Mike Shepard over to meet Wayne, Luke saw Janine, the marketing executive that he had invited, across the room, looking like she was guiding her co-workers. Luke hoped he could catch her later after he was done working the room.

As Luke approached Palmer to make the introductions, Wayne was in mid-sentence with his fair-average quality jokes: "I guess I'll have to come back next year if I want to meet Mr. Gabriel. I understood I was stood-up for a Bermudian mermaid of some sort."

Tom Gallier raised his Riedel stemware to his nose, inhaled a headful of the aroma of the 2009 Chateau Palmer, then lowered his glass, put an inquisitive look on his face and asked, after a beat - "John? John Fucking Who?" He cracked a laugh, and the new acquaintances all joined in chorus. Wayne Palmer immediately liked Tom Gallier.

Tom, who was used to schmoozing the rich and powerful in the world – they were his clients, after all – and thinking he was on a comedy roll, continued, "Shit, I mean darn… how rude of me. I haven't introduced myself. Mr. Palmer, I am Thomas Gallier, the host of this soiree. Please meet my colleague, Mr. Mike Shepard, of Super Secret World Domination, Inc." Wayne and Mike both laughed under their breath. "And I can assure you," continued Tom, "that John Gabriel has disavowed any knowledge of this event and denied all those defamatory statements by that no-good, lying, gold-digging mermaid strumpet in her *People* magazine interview."

"To be clear, are you referring to the mermaid interview, or the strumpet interview?" quipped Mike. "It's important to distinguish."

"Anyway, I've arranged for the mermaid and her friends to meet me over on Frenchmen Street around 10 tonight, so I'm not buying Gabriel's alibi about the mermaid," added Tom. "We can get the real story out of her after a few Macallan 25s."

"Nah, all you need is the '18. I mean, when she's with me, that is," quipped Mike. He was on a roll, or at least he thought so. The humor was average at best, but Wayne Palmer was starting to like these guys. He couldn't let that low-hanging fruit go to waste. Feeling a bit free of the formalities of his large booth on the convention floor, Wayne said, "So that garbled message that she left with me about needing an appointment this evening. Something about a hotel party with lobbyists, camouflage gear and a bows and arrows – I should ignore that?" It was a solid reference to the origin of the name of the Predators Ball, and just off-color enough to pass muster.

Like a comedy team that had worked the circuit for years, Thomas Gallier finished the thought for Wayne. "I don't think your bows and arrows are the kind of thing she was referring to, Mr. Palmer."

Even if it was B-grade convention humor, nonetheless many genuine hearty laughs ensued, all in accordance with the scientifically proven fact that jokes are actually funnier when drinking old Bordeaux wines in hidden chambers of ante-bellum buildings accompanied by a few billionaires, tech disruptors, smart attractive women and future captains of industry.

While the Gallier group was amusing themselves, Jill Serrano slipped into the room, having decided to attend even though John had texted her earlier that he had to bail out of town. Luke had been on the lookout for Jill but missed her entrance. Jill reviewed the wine offerings, accepted a few tastes and chose one, and then Jill recognized Wayne Palmer across the room, having met him the day before. She sauntered straight over to him, and not atypically when an attractive woman approaches a group of businessmen engaged in drinking, the group's attention turned to her. Jill raised her wine class and casually said, "Hi Wayne, good to see you again. Jill Serrano."

She had no idea – well, perhaps she had a little bit of an idea – of the social street cred that she had just conferred to Wayne Palmer. Even more than his being a billionaire space entrepreneur. And likewise, the others gathered around Wayne thought, "Who the hell is this?"

Jill and Wayne chatted, and Lindsey Zevon and two more of Wayne's colleagues joined the circle a few minutes later, and the conversation eventually reverted to the stellar wines. "Which one are you drinking?" one of Wayne's colleagues asked Jill.

"I'm back to the '06 Beaucastel CDP. The '90 Beausejour – a bona fide 100 pointer, no doubt - could have been fantastic with some air, but I think it might be losing the race with a little volatile 'brett,'" said Jill.[19] A wine geek would instantly understand that Jill was not being pretentious. She wasn't pretending the knowledge that she had just casually dropped.

Also, it took aplomb to offer an honest critique of a legendary old Bordeaux in a social setting. Pulling it off was a little bit of an exercise in declaring that the emperor had no clothes. But not only had Jill worked at a winery, she also had a good technical nose for wine. And furthermore, she got a quick assist from Thomas.

"Excellent nose, Ma'am," said Thomas in concurrence. "Tom Gallier, I'm one of your hosts of this sketchy gathering. To your point, lately about a third of these bottles have shown a tiny bit of volatility, rather than the normal 5 to 10 percent. It's 'brett' or a close cousin, and not a TCA taint issue,[20] but still it's a disappointment in a 100-point perfect bottle," concluded Tom.

"Well…I think we all just got schooled by the lady," said Mike Shepard, who held his glass up to Jill.

"Oops. My bad, I'm Jill Serrano," Jill said to Tom.

Tom extended his hand. "John Gabriel said that you'd be attending."

Unknowingly mimicking Gallier's earlier gesture, she then smelled her wine, looked up, and quipped, "What on earth is John Gabriel thinking, missing this kind of party to catch an overseas flight?"

The group chuckled again, with Palmer jumping right back in, "Oh, you haven't heard about the mermaid and John's parole officer, then?"

"John assured me that he had beat that rap," Jill quipped

seamlessly. Pretty good repertoire for a bureaucrat, thought Palmer. Mike Shepard and Tom Gallier thought the same thing.

The group continued their good-natured chatting for half an hour. As the party progressed, the group members all insisted that they follow up with each other, and exchanged phone numbers and business cards.

In absentia, John was the hit of his own party, even though few knew that it was in fact his party.

As the party began to wind down, Luke had made all the introductions on his list from John and was finally able to pick up his conversation with Janine, who seemed to have won extreme bonus points with her bosses for getting them admitted to Lead Head. "The band is going to break soon, but they'll do another set or two in the small bar on the ground floor. A few of their friends are gonna swing by. It should be epic. Any interest in staying?" asked Luke.

"Absolutely, I'm game," replied Janine, without hesitation.

BLUEPRINTING THE CYPRUS MISSION

Because of the exigency of the situation, John Gabriel's quickly-developing plan to destroy the false-flagged American jets copied a few elements from the anti-pirate mission he had run a decade earlier. John's plan was that a few simple, undetectable high-altitude balloons would, undetected, dump a couple of storage tanks of radioactive rain on the stolen F-16 jets, and the resultant radioactive painting of the skin of the jets and tanks would effectively light them up for a missile's targeting radar. Thus, when the captured jets were forward-deployed for a presumed 'false flag' attack, their general location - via their radioactive signature detected by daily satellite imaging - would be revealed. The Israeli Air Force could then destroy them by using their radioactive fuselages as homing beacons.

The night after the Lead Head reception, John arrived in Cyprus and two of his team members joined him a day later. Assuming the parts arrived on time, John estimated that it would take less than a week to assemble and stage the balloon arrays on the island of Cyprus, which he had chosen because of its ideal upwind position from the targeted area in Iran. Less than a week, he figured, so long as Majedah could arrange for the Mossad and IDF tech agents to do their part - to install the tanks of radioactive water and to provide the GPS and necessary radio telemetry for the balloon array.

As with his anti-pirate operation, winds aloft from the Cyprus launch point would carry the balloons hundreds of miles east into Northern Iran. The high altitude balloons' cargo loads were gliders fitted with tanks of radioactive water, which would be released to fly silently to their precise targets – the F-16s. Once there, the radioactive water payload would be dumped onto the jets.

The result would be a nighttime radioactive rain shower over the jets and tanks. The water would evaporate quickly, but the radioactive isotopes would irradiate the metal skin of the jets and the tanks. The irradiated jets and tanks – now 'infected' with radioactivity - would then glow brightly on several wavelengths, rendering them "hot" for targeting radar for months to come.

John had chosen a hidden mountainous site in Cyprus for the launch. But the winds were never precise, and these new balloon arrays would have a different payload than John had used in his Somali operation. The objective was aerodynamics and the achievement of "maximum glide slope." Basically, the water tanks needed to glide well enough to reach the target, perhaps hundreds of miles away. That was challenging, especially for a contraption carrying radioactive wastewater and conceived, designed and deployed in less than a week.

What most worried the team, however, was the scenario where the balloons were 200 miles off target. Then, the gliding tank would have to travel 10 lateral miles for every mile of altitude lost. That was almost impossible, especially in thin air and without propulsion.

Once John had worked through some numbers, he saw that the likelihood of a mission failure would be high unless the balloons moved in close to the targets. John thought he had a solution.

In a few follow-up calls, John explained to Majedah the supplies that her operatives needed to obtain for him. John also made a couple of key calls. One was to Tom Gallier. In his brief message, John relayed, "Tom, I'm sorry I had to miss our party. I'll tell you about it when I see you, but I need to ask a favor. Do you have any very close associates or clients in the government on the island of Cyprus? I might need some highly discreet, immediate expediting of passports. And someone in customs who can look the other way for a few days, especially if paperwork isn't entirely in order."

A few hours later, Tom called back. "Do you mean like importing a half million dollars of wine for the wedding of a rich Cypriot, despite the import ban, and making sure there is no customs confiscation?" asked Tom lightheartedly. "Uh, yeah. Got several of those folks there. Just let me know, John."

"I'll definitely need that hook up. Thanks Tom and I'll get back to you quickly."

John also called Frank Clicquot. After some brief small talk, John asked, "Frank, I read that there is a pipe organ on the island of Cyprus. Any chance it belongs to one of your clients?"

Surprised at John's continued interest in the obscurities of organs, Frank replied, "Yes, in fact we did some repairs on that one a few years ago. It's in the old church in Larnaca. It's a bit of a Frankenstein, built from pieces from all over the world. So, it's constantly breaking down. In other words, yes, I have a great client there. We had been subcontracted in a couple of times to do some work on it, and now we're the direct general on it. I'm sure we'll be back there soon."

"Well, if I needed to arrange for some cargo to come in very discreetly, through the international airport in Larnaca, extremely expedited and very confidential, do you have a reliable and discrete warehouse or transit company there?" asked John. "It would have to be highly confidential and secure."

"Absolutely, John. There is a very strong Catholic community organized around the Lady of Graces church where the organ sits. A couple of its patron families run import/export at the airport. They're very loyal. Centuries loyal. They'll help out, for sure," replied Frank.

"Thanks Frank, I think I'll need to get connected with them. I'll be back to you by tomorrow," said John.

Later that same night after one of John's calls with Majedah, several Mossad operatives staged a burglary on a recreational training center near the Lebanese-Jordanian border. Their flatbed trucks carted off parachutes, parasails and avionics, including three unpowered glider aircraft and various uniforms and gear. A couple hours later, the purloined loot went on sale in various online markets where stolen goods are fenced. The Mossad wanted it all to look like a routine burglary for profit. A few hours later, the stolen goods had all been bought up at a discount. And, for anyone who might come looking, there were electronic records of the goods having been offered, including the gliders. The gliders were purportedly sold to aviation club enthusiasts inside Syria. It was a sham, but it provided plausible deniability.

The stolen gliders would solve John' glide slope problem. They could glide vast distances, which vastly reduced the chances of mission failure. The stolen gliders could be modified to carry water tanks instead of people, and the superior gliding performance would allow an almost 250-mile range for the final delivery of the water tanks to the target.

Majedah was impressed when John requested the gliders, as was her technical team. Majedeh had ordered the burglary and sham sales without delay.

The operation was taking on complexity, involving a lot of interlocking pieces. But such was the essence of these operations.

THE NICOSIA TEAM

John was exhausted from the trip to Cyprus, in effect commenced on a hang-over day. He spent a day in Nicosia, the capital of Cyprus, making calls and completing some detail work. The Mossad team had already arranged for a small warehouse a few miles south of town, about halfway between Nicosia and the airport in Larnaca. John made plans to meet them there.

He met with his own team the next morning and briefed them for several hours before heading over to the warehouse command center. Milo Patton, Nick de Stijl and Brian Dietz had had a rest day in Nicosia before assembling. Luke Mandeville and the other balloon company guy, Scott Canto, would be arriving a day later.

When John and his team arrived at the Nicosia warehouse the next day, they were met at the door by Rebecca Biton, who introduced herself only as Rebecca, a colleague of Ms. Simon.

Tall and dark haired, Rebecca was a twenty-something woman dressed in an olive military uniform with no insignia, and which included a skirt rather than trousers.

She had the air of an executive assistant one might find working for a male executive who surrounded himself with an office of attractive women. But she also had the presence of a soldier in the armed forces, as did many Israeli young adults. She was a few years beyond college age and exuded a sense that she was serious about the military. After her initial greeting, she gave John and his team a disarming smile that could have the effect of making you forget that she was a soldier. Rebecca escorted them to an interior makeshift conference room.

As they waited with Rebecca, they were shortly joined by a woman who was also wearing an olive military uniform, which also lacked any identifying insignia. It was Majedah Simon. She was followed by a young man also in unmarked olives. As Majedah entered, Rebecca Biton turned and was about to begin some form of introduction. Although John had not served in the military, for a second he thought Rebecca was about to salute Majedah as she entered. In any event, no formal introduction was needed. Majedah Simon strode directly to John, extended her right hand and said, "Mr. John Smith, I am Majedah Simon. I extend my country's great appreciation and gratitude to you and your colleagues." The drop of a pin would register on a sound recording given everyone's rapt attention being focused on John and Majedah.

Majedah barely resembled the woman with whom John had spoken on the encrypted video calls three days earlier. Her hair was no longer blonde, but rather auburn and pulled back into a professional style that avoided being too austere or severe. The large eyeglasses were also gone, providing John a better view of her intelligent green eyes and her olive-toned complexion. John recalled that he had thought that he would not have been able to pick Majedah Simon out of a lineup, and he now realized that he had been correct. Her video disguise had masked her real appearance. John got the impression that she had also intentionally masked her attractiveness.

Twentieth-century mass marketing might have brain-washed men to think that blondes were more attractive or somehow sexier than brunettes. But blonde hair often directed attention away from the face or a facial feature. On the contrary, dark hair tended to frame and accentuate a woman's face and her features. John saw that was certainly true in Majedah Simon's case.

"I'm pleased to meet you in person, Ms. Simon," said John. "We've obviously just met your colleague Rebecca. Let me introduce a few of my team members." John then introduced Milo, Nick and Brian, using only their first names. John had briefed them that he was known only as "John Smith" to the others, and everyone would be known solely by first name. It was a rather formal circle of hand-shaking, but important.

John addressed Majedah directly. "We're a bit jet lagged, but if you could give us a place to unload our gear, we can be ready to meet in fifteen minutes or so."

"Yes, of course. Robert, could you assist John and his team," said Majedah. The male colleague who had entered with Majedah stepped forward and said, "This way, Mr. Smith. I'll get you and your team set up right away." John noted that Majedah was clearly Robert's ranking officer, even though there were no formal military indications.

"Ms. Simon, I do have one preliminary matter," said John. "May we speak a minute?"

"Of course," Majedah responded. She waved John over to a vestibule near the door.

"I'm not really sure of the protocols, and as you can imagine this is a bit of a unique situation for my team and me. We previously worked alone, as you surmised. So, I'll just ask this straight out, even if it seems naive. I assume you all are IDF officers. But there's no visible military insignia. Will we be working with the IDF or the Mossad? Or some other group?" John asked.

After a pause, Majedah said, "That is an understandable question. I'm not allowed to reveal certain things. And our security rules don't give a whole lot of guidance on this type of … cooperative venture. I can tell you that officially, the IDF is not involved in this operation. It can't be."

John recognized the conundrum for both himself and her. "You can appreciate the razor's edge this presents for my team, since we are not able to independently ascertain who you are, and where this all fits in the grand scheme of things. Like the Hague and Geneva Conventions and the like. Sanctioned military operations versus unsanctioned. I won't pretend to be an expert in it all," John said. "And I'll ease your mind that I don't think there could be an objectionable answer, either."

Majedah paused for a moment, and said, "Stay here

for a moment, I'll be right back." She walked out of the vestibule and returned momentarily and positioned her back to the room. "You didn't see this." Majedah discreetly handed John a leather wallet. He opened it. Inside was a military identification card issued by the Israeli Air Force. John was relieved that he had spent ten minutes at a Drone Convention booth chatting with its proprietor, a curator of international air force collectibles, and John had seen an IDF card. The card in the wallet contained a photo of Majedah Simon and identified her as being of *Sgan Aluf* rank. A stylized wing symbol designated her as air force. It was entirely in Hebrew, except beneath the symbol was the English translation, "Lieutenant Colonel."

"I've never seen one with any English on it," said John. While his statement was technically correct, he had only seen a single example at the collector's booth.

Majedah didn't quite know how to respond. John was correct – the ID cards generally did not incorporate any English. The English translation on her ID was a particularized instance and relic from a prior mission. She knew she was not at liberty to explain. "Mr. Smith, I understand your purposes in asking, and you can understand that my government's official policy is that you did not see this. Will this suffice, for your purposes?" asked Majedah.

"Yes, thank you. And forgive me, we didn't bring ours," quipped John.

A quick partial smile started to appear on Majedah's face, but she caught herself before it got too far. She thought to herself, this John Gabriel didn't miss much. "We'll see you in the briefing room shortly, then," she said.

A half hour later, both John's and Majedah's teams were assembled in a conference room getting acquainted. Majedah gave a quick introduction and introduced everyone on her team by first name. No other information was given as to their affiliation or rank. No one's clothing bore any insignia; in fact, they were all in civilian clothing, save for Majedah, Rebecca and Robert, who were in unmarked olive garb. The implication was unmistakable: Majedah oversaw the team and was the ranking officer. Despite their civilian clothing, her people were organized in military formality. Not a single member of her team was side talking or failing to pay attention.

At Majedah's request, John then introduced his team, and following Majedah's lead he used only first names. John indicated that a few others, including Scott and Luke, would be arriving later in the day.

Majedah then thanked John and addressed the group, which numbered about twenty people.

"Everyone in this room knows the importance of this mission, and the time sensitivity involved. And if that wasn't already a full burden, we will also be working with John's team members, who have made great personal sacrifices to be here with us. We've obviously not worked together before, and so I want to emphasize to everyone the need for efficiency and results. By the very nature of this mission, much of it will be worked out as we go along." Then she turned to John, smiled, and said, "Or as you might say in America, we'll be 'winging it,' but that might be too much of a double entendre for our first meeting."

John's team, not bound by rigid discipline rules, let out

a few chuckles and one groan, as was common. It human-ized the atmosphere in the room a bit.

Majedah continued, "John will now give an overview of the plan. Now is the time for everyone to step up with questions and comments. Two days or two hours from now is too late. We need 100 percent from everyone from this point until the successful completion of this mission. John, can you take it from here?"

John thanked Majedah and then presented his plan. Colonel Simon then asked her various team members to give briefings on the various details they had been working on.

The mission details were discussed and probed at length. John, Milo, Nick and Brian were there to assist, but they were in a support role, heavily reliant on Majedah and her Mossad and IDF personnel who were the core of the mission team.

Some details as to the basic gliding and steering mech-anisms were discussed. Because they had procured three gliders, John's plan was to use three balloon arrays, with one glider carried by each balloon array, and each glider holding two water tanks. This would provide six tanks of radioactive water to shower the two aircraft – in effect, six bullets to try to hit two targets.

After an hour into the overall presentation and discus-sion, John detected some skepticism on the part of a few of the staff when discussing operation details, and John was aware that Majedah was having to pull rank subtly over some junior operatives in the room. It was a tricky affair with at least four dynamics in play all at once: A woman was in charge; Mossad vs. military rivalry; the presence of foreigners – mercenaries at that; and more subtly, an institutional and emotional prejudice against improvised devices such as the balloon array.

John wasn't sure which of these conflicts was the main driver, but despite the subtle skepticism, Majedah kept her team focused. John wondered if the plan was really faulty, or whether the young operatives were just showing typical reluctance to be commanded by a woman or a foreigner. Or were they upset that they, and not some other group, had been assigned to this mission?

John got the sense that this team might be only one of several teams working to mitigate the captured-aircraft situation. That is, John's plan might be only one of several plans the Israelis were working on. John would never know. Perhaps Majedah herself did not know. But even if his plan had only a 20 percent chance of success, it would become "The Successful Plan" if it did work. John realized he had a little ego and pride invested in it.

Luke and Scott arrived later in the day, and John asked Luke to just follow him around, take excruciatingly good notes and be at his best. He introduced Luke to Rebecca and asked her to help Luke with any logistics assistance that he might need.

Majedah's team provided the engineers' modifications and logistics for building and assembling the materiel for the arrays. Their concern was to leave no Israeli finger-prints on the operation, which manifested itself in several ways, including the staged burglary of the parachute club. Another was the design of the water-tank drop. In his anti-pirate operation, John had simply made provisions for the fairing bolts holding the fuselage around the bomblets to be released into the ocean.

But now there was no deep ocean to hide the discarded parts, and the Mossad had to cover its tracks. Eventually, the materials would be found. The team had planned for each glider to continue its flight after dumping the water. The plan was to ditch them as far away from the target site as possible to avoid detection for days or weeks. The actual water payload bags were less of an issue. They looked like desert junk one might see blowing along any road.

The radio avionics were installed into the gliders, enabling them to be steered as needed to the supply depot target where the jets were stored. No one knew for sure whether the target depot had radar defenses.

The Mossad provided various other technical solutions, but they insisted on withholding many of the details from John and his team until a 'need to know' basis was achieved – that is, when launch was assured.

At the assembly and launch site in Nicosia, Cyprus, there was round-the-clock frenetic activity. It was battlefield triage, and if ever anyone needed to understand why chain of command mattered, this was a textbook example. Fifteen or forty-five minutes of technical and operational discussion would ensue, and then Majedah would announce the decision. No longer would any debate be on the table; the order had been given.

There were periodic group meetings, and their warehouse space had several offices and areas which were off limits to John and his team. So, too, did John and his team have their own office. John assumed it was bugged and advised his team of such. But at least there was the semblance of respect for his rogue team.

IN THE BREAKOFF ROOM

Late in the process, in a group meeting John was advised by one of Majedah's team that there would be a separate classified set of cargo on the third glider. Only four tanks of water, instead of six, would be available to John. The payload of the third glider remained "classified."

John was unhappy about losing the two water tanks, but there was nothing he could do. John looked up at Majedah as the information was announced. He did so right as she was looking at John, and her expression broke from one of concentrated professionalism, to a brief expression of unease as if she were becoming ill. "Robert," she said to her colleague, "let's take a short break, we'll reconvene here in 10 minutes" and she was already heading for the door as she finished her sentence.

John was fairly sure that no one else in the room had noticed Majedah's facial expression as she called a break. John knew that the entire team was experiencing exhaustion. Was that what he had just seen on Majedah's face, or was there something about this significant operational adjustment that disturbed her? His mission had just lost one-third of his payload. It was not a small matter. He was also miffed at not being consulted when this "audible" to his plan had been effected.

He waited a minute, and then casually strolled out of the room and to the conference room where Majedah had gone. He tapped on the door as he opened it and entered.

"Hi. I wanted to check and see if everything is okay," John said. Majedah's back was to the door, as if she were deep in thought. "Ms. Simon?" John asked. "Majedah?"

After a moment, Majedah turned and glanced at John. The distraught look on her face had not abated. She gave a small shake of her head as if to compose herself. Then she walked across the room to a keyboard in front of a screen and tapped a few keys. "I apologize," she said when she turned to face John. "The fatigue and the stress, it just… some old…circumstances came back into focus. I wasn't quite prepared for that. I'll be okay in a moment."

Silence hung for some time. John didn't want to pry, or trip up some gender spat by inferring that she was being emotional – that is, being a weak woman.

She might already have a dossier on John's real identity, but that wasn't the only reason he spoke up. "I failed to tell you something earlier," he said. "My name is John Gabriel." Silence again hung in the air for a few moments, and then he continued, "And both John Smith and John Gabriel are a bit rattled by this new secret payload and the fact that I'm losing a third of my ordnance," he said, trying to strike the balance between remaining professional and acknowledging her emotional distress.

Majedah composed herself and took a deep breath. She squared up to look at John and said, "I lost a family member. My brother. A long time ago. He was young, ready for college. He was killed when he accidently came across a couple of PLO fighters who were about to fly across the Lebanese-Israeli border in hang gliders. They murdered my brother and then killed a lot of soldiers. The attack became a national scandal, but his story was buried by the events, the bigger situation." After a pause, she continued, "He was just a kid, killed because he was in the wrong place at the wrong time. I had forgotten the details until just now… that his killers used hang gliders."

There was another pause, and John broke the silence. "The 'Night of the Gliders,'" he said, stating the name of a long-forgotten skirmish in a decades-long battle. He had run across that historical footnote when researching some details for this project.

"Yes," replied Majedah, appearing surprised that John knew the name of that event and still struggling to hold back tears. "It was the spark that started the Intifada. My brother was the first victim. A Lebanese civilian. And yet no monument bears his name." Her eyes were a bit misty, and she turned away for a moment.

John was somewhat at a loss to know what to say. He felt a twinge of guilt for having barged into the room, when Majedah clearly had just wanted a moment alone.

"I apologize, Ms. Simon. I shouldn't have asked." John felt like shit, and suddenly his adrenaline wasn't overcoming his exhaustion. "This is all – quite literally – so close to home for you. And your friends and family and colleagues."

Majedah turned and looked at John. "I'm just realizing, perhaps, that my brother is the reason that I joined the

IDF. It's so simple, now that I reflect on it. This mission and its use of gliders brings it full circle, in a way. I was a bit blindsided by that." She paused, and then continued, "The men who came and spoke with my family, they were so matter-of-fact, as if it was a routine investigation of a traffic accident. It's that business-as-usual thing, that's the devil. The devil that brought me here, and the devil I try to postpone dealing with," she continued. John sensed that it was out of character for Majedah to be revealing these thoughts and sentiments.

As John thought about what she'd said, a memory flashed through his mind. He'd been little more than a toddler when the military personnel had come to his house. The Navy officers had informed John's mother than her husband, Maximilian Gabriel, the "Chief of the Boat" or more formally the Senior Enlisted Advisor to the Commanding Officer of the *USS Crescent*, had been lost at sea and was presumed dead. At the time, John did not fully comprehend what the men were saying. He could recollect only that there were two, or maybe three of them, and that they wore uniforms. His mother began to cry. That was the key memory.

One of those men making the visit had been a young Mike Shepard. He had been an ensign – the most junior Navy officer - assigned to the *USS Crescent*, basically for training purposes. But Shepard had been waylaid for medical reasons shortly before the *Crescent* set sail on its last voyage.

The *USS Crescent* was lost with John's father among the 99 souls on board. Its disappearance followed the suspicious and unexplained losses of three other Cold War submarines and their crews in the prior weeks. The official inquiries into the losses of the four submarines were truncated. Whether the Cold War had temporarily turned into a hot war, fought by submarines hundreds of feet below the surface of the oceans, was never made public. Not even to the families of the hundreds of dead submariners.

John composed himself. He wasn't sure whether his flashback had transpired over two seconds or two minutes. He snapped back into a shared timeframe with Majedah. "This may sound out of turn, but this helps me," said John. "I just realized that a similar event in my past explains many of the reasons why I am standing here in this room. One of my own ghosts. I lost my father, perhaps in a similar manner. It was probably a tit-for-tat skirmish. The Soviets and the Americans. The Israelis got caught up in it, too. I was just a boy. Not even a boy," John's voice trailed off a bit.

"Then you know. I'm - I am sorry," said Majedah.

A few moments passed, and Majedah again drew a deep breath to compose herself. "I'm okay now. I'm okay. Your understanding helps. And I think knowing that you have a real name – John Gabriel – helps. Thank you for telling me that." After another pause, she said "Now, unfortunately, we have a current devil to deal with in the situation room right outside this door."

"Yes, we need to discuss the whole 'change of cargo' thing on the third glider. That's a bit of a curve ball, as we baseball-loving Americans say," said John.

"And now, you're going to witness my somewhat abrupt personality pivot as I restart our mission recording." She flashed an exhausted but genuine smile at John, and as she walked back over to the terminal, she asked John in a somewhat playful tone, "Now that I know your real name, Mr. John Gabriel, are you going to have to kill me?" They both chuckled softly at the worn-out movie cliche, but it relieved some tension. Then she entered a few keystrokes and said, "Let's pick back up on that briefing."

She proceeded to give John some crucial, need-to-know information about the change to the third glider and its secret payload. "I can only give you the most basic summary, but I want you to know. Actually, we need you to know. From your extensive operational experience in the Gulf of Aden with the balloon bombardment arrays, you may have some technical understanding or insights that we are missing," she said. It was a cold, technical but necessary inquiry. Exhausted and stressed, John struggled to process her request in a manner that he assumed was business as usual among military operatives.

The details were gruesome. Each of the gliders would be fitted with a few fragment grenades, using materials from Iranian anti-aircraft guns, or "flak." After the water tanks had been released from two of the gliders, those two gliders would be ditched, but right before the crash landing the flak explosive would detonate on each glider, which would make it appear that they had been shot down by local Iranian gunners. That was all well and good, as Majedah described it to John, and he thought it a clever cover.

It was the second part of the cover that offered a glimpse into the macabre world of black ops. Majedah explained that the third glider would carry three cadavers. Three cadavers of young anti-ISIS rebel fighters who had been extracted from Syrian morgues and airlifted into Cyprus. She was not able to give John all the details.

The three gliders would be made to look as if they had been shot down by Iranian guns, and the three cadavers among the debris would appear to be the glider pilots. Three gliders, three rebel soldiers and a set of fake plans detailing a behind-the-lines attack upon an ISIS target within Iran, would be found. It would look like a deadly sectarian attack by one Muslim group against a rival Muslim clan. And, it would likely take days or weeks before the rebel squad was ever located in the remote Iranian hills that were miles from the target, but if found the narrative would be compelling. And it would be almost impossible to trace the operation back to the US or Israel.

"I know this is a last-minute change, but can you and your team give us full assistance and support with any operational exigencies you might detect?" she asked.

"Yes… Ms. Simon, we will," John said, more for the benefit of the recording device than for Majedah.

He almost referred to Majedah as "Colonel Simon," in a sincere attempt to normalize the situation and make a gesture of respect for her position, professionalism and authority. But he'd quickly caught himself; he wasn't supposed to know that she held a military commission.

A small knowing smile appeared on her face. "Thank you, Mr. Smith," replied Majedah, putting a little accent on the "Mister" to acknowledge that she appreciated his catch in not saying "colonel" on the recording.

They went back to the room to continue their team

conference. As they walked, John glanced over at Majedah's assistant, Rebecca Biton, who was intently looking at Majedah. John could see the look of concern on Rebecca's face. It was obvious that the two worked closely together and that Rebecca knew her boss had been in distress, but didn't know why.

Together, the team continued their briefing. John noted that one technician was taking detailed notes and photographs. John's ego got a certain satisfaction imagining that future IDF and Mossad classrooms might feature this operation as a technical chapter in battlefield engineering. John softly said, "Just think what these folks would do with the CKS system… ." As soon as he thought of that, he realized that it was not a question of what they would do, but what similar things were they, and others, already doing?

John began to appreciate the various factors at play for the Israelis, and in particular that all the various agendas came together with Majedah. She was answerable to no one, yet everyone. The stress must be enormous. That kept John energized.

He glanced back at the room. He hadn't noticed it earlier, but it became obvious considering the stress the teams were under. He couldn't unsee it. John asked Majedah's colleague, Robert, how best to place a call to the United States. Should he use a special dial out code? He led John to a conference room and indicated it was a good quiet place.

John still assumed the room was bugged and that the call would be monitored. He had confidentially alerted his friend Mike Shepard a few days ago that he might be placing a call to him, uttering strange details and logistics.

Mike and John had often laughed about the "Cry Bastion" game from an old Clint Eastwood movie, and how it was really a version of playing "wingman." John had warned Mike that if John were to make such a Cry Bastion call, it was imperative that Mike should just play along with utmost seriousness.[21]

John dialed Mike's cellphone, and when he answered John jumped right in. "Mike, it's John here. I have only a limited time and I want you to relay this information into the Bastion network. The file is the Dropbox account in the folder "Cyprus," and the password is the Desire Street code. Again, the password to the Cyprus folder is the Desire Street code. Can you have Bastion extract that immediately and follow the instructions?"

Mike dutifully played along with the Cry Bastion ruse, not knowing whether John was trying to scare a kidnapper into dropping a gun or woo a beautiful woman. "Yes, John, copy that, I will have group Bastion effect an extraction of the Cyprus folder, using the Desire Street code as the password. May I clarify, what is the timeframe on this?" asked Mike.

"Immediately," said John.

"Copy that, John, immediately," said Mike.

"Thank you, Mike," concluded John as he hung up. He was counting on the room being bugged, because the call just ended was probably the cheapest group life insurance policy ever obtained.

BREAKOFF ROOM REDUX

A few hours later, John asked Majedah for a quick private meeting. There was a nagging 900-pound gorilla that needed to be discussed. They again moved to the adjacent conference room. As he prepared to talk, John casually picked up a copper coin from what looked like coffee change that was sitting on Majedah's makeshift desk.

"Ms. Simon, there is a matter which, for operational reasons and the security of our respective interests, we need to discuss under what we colloquially call the 'cone of silence.' All recording devices must be turned off. That's the necessary protocol."

Majedah already knew that John could be sincere, and thus his formality was intentional. He had just given her the requisite justification to openly disable any recording device in the room.

Majedah didn't hesitate for long. She said, "I will do that," and then walked over to a keyboard and, as she had done in their prior meeting, she entered a few keystrokes.

John now realized that she had turned off the recorder when they had spoken the day before. She had done so when she was about to discuss her deceased brother. She had cloaked her personal details from any prying. "Mr. Gabriel – I give you my personal assurance that we are under this 'cone of silence.'" She gave a small smile, and continued, "You can propose twelve things that you want to see done with a naked donkey, and I will be the only person on Earth who ever hears your secret."

John smiled. It wasn't said dismissively; it was her own reciprocal attempt to transcend cultural, chain-of-command and gender barriers, to give him her assurances.

"Ms. Simon, I am not a formal military man, nor are my team members. But my educated guess is that protocol might dictate that once this mission is completed, some might argue that it would be in the best interests of your country that me and my team be disposed of. Disappeared. Burned. We're expendable. We're mercenaries. We are dangerous loose ends that need to be cleaned up. You even joked about it earlier. I get that," John said.

"Now rest assured, your team is good, very good, but some things a guy just knows," continued John. "I know when a twenty-five year old kid working at the table in a room with me is demonstrably more agitated than he was just the day before, because he thinks that he might be the one who will be given the order to put a bullet in my head tomorrow. I also know when a couple of twenty-five year old kids have discussed the matter amongst themselves. Social psychologists call it the Common Knowledge effect.

"Rest assured – and I mean this - none of your squad said anything to me or did anything wrong or was in any way negligent. Again, trust me on that, they're good, they're professionals, they're keepers. Just chalk this up to the instincts of a ruthless pirate killer – who did many different things before he started killing pirates – which helped him develop a decent ability to sense a certain change in the ionization level in the air right before a rainstorm," John said.

Majedah froze for a moment; she did not move a muscle. Complete stillness—and silence. It was a non-verbal dialect filled with signal, not noise. These "tells" could be as revealing as any waterboarding, but only if you understood and focused upon the ritual and the conjugations of the language involved. "Non-verbal cues," as they'd say in a college course.

The message was loud and clear to John: "*Of course, this subject has been discussed.*"

John continued, "So, I want to advise you, Colonel Majedah Simon, that although my team is an amateur group, we understand this dilemma faced by you and your superiors. And as such, it is my duty to let you know – to let your country know – that a full file of my team's preparation for this operation, and the objectives shared with us by your government, has been placed with several third parties, and will be automatically released unless several Bastion-class DNR orders are issued by me before a certain date," John intoned.

John's 'Cry Bastion' phone-call ruse was the predicate to this discussion with Majedah. John hoped the call had been monitored, and if so, had been reported to Majedah. Either way, John's assertion - his bluff - now carried great weight.

He paused, took a breath, and then continued, dropping the stiff formality: "And, Majedah, I want you to know, with that recording machine turned off, that other than not getting shot in the back of the head, my highest priority is for this mission to succeed. And right below that, I have another priority, which is why I asked you to shut off that recorder. My priority - my wish - is that someday, somewhere, I am going to have dinner with you."

John then released a little pressure from the valve: "Even if it is only to reminisce about the unbelievable circumstances under which we launched some balloons to spew radioactive wastewater onto American jets that were stolen by the bad guys."

Not a word was spoken for the next ten seconds.

"Thanks for letting me get that out. You can turn the recorder back on," John said.

Majedah stood motionless. Her expression changed almost imperceptibly, millisecond by millisecond, as thoughts and emotions tumbled inside her. She looked at John, and they just stared at each other for a few seconds. Then she turned and walked to the keypad.

Just before engaging the keys to reactivate the surveillance recorder, she turned back and said, "Thank you, John. That's from me, Majedah." Then she just gazed at John for a moment with her green eyes. He realized that there was so much that could be inferred from those few moments. As did she.

A small smile again came to Majedah's face, and then dissipated. "I have to act like a Colonel now." She punched a few keys on the keyboard and came back to the table. As she did that, John put the copper coin in his pocket.

"I'm bound to note for my record that you have advised me of your team's precautions to ensure that details of this action would be made public if any harm were to come your way, and that certain protocols have been activated to that end. Presumably the same result will happen if your agreed-upon payment is not timely received." As she said that she raised her hand slightly, signaling John not to object to her embellishment. "Your team's expertise and cooperation have been appreciated and welcomed. No such harm would or will come to you or your team, and full payment has been authorized," said Majedah.

Now that Majedah had noted for the record that John's team had a failsafe in place, he knew that he and his team were safe. He appreciated that Majedah had shrewdly included the bit about John getting paid in full. The Mossad obviously did not want the world of mercenaries, upon whom they depended greatly, to conclude that the Mossad was a bad business partner.

They each drew a discreet deep breath and continued their discussion about the third glider. A few minutes later, Rebecca entered with some coffee. She fussed a bit with Majedah, displaying warmth and consideration for her boss, which contrasted sharply with the cold, severe professionalism of the Mossad and IDF team members in the conference room.

Before he could catch himself, John smiled at Rebecca, expressing his approval of her taking care of Majedah. She smiled back, but the stress she felt was apparent.

A SERIES OF COFFEE MEETINGS

John had set two early coffee meetings the next morning. The first was with a Cypriot sub-minister introduced to John by Tom Gallier on account of John's request. The Cypriot official had already caused the necessary paperwork to be delivered to John's team, so John wasn't seeking anything further in particular. The two met at a small café in Nicosia and made small talk about wine and Cyprus history. But in addition to a face-to-face expression of gratitude, John intended that his public meeting with a powerful government official would send an indelible message to anyone who might be tailing John – that he had at least one very powerful friend on the island. He was messaging that he was 'protected.'

When they parted, John took a quick walk around the Metochi Kykkou Gardens and then returned to the coffee shop for a second meeting, this one with Frank Cliquot's client. The man was a major patron of the Lady of Graces church in the town of Larnaca and he managed much of the import-export business out of the international airport there. A few days earlier, courtesy of Frank's intercession, John had routed a shipment into Cyprus through such company. The contents were listed as church organ parts. This meeting was also a face-to-face expression of gratitude. And again, the message was clear to anyone watching: John was under the protective wing of very powerful old guard communities of Cyprus.

Regardless of John's careful staging, in the end it was just that – staging. He had no real control over any sinister elements. Nor, and as he was about to learn, did he have control over what would transpire in the coming seconds.

It all happened in less than a minute. As John's second guest departed the coffee shop, John caught the glance of a man sitting across the room. The man quickly averted his eyes back to his phone. Within seconds, a woman with her back towards John sat down at the other man's table. She set down her coffee cup and placed a large purse on the table. Then she inserted her hand fully into the purse. From John's vantage point, it looked like her hand inside the purse was grasping a pistol and pointing it directly at the man. It was about as discreet as one could be when pointing a gun at someone in a public place. Her exact command to the man was not discernable above the background noise of the morning coffee shop.

The man being confronted remained frozen for a few seconds. Then he glanced at two men at another table, and with an almost imperceptible upward tick of his head he signaled them. He said nothing, rose up as he grabbed his bag and quickly walked to the door. The two other men did the same. In fifteen seconds, all three of them had exited the café. The woman, her back still toward John, took her hand out of the purse and raised her coffee cup to her lips as if nothing had happened. One would have to watch a security camera footage several times to try to understand what had just transpired. There had been no commotion that might otherwise have caused someone to snap a cell phone picture or video. John was struggling to comprehend the situation.

Moments after the three men had exited, the woman set down her mug and, purse in hand, rose and moved to the door. She was in no rush, and she even slowed at the bakery display. She turned and leaned forward slightly as if to get a better view of the baked goods, and her back was no longer towards John. She turned her head and glanced at John across the café. Their eyes met, and then without ado or any acknowledgement, Majedah Simon continued on and exited out the door.

A few seconds later, two other men sitting at another table - apparently Majedah's support team - put down their unfinished coffees and nonchalantly exited the café.

Over the ensuing few moments, John realized that his being alive had not been a pre-ordained certainty ten minutes ago.

A half hour later, John entered the command compound. The main room was filled with team members all busy with launch details. The operation was coming together. A launch might occur within two days.

Majedah was standing over a terminal, reviewing a screen with two of her technicians. She looked up and saw John and nodded her head towards the conference room where they had previously spoken.

John walked into the conference room and Majedah joined him a minute later. Without saying a word, she approached a computer terminal and again executed a few keystrokes. She took a breath, as if that might remove the exhaustion and stress from her face. "Off the record," she said.

"Yes," agreed John.

"I'm asking you to do the 'near impossible.' As if this entire operation isn't already full of impossibles. I'm asking you to ignore what you saw this morning. As if it did not happen. If ever I would ask for you to trust me, I'm asking now," said Majedah. To John, the request seemed to come from both Colonel Majedah Simon, as well as just Majedah.

There was a long pause as John's mind raced. But his over-riding understanding was that Majedah and her team had just protected John in some spook-laden situation he did not fully comprehend. To John, that singular assumption warranted trust.

The question just came to him, without much logical thought. "Are you safe?" he asked.

Another pause. Of all the things John could have asked her, she was not expecting that. She took another small breath, and replied, "Yes, absolutely."

"Is my team safe?" asked John.

"Yes," she replied. "Almost as certainly as is my team."

"Thank you," said John. "Any other questions are probably just …details and curiosity."

Another pause, and John asked, "Do we continue?"

"Yes," said Majedah. "Hell yes."

"Okay," said John. "It's ignored. And again, thank you, to both the Colonel and to Majedah."

"Colonel Simon is going to turn that machine back on," she said, as she walked over to the terminal and entered a few keystrokes. She looked back at John and a slight smile came to her face. She nodded towards the other command room as she left. John followed a minute later.

LIGHTING THE TARGETS

Later that day, all systems were cleared. The operation was a "go." Working backward from the desired attack time in the middle of the night, the launch was planned for the pre-dawn hours, when darkness would obscure the rising balloon arrays during their first half-hour of ascent. At 3 a.m., the three balloon arrays were launched from the hills in Cyprus.

Each array included about 40 weather balloons, about the size of a small commercial airliner. Below each balloon array dangled a glider, which looked like a modern drone but with huge narrow wings. Just a minute or two after launch, each balloon array had effectively disappeared into the black sky.

By the first light of dawn, the balloons had risen out of eyesight fifty miles downrange, heading northeast towards the southern Turkish coast. The team was tracking the arrays, which had risen hundreds of feet per minute and were now aloft at about 20 miles high – about three times the flying altitude of a commercial jet. In the meantime, new US satellite images became available, and the team was able to confirm that the depot where the jets and tanks were stored remained undisturbed some 750 miles east of Cyprus. Whether this mission was just a far-fetched fool's errand was still unknown. But there was certainly tension – if there was any chance the mission could succeed, each team member was focused on increasing the odds of that success.

The team expected the balloon arrays to be near the target about 20 hours after launch, and the teams took turns during the day getting much-needed naps. After the wait, it all came about rather quickly. Just after midnight, the full team re-assembled. The tracking reports from Majedah's analyst revealed that the balloon arrays had travelled in a relatively close cluster, about 10 miles away from each other. Critically, the balloons would each pass about 70-75 miles from the target. In golfer terms, it had been a good solid drive to the middle of the fairway, just a short wedge shot away from the green. Last minute triangulations and calculations were being done to determine the final release details.

Each glider was navigated from the mini-command center on Cyprus. It was the civilian version of a CIA pilot center in Las Vegas, flying and firing drones above the skies of Afghanistan. It was amazing what a decade of technological progress had wrought. Although no protocol required it, Majedah decided to ask John, in front of the assembled team, if he felt the operation was ready to commence. "Mr. Smith, my team believes things are in place. Are you in a position to recommend that the operation commence?" she inquired.

A few of Majedah's team glanced around the room. Colonel Simon was the commanding officer; why was she asking the American operative for his opinion, much less his approval?

"Ms. Simon, from my vantage point, the operation appears ready to activate. All systems appear to be a 'go,'" replied John. He gave Majedah a subtle nod as he finished, saying in effect, "Thank you for asking."

"Let's commence, then," ordered Majedah. "I approve the mission plan. Danny, please commence the operation and release the first glider per the schedule and sequentially release the additional gliders per the schedule." Her support officer, Danny, responded, "Commencing operation, releasing gliders in sequence per the schedule." Her team members began exchanging various commands and reports while watching several monitors.

"Glider one release confirmed," reported Danny a few minutes later. The second glider was launched five minutes later, and the third glider carrying the cadavers would follow about fifteen minutes later.

It was the middle of the night in northern Iran near the target zone. As each glider was released from the balloon array, it began its hour-long glide toward the target area east of the city of Tabri. Three IDF pilots had joined the group, brought in to fly the gliders via remote control on their final attack run. Right on schedule almost an hour after being released from the balloons, the gliders were just a few miles away from the target. The pilots began the final maneuvering of the first two bomber gliders to bring them to the slowest possible airborne speed, without stalling, about 700 feet above the target.

The first glider reached the target area and released its

1000-lb cargo consisting of two 50-gallon plastic drop bags, each about the size of a large garbage can.

Once dropped out of the makeshift bomb doors of the glider, each water tank bag had a long pull string attached to it, like a beginner parachutist who has a rip cord that automatically gets pulled as they leave the airplane. These pull cords ripped several seams of the water bags and caused a uniform disintegration of the bags, somewhat like a slow-motion film of a bullet hitting a water balloon. The bag walls disintegrated and the water began a downward explosion like a waterfall of tens of thousands of water droplets.

As the sheet of raindrops fell, they quickly disintegrated further into smaller raindrops and then drizzle. The result was 100 gallons of radioactive water had dispersed into a light rain over an area about half the size of a football field. It was a perfectly-executed precision drop.

A few minutes later, the second glider came into position and released its two bags. Its first bag worked flawlessly, and the second deployed a bit heavily so that some of its water did not aerosol as well, but the effect was almost the same, about 85 gallons being rained down upon the target.

Both captured F-16 jets, painted with Israeli Air Force insignia on their tail stabilizer wings, were blanketed with radioactive drizzle. Ten minutes later the drizzle had completely evaporated, leaving no clue that the fuselages of the planes were now glowing radioactive homing beacons. The metal skin of the jets had effectively absorbed the radioactivity of the rainwater.

After each glider released its water bombs, the pilots

flew the gliders as far as possible from the target area. There were no thermal updrafts in the middle of the night, so skillful piloting was needed. The pilots managed to ditch the gliders several miles away in the scrub of some foothills. The long ripcords on the water bags also acted as drag cords, moving the empty water bags a mile away from the target area before being released. They looked like harmless commonplace desert garbage.

The third glider followed a few minutes after the water bombing. It silently circled above at a higher 5000-feet altitude. In addition to its morbid cargo of cadavers, the glider carried a small reserve five-gallon water bag as a backup in case an F-16 had been completely missed. Also aboard were several hi-def cameras capable of detecting multiple spectra of light, including ultraviolet and infrared waves. The glider circled above the depot in the dark night sky taking detailed images and scans, transmitted them back to the mission control room. There, Majedah, John and the team sought to confirm that the radioactive water had hit its targets.

John felt a curious energy and expectation – it reminded him of those moments a decade ago, waiting to see if a pirate ship had been destroyed by a dart bombing. Or whether a CKS taser shot successfully disabled a fleeing vehicle. John realized that he was nonplussed by the gruesome cadaver cargo that was about to be dumped in the desert. He wondered briefly if his sensitivities had been forever warped by his pirate killings.

No expert x-ray technician was needed to interpret the images. The radioactive footprint of the water drop was obvious, with four roughly elliptical spill spots glowing brightly, overlapping each other like the concentric rings of the Olympics symbol. The stolen F-16 jets as well as the tanks and other armaments had been painted with the radioactive marker. To any number of electronic sensing devices they were now the equivalent of a car whose auto alarm had been activated. Loud as hell, and incapable of being concealed.

After the third glider had captured and transmitted its images, its pilot glided it to the ditching site where the other gliders had been crashed. The pilot circled the ditching site at low altitude and released the cargo of three cadavers through improvised trap doors on the underside of the glider. The pilot then scuttled the glider near the other two gliders. Just before it crashed to the ground, the pilot activated the explosive flak charges aboard all three gliders to simulate them having been shot down. The flak explosions were a muffled boom that was indistinguishable from a truck backfire on a distant roadway.

By 2:00 am, the mission was successfully completed. As Majedah watched the final flak explosions, she did an encore of her previous command theatrics. She raised her hand to bring her team to attention, and then asked, "Mr. Smith, I believe we have successfully completed the mission and achieved all of its objectives. Do you concur?"

There was excitement in the room, and Majedah's performance seemed to focus it. This time, the glances around the room did not connote any disapproval or questioning of Majedah's giving command co-credit to this "John Smith."

John recalled his earlier response and largely repeated it, knowing the recordings of this event would be studied by future IDF and Mossad operatives. "Ms. Simon, from my vantage point and extensive field experience in these types of operations, I confirm your conclusion that the operation appears to have achieved all of its objectives and is a complete success."

"Confirming, this mission is now completed. Thank you all, and let's break down this site per normal operational procedures," said Colonel Simon.

There was a mild uproar as congratulations and high fives were exchanged. Several of Majedah's team had already packed their gear prior to the final bombing run as if preparing to move on to their next assignment. For all John knew, Majedah's team might be staying together to go destroy those jets in the coming days. John thought it important to celebrate their mission success, even if briefly. He knew that these missions were completely dependent upon the human element, and a celebration was part of it. He recalled the Paris after-action party for his anti-piracy team and made a note to himself to plan another one for his Nicosia team.

Although this wasn't "his" mission or his room, John had arranged for three bottles of Israeli champagne to be delivered a few hours earlier. After Majedah declared the mission completed, John raised his arm and, in an elevated voice as he put the bottles of Yarden Blanc des Blanc bubbly on a table, he said, "Everyone, I know that different groups have traditions. On behalf of my group and myself, I'd like to share our after-action tradition with you. Perhaps the exigencies of your mission won't allow for a proper three-day celebration. But in the spirit of that celebration, which we must never forgo, my team and I offer you a toast," said John. With that, he quickly pulled the cork out of the first bottle.

Rebecca looked at Majedah and nodded her head enthusiastically, signaling to her boss that she should go over and accept the first glass.

Majedah went over to John, and he poured her the first glass of bubbly. She smiled and raised her glass. "L'Chaim," she said to John, somewhat quietly. And then she turned to her team and said, with a little more volume, "To life… and that's an order! Get over here!"

The IDF and Mossad team members broke into smiles, and a few clapped. Both teams came together, and the Israeli bubbly was poured.

It was an altogether fitting and proper gesture on all sides.

John congratulated Luke, Milo, Brian, Scott and Nick, and advised that they should be ready to bug out within the hour. As the team members slowly began to filter out of the room, Majedah said, "Mr. Smith, may I have a quick after-action briefing with you?" They entered the room a few steps away, and as they did, she closed the door.

"Mr. John Smith, on behalf of the State of Israel, I thank you deeply. I also thank you on behalf of the civilized people of the world, although no one has authorized me to offer that bit of thanks. Because of the nature of your help and you're not being a member of the sanctioned defense organizations of my country, my words may be the only expression of appreciation that you will ever receive. Thank you," she said again, with all sincerity.

"You are most welcome, and I thank you and your colleagues for allowing us to assist," John said in the same formal tone Majedah had used. "The best interests of our United States were also advanced by this operation." That little addition by John was a for-the-record CYA.

Majedah then walked over to the computer terminal and hit the same keys she had previously disengaged at several other times. The recorder had stopped recording. She took a deep breath. Then she took another.

"John, this, this is just me…Majedah, talking now. I… I don't quite know what to say, so I will just say, 'Thank you,' again, and tell you that I appreciate how you handled everything these past few days. There isn't any field guide that covers these types of missions. Or these…. things. And, also that… I do… I do look forward to being able to have that dinner with you. I just want to make sure that you know that I want to do that."

A lesser man might have leaned over and kissed her right then. And it would have ruined an extraordinary moment.

They just stood there and let it hang. For three seconds. Or maybe three hours.

Right before the silence became uncomfortable, John said, "I get to choose the wine," with a wry grin breaking on his exhausted, unshaven face.

"The first bottle, yes," Majedah replied, as a big smile melted over her similarly exhausted face.

Majedah then reached and out grabbed John around the shoulders and hugged him deeply. She held on to him for several seconds, with her head pressed against the side of his head.

When she released him, she turned and walked back over to the terminal, looked at John and said, "Sometimes, I hate this fucking thing and right now is one of those times," before hitting the key and re-engaging the recording system.

"This confirms that Majedah Simon and John – Smith – concur that the mission is completed," she said for the record. Then they left the room, smiling.

A few minutes later, John and his team departed as various members of Majedah's team were removing terminals, screens, files and the like.

Within an hour, the warehouse command center was empty except for a single Mossad agent tasked with eliminating any trace left behind.

A MAKESHIFT HANGAR IN SYRIA

A few days after John's mission had successfully painted the captured jets with the radioactive marker, the updated daily US satellite photos had been transmitted to various allies, including the IDF. The stolen jets had been relocated hundreds of miles closer to Israel in eastern Syria, and their radioactive beacons were visible on the new set of satellite images. After analyzing the photos and calculating logistics, the IDF dispatched two of its F-35 stealth jets armed with Hellfire homing missiles along with two F-15 fighter escorts. The F-35's guidance controls of their missiles had been recalibrated to home onto the plutonium beacon emanating from the captured F-16 jets.

Salah Yassin had organized rocket launches into Israel civilian areas for almost two decades, and he helped build tunnels to move fighters in and out of Israel. With funding from Seymour Gacy's 'Together Forward' front group and the Iranians, Yassin was now running an intifada organizing operation. Today, Yassin was visiting the Syrian hangar now housing the F-16 jets.

His latest plan had progressed flawlessly. His carefully choreographed false-flag attack on Mecca would unfold over the next few days. Yassin stood proudly in the warehouse where he was concealing the two captured F-16 jets that had just arrived by flatbed truck from northern Iran. Yassin knew that the next 36 hours were critical, and his top aides were present to run through the final plans before the pilots were tasked. The attack on Israel would then begin, and his greatest ever plan – to fly the stolen jets over Israel and then on to Mecca in a simulated attack by Israel upon the Kaaba shrine - would trigger the all-out Islamic-world war against Israel. Today's meeting was to gauge whether there was any vulnerability of the jets to electronic jamming or other countermeasures that the Israeli Defense Forces might employ.

Yassin's enthusiasm was barely containable as he scrambled up a ladder towards the cockpit of one of the F-16 jets, painted with stenciled patterns to mimic an Israeli Air Force jet. He barked a series of questions to one of the technicians who he had flown in from Germany to assist in final preparations.

Suddenly, in the middle of Yassin's rapid-fire questioning,

a thunderous jolt more powerful than an earthquake threw him forward. A deafening roar and flash accompanied it, and a millisecond later the sensation of a heat blast washed over him. Thrown down hard to the concrete floor, Yassin raised his head and surveyed what had happened on the other side of the warehouse. That was the last volitional muscle movement that Yassin would ever experience. He would not live for the several seconds necessary to process the fact that a Hellfire missile had just exploded in the far end of the warehouse.

Another explosion erupted just two meters away from Yassin, a direct hit dead-center on the fuselage of the F-16 above him. The 8-kilo explosive charge of the second Hellfire missile disintegrated the jet into almost 200 separate metal fragments, although the resulting firestorm made identification difficult. Half of Yassin's body was vaporized by the Hellfire's warhead, and the remaining half was shredded into walnut-sized pieces which were blasted 75 meters in each direction. Yassin's six closest aides– the entire leadership of his terror organization - were immediately killed by the two blasts, their bodies cut into thousands of pieces beyond identification. In all, almost two dozen jihadists in Yassin's makeshift hangar died an instant death. Another half dozen - many were technicians and other trained specialists - would die of their wounds within a few hours.

A few minutes after the Israeli F-35 jets had fired their Hellfire missiles and turned towards base, an Israeli Hermes reconnaissance drone overflew the remains of the targeted warehouse and recorded images of the burning remains of the destroyed F-16 jets and other captured armaments stored in the hangar. A second mop-up wave of aircraft would arrive in five minutes, targeting the other weapons stored in the cache. By mid-day, all of the captured tanks had been destroyed, and the remaining stolen weapons cache was largely eliminated.

Shortly after the strike, the Mossad leaked through various channels that the strike was a suicide sabotage which had been carried out by a dissident sect of Syrian-based Sunni Muslims, armed by Chinese interests who were trying to secure new oil deals. In support, various spoof militant websites began to leak videos and forged documents claiming to expose an elaborate ISIS-related scheme. This propaganda narrative was that the two jets were Russian-made Sukhoi SU-27's obtained by ISIS, and that they were about to be used by ISIS to attack the Kurdish and northern Iraq area as part of an ISIS offensive to take control of the oil fields. The story also claimed that such an attack was intended to interfere with the current oil sales being made by the Kurds and Iraqis to the Chinese.

It didn't matter whether or not the propaganda details were true, or even made complete sense. Mass communications were done on an emotional level, not a logical level, and targeted the ignorant masses. The leaks supported the narrative that there was a burgeoning Muslim civil war and that China was now picking sides. This triggered nerves and caused the story to gain traction like a fire in a dry warehouse.

The American State Department was furious, foremost because it had no knowledge of the operation. Further, it made the sitting American President Howard Jackson look like he had no control. Worse, it implied that China was meddling in what had been an American area of influence. China issued forceful denials. Through all of it, neither Israel nor America was a primary suspect in the attack. Instead, China and the jihadists were battling the war of words.

Ilene Meinhoff watched the news of the destruction of the captured American jets with apprehension. Her hubris made her question how there could be such an attack without her and her boss Seymour Gacy knowing of it in advance. It was completely outside of the apparatus of control that she and Gacy had put in place under the Transparency Act.

Ilene made several calls to apparatchik bureaucrats who Seymour Gacy had installed in various posts, directing them to communicate that the US government was extremely angry with this "violation of international law," that "there are likely violations of the US Transparency Act," and that this "showed why the Transparency Act was so important for world peace," etc, etc. She also called a few key senators and congressmen who had accepted millions from Seymour Gacy and demanded that they publicly call for a "Transparency Act investigation into this violation of international law" by "cronies of irresponsibility."

As John Gabriel prepared to depart Cyprus, he realized that Kirk Woodbury had introduced Majedah to him less than two weeks ago. He didn't know whether to be angry with Kirk or to bring him a case of old Bordeaux. He decided that the latter was the proper course of action. He quickly changed his flight plans to include a stop in Bermuda.

SAFETY CHECK OVER THE OCEAN

On his flight to Bermuda, John's thoughts pivoted to 'drone cops' generally. John had read a few reports about the Los Angeles Mayor's campaign to stop the 'criminal drones,' and his increasing the bounty on capturing whoever was behind the vigilante drone system. It gave John some pause. He called Nick de Stijl, who managed the CKS project. After some small talk, John quizzed Nick. "Nick, is there anything we've overlooked on the digital side? Some Achilles Heel whereby CKS can be traced?"

"I don't think so, John," said Nick. We're constantly reviewing it, and we've engineered to assume we were up against the NSA. We'll keep looking for any risks, but we're good."

"This bounty stuff got me thinking, Nick, about a couple of things. One, what if a CKS bidder hijacks a drone? Meaning, maybe a bidder pays 25 or 50 grand in order to take control of the drone, just to kidnap it and capture it, thinking it will be worth the bounty. Or worse, that CKS can actually be traced back?" asked John.

"Well, we've got the take-over override feature already in the drone software, so we can take back control if a pilot goes rogue. And the entire electrical circuitry self-destructs if contact is lost for more than 20 seconds. Like with a capture or a crash," replied Nick. "But let us rethink the scenarios and see if we've missed anything."

John continued, "One more thing, Nick. I was thinking about military aircraft and attack formations. The CKS drone operates alone. We've never considered using a wing man, or a tail gunner or rear guard. Do we need some kind of armed 'escort drone'? Like fighter jets escorting bombers? I don't like the complexity, but let's consider whether it may be needed," said John. "Particularly if we might be facing bounty hunter traps."

After a pause, Nick said, "You know, the tail gunner idea is interesting. I agree it's probably redundant, but what if we just mounted a short light barrel with a shotgun shell onto a drone? If some attacker approached too closely, one shot would disable it."

John thought for a second before responding. "The taser unit on the drone is supposed to be non-lethal. But I guess it could certainly kill a vulnerable person if we intentionally shot them. But I'm still hesitant to load an actual gun shell onto a drone. It seems likes it crosses some imaginary line." He paused, and then finished, "Regardless of whether it's appropriate over freeways in California, it's coming, whether we like it or not. So yeah, take a look into some kind of tail gun feature for the drone. We may need it sooner than we think."

"Will do, John," said Nick.

And with that, the blueprint was created for a fleet of armed drones.

DOHA - A SECOND MEETING WITH A BUYER

A few weeks after his initial meeting with Mr. Abdullah, Taras Shimko had been summoned to a second meeting. Once again, Taras was sitting in a hotel room in Doha, having gone through the same security routine he'd experienced at his first visit. Mr. Abdullah entered the room and sat with him.

"My client is inclined to accept the terms of your offer to sell the satellite weapons array. It will take some time to arrange untraceable funds. Assuming we can agree on the timing, my client proposes to pay you one-third in gold bullion, one-third in Chinese renminbi, and one-third by delivery of Dubai benchmark crude," said Abdullah.

"However, there is one other condition, in addition to the technical diligence and verification that the satellite is what you say it is. My client is not willing to suffer the ignominy of having the United States destroy this weapon with some 'Star Wars' device after purchasing it," continued Abdullah. "My client will require proof that the United States does not have an anti-satellite weapon in orbit."

Taras thought about that, and then said, "I understand the concern. I cannot prove a negative, of course. So long as we agree that such impossibility is not required, then yes, I can and will provide credible official backup that no such 'satellite killer' exists."

Abdullah paused for a moment. Shimko's answer had

been, frankly, perfect. A con man would have promised a unicorn at that moment. But this man, who promised a satellite nuclear weapon system, was reluctant to agree to "prove a negative," as Shimko had said. "With acceptable official backup, we have a deal," said Abdullah. He rose and in the Western business style which had become the accepted norm when conducting business in the Middle East, extended his right hand.

Shimko rose and shook his hand. "We have a deal," Shimko said.

Back in his modest hotel room an hour later, Taras made a call on his cellphone. "Yoko. It's Taras. I need you to get something for me. Fast, and the pay will be good."

A MODERN MATA HARI

Yoko Senstra was the closest thing to a Western industrial spy that Taras Shimko knew of. Whatever her real age, Yoko had the air of a late thirty-something exotic denizen of the executive suite. Her given name was Jenny Lipton, born to a Korean mother and an American father. She had taken the name "Yoko Senstra" when she left New Jersey after high school. She married a British diplomatic officer stationed in Moscow during the chaotic 1990s. She sought – and found – the fast life, and the sketchy characters who inhabited that world during the rise of the Russian oligarchs. Living that fast life led to a divorce.

Yoko stayed in Moscow, moving from boyfriend to boyfriend. As her youth and beauty faded, she gradually lost out to ever-younger contenders from various parts of the globe. Like any number of Washington DC lobbyists who were former bureaucrats or diplomats, Yoko had become a conduit "advisor" for people needing things or introductions in Russia, and vice versa. If you were somehow involved in throwing embassy parties or arranging international business, you sometimes needed a sub-official go-between, and Yoko was willing — for a price.

And though she might feign indignity when asked, she could also arrange for call girls and drugs. And other things.

Years earlier, Taras had become acquainted with Yoko at a function in Moscow attended by the top administrators of the vestiges of the Soviet space program. Yoko was there working the room. Taras was glad he'd cultivated an acquaintanceship with her and could turn to her now.

Taras explained to Yoko what he needed to obtain, and she envisioned the perfect source from whom she could obtain it. One of Yoko Senstra's specialties was identifying individuals with access and exploiting their weaknesses. Yoko had met Percy Lacksman at several Washington lobbyist events in the past few years and had identified him as a fruitful target. She had determined that she could appeal to his vanity and his misplaced sense of entitlement. He also seemed to appreciate cash, because a young mover and shaker like Percy needed to display the material trappings of success.

Yoko wagered that she could contact Percy for the information that Taras was seeking. Her pitch to Lacksman

would be simple: That a venture capital group was reviewing some space-related investments and trying to decide
in what jurisdiction the investment fund should be incorporated. To that end, one factor was predicting what laws
might be passed in the future, and by which countries.

Her cover story to Percy would be that one of the venture capitalists wanted to understand how a country could
enforce its laws, particularly with respect to the internet
server farms located offshore (i.e., "you and what army?"),
and one of the investor's follow up questions was, "Does the
US have a military vehicle in space, i.e., a satellite killer?"
This might affect the ability to regulate (or threaten to
shut down) the Internet traffic routed through satellites.
Yoko would tell Percy that the venture capitalist wanted
the answer to that question in order to satisfy the board
member who had asked it.

The next day, Yoko made her pitch to Percy. She offered
Percy $50,000 for a report that identified any US govern-
ment or US private contractors who could track and kill
an orbital satellite, or confirmation that no such capability
existed. After some haggling, including about how busy he
was, Percy Lacksman got her to raise the price to $100,000
– but to be paid after delivery of the memo. Because of his
position on the staff of a Senate aerospace committee, Percy
already knew that there was no "official" US program; thus,
he knew that his task was just to manipulate or intimidate
the bureaucratic levers to get some official-looking report
to confirm what he already knew.

This was easy work for such a brilliant guy like him,
Percy Lacksman thought. Easy money for a meaningless

report that says what everyone already knows. What fools, these rich venture capitalists. Percy readily agreed with Yoko to provide the report, and he began plotting how to get such a report drafted.

THE PROMOTION

The past few weeks had been a bit of a blur for Jill Serrano. Seemingly out of the blue, she had been tapped for a promotion. A new post had been created, almost overnight, within the Department of Homeland Security. She had accepted the promotion the day after it was offered to her. It was an interim appointment, meaning she started right away while the months-long formal process ground forward.

The new sign on her door read, "Director of Drone and Airspace Operations – DHS (Interim)." Jill was surprised that she had been tapped for the post. Over the years, she had never devoted any energy to playing the political promotion game at her agencies.

Unbeknownst to Jill, Ilene Meinhoff had secretly arranged her promotion using several of Seymour Gacy's cronies, right after she had had watched Jill at the Kitty Hawk panel at the Drone Convention. In addition to her engineering background and her experience in government, Jill, as a Hispanic-named female in a traditionally male-dominated field, "checked all the boxes" with respect to government hiring. This was a common *modus operandi* for Ilene Meinhoff and her boss Seymour Gacy – they identified operatives and patsies who were practically impossible to oppose, using such person to justify the creation of a new regulatory post. To oppose the new bureaucracy post was to oppose the sympathetic person who was being designated as its first head. Any critic would immediately be branded as sexist or racist.

Under the guise of border security and immigration/ICE use of drones, Ilene Meinhoff had spread the word that the justification for the appointment of Jill Serrano was that a Latina woman was needed in the post to show sensitivity to the 30 million immigrants of Hispanic descent residing in the United States. Because of her pre-drone era work in aviation, Jill was the obvious choice. She had never met Ilene Meinhoff or Seymour Gacy, nor did she know that they considered her a patsy.

Nor did Ilene Meinhoff know that Jill Serrano was a very poor choice to be anyone's patsy.

PERCY SEEKS A MEMO

In her first weeks at her new post, Jill Serrano conducted a series of briefings for agency staffers as well as for people in related posts to foster inter-agency cooperation. One such group meeting was attended by Senator Baxter's chief aide, Percy Lacksman. Percy was thrilled about Jill Serrano's promotion. He now had a direct target from whom he could seek his official looking report on the lack of any satellite killer in the American arsenal.

Under the guise of preparing his boss for the upcoming schedule of hearings on electronic warfare, drone capability, risks to the electric grid via electro-magnetic pulse/EMP attacks, etc., Percy reached out to Jill for some background help.

"I need a backgrounder memo. Basically, the Senator wants to know whether the US maintains any contracts for maintenance of these types of operations. He doesn't want to come off like a dumbass in the hearings if there are existing programs that he should know about. He'll look like a fool, and with next year's election coming up, that's not anything we will risk," said Percy.

Percy then asked if he could get the report within the next ten days because of a committee deadline and "before everyone else realizes what a fantastic group you have there and fills up your pipeline." He was quite the smooth operator.

"Of course," replied Jill. No sooner had she agreed than Percy forwarded her a formal committee document request, which was slightly different from what he had just said in their call, as it asked for information on the existence of "any research or reports regarding the governmental or contractor programs for anti-satellite weapons programs."

On the spot, Jill decided that she would avoid Percy in the future.

THE DOHA MEETING - III

Taras Shimko was again in the Doha hotel room with Mr. Abdullah.

"My client is ready to consummate this proposed transaction. They have made various arrangements to have their announcement of the acquisition coincide with upcoming cultural and religious celebrations. I would like to arrange the specifics of the closing of our purchase, including the receipt of the report verifying that the United States lacks any satellite disabling capability," intoned Mr. Abdullah.

The rogue Soviet Firebird satellite was the perfect tool for the avid jihadist Nadim Rachid. Unbeknownst to Taras Shimko, Abdullah was representing Rachid as the purchaser of Firebird.

After first learning of the Firebird opportunity, it had taken Rachid several months to line up a few discreet partners to help finance the purchase. It truly was the perfect weapon. It was flagged as a Soviet/Russian vehicle, so the United States could not attack it without risking the appearance of making a first-strike against Russia. Further, because its orbital path and radio telemetry frequency were known only by its owner, it was likely safe from black-ops countermeasures.

In response to Abdullah, Taras Shimko said, "The report has been prepared and is being updated to include the latest information. Now that your client has made arrangements for an untraceable payment, we can arrange the closing details, including delivery of the report, within two to four weeks," promised Shimko.

After his meeting with Abdullah, Taras called Yoko Senstra to ask for accelerated delivery of the report. Yoko then called her operative, Percy Lacksman, to lean on him.

"A week, maybe a couple of weeks at the outside," Percy promised Yoko. "The research is done. My people and I are working on the last little pieces, 'dotting the i's and crossing the t's,' as we say. Rest assured, the report will show that there is no killer satellite program." Percy hoped that he could deliver on his promise.

In a staff meeting with her researchers and analysts later that day, Jill assigned numerous backgrounder reports. Jill asked one of her researchers for a report addressing whether there were any contracts for anti-satellite weapons programs or similar weapons that might be governed by the ABM and other arms treaties, "including any contractors we have on the books that run any of these programs for us."

Jill told the staffer, "I'll forward you the subcommittee request. Just collect and survey what work has already been done, probably by a dozen different agencies, and summarize the status quo. I seriously doubt there are any such programs. Any that existed would be long-dead programs started decades ago under Reagan. You might start with the 1980s 'Star Wars' space laser program that was defunded when the Soviet Union fell apart. Probably lots of primary materials there."

DRONE WARRIORS IN THE MOJAVE DESERT

The sun was high in the sky of the desert of eastern California. John Gabriel, Mike Shepard, Nick de Stijl, Luke and Milo were standing under a pop-up tent next to a flat stretch of desert. A number of technicians were manning the open field. A large luxury motor home was parked close by.

A group of CKS players from around the globe – untraceable but supported by John Gabriel - was holding an invitation-only Red Team-Blue Team shootout competition being staged for twenty of the best CKS taser gunners. Half the participants were assigned to Red Team – the targets. The other half were assigned to Blue Team – the hunters. Like the CKS car chases, each pilot controlled his drone through the CKS link.

Red Team members flew a model-airplane-sized drone similar to the CKS car chase drones, but without any taser device. Each Blue Team member operated a similar small drone, but attached under its fuselage was a two-foot-long pipe about one-inch in diameter, very similar to a gun barrel. A single 12-gauge shotgun shell was arrayed at the back end of the pipe-barrel. In effect, each Blue Team member was piloting a drone with a loaded shotgun attached to its belly.

The objective of each Red Team flyer was to pilot his model-airplane-sized drone over a one mile course to the finish line, without being shot down by Blue Team. The objective of each Blue Team member was to shoot down a Red Team drone. Any Red Team member who piloted their drone past the finish line would advance to the subsequent round. Similarly, any Blue Team member who successfully shot down a Red Team drone would advance to the subsequent round. Any piloting technique of diving, ascending, turning, looping or aerobatics was allowed. These live-fire aerial drone dogfights were being conducted over the CKS platform.

John and his team tested and retested the CKS communications links. The all-clear sign was given and the Blue Team drones were released into flight, each controlled by its own pilot. A minute later, the starting gun sounded and the Red Team's drones were released, beginning their mad dash for the finish line a mile away. In addition to the high-def cameras aboard each drone, ten high-def videocams along the route would record the various dogfights.

The pilot of Red Team drone #3 dropped the drone's nose in order to increase speed. The finish line was only 75 yards ahead. Blue Team pilot #8 was above and behind the Red drone, and was diving fast in order to take a kill shot before the Red Team drone #3 made it to safety. Then, just seconds before the Blue Team drone moved into a perfect kill shot position, Red Drone #3 pulled a classic dog fight maneuver – the pilot suddenly pulled the drone's nose up towards the sky and turned left. Blue Drone #8 had already committed to its dive and could not pull up quickly enough, and Red Drone #3 rose above the Blue Drone's firing sightline. The airspeed of Red Drone #3 dropped precipitously towards stalling, but the immediate threat was abated. Just before stalling, Red Drone #3 dropped its nose straight towards the ground while banking hard left. The drone was momentarily without lift and began freefalling, until gravity restored airflow over its wings. Red Drone #3 continued its dive toward the finish line not far above treetop level. Blue Drone #8 performed its own gravity-defying loop-and-dive, and in seconds had the Red Drone back in firing range. But it was too late, as the Red Drone #3 skirted across the finish line with only seconds to spare before Blue Drone #8 would have shot it down. Blue Drone's CKS targeting screen now flashed "Ineligible Target" over Red Drone #3. That dogfight was over.

A few minutes later, all of the dogfights were completed. Five Red Team drones had successfully been piloted across the finish line. The other five had been shot down by Blue Team drones.

A half hour later, John, Mike, Nick, Luke and Milo were in the motor home next to the dogfight field, summarizing what they had just watched. Mid-day beers were in hand.

Mike Shepard had a perplexed look on his face. "John, it's a fucking drone air force. It's like watching a sci fi movie. Now I get why you called this whole thing CKS. 'Civilian Kamikaze Squad,' 'Civilian Kill Shot,' whatever."

John paused and then went into a mini-lecture. "I kept coming to the same conclusion: Attack drones are coming. Soon. Cheap, off-the-shelf technology with remote piloting by gamers. Outlawing them won't mean anything, it's like trying to outlaw drinking.

"Like it or not, the world is months, or at best a couple

of years, from someone releasing dozens or hundreds or thousands of armed drones, with crowd-sourced shooter pilots. Hell, you just watched 20 of them in a battle, literally piloted from all over the globe," John said.

He continued, "And we'll all say, 'we'll just have to make sure that the wrong person doesn't get the capacity to do this.' Well, good luck with that. There are 500 million assault rifles floating around the world. Are any of them in the hands of the wrong people?" said John.

"So … who are the wrong people? Who decides that?" asked Luke.

John was worked up now, and the guys were seeing him in rare form, almost like a rant with Mr. Freddy. "Perfect questions, Luke. Jihadist terrorists? Chinese hackers? Domestic police? The Stasi, KGB? Or our own FBI? The 17 year old incel geek in the basement down the street? I've gone round and round on this. I always seem to return to the idea that a reserve citizen army – like the Minutemen - a defensive force, always lying in wait but existing in plain sight. That's really my answer to both questions – 'Who are the wrong people?' and 'Who decides who the wrong people are?"

Mike weighed in, saying, "I get that drones are new-fangled and they're everywhere, and shortly there will be ten or a hundred times as many. But turning thousands of gamers into potential Minutemen? They're training to be drone warriors while playing CKS, but they don't even know they're training?"

"Yes," said John. "Do you know the Chinese have 80,000 state-sponsored hackers? How many weeks would it take to train them to become a corps of 80,000 pilots? Drone pilots, that is. One week? Three days?"

John continued, "As super cheap drones populate the skies, the skies will become lawless, chaotic. For at least some period of time. Good results may follow, or bad ones. A gilded age, or a medieval dark age? Tech heaven, or an Orwellian/Matrix dystopia? Decay or rebirth? Order arises from chaos? It's a razor's edge.

"Think of any advanced culture that was overrun by bad guys," John continued. "Do you think France was grateful to have a corps of trained Resistance fighters?"

"If this is the future, why isn't someone doing anything about it?" asked Luke.

John answered, "Another good question, Luke. First, who is 'we?' Maybe we are doing something about it," as John gestured to the dog fight field outside. "Maybe the 'we' is 'us'.

"More to the point, it's a lack of foresight. Let's game-play it out. If you took a dozen jihadi leaders, gave them funding, a team and a timeline, and put them on a game show to win the prize of "Villain Who Does the Most Damage to The United States," what would the winning bad guy do? Or think of the same show, combine five college kids, a couple bottles of vodka, two joints and a stenographer, and they'd quickly have half a dozen diabolical but totally feasible ideas," said John.

"I get your point. I wouldn't even try to use a nuke. I know I'd fail. I'd do something achievable," said Luke.

"Exactly," said John. "My point is, half of the winning ideas would involve drones and micro-weapons aimed at soft targets. And worse, the operations are completely doable. That's the danger. That's our blind spot.[22] But our big professional military industrial complex killed off the Minuteman ethic. That's why nothing is being done. So we're exposed and not doing the thinking that one would expect on a routine game show offering prizes to civilians. We have no defense to the drone attack you just watched, and it could happen next week," said John.

"That is, no defense other than having a ready reserve force that can shoot them down," said John. "OK, so maybe I stop with the lecture now, huh?"

Nick had been silently listening. "Fuck, wow," he said.

Milo spoke up. "John, please tell me that bad guys can't hack CKS and highjack those attack drones."

"Okay, you guys are scaring me now," said Mike.

"That's the nature of these things," said John.

A POWER CALL FROM DHS

As part of her new job at DHS, Jill had been making routine introductory calls to various players, including private industry. Since her promotion had come after the recent Drone Convention, she wanted to touch base personally with some of the people she had met there.

One of Jill's calls was to Wayne Palmer. After participating in the Kitty Hawk panel that his company sponsored, and then knocking back some fantastic wines with him at the Lead Head party, she wanted to tell him about her new post. She assumed that Wayne or his assistant Maggie Needham would fob her off to a functionary assigned the pesky task of dealing with regulators. But Wayne had given her his private number – why waste it? When she called Wayne, he greeted her warmly and they exchanged stories about the Drone Convention.

"Jill, I gotta tell ya. When you called out that bottle of Bordeaux because of the 'bret', you'd have thought a suckling calf had been slaughtered right then and there with a knife fashioned from its mother's leg bones," said Wayne. "But then that Tom Gallier fellow says you're right! Damn, I wish I had done that."

"Wayne, if you don't mind my asking, I did spend a little time in Texas when I was young. There was some salty language around, and God knows there were barbeques on a weekly basis. But I have never, ever heard the expression of a calf being cut with a knife fashioned from its mother's bones. Did you just make that up? I mean, has that phrase ever been uttered, except for the first time just a few seconds ago on this call?" asked Jill, with a playful intonation.

"Well, so much for my Texas act," said Wayne with a chuckle. "I guess I know what Tom felt like when you called out his mud wine."

"Well, I did work at a winery. But not at a rocket factory. Maybe we can agree that I'll give you my crib notes on wines, and you keep me up to speed on the rocket science?" Later in the call, Jill mentioned the research memo she had just received and asked Wayne, "Hey, does General Space do any black ops contracting for the government?" A naïve or impertinent question, perhaps, but Jill asked in good faith.

Comfortable with Jill, Wayne Palmer was quick on the uptake. "No way," he intoned. He explained that while the financial side of him would love a fat, pork-laden contract with the US government, it would be a deal with the devil. "We bid on contracts and we win our share. Lots of audits and paperwork. I've got no problem with that. But it's these new provisions of the Transparency Act that say that any conversations that we might have had, or might have, about any clandestine program make my whole company subject to some backroom Transparency Act Council. My company is already a target of every lobbyist and everyone else we've beaten on some big contract they thought they had bought by giving money to some politician. I'll put up with all of those fights, but it's just not worth the trouble, from a financial or an operational point, to make every conversation of every employee with every wanna-be spook or informant, somehow a problem to be controlled by whoever happens to have bribed that's year's Transparency Act bureaucrats.

"If I wanted those fights, I'd run for office," he quipped. "The Chinese successfully stole half of our missile technology back in the '90's through White House shenanigans. Think they aren't still trying? I guarantee they've bought and paid for half that so-called council."

Wayne was never shy about expressing his opinions, and told Jill that General Space was under a directive from Palmer to steer clear of any contracting with any spies or covert programs, or anything else that would bring the non-public operations of General Space under the purview of the Transparency Act. "In effect, that law is a hostile takeover, a proxy fight where the vote is stacked against me; I'd have to give away the company, but no one would pay for it," said Wayne.

Wayne had given her an earful, unvarnished. She was just beginning to learn the nuances of the issue, that the Transparency Act and the President's anti-cronyism Executive Orders had far-reaching, unintended consequences. Or as Wayne Palmer had hinted, consequences that were intended.

Jill then switched her tone with Wayne to that of a grad student who needed help with a topic. "So, do the Chinese worry about you? Could you take down a Chinese satellite?"

There was a pause. "Who is the 'you'?" Wayne asked back. "A private citizen or the government?"

Touché, thought Jill.

Then he answered his own question, continuing, "Well, the 'you' would be the United States, or its under-cover operatives, or an ad hoc coalition of nations, or I suppose a big NGO. Make no mistake, it would be a clear act of war if a political entity were involved. Or a terrorist act, like an embassy bombing or airplane hijacking, if it was done by an NGO."

Wayne continued, almost as if thinking out loud, "The US probably would not do it, because it is banned by treaty. But if the Chinese satellite in your hypothetical was itself violating a treaty, the enforcement mechanism might be unclear. But again, this is in 'act of war' territory. Honestly, right now, what 'we' do is keep our fingers crossed that

China or Iran or Russia or Pakistan doesn't put a noxious bird up there, or that if they try, it's an expensive and embarrassing debacle, as bad as the North Koreans' long range missile attempts. All the hypersonic cruise missile stuff is bad enough. Having them up in orbit, that's a nightmare.

"And by the way, your question links to my point about the Transparency Council. Of course, the bureaucrats want jurisdiction over my company. Then they could sell my secrets in bits and pieces to the Chinese," he said.

As an endnote, Wayne added, "Anyway, any weaponized Soviet birds from the 1960's burned out long ago. They couldn't afford to keep 'em up in orbit. That's the real 'peace dividend' from the end of the Cold War, for sure." Wayne never shied away from controversy.

"Well let's hope we never have to face the Chinese putting weapons in space," said Jill.

"We will have to face it. The question is whether we'll even know about it," intoned Wayne.

Jill and Wayne wrapped up their call, promising to spend some time together at next year's Drone Convention. Wayne promised her a throne on the panel dais, now that she was such a big shot.

"I'll settle for getting to sit next to a couple of princes, please," replied Jill. "And not the frog-type of prince." As Jill hung up, she realized that what Wayne had just told her was all relevant to her new job. What part of it was her responsibility? With whom did she share those responsibilities? What was this whole Transparency Act regime, anyway?

Jill was getting a fast education. She looked at the stack

of work in front of her, including the draft research memo requested by Percy Lacksman for the Senator's subcommittee. She wondered, what was Percy really after? Was Percy's boss, Senator Baxter, about to take up these issues as a policy initiative? Or politics? Jill pondered whether Percy Lacksman might have more substance than she gave him credit for. She had considered him to be just a preening creepy guy.

Jill reviewed the research report draft. One section cataloged the existing studies and reports over the decades addressing killer satellites, and to the point, America's lack of satellite-killing capabilities in the area because of various treaties. Referenced in the report were decades-old Soviet "Fractional Orbital Bombing System"[23] summaries about an early Soviet nuclear weapon in space, as well as more newfangled "Kinetic Bombing Systems" and whether those would technically be a violation of space weapons treaties. In a way, the memo basically presented an argument that supported what Wayne Palmer had told her —that there was nothing the US could legally do regarding countermeasures against a weaponized satellite. And almost as a matter of circular logic, the memo therefore concluded that the US had no capabilities or assets in place to do so.

After she finished reading the draft report, Jill asked herself, "Why would Percy Lacksman be asking for a report on something that would be illegal?" Her thought train continued. "Everyone I bother to ask will react like Wayne Palmer. I'll come off like a bimbo. It's an embarrassing waste of time. So, I'll give this jerk Percy the obvious answer to his question: 'It's illegal, so no one is legally doing it.'"

Jill then sent an email to her research assistant, outlining a few edits to the final memo, and asked that it be finalized for her signature.

A STARK REALIZATION

Weeks ago, John's Cyprus mission had caused him to bail out of the Drone Convention and his own Lead Head party. Near the end of the mission, he had gotten a text from Jill Serrano with the news item announcing her promotion, and Tom Gallier had arranged a congratulatory bottle to be sent to her with a card that read simply, "Congratulations from the Lead Head team at the Drone Convention." Three things dawned on John.

First, he realized that it was now Jill's job to regulate his CKS program, which had successfully eluded the best hackers in the world as well as the efforts of the Los Angeles mayor. Actually, it was now Jill's job, as well as the job of the FBI and every other law enforcement agency.

Second, he realized the importance of CKS and his other operations remaining undiscoverable.

Third, John realized that those were the rules he would continue to live under, as hard as they might be to follow. Milo Patton had reminded him of that, with a phrase from the pre-digital era: "Hiding in plain sight." But in the digital age, hiding in plain sight required something more. Algorithms were becoming too good at detecting things.

Hiding in plain sight now required that patterns must not be discernible to algorithms. In short, John's CKS needed to be indistinguishable from background noise – off of the algorithm. "Off the algo," John thought to himself.

John's thoughts turned back to Jill and their dinner at the Drone Convention just weeks ago. After so many years, a strong connection remained between them. But now, Jill was the Director of Drone and Airspace Operations. One of the chiefs of the algorithm. The Director in Charge of Regulating John Gabriel.

It needed a bit of managing to not become a zero-sum situation where Jill's professional gain was his loss, and vice versa. "Crap," John audibly said to himself. "This is delicate."

A SHERPA AT DHS

As part of her new job, Jill Serrano had her first official albeit routine meeting with Vernon Cutcher, the general counsel of the Department of Homeland Security. Cutcher struck Jill as a wise, steady hand as he explained some of the functions of her new position. She learned about her authority to put suspected terrorists on a terror blackball list, including banking freeze lists and no fly lists. She inquired further about precisely which functions and authorities had been delegated, officially or unofficially, to her post. Jill genuinely wanted some guidance on the written, and unwritten, rules and boundaries that she was subject to, and the DHS general counsel seemed the right person to ask.

Vernon Cutcher had not expected such a detailed inquiry from Jill, and almost reluctantly began to give her some context. He realized that when he had first learned of Jill's appointment, his reaction had been, "Who is she sleeping with? How did she get this job? Or is she just window dressing, because she checks all the boxes from a political perspective?" But as he sat and conversed with her now, Cutcher didn't get that vibe at all from Jill. He felt a twinge of embarrassment. He had stereotyped her.

"Actually, Ms. Serrano, you occupy a brand new and therefore a powerful office, and its boundaries are somewhat dynamic. Your duties, and the duties of those who follow you, will largely depend upon what you choose to do, the precedents you set, the pushback you get from others, and the systems that you put into place," Cutcher offered. "You could be a public punching bag or a patsy while allowing decisions to be made elsewhere. Or something in between."

Cutcher continued guiding Jill through the "ecosystem" that was now Jill's daily environment, including the neighboring agencies and their personalities. He also highlighted the fissures and gray areas. "It's a bit of the wild west. The politicians can draw the boundary lines, typically big straight lines that cut through vast swaths of prairie or mountains or desert, but in reality, those lines often overlap and bureaucrats fight over them. As I said, it's the wild west," Cutcher analogized.

Jill was taken aback and almost awe-struck by Cutcher's

curmudgeonly manner and cut-through perspective. He had not minced words with her. As they wrapped up the meeting, Jill couldn't help herself. "Could I ask one more thing of you, Mr. Cutcher?"

"Of course," he replied.

"Can you please call me Jill?" she asked.

Vernon Cutcher thought for a second, smiled, and realized that he really had just conducted a bona fide mentoring class.

"Yes, Jill, I would be honored to do that," he said.

Inspired by her meeting with Cutcher, in her new role Jill became a voracious reader of staff reports on all things respecting aerospace, aviation and drone regulation, including the crossover areas of satellite launches. It was a fascinating history, particularly given how NASA had decades ago rolled up a dispersed group of allied but competing factions into one agency. Perhaps a NASA II would soon become necessary, and perhaps Jill would have a hand in that.

A BUFFET LINE OF INSIDER INFORMATION

While she was doing her research and reading, Jill noted a few additional mentions of the old 1960's Soviet Fractional Orbital Bombardment Systems, or "FOBS" programs. Because of her engineering background, she found it interesting. That epoch seemed analogous to the present, with rapid technological developments which were weaponized (but never used) by one side in a technology arms race.

Because these old programs largely predated the internet and details were behind Cold War-era vault doors, Jill called upon an underused resource to which she, and others in government, had long ago been made privy: The Congressional Research Service. It was well funded by Congress, because it churned out non-partisan research papers on issues before Congress. An untold number of Congressional staff and members had spent untold thousands of hours in the waning moments before a hearing, cramming on CRS research reports. An old college professor of hers, Dr. Poseidon Jaffe, had been one of its outside contractors for years. As good as the research reports were, no Congressional funding had ever been provided to publish the reports on the internet. To most, it was as if the reports didn't exist because they hadn't been indexed into the algorithm. They were knowledge existing "off the algo."

Jill called Jaffe, caught up on the past few years, and then asked him if he had any old analysis papers on Soviet FOBS, kinetic bombardment, and the regulatory environment thereof. Jaffe replied that indeed, they called them the "Star Wars" files, referring generally to the Strategic Defense Initiative of the 1980s. Most of them were archived in PDF format, but Jaffe promised to upload them to a cloud account and to send Jill a link to the files.

In her new job, Jill Serrano was on the distribution list of daily and weekly internal report feeds and regular staff reports, many of which were classified or confidential, including long lists of events and timelines affecting the world of satellites, drones and aerospace, from the routine to the curious. One summary report included dozens of references to anomalies. It was nicknamed the "UFO" category by various staffers. It purported to omit "military operations in known theaters of war." Listed methodology was "unknown – air-to-surface vector, potential drone-linked missile system or targeted bombardment." Out of curiosity, Jill reviewed some of the links in the report, which cross referenced other unexplained events with various qualifiers, such as "unknown – potential drone-linked targeting vectors." Many of the files simply stated, "no information contained in associated files." Jill wondered if those were covert operations. Several files also noted they were "unexplained enigma." Jill wondered whether that was new jargon for UFO-type mysteries.

Jill also received a portion of a daily confidential inter-agency news summary. It was not highly classified like the President's Daily Briefing, but even its watered-down content was illuminating. Most of the items Jill saw were keyworded with the word "drone," "satellite" or similar items. As Vernon Cutcher had explained to her, the agency lines of authority were indeed murky. The report included references to continued State Department activity respecting a recent bombing of buildings in Syria, and a suspected radioactive spill which the anti-nuclear proliferation US daily satellite sweeps had picked up. The State Department was lamenting that radioactive materials had been tracked across various routes in the Middle East, with the consequent related explosions in Syria. They remain "unexplained enigma, currently unconnected to US operations" but in almost every notation, "possibly related to Transparency Act issues."

Jill reflected on what Wayne Palmer had said about the Transparency Act. She walked over to the window in her new office where some storage boxes sat on a table waiting to be unpacked. She thought about how Wayne had described the Transparency Law regulatory regime as being an unabashedly bad thing. She realized that Vernon Cutcher and Wayne Palmer had given her the same message. Palmer had done so in his over-the-top manner, and Cutcher in a more balanced, wise-man approach.

She glanced down at the cluttered table and saw some congratulatory cards and gifts that she'd forgotten about, including the bottle of wine that John Gabriel had sent. Jill realized that with her promotion, things had been a blur the past few weeks. Or was it already measured in months? She recalled her dinner with John, and that they had promised not to let months or years pass before doing it again. As she thought about it, that dinner with John had been great, but slightly weird. More correctly, she thought, the dinner and company had been awesome, but John's quick, unexplained disappearance had been weird. She couldn't help dwelling on that a bit. What a fantastic evening it had been. What was the protocol now for her to follow – officially as a DHS subagency director, or personally, as an old friend– with that bottle of wine in hand?

As she recalled admittedly foggy details of their dinner - after all, a lot of wine had been drunk - Jill remembered a few references John had made, something like: "One of those technology projects helped our people overseas. There weren't any government solutions available, and we helped make the impossible happen, quietly and privately, a little bit Leonardo da Vinci style."

Jill thought, What in the hell was John referring to? How come John Gabriel, Wayne Palmer and even Vernon Cutcher seem to be all over this stuff, and I feel like a clueless freshman?

AN OLD MEMORY REDUX

As Jill thought about those dinner details, she suddenly shuddered as that memory file booted in her brain. She'd felt grateful that John hadn't brought it up at dinner. Sometimes a gorilla is best left undisturbed in a room.

The memory wasn't repressed, it had just been ignored. Jill remembered that night, decades ago. John had forcefully insisted that he, rather than Jill, claimed to have hit her insane and dangerous uncle Jimmy with a kitchen pan. At the time with all the blood, both she and John had thought Uncle Jimmy was dead, and John had quickly reasoned that because John was a juvenile, he could not be charged with murder. Jill had gone along because she was in shock.

Jill wondered if their lives might have been different, had her uncle not attacked them that night? They certainly would have made out on a couch together. Maybe she would have lost her virginity to John. Who knows? But it had all just unraveled because of her no-good uncle. Then she wondered, would her life have been different if news had broken that an eighteen-year-old girl had killed an older man in a bloody kitchen battle?

Almost immediately, Jill realized that she trusted John Gabriel in a primal way. And she still trusted him because he could keep his shit together and capably handle a bad situation. In the heat of the moment, not even eighteen years old, he'd made an excellent judgment call in a split second and had taken appropriate action. 'One cool customer,' as a submarine captain had quipped in a film. Not bad for a seventeen-year old kid, with a contusion and blood pouring from his head, close to clinical shock and standing in a pool of blood. The kind of trauma to which young soldiers of prior generations were routinely exposed.

Jill's recollection of their long-ago past over-rode any protocol. Jill then decided that the right "protocol" with John Gabriel would be whatever protocol she decided upon. She would invite him, her high school boyfriend – okay, almost a boyfriend - for a personal dinner to drink the fantastic wine he had sent over.

But Jill smartly realized things were a lot different now that she had been promoted. She wasn't sure exactly why yet, but her intuition was pretty strong – if John was actively in the drone business or intelligence community or had an investment portfolio of drone and satellite start-ups, it might not be copasetic to be seen out for dinner with John. Perhaps it was too close to the cronyism slippery slope. But because she realized she fundamentally trusted John so thoroughly, it felt perfectly fine.

Jill still had to finish reading through the formal

records retention rules for her emails and calls, so to avoid any missteps, at lunch time she bought herself a disposable cellphone - her first – and downloaded a popular encrypted call app. She used it to call John. She thanked him for the wine and she invited him to dinner.

"We didn't finish our catching up, and you left the Predators Ball early," she said. "Did you stand me up, John Gabriel?" she teased.

"I did read that someone stayed around long enough at the Lead Head party to be named queen of the ball, promotion and all," John replied.

"I'll tell you all about it," Jill promised. John was going to be in Washington in a few days, and they made their dinner plans.

A SECOND DINNER

When Jill arrived at the restaurant, John Gabriel was already there. It was a new restaurant in the gentrifying 14th Street area of the District. One of Jill's co-workers had recommended it as "the exact opposite of one of those stuffy power-broker places." Jill was carrying the gift bottle from John. It was the same vintage that Jill had worked on at the Sonoma winery.

Jill looked great. She had always been a naturally attractive woman but then again she typically was around engineers, bureaucrats and soccer moms, and dressed down to the part. Tonight, she had gussied up a bit, with a summer dress, a few pieces of classy yet discreet jewelry and a tiny bit of makeup so sparingly applied that half of a jury would say she was wearing none at all.

Jill broke into a big smile when she saw John. "Hi, John," she said simply, as she approached him, and he rose from his chair in the waiting area.

"Jill," he replied, and he gave her a little international kiss on the check. As he did, she then kissed his other cheek. "I do the double cheek thing," she said, in a singsong, "I'm happy and in a good mood" sort of way. They were both happy to see each other.

The maître d' asked them to follow him to their table and asked, "Shall I have the sommelier take care of those for you?" He was referring to both the gift bottle Jill was carrying and the bottle of aged champagne that John had brought. "Yes, thank you," said John, and both bottles were handed to the maître d'.

"Sorry I'm a bit late. I had some parenting duties to attend to," Jill said, referring to some coaching she had to do with her son, Jamie. "With the new job, the routine has changed a bit – a lot more work, frankly, and I forgot how easily the world of a 14-year-old can get upended," she said. "A zit on the chin is a problem, but being ignored by a girl for a few hours on social media is a tragedy. So, a little quality time was needed."

"Sounds like you're handling it perfectly," said John.

A little smile came to Jill's face, which then melted into an even bigger smile. John always did know the right thing to say, she thought.

They settled in at the table and the sommelier poured

two glasses from the half bottle of 1999 Salon champagne that John had brought. Jill was the one who raised her glass to propose a toast. "To my friend, John, and…" She had not prepared a toast and she couldn't quickly think of any words. But she had a graceful, serene and happy look on her face, even though she was stuck in mid-toast.

"I think that's worth toasting to," said John, and he moved his glass to hers, clinked, and they sipped.

"Now, sometime after you tell me about this fantastic champagne, we get to discuss why you are not easily categorized when I try to toast you!" intoned Jill, perfectly setting the table for the conversation that she wanted to have, even if she was jumping the gun a bit.

"That's what the Bordeaux is for," John replied.

They were brought course after small course. Jill spent a lot of time giving the details of her promotion, how it had happened right after the Drone Convention. She gave some details about the rest of the Drone Convention and the Lead Head wine tasting.

"I have a revelation for you," said John. "I've decided that after all these decades, I'm going to share the truth with you. Or just 'take the Fifth,' as they say. That Lead Head, it's my event. Tom Gallier is my front man. I really, really did not skip out on it lightly. So there, the truth."

Jill nodded her head, and raised her champagne glass again. "To my truthful friend, John. Damned few left."

Soon the champagne from the small bottle was gone, and the sommelier returned and opened the gift bottle, a Lafite Rothschild Bordeaux.

As promised, there was a conversation that had been

saved for the Bordeaux. John offered the toast. "To my friend, Jill. The decades make for even richer stories to tell," said John.

"Jesus, John, did you just call me old?" asked Jill.

"That was a mouthful, and I can't believe I got it out without flubbing it," he said and then laughed. Their laughter opened the door to discuss their impressions of what had happened so long ago.

John started it simply: "So with all these new things coming at you, it seems like the perfect time to reminisce a few decades back. What in the hell happened that night, that summer? And afterward?" John asked.

And so, they shared how in retrospect they had both just "moved on" from their memories. Each of them described a few nightmares in the weeks after the attack, but they had faded into a flurry of new friends and activities in college, and Jill's family moving to a new town while she was a freshman in college. They both shared some thoughts about the long-term effects of that night – good and bad.

"I remember feeling that my dad would be ashamed of me for failing to stop your uncle on my first shot," said John. "Like he was watching from heaven and saw me failing and leaving a girl defenseless. And I felt that way even though my dad had passed away when I was a kid. A whole graduate school of psychology students could occupy themselves with that one."

"Honestly, it's hard to remember. But you did tackle him first, and then I smacked him with a pan after you took him down," replied Jill. "Without your tackle, I wouldn't have been able to use the skillet."

"Yeah, but I thought, I was the guy, and I was supposed to protect you. And I failed because if you hadn't hit him, who knows what would have happened," said John.

"You know what?" continued Jill, "With years of hindsight, I felt a lot of guilt, too. That seems odd now, but it was very real then."

"Why did you feel guilty?" asked John.

"I felt guilty about my uncle. He was a no-good shit, but somehow, I felt that I was responsible for his condition. And I know my mother felt guilty that she'd kept her problem brother around, and that he'd attacked us," said Jill. "And then just a bunch of other guilt, maybe the whole Catholic guilt thing. That maybe I was a bad person, because this had happened to me. You know, all of those irrational things that are nonetheless real things," Jill said.

"Isn't it odd that we both felt guilty?" observed John.

"Guilt is powerful," said Jill. "I guess that's why it gets used as a weapon so often."

"That's a pretty good take-away," said John. "That's a good lead-in. Honest John, here. I told you a bit of a half-truth at our last dinner. I was married for a short time, but I'm not divorced. I'm a widower. My wife had died a few weeks or months before I got your wedding announcement, and … well, I guess I just wasn't in the mood to discuss that, or something. In any event, can we consider the record 'corrected' for now?"

"I'm sorry to learn that, John. I had no idea. And thank you for telling me that. It sheds a little light on this mysterious guy from my teenaged past, known as John Gabriel."

"At least my name stayed the same," quipped John.

"Touche, fair point! Perhaps my having a different surname than in high school pins me down to a certain consistency in telling my matrimonial history," said Jill.

As they wound down their talk about the tragedy and its aftermath, Jill noted that John's phone had not been pestering him tonight as it had at the Predators Ball. "And hey, what's the real story of why you cut out of town and missed your Lead Head party?" Jill asked, in a direct, slightly buzzed manner. "I was worried that you were sick. And now I realize it was like missing your own birthday party. Was it really for some deep-sea wreck dive? That was the scuttlebutt someone mentioned," said Jill.

John paused. He didn't want to lie to Jill but given the circumstances he couldn't tell her everything.

"I started doing those dives in college. Probably because I'd thought about it ever since my dad died in a submarine accident. As a kid I used to read books about divers who recovered sunken treasures, and I'm guessing my interest in that kind of adventure stayed with me. So, I have done a couple of interesting wreck recoveries, but that's not why I left the Drone Convention early," John admitted. "My knee-jerk reaction is to 'take the Fifth' on this, since I'm not a minor anymore. I'm not sure I can still beat the rap for a felony assault with a deadly frying pan," said John with a wry smile.

"Well my frying pan attack skills are a little rusty, so I might not be able to rescue you…again," said Jill, also with a wry smile.

"OK, truce," said John, as they both chuckled. "Actually, a client thing came up, but they were a new client.

It was an emergency, and they were in a jam, a really bad jam. I did get an unexpected quick education as to how this whole Transparency Act regulations thing has really, really made a hot mess out of a lot of things."

"How so?" asked Jill.

"The – client – was so paranoid that they would only speak on an encrypted line," John said.

Jill then described her call with Wayne Palmer, and his insistence along the same lines that the Transparency Act and regulations were such a problem that he was now obsessed with avoiding interaction with government agencies. "He gave me his private number. We had a good chat a few days ago. A good schooling for me, I should say," Jill said.

Jill recounted that Wayne claimed that because of the Transparency Act, his company avoided involvement in any covert operations or black ops, and more importantly, what she called "white ops." Jill offered up several examples she'd seen in her new post of the problems the Transparency Act was causing. "The number of unintended consequences and even incompetence is kind of alarming," she confided to John.

Jill had not yet discerned that the consequences were intended, unfolding according to the designs of Seymour Gacy.

A STRIP TEASE AT DINNER

And then it began in earnest. The new bottle had been opened and they had come to realize that they trusted each other. John and Jill began an unrehearsed sort of strip tease they never got to play as teenagers.

Jill told John about one of her reports, the one she'd done at Percy Lacksman's request. "I can't reveal the classified stuff, it's like the saying from the movie, 'I can't talk about Fight Club,'" she said, "But most of it is not classified, it's just putting two and two together, most of it is all out there in the public record." She lamented how the government seemed to be clueless about a lot of things that were going on, even when they were sitting out in plain sight.

And then Jill tripped upon the proverbial gold nugget in the ground. "When we were digging around for that report, I ended up with a list of unexplained enigmas from around the world. The staff calls them the UFO Files. Shit, John, one of them was like reading about undetectable alien astronauts dropping magical disappearing space bombs on Somali pirate ships. I'm not sure if anyone is keeping track of things. There's no ghost in our machine, I think. Just some archival tags feeding into an algorithm that might happen to link things together, if you are lucky. Hit and miss. Am I supposed to become the expert?" Jill said, as she sipped more wine.

As she lowered her glass, John engaged in a little drama.

He looked at her, and said plainly, "Well, I've attended a Fight Club thing or two, and I know a little something about those Somali space alien bombs."

"You know? What do you mean, you know?" asked Jill, surprised. She jokingly gave a furtive glance around the room, and then leaned forward. "Do we need a cone of silence, John?" She chuckled a bit. "Sorry, I had to do that," she said, still amused with herself.

"There are a whole lot of customers for a lot of this new technology. And to know who is doing what, and who is buying what. So, knowing those things can be really valuable, more valuable than the technology itself. And just as important, keeping things absolutely confidential is just as valuable. Actually, more valuable than the technology, sometimes," said John. He caught himself, leaned back and said, "Okay, that sounded way too ominous and dark and bongy. But anyway, it's been a bit of a surprise to me."

"I think you avoided my question with the 'bongy' reference, said Jill, with a smile that defied description. "John, John, John…. You are an international man of mystery I'm beginning to realize."

As they talked further, John gave her a few more pieces of information, sometimes keeping it vague as to whether he had first-hand experience in the field with those pirate ships, or whether he was more indirectly involved through acquaintances.

Jill added in her own take on how fast things were happening, almost spinning out of control in some sense: "I've had to deal with TV stations using electronic jamming to block the signals of their competitors' drone and helicopter cameras, for chrissakes, so they can have exclusive crime scene footage for the news lead. Online retailers fighting to airlift you a box of aspirin for your hangover. And what thirteen-year-old kid will resist slingshotting those little drones right out of the sky?" Jill said as she catalogued a few headlines of the past month. "Is that little league terrorism? You'd be surprised what some people think inside my agency. They're little dictators.

"And they've already got the Los Angeles mayor and police up in arms, because someone is actually solving the problem of this parade of morons doing the weekly car chase theater. We've had that taser-zap technology available for a decade and a half; and now it's a crisis because the local governments just sat on it, and now they're pissed because some private company is minting money using it. What, like letting idiot criminals drive 100 miles per hour in getaway cars is a better solution?

"Jesus, where will all this be in two years? Anyway, I guess I am on the hot seat now, being a bureaucrat that politicians can yell at when something happens," complained Jill. "Oops," she added, "that sounded like a rant, didn't it? I think I'm supposed to have a disclaimer, that 'things that come out of my mouth do not necessarily represent the viewpoint of my employer.'"

John then mentioned, "I know one of those car taser guys. There are all kinds of stories supposedly explaining the various acronyms, 'backronyms.' Fanciful stories that sound plausible. Like folklore of old. They are too good not to be true. They've built a huge worldwide digital community."

John continued to refer to it as being a project "of a guy

he knows," rather than his own project. "The taser guys see their program as training resistance fighters, most of whom are gamer types. Like the resistance cells that formed before D-Day in World War II. Everyone knew the Allied invasion was coming. It was only a question of when and where.

"And the taser guys don't think they are 15 years ahead of technology, the way that video gamers of the 80s and 90s were a decade or two ahead of drone technology. The taser guys think that they are more like only 15 weeks, or maybe 15 months ahead, not 15 years. They refer to '9/10 thinking' a lot. Anyway, that's what the taser guys are thinking," said John.

Jill let that sink in. Her face showed the enthusiasm of an underclassman enjoying their first "grad student" level jam session, just realizing the breadth of fascinating issues within their chosen major. Then she leaned forward a bit, as if she wanted to lower the chance that someone at the next table would hear her, and said, "I'm not sure if your taser friends are scary or fascinating. Maybe it's like Batman, Robin and the butler guy," she said. "Or maybe it's a bunch of cat women," said Jill, intentionally injecting a bit of excited inflection into it. "Maybe you are like Commissioner Gordon, who could arrange for these taser guys – or cat ladies - to give me a tour of the bat cave someday," she teased.

John tried to avoid a wry smile, but the wine forced it to make an appearance. "I'm not sure how the bat people would feel about the drone cops stopping by for a tour of the outlaw drone cave."

Jill leaned back in, for effect. "I get the sense that you

can be very persuasive with your friends. Space alien pirate bombers. Freeway drone pilots. Batman entourage. Deep sea wreck divers. Smoke-filled power broker rooms with no smoke. You are a one-stop shop, John Gabriel."

"Let me ask you what my friend would ask you," John said. "Those car zapping drones, or the space alien pirate killers – are they bad? Or are they bad only if there are too many of them?"

"That might be above my pay grade," quipped Jill. After a moment, she corrected herself. "Oh shit, maybe it's not anymore. Are you leading the witness here, John? I've gotta watch out for you."

John continued, "Did the East German Stasi start out as a group of well-meaning purists and patriots, who let things get out of control? Were they bad men from the get-go, or did they turn evil over time? And for the average guy, did it matter? Was life under the Stasi or the KGB somehow any better because some of the overlords started out a decade earlier with good intentions?" John asked, somewhat rhetorically.

They both nursed their glasses, following John's professorial rat-a-tat-tat of questions.

"With this new job, I've somehow gotten front row tickets to a whole show, but I just arrived five minutes ago. For all I know, maybe I am expected to perform on the stage. Is this all just random?" pondered Jill.

They both paused.

"I'm looking for some help getting read into it all. And maybe, just maybe, you might need a little assistance now and then, say, when there's a drug addict wielding a knife in a kitchen?" she chided.

"Touché, Catwoman… touché." John said.

John continued, "And maybe it's not random. Maybe there are a few ghosts in the machine, and the ghosts put you there. You're being groomed."

In the bustle of the past month, Jill had never thought of that. She trusted John's insights into things. "Groomed? So, what use would I be to the ghosts? I don't plan on being corrupt. Or maybe I am just a pawn, put in place to take a fall or get steamrolled when needed?" Jill observed.

"Or you are the good wedge for the bad guy who follows you?" John asked.

"You know, a wise soul just explained that process to me a few days ago," she said, referring to her talk with Vernon Cutcher.

"I think we just reverted to college dorm bong talk," said Jill. "I don't do that enough anymore. I got a lot of it when I worked at that start-up winery."

"Do you think that talking about college bong issues could be a problem for you now, given your job and all the layers of security and threat-screening?" asked John.

"Probably," said Jill. "No, actually, make that definitely." She laughed a bit. Jill told John about her first purchase of a disposable 'burner' cellphone with one of the encrypted call apps installed, allowing for encrypted non-traceable calls. "Get yourself one and install the app before they are illegal under the Transparency Act." She chuckled, even as she realized that it wasn't that funny or outlandish as a prediction. Jill was starting to get it.

"I'll do that. You'll be my first test call, I promise," John said. He knew all about burner phones and encrypted call apps. He already used them but didn't want to interrupt the moment.

"We sound like spies," said Jill.

"No, we just sound like people who know what the Stasi was," said John.

Their heavy philosophical and political talk dissolved to overviews of their respective engagements and eventual divorce and widowership, some stories of Jill's kid, and then to lighter banter about a few characters from the final weeks of high school, the "where are they now?" chit chat.

As the evening ended, John and Jill stood outside the restaurant. Jill confided to John, "I have really appreciated our dinners. I don't mean that in the past tense – I mean I really appreciate them. Present tense. And hopefully future tense. I'm not so good with words sometimes."

Jill continued, "You know, when we were young, I associated you with danger and stress. It was just the circumstances. And now, I associate you with the opposite. There's a calm and strong resilience, a sort of peace within you. It rubs off on me. I just – just want you to know that I really appreciate this."

John was quiet for a moment. It was an extraordinarily kind thing for Jill to say to him. They were all grown up now. Or at least Jill was. He felt a small smile of contentment about to come to his face, which coincided with Jill thrusting herself into a long warm hug with him. She then moved her head over and just held her cheek to his, as if she was recharging a battery.

It was better than kissing. It was anything but ordinary. It was not the stuff that needed to be verbalized; in fact, words would only detract from what it was. It was fair to say that John and Jill were making it up as they went along. It was perhaps weird and ambiguous to an outsider, but in other ways there was crystal clarity. After a traumatic history that dated back decades, neither of them would particularly care what labels might be applied by other people.

Jill pulled back a bit, and there was a hint of a tear in her eye. "Can we just agree that this will happen more often than every couple of decades?" she said.

"A lot more often," replied John.

"Okay," said Jill. "Is it illegal yet to check a teenager's homework while slightly inebriated?" Jill asked, in a slightly lighter tone.

"Big day coming up?" John asked.

"Every day is a big day," she replied. "I'm an expert on that. I'm a Catwoman."

They both knew that these dinners stood a good chance of becoming regular events.

PREPARING A SATELLITE SALE

Taras Shimko was anxious to close his satellite sale. He had spent the past two days running through the Firebird controller dashboard with two of Abdullah's engineers. They were learning the ins and outs of the satellite and its control program and continuing to conduct diligence to ascertain if there were any problems with Firebird.

Taras and Mr. Abdullah – on behalf of his secret client, the terrorist Nadim Rachid - wanted to close the sale as soon as the technicians were ready. Taras still needed to provide the proof to the buyer that there was no satellite killer lurking in orbit that would deny them the fruits of their nuclear weapon. Taras Shimko called Yoko Senstra to try to get a hard delivery date on the report so that the closing could proceed.

Yoko in turn called Percy Lacksman and pressured him for a firm delivery date. In turn, Percy Lacksman sent an email to Jill Serrano, asking if that report would be ready prior to his upcoming scheduling conference for the Senator. He called Jill's office a few minutes after he sent the email. He didn't get through, but Jill emailed him back an hour later, stating that the report was done and was being proofed, and that she'd give him and the senator a copy by the end of the week.

Percy reported this schedule back to Yoko, who then reported to Taras that he would have the report within the next week, perhaps sooner. If that were indeed the case, Taras realized, then he could schedule his sale closing in less than a month. All these months of work were about to pay off, he realized. He just needed to stay focused and see it into the glove, as the baseball expression went.

Later, Jill hit "send" on her email, after approving the final draft from her team. It was now an official memo of the Director of Drone and Airspace Operations of the Department of Homeland Security.

The memorandum from Jill's office included several conclusions, one of which was, "There are no contractors who have any agreements with the US government to maintain any orbital, aerial platform or surface-based weapons intended for use against an orbital object."

A FOILED DRONE KIDNAPPING

The notation in Jill Serrano's daily internal DHS report was buried near the bottom of the items, and it was an oddity. It referenced the coordination of media assets respecting a "drone interdiction" in Los Angeles and the "Mayor's Office Press Event." She suspected that her office was going to get dragged into it at the last minute, whatever it was, particularly because Los Angeles Mayor Gonzales' office was constantly bombarding her and other federal offices about his pet campaign issue, the rogue drone situation in Los Angeles. The mayor was up for re-election, and his response to the drone issue was on the wrong side of public opinion. He needed a quiet bail-out that he could take credit for, and the Feds were the perfect solution.

Jill clicked on the briefing item and in a few minutes learned of the mayor's plans for the following morning. Apparently, a local meth lab drug bust in east Los Angeles led to a police search of a building's rooftop. Inside a garage-like roof unit sat one of the CKS drones poised for deployment in a future operation. The discovery was not yet public, but word of it was passed along to the Los Angeles mayor, who was now planning for an on-site press conference to announce his re-election campaign, staged against the backdrop of his administration's "capture" of a rogue drone. The good mayor was seeking to have as many members of federal and state agencies as possible appear at the press conference, each bedecked in their organization's uniform. Of course, the mayor's request did not reveal that the officials would be serving as actors in the news video that would launch his re-election campaign. Jill was getting used to the political capture of law enforcement, but she almost winced as she read the internal briefing item.

Her decision came to her instantly. It was neither logical nor emotional. It was based on trust. She walked out of her office to a park a block from her office and called John Gabriel on her burner phone.

"Hello again," John said, somewhat surprised to get a call so soon after their dinner.

"Hi John. Listen, I was thinking about what we talked about at dinner. I want to pass something along to you. Anonymously. Very anonymously. Mermaid and Catwoman stuff. Maybe it would be of interest to your close friend who might know something about those Los Angeles drones."

John could tell that Jill wasn't in a position to linger long on the call.

"It seems the Los Angeles mayor will be launching his re-election campaign tomorrow from a press conference on a rooftop in east Los Angeles, where a narco squad on a drug bust stumbled across a rooftop shed with a drone in it. The building is on East 46th Street. The event is scheduled for tomorrow morning. The mayor is calling in chits with every state and federal officer who will stand in uniform for the spectacle. I guess he thinks it will make for a great campaign video," Jill said.

"Catwoman or not, I didn't take this job to end up as a publicity prop for the next twelve months for … some douchebag mayor," said Jill.

John asked her a few questions, and she answered as best she could.

"I've got to run now, John. Just, please, this call didn't happen," said Jill.

After a pause, John, said, "Thank you. For my friend. Seriously, thank you. No one will ever know this call happened. And by the way, clear the call history on this app," said John.

"Happening in thirty seconds," said Jill. "Talk later." As she walked back to her office, she hit "delete" on the call history button on the encrypted app of her burner phone.

Later that night, an LAPD officer sat in a cheap picnic chair on a roof in east Los Angeles guarding the drone shed. Suddenly a sound broke the night calm as a half-door that resembled a roll-up garage door opened up on the side of shed. A few seconds later the drone flew out of the shed into the night sky. The officer briefly pulled his gun, wondering if he should fire at the drone. The officer swore and watched in disbelief as the drone disappeared into the night sky. He knew there was going to be hell to pay. He radioed his partner in a squad car parked down on the street.

"Shit, did you just see that?" he asked excitedly.

"See what?" his partner responded.

A few hours later, Jill's eyes paused on a short item buried in her morning email briefing. The press conference planned by Los Angeles Mayor Gonzales had been "postponed until further notice." She smiled and wondered how John had broken the news to his "friends."

PLANNING ANOTHER DRONE KIDNAPPING

Mayor Gonzales' campaign was in near-panic attempting to refocus the press and the public after his cancelled press conference highlighting his anti-drone re-election campaign. The mayor's reading of popular sentiment was bad enough, but his new plan involved a stunt that was even worse. The plan was to forcibly capture a CKS drone during a sting operation. Once in hand, the drone's electronics might help trace it to the rogue drone operators. And, it would be a great prop for a press conference.

Just days after Jill had tipped off John about the mayor's planned press conference, another item appeared in Jill Serrano's daily DHS update. As before, the item mentioned a "drone interdiction" and "Los Angeles Mayor Operation." She reviewed the entry, but details were lacking. Two ICE-owned drones had been requisitioned to the El Monte regional airport in Southern California, close to where two major Los Angeles freeways intersected. The item noted "NOTAM EMT 1000 PDT," "operation window 1000 – 1200 PDT," "LE i/CD77"and "media assets 1300-1500 PDT." This meant that an advisory to local pilots would be issued at 10 am, with some operation (perhaps involving the drones) taking place from 10 am until 1 pm, and a likely press conference between 1 and 3 pm. No action was required of Jill or her section of DHS, which seemed odd to her since coordination and policy concerning drones, airports and different jurisdictions was exactly the type of event her office was supposed to handle. Something was off.

Jill decided this was likely a do-over scheme by the Los Angeles mayor, similar to his aborted press conference a few days prior.

She again called John Gabriel using her burner phone. He picked up right away. "Hi Jill," he said. "I'm torn between being happy to hear from you, and worried that it's coming in on the encrypted phone app of a burner phone. How are you?"

"Hi John," she said with a bit of applied warmth. "Everything is good here, and you're right I should just call to say 'hi.' So, 'hi.' But there's another item I came across, and like before I want to pass it along to those close 'friends' of yours. The drone friends."

John was silent, waiting for Jill to continue. She continued, "It's not much, but there are a group of items scheduled for next Tuesday. They seem odd, like before, some drone thing linked to the Los Angeles mayor. But the fact that this is being run by someone else at DHS, instead of my office, is a tip off. Something is odd about it." She gave John the details from the notice. "If this were some legitimate law enforcement operation – which it would be if it had been sanctioned properly - it wouldn't appear in this particular DHS catch-all feed. It's almost as if it was included there so that no one would notice it. No one who has control over it, that is. Which should be my office. That's why it sticks out," she said.

"And John, about the 'LE i/CD77' part of the message. I'm not positive, but that might mean that any notices to local law enforcement should reference code 77, which signals a possible ambush. But I'm not certain that's what this means," said Jill.

John asked a few questions, and after some small talk he again thanked Jill and told her this was all off the record.

After they hung up, John spoke with Nick de Stijl. "Nick, other than a good upland bird load, what would be the best shotgun shell to use to take out a helicopter-style drone from, say, 20 yards? Using an extremely short barrel?" John asked.

"Believe it or not, there are several brands of them," replied Nick. "The trade knows them as 'drone defenders.' It's a 12-gauge shell that shoots out a door-sized net of wires. It tangles up a drone and downs it. Safe, too. No one gets hurt by errant shots."

"Nick, if we needed to, could we dispatch two of our CKS drones simultaneously to a chase, and load each with a couple of those drone defender shells? There wouldn't be any tasering. Maybe replace the taser unit with a short barrel and those shells? Like coming to a gunfight. Probably with two other helicopter drones trying to ambush us," asked John.

"Shooting a couple of shotgun shells is far easier than our taser shock, for sure. It would be easy to rig, John. Just let me know. And yes, if I can disable the taser units, it's really easy," said Nick.

Let's do it, get a couple ready to deploy in a gunfight next Tuesday. Each with a forward and tail shell, ready to go. Stage them close to the El Monte airport for an expected gun fight. We'll ambush the other drones. It has to work, so test it out between now and then," said John.

"No problem. Let me give you a report in a couple of days," replied Nick.

AMBUSHING A SNEAK ATTACK

Jill Serrano's hunch – and tip-off to John - had been correct. An Amber Alert was issued at 10:15 am the following Tuesday, when the freeways had cleared of rush hour traffic. The alert identified a white van driving out of East Los Angeles north on the 60 highway which then turned eastward onto the 10 Freeway. On this route, the van would pass less than a mile from the El Monte airport.

The short alert messages to the California Highway Patrol and to local police in Rosemead and El Monte included the requisite "Amber Alert" coding, which was quickly relayed into the public notices on billboards and cellphones in the area. Buried in the non-public part of the alert message was, "Code 77" – meaning, "possible ambush, use caution."

John Gabriel and Nick de Stijl had been waiting for this ambush and assumed it was an attempted downing and capture of their CKS drone. John approved Nick to launch the two special CKS drones. Both were loaded with 'drone defender' shotgun rounds. One immediately began tracking on the CKS platform, notifying tens of thousands of users across the globe that a car chase was up for auction. The second CKS drone ran silent, not tracking on CKS, but lurking several hundred yards behind and to the north of the lead CKS drone. Less than 10 minutes later, one of John's CKS team masquerading as the winning bidder in the auction took control of the CKS attack drone and positioned it above and behind the target van. The CKS auction site worked per usual, and one TV station helicopter appeared to cover the Amber Alert vehicle, having just ended its rush hour reporting at 10 am.

The two CKS drone pilots scanned the horizon for potential incoming drones. And without surprise, as the lead CKS drone was almost due south of the El Monte airport following the targeted van, two helicopter drones appeared, incoming from the airport's direction. They were flying together, straight towards the CKS drone at about 200 feet altitude.

The pilots of the two ambushing drones did not know that the 'rear guard' CKS drone was present. The rear guard CKS drone increased its speed as it vectored directly towards the two drones. The intercept point was about 100 yards away from the lead CKS drone.

As the rear guard CKS drone vectored towards the two drones, the lead CKS drone suddenly turned north, straight towards the incoming ambush drones. The high def cameras on both CKS drones were fully engaged.

The two attack drones were now surrounded by the CKS drones. As the rear guard CKS drone closed within 30 yards from the side of the attack drones, it fired its forward-facing 'drone defender' shotgun shell. It was a sneak counter-attack upon an ambush attack. The projectile tangled itself with the propellers of one of the attack drones, and within a few seconds the attack drone veered into a steep dive towards the ground and then shattered into pieces on a cement parking lot. Video of the one-sided dogfight was broadcast over the CKS game platform to tens of thousands of viewers.

After firing, the CKS rear guard drone pitched sharply upward and then turned right as it dove back downward, so that it was now directly behind and above the remaining attack drone, whose pilot was not yet fully aware of what had just happened. Nor did the attack drone pilot realize that the CKS drones were flying gunships.

The attack drone now had an armed CKS drone behind it, and an armed CKS drone ahead of it. It was sandwiched. The lead CKS drone fired a 'drone defender' shell straight into the attack drone and then dove sharply left. The rear guard CKS drone's camera recorded the direct hit on the attack drone. The shotgun shell net wrapped around the forward propellers of the attack drone, which broke into a short and mortal dive to the cement a few hundred feet below.

The ambush had been thwarted, and tens of thousands of viewers had watched it real time on the CKS system.

It was the debut of a new era of privately armed drones. But unlike the revolution that would 'not be televised,' this revolution had indeed been televised – live – to a world audience.

By mid-afternoon, every local television channel and radio station was covering the failed drone ambush as their lead breaking story. Some pre-empted their regular programming to cover the event, complete with high-def footage of that attack. This had legs; it was not going to abate any time soon.

The Chief of Staff of Mayor Gonzales, Vera Cruz, watched the debacle as it went viral across social media and local television. Within thirty minutes Cruz had made her decision. She was quitting her job. Gonzales' re-election campaign was as dead as those two smashed drones. Vera would feign outrage at Gonzales's bad judgment in authorizing such a horrible attempted ambush attack over Los Angeles.

Conveniently, just a week prior Cruz had received an exploratory reach-out from an insider for Anna Solare, who was Gonzales's strongest opponent in the upcoming election. Solare was obviously looking for campaign assistance. Her decision made, Cruz wasted no time. She texted the

Solare agent who had reached out to her. "Let's meet this evening," her text read.

INSIDE THE GARDEN WALLS

Rebecca Biton had ordered a copy of an out-of-print book, *Field Guide to the Plants and Grasses of Palestine*, after noticing that her boss, Majedah Simon, had stopped bringing flowers and arrangements to the office from her home garden. Rebecca had sensed that Majedah was a bit distracted - and possibly off of her game - the past few weeks. Rebecca thought her boss worked too hard and might succumb to burn-out. And she wasn't pursuing much of a personal life. Rebecca wanted to help, but didn't think it appropriate to invite Majedah to attend gatherings with her fiancé or their small group of friends – it might prove awkward for Majedah as the odd-person-out.

And so, the ever-resourceful Rebecca had devised a plan, which was bold without being too intrusive – or so she thought. She would be force-visiting Majedah that coming weekend, when her fiancé would be busy watching a televised soccer match – something Rebecca had zero interest in doing.

With field guide in hand, Rebecca knocked on Majedah's office door and then stepped in and asked, "Colonel Simon, I wanted to ask a favor. May I can come by your place on Saturday to do some serious gardening? I want to see whether that field patch in your backyard might have some of the more exotic native species that I've been looking at," said Rebecca. She held the worn copy of the field guide in hand as a prop for her proposal.

"Gardening? At my house? This weekend?" asked Majedah. She paused a second and looked at the book that Rebecca was holding. "You sure you want to do that? I mean, the garden is a mess right now. I've been…" Her voice trailed off, and then Majedah re-focused herself and said, "Absolutely, Rebecca, that would be great. Saturday would be great."

"Great, and thank you," said Rebecca, as she slipped away down the hall.

After Rebecca left, Majedah glanced at the empty flower vase on the table in her office, and realized that for weeks she had not brought in any flowers. In fact, she hadn't really been tending her garden, probably since before travelling to the Cyprus operation. Then it dawned on her what had just happened, and she smiled at how adept her assistant Rebecca really was.

Jeez, am I becoming a cat lady? Majedah thought to herself.

She got up and walked the short distance to Rebecca's cubicle a few meters down the hall from her office. "Rebecca, perhaps I'll whip up something for us to eat afterward. After gardening. Maybe from the farmers' market. So maybe mid-morning?" suggested Majedah.

"I'd love that," replied Rebecca.

A SNIPPET OF INTELLIGENCE COMES IN

The clerk at the hotel in Doha was in the parking garage of the hotel, feigning a cigarette break. He finished his telephone call, put out the cigarette, and then smashed the burner phone against the cement post and tossed the remains into the garbage can as he exited the garage. A thousand dollars a month was good money, he thought. But the Mossad agent on the other end of the line thought just the opposite – how unbelievably cheap it was to obtain information like this.

The intelligence report was initially sketchy, but of massive consequence. When the Mossad received information that an old Soviet satellite weapon might be for sale to a jihadist organization, it forcefully underscored the maxim that a successful spy organization needs "assets in the field" to be effective.

Mr. Abdullah had been a person of interest to the U.S., as well as Interpol and the Mossad, for several years because of his known association with the radical Nadim Badr Rachid, but he was almost impossible to track. The most recent information on him was always tenuous.

For some time, the Doha hotel clerk, dutifully on the Mossad's informant payroll, had kept watch on Abdullah, reporting to the Mossad after each visit. From this, the Mossad had become aware that Mr. Abdullah made regular monthly visits to the hotel. He tended to prefer the same prostitutes, so they had to be arranged in advance.

Recently, there had been a change to Mr. Abdullah's regular visitation schedule at the hotel, and the informer had advised the Mossad of such. The Mossad made sure that one of Mr. Abdullah's preferred prostitutes was not available according to the changed schedule. A substitute was needed. The Mossad then arranged for the replacement prostitute to bug the hotel room.

The bug recorded a snippet of intelligence spoken by one of Abdullah's associates. In it, the associate referenced the upcoming ISIS anniversary and the need to close the purchase of the satellite weapon before the anniversary. A second snippet referenced a Soviet nuclear weapon, and a third fragment of conversation referenced a satellite purchase.

Combining these intel fragments led to the possible situation that ISIS might be planning an imminent purchase of some sort of Soviet nuclear weapon and possibly a nuclear satellite. Nothing more was known; it was enigmatic and not actionable by the Mossad. Also, the information was single sourced via the Doha hotel intercept and had not been confirmed or corroborated through any other source.

ANOTHER INQUIRY THROUGH BERMUDA

The Mossad command asked Majedah Simon to help analyze the new intelligence data from the Doha hotel bug. The Mossad wanted all potential avenues reviewed to try to turn the cryptic intelligence into an actionable item before it was shared with allied governments.

Upon receiving the briefing, Majedah immediately thought of John Gabriel. She then wondered whether she was inventing some excuse to contact him and might inappropriately be using this situation for that purpose. But upon reflection she realized that he was a bona fide potential source, and that she could contact him in a manner that did not compromise him in any way. She had his personal contact information – they had exchanged it before he had left Cyprus.

But Majedah didn't want any of that information about John being included in any Mossad report. Instead and oddly to protect John, she decided to use the same formal avenue that she had used before – the Bermuda insurance intermediary. It protected John. Her colleague made an inquiry to Kirk Woodbury as before. This time, however, a different message was given to Kirk. It was a request that John text his availability for a conference.

Kirk Woodbury called John, thanked him for his recent visit to the Devil Island, and said that their mutual friend had contacted him again. The caller wished for Kirk to pass along a message to John. It was a telephone number for John to text with a time when he would be available for a call. Later, John texted that number from one of his burner cellphones, and at the appointed time he received a secure call from Majedah Simon.

John felt a slight energy boost – he wondered if Majedah was calling to arrange that dinner they had discussed in Cyprus. He had assumed that months would pass before any such arrangements might be made, if ever. But John realized that by using Kirk as an intermediary, she probably was not calling John about a dinner date – not directly, anyway. This would be business.

Majedah briefed John on the intelligence snippets that the Mossad had received, and that such intelligence would shortly be passed along to the U.S. pursuant to existing intelligence protocols. In the meantime, Majedah asked John if the information made any sense to him or whether he might have a suggestion as to how to get some actionable intelligence from it.

"John, you run in some very esoteric circles that appear to be outside of our usual network of knowledge. I know it sounds far-fetched, but so far everything that we know about you is also far-fetched. So, I thought it would be valuable to run this by you, just in case," Majedah said.

John told Majedah that he knew nothing about it, that it was complete news to him. He promised to sleep on it to see if any revelations might present themselves, and they agreed to reconvene the next day.

At the end of the call, Majedah asked her assistant, Rebecca Biton, to drop off the call to give them privacy.

When Rebecca had exited the call, Majedah said, "John, I wouldn't have called you on this if it weren't a time sensitive and extraordinary matter. I'm still processing a lot of things from our time together in Cyprus, and I didn't intend for this call to take the place of the follow-up that will happen" – she paused for a moment, then continued – "the dinner that we want to have, that we're going to have, in the normal course of things." The sincerity and directness of her statement was refreshing to John, even if it didn't qualify as a Hallmark greeting card inscription.

John thanked her for her words. They would talk the next day.

THE MEMO STARTS THE DOMINOES

As Yoko Senstra finished her call with Taras Shimko, confirming that Taras had received the classified memo addressing the lack of any killer satellite program, Taras thanked her and promised that the remainder of the payment would be made to her shortly.

As Jill Serrano reviewed her daily briefing, a small item caught her attention, referencing a possible "unlawful transfer of satellite technology to a jihadist group." Jill knew that the keyword sorting protocols had included it because it contained the word "satellite."

To Jill's surprise, her group's report of a few days earlier – the one she had initiated at the request of Percy Lacksman

– was footnoted in the summary of the item, as one of the most up-to-date background briefing papers in this area. At first, Jill considered that footnote an incredible coincidence. But then she reconsidered Percy Lacksman's very odd reasoning to her when he asked for the memo, and her initial reaction just to get the thing done and get the somewhat annoying man off her agenda. With this classified news items, she wondered how Senator Baxter's committee was involved.

She considered the prospect that the timing of her report and the classified info about the sale of satellite technology to a jihadist group was 'too perfect' to be a coincidence. Would Senator Baxter use her report to justify another billion dollar program at the Pentagon to be proposed in some politician's home district? Was it planted to lead to a new Star Wars spending program? Was that what Percy Lacksman's boss, Senator Baxter, was really after, and the reason why his request had been so formless?

Jill thought back to her dinner with John and his comment that, "There may be a few ghosts in the machine."

She made another snap decision. She called John on her secure-call app and shared with him the basics of the memo she and her group had prepared and her suspicion that she was being played by Percy Lacksman or his boss Senator Baxter, as the report was just too perfectly timed with the classified briefing note that she had just received.

Jill asked John whether he thought she was being 'set-up' for something, and for advice on what she should do if indeed she was being set-up. "It all seems too close to the scenarios we spoke about at dinner," she intoned.

"Listen, Jill, just sit tight today. Let me do a little

digging around. I'll call you back - tomorrow at the latest," John promised. Jill cautioned John that the briefing item about a possible satellite technology sale was classified, so to be judicious in mentioning it to anyone.

"I've got the research reports from CRS that my office used to write the memo for Senator Baxter," said Jill. "They aren't classified. I'll upload them to the cloud and send you an encrypted link."

John Gabriel did not know Percy Lacksman other than from the Kitty Hawk panel at the Drone Convention, and frankly he had no idea if Jill was being played by Percy or his Senator Baxter as some sort of justification for a new pork barrel spending bill or otherwise. But when combined with what Majedah had told him the previous day, the coincidences were just too strong to ignore.

SNIPPETS OF INTELLIGENCE AGGREGATE

John called Majedah Simon back later that night. It made him smile thinking that he was calling a Mossad agent to help her out despite his bona fide worries just a few weeks ago that she was going to have him killed. Based in part upon Jill's suspicion, John told Majedah that he might have a couple of names to toss into the mix in the Mossad's analysis with respect to the potential satellite transfer: Percy Lacksman, and the U.S. Senator he worked for, Robert Baxter.

Just thirty minutes later, Majedah was back on the phone to John. She told him that the name "Percy Lacksman" had garnered some leads from the Mossad's relational analysis algorithm.

"We've got some communications between a sometime lobbyist and influence peddler named Yoko Senstra and a Percy Lacksman. She's based in the Washington area. We also can connect this Yoko Senstra with telephone communications in the same time period with a Russian national named Taras Shimko.

"John, thank you. It's not much, but it might be a lead."

"Who the hell is Taras Shimko?" John asked.

"We don't know anything more yet, but in any event, we're digging into that. Again, thank you, John. I'll update you if things warrant," promised Majedah. "And please, if you come up with anything further, let me know," Majedah asked.

"Okay, sit tight, I'll do a little more digging around," said John.

Moments after they hung up, it dawned on John that he had just used the exact same phrase – "sit tight" - with the two women with whom he'd had any semblance of having had a date during the past year. His main worries were that one might need to kill him, and the other might arrest him.

"You are anything but predictable, Gabriel," he muttered to himself.

John was intrigued and gave some thought to Majedah Simon's request. He knew that Jill had sent over a link with old CRS research memos about satellites. He pulled them off of the cloud and reviewed them. Many were Cold War era Congressional Research Service memos and other briefing papers.

John was fascinated by the background memos. He scanned through them and was surprised how ignorant he was of some early ventures regarding alternative weaponry and space. But he was looking for names. One CRS briefing memo from 1987 about Reagan's "Star Wars" program included an appendix listing all of the known Soviet scientists advising the Soviet leadership about Star Wars technology. The entry for "Pavel Gurin" listed his second wife as one "Ivana Shimko." The name grabbed his attention – someone named Shimko married to a top Soviet satellite and missile operative, Pavel Gurin. If this Ivana Shimko was related to the Taras Shimko who Majedah had mentioned, then there was a likely family connection of Taras Shimko with Pavel Gurin, an officer in the Soviet rocketry and missile corps.

John thought about Majedah's initial call to him outlining that there were three pieces of intelligence linked to a Mr. Abdullah, and that "sale of a Soviet nuclear satellite" was one possible combination of the information. John realized there was a good likelihood that if there ever had been any Soviet nuclear satellite, and if it was still in orbit, it surely would have involved the inner circle of Soviet rocketry – and thus may connect to the Pavel Gurin listed in the appendix. The timeline was right. It was certainly possible that this Taras Shimko might be related to Gurin's wife. With all the crazy instances of billions of dollars having been siphoned out of Russia by Putin and his cronies since the 1990's, why not another instance of technology-looting by the son of a former Soviet missile program insider? It certainly was not a crazy suggestion.

John paused and weighed the competing concerns and risks he now faced. He realized that giving this information to any official channel – including any U.S. law enforcement agency- could likely result in the information being given to the Russians, which ironically meant that the Russians could simply recover and keep the nuclear bird if it existed. Was this better than its being sold to the highest bidder? After Putin's recent expansionist invasions in the Balkans and Ukraine, the prospect of Putin having a nuclear weapon in orbit was almost as bad as the prospect of a jihadist having such a weapon. There was no right answer.

But if the US or the West came into possession of the Soviet bird, it would be tantamount to an act of war, similar to that of the US taking over a Russian submarine or aircraft carrier. There were also numerous potential bad outcomes where the US might try to keep secret that it possessed the Soviet weapon. But the sheer number of spies and idiots in the ecosystems virtually guaranteed that it would not remain a secret. The outcomes were all slippery slopes towards war.

John then realized there was only one viable solution: If such a satellite existed, no one could have it. It needed to be disabled or destroyed, and it needed to happen soon.

And he also realized that no government actor was in a position to destroy the satellite. It was both too "precious" and for clever humans, too tempting to want to play the game of "pretending not to know."

If it existed, it needed to be destroyed with complete stealth, so that all could pretend not to know.

Great idea, but how could that happen? John asked himself.

THE ZONE

Different people have different triggers which put them into the "zone" - a mental state in which the brain makes better and faster connections than under normal circumstances. Athletes spoke of achieving the zone, but science remained unclear as to what triggered or maintained it. Whatever it was, John went into his zone.

The engineer Nick de Stijl, who managed John's CKS drones, was the first person John called. "Will the CKS taser array work in a vacuum?" he asked. "Yes," answered Nick.

The next call was to Jimmy Bedford, the ICE-3 satellite hobbyist who John had met at the Drone Convention. John had called him several times since the convention asking what the group planned on doing next, etc. On this call, John jumped straight to the point with Bedford: "What level of voltage and amp pulse would be needed to fry the circuits of a 1970s or 1980s Soviet or US military satellite?" asked John. After some tech talk and questions, Bedford answered with a minimum – at least 55 thousand volts static, 200 amps or more.

John called back Nick. "Is it possible to configure the

CKS tasers in parallel or series in order to get a tase of at least 55 thousand volts with at least 200 amps?"

"Yes," came back the answer. "Basically, we are already doing that."

"Can we do it with a battery that weighs five pounds or less?" asked John.

"Yes, but that would limit us to less than a half-dozen zaps, maximum," said Nick.

"Would the battery be stable in a vacuum, near absolute zero?" asked John.

"A vacuum would be okay. A couple hundred degrees below zero… that's tough. In space? It could depend upon the solar light aspect. It might need a heat shield. If possible, you'd want a continual current throughput or the battery would fail," said Nick.

"How much throughput?" asked John.

"Not much. Probably the equivalent of dripping water during a cold spell so your house pipes don't freeze. A fraction of an amp would suffice for a few days," said Nick.

"How big of a solar array would be needed to provide that?" asked John.

"Umm, maybe a square foot would do," replied Nick.

John called Jimmy Bedford again. "If I had a taser powered with 55,000 volts and at least 200 amps with three discharges max, could I fry the circuits of a U.S. satellite or Soviet satellite if I only had contact with its outside fuselage?"

"Yes, of course," replied Jimmy. "That's the number one risk to rockets and satellites – lightning on the way up, or radiation surges while in orbit. Hitting hard debris is a distant second."

John's plan continued to gel. The satellite didn't need to be destroyed, just disabled. He could electrocute the rogue satellite with the taser-type shock – that is, fry its circuits. No explosives were needed, which would save hundreds of pounds of rocket weight and the several tons of rocket fuel otherwise needed to get the explosives into space.

In his zone, John was satisfied that he had his basic weapon: A taser, not unlike the tasers his CKS drones used to disable car-chase criminals in Los Angeles.

Now, he needed to get that taser unit into space, positioned to short out the satellite. A satellite that he had no idea where or how to find. And he needed to do it fast. John chuckled as he realized that sounded like the opening of a bad lawyer joke.

At best, John realized that he would only have access to a small rocket or missile. Most of a rocket's weight was comprised of the fuel needed to get the rocket into orbit. John quickly thought about how he could bypass that, by launching it from a high platform. A launch from a jet seemed most plausible, like a missile fired from high altitude. Already travelling at 500 mph and at 30,000 feet or more altitude, such an elevated and fast-moving platform would significantly reduce the size of the rocket that was needed.

But launching a high-altitude attack rocket from a jet was not an immediate possibility. He'd need the US military to be involved, and the entire project was to prevent any government from being involved.

John then thought about the high-altitude balloons he had used in his other missions. He was adept with those

– they were a possibility. As with his Somali operation and his false-flag operation, he could try using a heavy-load balloon array to get a small rocket to an elevation of 100,000+ feet, where the air was so thin it was almost a vacuum. That would be significantly higher than the 30,000 to 40,000 feet altitude that a jet could achieve. From that high balloon platform, he could then launch the rocket with almost zero drag. With such minimal drag, a rocket would not need the massive size necessary to achieve the first 20 miles of altitude, so a vastly smaller missile might suffice. But that missile would have to be capable of burning without atmospheric oxygen.

It was a possibility.

John realized that the other problem with using a balloon array instead of a jet was that the balloon was static, whereas a jet would be travelling at 500 mph or so. The rocket would burn a lot of fuel accelerating. But upon reflection, he realized that was somewhat of an illusion. A jet's speed was less of an issue when gauging its speed against an orbital trajectory. What could accelerate a missile off of a jet or a slow-moving balloon platform at 20 miles altitude in almost zero atmosphere in zero drag, without using the precious missile fuel? The 'tyranny of the rocket equation' was a frustrating reality – that rockets used lots of heavy fuel, which triggered a feedback loop requiring even more fuel.

John knew that one of the key factors in rocket launches was that although literally tons of fuel were burned getting the rocket or payload up to a zero-drag altitude, the rocket at such altitude was moving at a speed of several Mach – a thousand, or many thousands, of miles per hour. So, if John wanted to launch a rocket from 100,000 feet to save all that rocketeering and fuel needed to get the payload up to that altitude, he would have to compensate for the very real fact that the rocket launching from a balloon array would start with a velocity of zero rather than Mach 3. That was a very big disability.

John wondered if he could slingshot the rocket off the balloon array? And if so, how fast would a slingshot accelerate the rocket?

HOW TO DISABLE A SATELLITE

As John thought about a slingshot, it occurred to him that there were similar devices. Every year on TV John had watched the Pumpkin Engineers show where engineers used medieval siege machine designs to toss an object – a pumpkin - over a mile in distance. One category of devices was like a slingshot, and John's thinking about the sling-shot shifted to the other contraptions used by the Pumpkin Engineers. Any of them could be a solution, if only they could be lifted 20 miles high by a balloon array.

John knew his choices from the TV show: a spring, catapult, cannon, centrifuge, torsion or a trebuchet. An actual slingshot or a bow might also be possible. For technical reasons, John narrowed the candidates to the three best possibilities: A catapult, a trebuchet or a centrifuge.

Perhaps stoked by the memory of his teenaged prank with the crashing Skylab station, he recalled he had used a spinning arm, which essentially was a centrifuge. John's teenage prank for the Skylab party became the wellspring of his Eureka moment: A catapult and a trebuchet were both heavy. And weight was the one thing his balloon platform could not tolerate. But a centrifuge could be light – very light if fabricated from an aluminum, titanium or a plastic alloy, the centrifuge arm could be 100 lbs. or less.

John had his proposed solution: A taser-tipped missile launched into low earth orbit from a centrifuge accelerator off a high-altitude balloon array.

John sketched out a basic design of the centrifuge. It was a motor which spun like a twin-blade propeller. The rocket was attached at one end of the propeller and a counterweight was at the other end. The guys on the Pumpkin Engineer television show could throw a pumpkin at hundreds of miles per hour with full air resistance. In a 99% vacuum, that same centrifuge should accelerate the rocket to over 1000 miles per hour, and … well, thought John, with any luck, greatly reduce the amount of fuel needed to get the rocket into orbit. The numbers would have to be proven up, but the basics seemed solid to John. And from there, it progressed.

John calculated approximately that the rocket engine burn alone would take the rocket to an altitude of 25 miles or so, which was too low to make orbit. Calculating the leveraging effect of the centrifuge with a simultaneous rocket burn was a bit above John's pay grade, as the saying goes. But John found a formula that his engineers had used on some other projects, and after removing the drag factor in a spread sheet, he guesstimated that his rocket and payload would be able to reach an orbit somewhere around 275 to 300 miles high with the spinning centrifuge.

If this rogue satellite target was in low earth orbit, it would likely be at about 150 to 200 miles high. But if the nuclear satellite's orbit was higher than 300 miles, then the satellite would be out of reach.

John figured that he would need a two-stage rocket. Basically, a missile with a booster attached. He wondered if Wayne Palmer might have such a contraption. After ejecting its spent booster stage, a small second stage consisting of an array of retro rockets and a small primary burn would accelerate the rocket to orbital speed to intercept the orbiting satellite.

Then John stopped. So what? he thought. He had come up with an interesting idea as to disabling a nuclear satellite. But who would act on it? Why was he wasting his time and mental energy – because he had a crush on an attractive Mossad agent who had called? Or because his attractive high school almost-girlfriend had called?

Then he thought of his recent war-gaming session and Luke's question: "Why aren't we doing anything about it?" To which John had responded, "Maybe the 'we' is 'us'."

With a nuclear satellite, maybe the 'we' was John and his circle. John slipped back into his zone.

John inventoried the people potentially available to him to orchestrate such a plan. He would need his balloon team. His CKS manager Nick de Stijl would provide the critical taser and targeting know-how. He'd need Jimmy

Bedford and his colleagues with their know-how in respect to communicating with failing satellites. All of this would have to be under the navigation of Jimmy Bedford and his ICE-3 team. He'd need a rocket, the only source of which was Wayne Palmer. Jill Serrano could serve as an intermediary to Wayne. For all the technical hardware and the software, he could call upon Majedah Simon.

John thought back to the quandary: There was no nation state that could touch this – they were damned if they did. And the Transparency Act made it impossible, or at least felonious, for any black-ops contractor to handle the matter "off the record" for the government.

Perhaps John was uniquely situated to handle this.

PUTTING THE BAND TOGETHER AGAIN

Back in his zone, John quickly began assembling his team. Again, he called Jimmy Bedford, and without revealing the actual target, more or less proposed to Jimmy an extremely well-paid commercial venture, whereby John would hire Jimmy and his private ICE-3 satellite tracker geek team. Jimmy and his colleagues were hard-core engineers and ex-NASA/Jet Propulsion Lab technicians who tracked interesting space garbage as a hobby.

As John and Jimmy began to discuss the venture, John told Jimmy straight out that he didn't believe the ICE-3 story.

"Jimmy, I haven't been calling you because you and

your group recovered control of that abandoned satellite for a few weeks and then lost it. I've got a hunch that the press stories about losing contact are a bunch of BS. I don't think its batteries went dead. I'm pretty sure you guys still have control over that supposedly lost ICE-3 satellite and that you're trying to figure out what to do with it, without reporters calling you every day asking for an update. So, this would be the time for you to tell me what the heck you and your guys have going with that ICE-3 platform," John said.

"What makes you believe that?" asked Jimmy.

"I'll appeal to your scientific prowess and tell you that your algorithm for telling half-truths to strangers has some serious bugs," replied John in a matter-of-fact deadpan tone. "My guess is that you know that."

"I refuse to play poker with my buddies because they can read me like a book, that's for sure," confessed Jimmy. "For the longest time, I wondered why they all folded when I held a killer hand, and they all doubled down when I was bluffing. So, let's just say that I wasn't really comfortable with the prospect of having to talk to snooping reporters and tell them all kinds of stories. Especially when they'd start asking about Transparency Act stuff. It was just easier to issue a press release that we'd lost the bird."

"Is it still operating?" asked John.

Without hesitating, Jimmy replied, "Yep. We're upgrading it bit by bit, but it's quite a relic, as you can imagine. We've got three basic problems with ICE-3: Slow bandwidth, deteriorating power, and the Transparency Act. Like, was I supposed to register with the government if I bought a software patch online that we might use to update some old software on ICE?" opined Jimmy.

"My guess is that getting a mushy answer to that question would cost you six months and $50,000," said John.

Jimmy continued, "More to the point, a couple of my guys have zero appetite for their finances and telephone calls being subjected to a political magnifying glass. This is a hobby, not a political campaign. So, we took a vote and decided to announce to the world that we had failed, that we'd lost contact with the bird. It's funny how quickly reporters will believe you when you say you've failed at something," Jimmy noted. "Their calls just stopped. But we continue to get lots of emails from hobbyists and fans who are super interested in the minute details. We deal with those case-by-case," said Jimmy.

John and Jimmy then discussed the details as to whether the ICE-3 satellite could serve as a command-and-control platform for a low earth orbit operation, or whether the platform would have to be Earth-based. ICE-3 was in a deep elliptical orbit of the Earth, sometimes near, other times farther away. Jimmy needed more details and said he'd have an answer within a few hours. He readily agreed to take up John on his offer to be engaged on his new project.

In reply to Jill's earlier call to John about the Percy Lacksman situation, John's return call to Jill was not quite the response that Jill had expected.

"Jill, this is going to seem like it's coming out of left field, but I have an urgent need to sit down with Wayne Palmer,"

John said. "This is definitely a Fight Club thing. I can't and won't talk about it…. Yet. This is not transparent. Not right now, that is. I hate to say, 'Trust me,' but…can you 'trust me' on this and get me in front of Wayne? In the next 24 hours?"

It was an unsettling request in some respects, but Jill trusted John.

"Okay, I'll call him," responded Jill. "But John, you are not a juvie anymore. Tell me you know what you are doing here."

"I'm in new territory – I know that – and it will be completely undetected by anyone. I will make sure of that," he promised. "I'm pretty sure it relates to your question about Percy, but I'll know more after I meet with Wayne," John assured her.

Once again, John quietly fretted about lying to Jill or telling her half-truths. He rationalized that he was at least half-certain of what he'd told her.

Jill Serrano called Wayne Palmer, and after some chit chat including Jill's thanking Wayne for giving her a heads-up on the Transparency Act and her new spirited criticism of it, she asked Wayne to meet with John Gabriel. Strictly off the record, as a favor.

"Oh yeah, I wanted to meet John, he invited me to that fantastic wine tasting with that guy Tom Gallier," said Wayne. "I wanna know what the real story was, none of this mermaids-in-Bermuda nonsense," Wayne joked. "Have him call me; you can give him my private number."

Jill thanked Wayne and reiterated that obviously this had nothing to do with the DHS, it was "even more private than the wine tasting."

"What wine tasting?" asked Wayne in his most earnest sounding voice.

Jill connected back with John and gave him Wayne's number. John immediately called Wayne and set a meeting for early the next morning. The half-day interlude gave John the chance to catch his breath and to put some details on the basic plan, so that he would not come off as a lunatic.

John also placed another call to Majedah, as he had also asked her to sit tight. He told her that he was doing some due diligence for her, and somewhat like the situation that morning in the café in Nicosia, he could not give her any details right yet, but it involved the Russian satellite. "Do you have any pull with Wayne Palmer over at General Space?" John asked. "I've got to ask for a little confidential 'assist' from him in a few hours, but we're not closely acquainted. Off the record, can you let him know that it's okay for him to speak with me, and even better if he can find a way to help me? I mean, I'm not asking for any national security favors or that you spend any political capital. But an assist would be helpful, if it's not a big deal," intoned John.

It seemed to John that all Mossad agents had been programmed with a real-life version of the television "tape delay," whereby they double-checked what they were about to say to ascertain whether it included classified information. John envied that trait. After such a pause, Majedah said, "We've got a good line of communication there. We'll close the loop for you." Majedah's clinical response, even though good news, was slightly unsettling to John. He realized he wanted more than a business-like response from her.

"Thank you, Colonel Simon," John said, and he caught himself a bit as he addressed her by her military title.

"John, for you, it's nothing," she replied. That's better, thought John, until he realized he was reacting like a pimpled schoolboy.

Moments later, Majedah called Wayne Palmer. They had not spoken in a while, and the last time her office had contacted him was to ask for the satellite reconnaissance shots of the Iranian depot where the stolen planes had been stashed. That had been a huge favor.

Majedah obliquely referenced how valuable Wayne's information had been in that operation. She mentioned that "one of our friends" would be contacting Wayne, and although he was not an operative and not connected with Israel, she asked if Wayne could field a call.

"This friend is good people, and we know that first-hand. Frankly we wish we knew 100 people like him," attested Majedah.

Wayne replied, "Of course I will. Your guy is my guy. And he invited me to the best party of the year so far."

Majedah paused for a moment. "So, you know who I am referring to?"

"Yeah, I'm sure you mean John Gabriel. I just got off the phone with him, we're meeting tomorrow morning," Wayne replied.

There was a pause. "Well, in that case, consider this to be our vouching for him," Majedah said. After she hung up, once again she thought to herself, This John Gabriel is an enigma.

A SPACE COWBOY MEETS
WITH A GUNFIGHTER

John caught a Netjet flight to Houston and met with Wayne Palmer early the next morning. In preparation for the meeting John assembled a 15-page slide presentation. To establish a fail-safe level of security, the "target" was simply described as "top secret platform experiencing critical data breach." That could describe any number of about 3,000 satellites currently orbiting the Earth.

Wayne Palmer's office was at his office park campus outside of Houston. It was large and well-lit, seemingly designed as a room to host small contingents of business leaders. The walls were adorned with classic NASA space art, as well as photographs of General Space rocket launches. A couple of cheeky old science pulp fiction magazine covers depicting 1940's conceptions of space travel punctuated the otherwise historical displays. It was a room fit for a museum. But no museum would do justice to Wayne Palmer – his live act was part of the show.

Because John had left the Drone Convention early and he had not attended his own Lead Head wine event, naturally it was the first topic of conversation with Wayne as they got to know each other. Wayne gushed about the event and thanked John for including him. "And a special thanks for the 'plus six' on the invitation. Some of my people think I'm Christ reincarnate for getting them into that room. Those were the hottest, must-have tickets of the whole damned event. I mean, I'm jealous, man," said Wayne. "I had my people take note that this is how you throw an exclusive party."

"Well, you're welcome. Let's make it an annual rendez-vous," said John.

"Hell, I spent over half a million on sponsor fees and costs for all my booths, but your party snipered me and won the top prize. Well, maybe second prize after that stripper circus thing, but that didn't start until two a.m. …I'm told. Some of my sales reps – they're young guys, most of 'em – kept this sort of tabulation, like fantasy baseball, of all the best-looking ladies at the event. And I'll be damned, they claim that the majority of them were at your party. Well, Tom Gallier's party, officially anyway, but I'm pretty sure you're the one who quietly made it all happen. Anyway, I'm gonna catch hell next year with any of my salesmen who don't get an invitation to it. Maybe a sales contest. Lead Head is for winners!" Wayne chuckled, relishing being slightly politically incorrect. Or a whole lot politically incorrect.

"And I'd like to know the real story about mermaid hunting in Bermuda? Racing to beat South Africans to a sunken boat? Sounded a little wet to me," chided Wayne. "But we all have our reasons sometimes."

"Well, Wayne, next year perhaps you can co-host that wine event with me. It's off limits to the Transparency Gestapo, which makes it even more fun," goaded John. "And if you do, I promise to tell you a bit about Operation Mermaid."

"Don't get me started on those Transparency bastards," Wayne said. "I was talking with that guy at the event, Frank – Frank Clicquot - he gets to run around the globe, fixing old organs. Gets to name his price. Fuuuck me! No bureaucracies, except maybe the trustee boards of those churches. I wonder when the U.N. will decide that church organ repair needs to be regulated? Or outlawed because it unfairly triggers the tone-deaf," said Wayne. "But he sure has it good right now. Sometimes I wish I'd gone into a trade like that. Just me and my craft, no one snapping at my heels or protesting me year-round because I gave five bucks to the wrong politician," lamented Wayne.

For a moment, John realized that his own rants with Mr. Freddy covered some common ground with Wayne's. Perhaps Wayne had fewer inhibitions when he was safely ensconced in his office with someone with whom he felt a kinship.

"I think we're of the same mind on that subject," replied John. They both shook their heads as they reached for a gulp of coffee.

"Let me show you what I've got," said John. He put a small screen tablet in front of Wayne and instantly booted the slide show on his own tablet. For the next few minutes, John narrated the basic presentation. The last slide included the timeline, measured in a few days, not years.

John's presentation took just five minutes. Wayne rubbed his jaw a little bit, thinking. Apart from Wayne's showmanship, one got the unmistakable impression that Wayne's brain was a high horsepower machine. Wayne then said, "Y'know, John, I was kinda expecting that last slide to have that music, that goes, "dada da da dada da da da…." He mimicked the famous theme track from the 1960s "Mission Impossible" television show.

"It is ambitious," admitted John.

"'Ambitious' is a whopper of an understatement, I think. So why are you showing this to me?" Wayne asked.

"I've got everything except the rocket," replied John. "I need a small rocket and booster, able to burn in a zero-oxygen environment. And I need it yesterday."

Wayne paused, looked at the screen and then looked at John. "Who is your chief engineer on this?"

"Which particular part of it?" replied John.

"The conception part. The architecture of this. The blueprint brains," replied Wayne.

John paused a moment, and replied, "Me."

"You designed this? By yourself?" asked Wayne.

"I take it I'm about to get schooled – in a bad way - in basic telemetry and physics," said John, "by the most successful rocket guy on the planet."

Changing tack, Wayne asked, "Are you weaponizing space?"

"No. We want to de-weaponize it," replied John. He made a mental note to remember that phrase; he had pulled it out of thin air, on the spot.

Wayne set down his coffee and sat back in his chair. "Look, Mr. Gabriel. John. The presentation here would be a decent entry into a high school science fair, or even a college competition. Or even a NASA call for proposals. Actually, it's better than that, it's pretty fucking good, so shame on me for damning it with faint praise. It's intriguing, but it would end right there under normal circumstances."

John was seasoned enough to know that there was a "but" coming, and that such "but" was his only chance with Wayne.

"But today ain't normal, that's for sure," Wayne said, as he leaned forward and gulped another half-cup of coffee.

"Listen, John, there are four or five things that make this not normal. The first is, I got a call from the drone office at DHS, asking me to meet with you. That's pretty special, right there. Second, I got a call from a highly placed IDF officer, asking me to meet with you. Now that's pretty special, too, and I'll admit that the likelihood of those two things happening the same day, is about as likely as…. well, it got my attention," said Wayne.

"But the third thing is, getting those two calls from two quite attractive women, within a few hours of each other. Well, my stat guys would call that a 'five standard devia-tions' sort of event. Black swan stuff," said Wayne. "So, you got my attention, I am taking this damned seriously. Black swan serious.

"But John, all that doesn't make a rocket fly," Wayne said. "Regardless of what science fiction Hollywood puts up on the screen."

There was a pause. John wasn't sure if there was another "but" on the horizon, or whether he had just been told that he was an idiot.

"But," continued Wayne, "and here's number four, I gotta admit to you, there's something in there. Honestly, we've given some attention to balloon-based launch platforms, which are interesting, but for our corporate purposes those platforms aren't of much use because they are limited by the weight constraints. We're typically in the business of trucking big heavy cargo into orbit – communications satellites, that sort of thing – and they're kinda heavy, and the balloon payload numbers just don't tie for those big jobs. Not even close. The balloons would need to be too big, the walls too thick and inelastic. But we do understand the basic concept, and it is a sound idea for some smaller applications.

"But that's not the important thing. Number five is the two-by-four board that you slapped my head with - this centrifuge arm and the gradual RPM acceleration concept. A battery with a small solar panel might actually achieve that, and especially in zero oxygen," Wayne mused.

"Listen, John…. in technical terms, that's genius. I mean, that's just fucking genius. I've got a team of researchers who look into this stuff, that's all they do, 24/7. And not a single damned one of them has thought of putting a spinner centrifuge as a launch accelerator on a sub-orbital platform. Dammit, now that I see it on a screen, it is so obvious. So…fucking obvious!" Wayne said, a little worked up.

"The entire concept of orbit is centrifugal force, and we can slingshot ships around planets using the same concept. But somehow it hasn't been used in the stratosphere – or mesosphere – to get a vehicle into orbit. We just missed it. Boom, plain and simple," confessed Wayne.

"I'll give you one addition that's not in your Power-Point. The centrifuge can also act as a generator to increase the charge of the taser battery. Like those battery-powered cars that the young hipsters all drive. Same principle. More zap power," offered Wayne. Wayne was excited and agitated. He loved this stuff.

Wayne leaned forward. "Look, John, I'd probably short your chances of this thing working, if there were a market for it. But I'm fascinated by this centrifuge arm. So, whiskey tango foxtrot, I'll give you your rocket. Obviously, this 'gift' never happened, officially. I'm pretty sure we have a prototype in a warehouse that will fit your bill here. But I'd like to trade my rocket for two things. And no, I don't mean those two hot women you had call me," assured Wayne.

"Absolutely, just name them," replied John.

"First, let my team run with this spinner arm idea. No one else created this, just you, right? I mean it's not patented, is it?" asked Wayne.

"Just me. And no, it's not patented. It's only a couple days old. It's yours, you can make it a General Space invention; but you and I agree that if I ever need to use it, you'll give me a free license to use it, gratis," replied John.

"And you can stand on the stage when the techie awards are given out, too," promised Wayne, obviously smitten by the technological possibilities that lay ahead.

"Okay, so long as I'm within arm's length of where you get to stand," said John.

"Right next to me – so long as no Transparency Act report is required for that," said Wayne.

Wayne continued, "Second, I would guess that someone who can get both DHS and Mossad on the phone to me – and the good-looking ones, to boot - asking for the same thing, must have a few tricks up his sleeve. So, my second thing is this. Can you give me a little help - no guaranties – just some help and a good college try on your part. I need some help flipping the vote of one more senator on the Transparency Act repeal. If I flip one more senator, we've got the votes to override a veto, and I can make the whole Transparency Act go away.

"I've got three senators who still support the law solely because they need something from the president. But they are persuadable. Just one, and then you and I don't have to commit a felony just by talking about rockets," Wayne said.

"I'll do what I can, but it's not really my area. Who are the three senators?" asked John.

"ABC. Anderson, Baxter and Castillo," said Wayne. "There are others, but these are the three we think are the best targets, where there is at least some chance that one can be flipped."

As Wayne spoke, John realized that Percy Lacksman – the guy that Jill had been complaining about – was the chief of staff of Senator Baxter's committee. It was an incredible coincidence. Or not.

"Wayne, I can add a little frosting to this. I may be able to deliver that second request, right in this meeting. Senator Baxter's chief of staff on the aerospace committee is a guy named Percy Lacksman. In the very near future he'll probably be busted for espionage. Is that enough information to allow you to flip Senator Baxter?"

Wayne asked, "How near?"

"Days, maybe a week or two at most," replied John.

"How good is your information," asked Wayne.

"I've seen the underlying evidence. It's damning and there is no innocent explanation," said John. "70% or better."

"Okay, okay, that's good. I think my people will know what to do with that. I assume that information is... highly sensitive."

"Yes, I think it's fair to say that a few guys in uniform with unpleasant demeanors and working side arms would come knocking on your door if you were to print that information in your company newsletter," said John. "And you'd be getting the nice-guy treatment, compared to a few others whose heads would roll. And I've made promises to the people whose heads would be at risk. So yes, it's highly sensitive."

"John, can you do your best to give me a day or two advance notice before that bust goes down?" asked Wayne.

"Jeez, I've gotta buy back everything?" chuckled John. They sipped coffee, happy that their business was aligning so closely. "Sure. Just throw in an extra one of those rockets you have in the warehouse as my frosting-on-the-cake bonus."

Wayne then lowered his voice a bit. "With all this Transparency Act nonsense, there's a small team I work with. We have our own reference to this movie, where a bunch of underground clubs spring up, basically just guys bare-knuckle boxing other guys. But my guys do rockets. The first rule of our rocket club is, 'Never talk about Rocket Club.' And the second rule is, 'Refer to Rule number 1,'" said Wayne.

Beneath the humorous reference, John understood that Wayne was not playing around.

"Agreed. First Rule and the Second, too,"[24] replied John.

"Can we do some immediate coordinating on that centrifuge arm?" asked John. "I'm going to need a working model within a few days. Any insight from your guys would be helpful. Plus, a crisis is a terrible thing to waste."

"I was already planning on who would be coming in here this afternoon to be assigned to the project," said Wayne. "And John, you're gonna need a command center. A flight operations center. Got one?"

"Um, no," said John.

"Where's the launch site?" asked Wayne.

"Los Angeles seems best," said John.

"General Space has one just south of Los Angeles. I'll let you use it. Again, no one gets to know," intoned Wayne. Palmer was clearly coveting the patent of the centrifuge arm launcher.

"Thanks Wayne. Yes, that would help us a lot," said John.

When their meeting broke, Wayne connected John with Wayne's technician who would coordinate the delivery of the rocket. "It goes without saying, use encrypted communications," warned Wayne. "Steer clear of the Transparency Gestapo."

"Off the Algo, I promise," John replied.

At the airport following the meeting, John called Luke. After running through a few matters, John said, "Luke, get in touch with Tom Gallier. I'm going to need a few bottles of some of his best wines. See if he can find any of these: 1900 Margaux, but only if he has a certified Nicolas cellar bottling. A '28 Cos. A '47 or '49 Cheval. A '55 La Mission. A '59 Lafitte. A '64 Cheval. Any of the usual '61s and 82s. '90 Latour. A couple of those bottles need to go to Wayne Palmer at General Space. Tell Tom to use the New Castle Protocol[25], he'll know what that is. Make absolutely sure that his dispatch is from an untraceable source, bill of lading and all. The sender should be, "Rocket Club."

"Sounds like an awesome tasting group," ventured Luke.

"That stays in the Eyes-Only file," said John.

"Must be some great juice," said Luke.

"Damned little left," John assured him. "We'll try one sometime soon."

WORKING THE TRIBE IN THE ZONE

As promised, John called Majedah again on an encrypted line. He thanked her for her introduction to Wayne and told her about the probable linkage between Taras Shimko and Pavel Gurin and its potential relationship to a rogue nuclear weapon array on a Soviet-era satellite. He gave her a brief overview of the plan. Majedah was as skeptical as Wayne had been, but also careful not to come across as a naysayer. She was well aware of what John had pulled off in the past.

"John, you know we cannot be involved in that, we

cannot be within a hundred miles of any operation like that," Majedah intoned. "I shouldn't even be on this call with you."

"I know that, and you aren't and won't be. But Majedah, I need your help on a couple of small items. Discrete items, that won't connect to the mission. You've got access there to some of the best precision machine shops in the world. I need a few things, like a medium sized servo motor, with a state-of-the-art lightweight battery with a matched solar panel. And a high gain radio array, some of it no doubt classified. And I need them to be delivered to Los Angeles in a couple of days. And one other thing. I need to borrow a couple of your team members who can help with the assembly of the array."

"John, do you also need a Shetland pony and a cheeseburger with that?" Majedah asked.

It broke the tension, and they chuckled. "You know the first rule about Shetland Pony Club?" asked John.

"I'm not supposed to let you know that I know anything about the Shetland Pony Club," answered Majedah. "Look, John, even if I could manage to get you those things, it's nearly impossible for us to get them into America. And smuggling things – that's a tall order, even if we could be involved in this, which we can't," said Majedah.

There was a pause, and Majedah thought back to just a few months ago, when John had answered her cold call to help with the false flag attacks being planned against Israel. She realized that in some way, she – and her colleagues – owed something to John even though they couldn't assist.

John paused. "If I can get your people and cargo here,

can you do it?" he asked. John's timing and tone were pitch perfect.

With only a moment's hesitation, Majedah said, "Let me get back to you. How quickly?" asked Majedah.

"Three days," said John.

"This is where I should scoff and laugh, except you'd probably politely remind me that your balloon team arrived here within that timeframe," said Majedah, acknowledging how quickly John and his team had arrived in Cyprus with an operational plan.

"Reminding you would violate a Shetland Pony Club rule, wouldn't it?' asked John.

"Let me do some checking. I can't promise on this one. But I'll check. And John, even if I can, it's no simple matter, no matter how high up your friends may be," cautioned Majedah.

"All I can ask is that you try," said John. "And this is completely off the books. No one except me will know where any of this came from. And let me work on that transit issue. Let's talk in a few hours."

After they hung up, John stared straight ahead, as if intensely concentrating or just blanking out. Then he said out loud, "Fuck it, the choice is easy when you don't have any choice."

He dialed Frank Clicquot. After some small talk, John said, "Frank, suppose there was some emergency repair work needed on an important American organ. Hot rush and all of that. How quickly could you and your team get into the United States if you had to bring along a bunch of organ parts and maybe even a couple of new team members?"

"John, I'd like to pretend that I've never been asked anything like that, but I'd be lying. The U.S. is easy for us, actually. We've got customs and immigration and other credentials for emergency work. We've used them several times, usually right before Easter, Christmas or graduation season when the show must go on," said Frank. "Especially when some big shot's kid is involved. What have you got cooking?"

"Well, this one might sound unusual, but given the stories you've told me, maybe not." And then John described the need to hide his high-tech satellite parts with a cargo of tracker organ parts that Frank and his team would bring over from the Continent. Plus, a couple of new team members who would need to dress the part."

"This one would cost a pretty penny, John. I can do it for you, but…this is…bold," said Frank.

"Frank, I am indebted to you and I know a bank account or two will take a hit over here," said John. Let me get back to you with specifics, and you'd fly in here in about two to three days."

Amid a flurry of other calls, Majedah called John a few hours later.

"John, the good news is that I can probably provide that equipment and a couple of technicians. You've already worked with them on that F-16 operation," reported Majedah.

John replied, "Thank you. I've arranged transit into Los Angeles for the gear and your technicians. Have them do a quick study of old pipe organs. The kind in old churches. They'll be coming in as part of an emergency repair team for a tracker pipe organ. We'll bring in your gear mixed in with a bunch of pipe organ freight," said John. "I'll have the details by tomorrow."

"Pipe organ repairmen?" repeated Majedah. "You're using pipe organ parts for a low earth orbit satellite operation?"

"Something like that," said John.

"Also, one other dead end. I don't have any smoking gun communications linking this to Taras Shimko. We were unable to hack into Taras Shimko's computer," Majedah conceded. "So, we don't have any information or proof that he's involved with any supposed satellite."

"Okay, I'll get that covered another way," John assured her. His statement was more of a hope and expectation than a fact. But his determination was undaunted.

GUESSING A TARGET

With its huge port, two busy international airports and sprawling industrial warehouse districts larger than entire cities, Los Angeles was an easy place to arrange a pop-up light manufacturing operation without attracting attention. After all, John's CKS drone hangars were successfully hidden in the nooks and crannies of the vast industrial rooftops. Southern California was still home to many specialty machine and supply shops which catered to the aeronautics, maritime and entertainment production industries.

Because John's small CKS drone team was already located in Los Angeles, it seemed a practical place to stage the assembly and launch of the anti-satellite array. He chose a warehouse space in the suburb of Duarte, near the base of the Angeles National Forest, a mountainous area just east of Los Angeles. Huge afternoon cumulus clouds formed columns over the mountains, rising tens of thousands of feet high. John could use the cloud cover as a cloaking device for the launch.

John briefed his CKS manager, Nick de Stijl, about the current project. They decided to put the CKS on hiatus to devote the mental bandwidth to the Firebird project, particularly in designing the taser array and its camera and targeting systems. It was very similar to CKS except that it would take place in orbit and be controlled by routing and relaying the signals through another satellite, the ICE-3. Nick would be working with the ICE-3 folks, Wayne Palmer's rocket technician and a couple of technicians from Majedah's team.

Over the ensuing three days, John and his team were very busy ordering parts and supplies from the area's engineering and supply companies. The procurement list included an aluminum mast serving perfectly as the balloon array's spinner arm, parts for the battery housing and a precision release mechanism for the rocket.

John arranged the command center at General Space's Redondo Beach control room facility that Wayne Palmer had provided. Some communication links were set up between the rocket assembly and launch site in Duarte and the control room in Redondo Beach. The surplus rocket from Wayne Palmer's General Space warehouse arrived by truck a few days later from its secure desert storage site in New Mexico. Discreetly, two large SUVs had accompanied the truck and its precious cargo all the way into the loading dock. Along with the hardware, the General Space convoy dropped off Terry Sands, a General Space technician who would assist with the rocket's controls. Wayne Palmer had indeed sent a rocket scientist to accompany the rocket.

The evening after the General Space delivery was made, an Austrian Airlines flight landed at Los Angeles International Airport. Frank Clicquot and his main assistant deplaned, as did two additional technicians who had done some homework on the mechanics of pipe organs. They were both mission operatives with the Mossad traveling under fake names as craftsman associates of Clicquot Organ Services. Frank and his three colleagues wore clothing with a company logo attached.

At the Customs window, the agent glanced at Frank and the EU passports of his group. As he scanned them, he asked, "You guys doing transplant delivery?"

"Different kind of organs. You heard of El Capitan Theater?" asked Frank. "One of the biggest pipe organs in the world is there, and apparently Disney and the mayor are panicked because it's broken and there's some televised award show coming up," deadpanned Frank.

The immigration agent was only interested in moving his line along. "We specialize in those, that's for sure. Have a great visit," he said, and they moved through.

Frank was familiar with the workings of the import warehouse where their freight was directed. It was after hours, and Frank presented impeccable paperwork to the clerk. A few comments about the delays with ships at the Port of Los Angeles punctuated an otherwise unremarkable pass-through. The servo motor, battery and solar arrays, all packed together with some vintage organ parts and pipes, were released to Frank and his team within an hour.

John and Nick met Frank and his team at a nearby LAX hotel and handed them their hotel and rental car keys. Frank gave Nick the truck keys.

"Well, I imagine this is going to be a story we'll tell on Tom Gallier's Paris barge someday. I'm gonna catch some sleep, though. Let me know when you have any time," said Frank, knowing that John was likely fatigued.

"That's a plan. And Frank, thank you. I'll settle up with you shortly," promised John.

The next morning, Majedah's associates, Ben and Liam, arrived at John's warehouse in Duarte.

As John worked with his balloon team, Brian, Scott, and Milo worked on the assembly of the balloon platform, centrifuge spinner arm and rocket release mechanism, with assistance from Ben and Liam. John also spent time planning alternatives with Ben and Liam, as well as Nick and Jimmy Bedford, trying to architect the best way to find the location of the Soviet Firebird, and how to zap it in outer space with a taser array like the CKS squad had been using. They all pulled back-to-back all-nighters excitedly talking though the details, with naps caught here and there.

John provided Jimmy Bedford with all his file material on Pavel Gurin. It contained a lot of minutiae, some of it still in Russian. Jimmy's team, being the obsessive enthusiasts they were, already had in their historical database many gigabytes of data from NASA, detailing all known Soviet satellite launches.

NASA had warehoused all data on Soviet launches, including the ones that were unannounced or which were announced but with dubious authenticity as to their payload. After the Cold War ended, the files had been declassified. Over the years, Jimmy and his team had received copies from various Freedom of Information requests. It seemed amazing to John that Jimmy and his colleagues had already collected all this available data, which otherwise might have been lost somewhere in misfiled NASA data archives, or even discarded at a municipal dump in Houston.

Jimmy Bedford explained to John, somewhat defensively, that, "Butterfly collectors know butterflies and have huge collections of butterfly pictures and specimens. And we are satellite chasers. We have huge collections of data on satellites. Hell, there only about 15,000 launches in history, with a few hundred added each year. It's not a large data set."

Working with John, and their own extensive database, Jimmy had compiled a list of the best possible candidates for a nuclear weapon satellite launch by the Soviets. The A-list included six birds; the B-list included another 23 birds. Beyond that, several hundred were on the "possible, but not likely" list.

Four candidates on Jimmy's A-list were put there because they were secret or "dark" launches that had not subsequently been inventoried or their payloads revealed, either by NASA or any other agency. All of them emitted signatures of working spy satellites. Jimmy reasoned that it would have been a technological feat to have launched such extensive spy satellites and to have also armed them with nuclear weapons without altering the various electronic and radar signals of the launch vehicles. In other words, nuclear weapons were too big and too heavy to fit into typical Soviet spy satellite rockets. It would have violated Occam's Razor. If they were the size of spy satellites and behaved like spy satellites, they probably were spy satellites. These were agreed to be downgraded to the "B-list."

That left two remaining candidates on the A-list. One was a 1969 satellite to which the Soviet Soyuz astronauts had twice been dispatched in the 1970s, and again in the mid-1980s. Jimmy had discerned that the Soviets had never permitted any joint mission to that bird. That is, the International Space Station joint mission did not make any repair or maintenance calls, even though a few sole Soviet visits had occurred in the 1970s. It was in relative middle earth orbit, at 435 miles in altitude. It was an obvious and strong candidate as being Firebird.

The second possibility was a Soviet satellite apparently from a 1983 launch but reportedly damaged and disabled in 1991. It was still in low earth orbit. Jimmy noted that the chance of damage to a satellite in LEO being caused by an asteroid was low. It had been set initially into orbit at 220 miles, and with three decades of orbital decay, would be at about 195 miles today. But if it had been hit by an asteroid, all bets were off.

As Jimmy explained to John, if they had just two areas in a haystack to look for the proverbial needle, these two birds would be the two places to start.

John and Jimmy conferred, and John needed to decide. In the end, it was an easy choice. The 1969 satellite in a middle Earth orbit was out of range for John's clever balloon contraption. John could re-engineer things, but it would likely take weeks or months. The 1969 satellite was like a planet that was too far away, so why try? It just wasn't possible on any reasonable timetable.

There was another dispositive factor. If the 1969 satellite was the rogue nuclear weapon, then that meant that the Soviets would have expended precious and scarce resources to put it there at the height of the 1960s race to the moon. Doing so would have sapped enormous money and energy from the Soviet lunar program.

The 1983 satellite, however, was consistent with the politics of the era. Launched during the chaotic time of de facto coups in a destabilized USSR, it certainly had "rogue" indications, meaning it may have been launched under factional, but not necessarily full, Soviet control.

John decided that the 1983 satellite in low Earth orbit was their target.

Jimmy and his ICE-3 satellite began to ping the suspected orbital path of the 1983 bird. In effect, they were trying to locate it by radar. Initially, Jimmy found nothing where his calculations indicated the 1983 bird should be.

On the chance a space debris collision may have occurred as reported, Jimmy widened the search by adjusting the satellite's orbital decay rates. If the satellite had indeed been hit by some space junk, it could be out of its original orbital path. The ICE-3 satellite communication link was a bit slow, but the data did finally arrive.

Jimmy Bedford huddled with John at the screen and explained what the columns of data meant.

"So, there are many orbital paths up there. Imagine a three-dimensional interstate on-ramp and off-ramp where 100 exits and on-ramps all converge at the same place," explained Jimmy. "It looks like a mess, but the satellites all follow the same track, like cars racing around a speedway, again and again, year after year. So, if we are looking for the damaged bird, we can simply edit out any vehicle that we see has stayed on a consistent track.

"Like any satellite, we have some data for the 1983 Soviet bird. We know the speedway it was on with location data from 1983 through 1991, so we can predict where that bird would have been, or should have been in future years, the same way Copernicus or Kepler or any others could predict where a planet would be or when an eclipse would happen. With computers, it's quite simple," continued Jimmy.

"So, we had ICE-3 bounce a few radio signals, like a radar ping, to some of the spots where the 1983 bird should have been according to its track from 1983 to 1991. But it just wasn't there, and that would make sense if it had been hit by some space junk or an asteroid. There are all kinds of factors involved – potential energy, energy loss because of cavitation "wobble" or impact displacement, like a billiard ball hitting another. The billiard ball analogy isn't bad; there are a lot of places the satellite could end up," explained Jimmy.

Jimmy was using the screen to demonstrate his explanation to John, who was mesmerized by the presentation. "So, we widened our search. Actually, we sent out a burst of signals, covering a much wider area. A bigger cone, if you will. And we filtered out all the other normal satellites that we have already identified. And we found something," said Jimmy.

John looked at Jimmy's screen, which was a bunch of columns of data. Impenetrable. "How can you tell that, from this?" asked John.

"Oh, wait," said Jimmy, as he hit a key. The screen toggled to a new screen, which was a graphic interface. "This blue line shows the old orbit of the 1983 bird. The red line shows the orbit of the one we found."

"It's pretty close to the blue orbit. So that's it, the 1983 bird? Unless there is some other candidate close by?" asked John.

"Well, here's the thing. If you asked 100 scientists to place a bet, with their own money, as to where they thought the 1983 satellite would be after a strike, probably 99 of them would pick an orbit that was below the original 220-mile orbit. They would predict some kind of orbital decay, because of all those factors I mentioned. But in the highly unlikely scenario that the 1983 bird had been struck by an asteroid directly from behind, in effect giving it a shove forward, then maybe there would be less decay, but it would likely still be lower than the original orbit track – that's what three decades does," explained Jimmy while pointing to the graphics on the screen.

"But look at this, John. This new one we found; its basic orbital path is at 233 miles."

John looked at Jimmy, trying to understand the ramifications of what Jimmy was saying.

"Remember my billiards example? The collision of billiard balls can result in millions of new positions. But they have one thing in common – they are all sitting on the green felt of the pool table. This new bird we found – this is like the billiard ball floating three inches above the green felt of the pool table. Just suspended in the air. It just…it just isn't really possible…unless it was hit by a cue ball that came up through the felt," said Jimmy.

"Do you mean that this isn't the 1983 bird, because its position is impossible, even if something hit the old 1983 satellite?" asked John. His old law school teaching skill of homing in on the real issue was showing.

"Exactly," said Jimmy.

"Doesn't that simply rule out an asteroid hit if these are the same satellites?" asked John.

"Almost 100%," agreed Jimmy.

"Let's suppose, though, that the blue line and the red line are the same bird. What could explain it?" asked John, again focused on asking the right question.

"About 5 million joules of energy," replied Jimmy, sounding like a rocket scientist. "Basically, a whole bunch of power. A big energy input was needed to raise its orbital path. That could come from several sources, but the simplest explanation is usually the best," said Jimmy.

"And that would be?" asked John.

"The onboard rocket engine. The easiest explanation – what Spock would tell Captain Kirk[26] – is that the 1983 satellite fired up its engine and moved itself to a higher orbit."

"So that would mean the 1991 report of a disabling

strike was false," noted John. "It's not a dead bird. Someone fired it up, or the bird was auto-programmed to do it itself?" reasoned John.

"That's where I would place my money," said Jimmy. "The bird powered itself into a higher orbit."

"Did the 1983 satellite have a name?" asked John.

"The 1991 report referred to it as being part of a Firebird program," said Jimmy. "That's the only reference I see."

"What month was that 1991 report?" asked John.

"Let's see. October 1991," replied Jimmy.

"Jesus," replied John. "The Soviet armed coup happened in August 1991. Pure chaos. And a perfect time for someone to pilfer a nuclear satellite by simply moving it. Hiding it in plain sight," deduced John.

"That's gotta be our bird, Jimmy. Firebird. That's where I'd put my money, too. In fact, that's exactly what I appear to be doing already!" John said as he raised his arm showing off the operations in their small warehouse headquarters. "Let's tase Firebird."

"Y'know," said Jimmy, "Generally I like to avoid being waterboarded or being called a terrorist, but I don't mind a few old commie bastards being pissed off at me. Let's go."

MAKING IT ALL HAPPEN

John summoned a meeting of his entire team. It was the "25 hours" meeting. The timing was "emergency." Every hour mattered.

John had his key team together: Nick from CKS, Jimmy Bedford and two of his ICE-3 associates, Terry Sands from General Space, Brian and Scott of the balloon company, Milo Patton, Ben and Liam on loan from the Mossad, and Luke. John had also asked Mike Shepard to join the group; he had arrived a few hours earlier. John felt a twinge of guilt when he realized that neither Jill Serrano nor Majedah Simon was there.

John ran his team through the high-level plan and some granular details. As a group, they addressed various technical issues and workarounds. "Gentlemen, I'm just asking that you give me twenty-four hours of working as hard as you can. I promise that the twenty-fifth hour will arrive," John offered as encouragement.

"There are a couple of rules you must know. You are part of Rocket Club. The first rule of Rocket Club is, don't talk about Rocket Club. The second rule of Rocket Club is…" John didn't need to finish the line; everyone had heard it in beer commercials, dirty jokes and motion pictures. Everyone chuckled, and the message was clear.

John urged his team to simplify, simplify, simplify. They were not landing a man on the moon or trying to get three men back from the moon. They were playing a game of "tag" with an orbiting spacecraft. That was it. The tag could be sloppy and embarrassing, it didn't matter. Anything more elegant was wasted effort, and they didn't have any margin for wasted effort. For now, John decided not to mention that the target was armed with nuclear weapons, or that it was Soviet. He would drop in those details later. The team generally knew that they were intercepting a satellite and decommissioning it. Individual members had pockets of knowledge, but John was truly trying to keep things compartmentalized as much as possible, as in any decent military operation.

He ran through a modified version of the power point presentation, updating with details that had been learned. Nick de Stijl, along with the balloon entrepreneurs Brian and Scott, managed the balloon platform as well as the taser unit and telemetry systems. They were to work with Jimmy Bedford's team to make sure the signals could be routed through ICE-3 once the rocket launched off the balloon platform.

The ICE-3 satellite relay was beneficial because it avoided atmospheric interference, and it also could maintain constant line-of-sight communications with the 1983 satellite when it was on the other side of the Earth. It also kept the critical signals away from the NSA and Russian and Chinese spy satellites.

Milo, Ben and Liam were working on the rigging for the centrifuge arm and would assist Terry Sands of General Space in syncing all systems for the release of the rocket as it spun off the centrifuge arm. Nick was in charge of arming the rocket with the taser unit. Mike Shepard filled in for John when needed, and Luke similarly assisted with coordination.

A six-month process would have been challenging enough. But as with the Army Corps of Engineers or the Seabees, critical time deadlines were the necessity that was the mother of invention. And necessity here meant "immediate."

John asked the teams to reconvene every three hours for a 10-minute status conference. John was the conductor of the orchestra, interacting with all the teams, shuttling among them.

The tasing objective was simple. The missile's retro rockets would be used to position the rocket alongside the Firebird satellite. The taser would give the Firebird satellite an electrifying kiss of 55,000 volts. Maybe two or three kisses with any luck. There might not be any reliable indication that their mission had worked. How do you prove that a dark satellite is dead? John met with Nick and Terry Sands to discuss details of the taser, how it would mount on the missile, how it would draw the charge from the battery and its command and control. Elegance was jettisoned in favor of "what worked."

A few hours later, Majedah Simon was on the phone with John.

"A little good news for you, John. Those names you provided were helpful links. We've managed to assemble a fuller communications file among Taras Shimko's associates. The circle includes Percy Lacksman and a go-between named Yoko Senstra, who connects Lacksman to Shimko.

There are some payments to offshore banks involved," said Majedah.

"Bullseye," said John, thinking of the request made by Wayne Palmer. It seemed to John that Majedah had constructed her dossiers from NSA-type wiretap data, the existence of which was undoubtedly classified. "Majedah, can I get a copy of that and – if I have to – give a copy to someone who is not part of the US government?"

Majedah paused, and then said, "Yes, John, but you and that person must be able to sanitize the source. It's critical that it be anonymous and untraceable."

"That's been arranged, not a problem," promised John. "Can I get that in the next couple of hours?"

"Would you like another brown Shetland Pony with that, too?" she said.

"I forgot to say, 'thank you.' I'm sorry, thank you. A little stress on this end of the pond," said John.

"Yes, John, I can make that happen." After a pause, she said, "You must be an absolute monster when a restaurant has run out of the wine that you ordered."

John appreciated her subtle attempt at humor. "Thank you, Majedah. I… I will fill you in as soon as I can. Your guys Ben and Liam are a great help. And with any luck, this satellite sale will be stopped. Here's something to think about. This Percy Lacksman fellow, his involvement will be publicly revealed in a few days. It will be a spectacular political scandal here in the States, and I can imagine that the blowback elsewhere will be strong. A real blast radius, so to speak. So, make sure any of your important assets get clear of him and his world, and that you're ready for the shakeout of our busting up this satellite sale. Everyone should cover their asses and get out of the way."

"Thank you, John, we'll make sure we're out of the blast radius," she said.

"And Majedah, I assure you that I would be a consummate gentleman if a restaurant didn't have the wine I ordered. So long as the substitute bottle was on-the-house."

"Well, I guess that's something I'll get to corroborate someday, right?" she teased.

"Thanks, that does help lessen the stress a bit."

John then called Wayne's private number and was put through to Wayne. "Wayne, it's John. I'll keep it short. You wanted a heads up. This is the heads-up. That package we discussed regarding our mutual friend's problems with obeying certain national security laws. Your office will receive a hard copy tomorrow. It's critical that you anonymize it by re-photocopying or whatever is necessary. It will be messy and noisy. International eyes will be all over it. So no fingerprints, real or digital, that's the condition attached. And burn and reburn any record of how you got it. Assume that Transparency cops might come looking. Actually the Transparency cops will seem like pikers compared to the heat that will be scrutinizing this dossier. I'll follow up with any more precise information as to when it's going to go down."

"Understood, John, I'll personally oversee it and make it happen. And thanks," said Wayne.

CLEARING A PATH AND
SETTING SOME TRAPS

John then called back to Jill Serrano. He'd last asked her to "sit tight."

He revealed some key pieces of information about Percy Lacksman, basically, that he was dirty and was selling classified information.

"That memo he had you do was likely tied into one of his bribery projects," John said. "He used you, Jill, I don't know how else to put it. Your instinct that your memo was being used for some other purpose was spot-on correct."

He explained to Jill that she needed to act immediately to distance herself from Percy, ideally as a sort of whistleblower.

"There is going to be a wicked witch hunt. The truth doesn't matter sometimes. There are only hunters and prey. So, you need to be out in front of it – one of the hunters. Your best defense is aggressive offense as a whistleblower. An aggrieved whistleblower. Otherwise, you'll be blamed. Tarred and feathered as a conspirator or a patsy," John opined. "Neither of those is good."

John told Jill that he could not give her a copy of the file that he had on Percy, because everyone had to be protected from the blowback and recriminations of an upcoming investigation. They worked through some potential specific actions that Jill should take in the coming hours. She mentioned her mentoring session with the DHS general counsel, Vernon Cutcher, and they both agreed that it was the perfect course for Jill to pursue. "You need to position yourself as the consummate professional who was the canary in the coal mine, as well as a bit of an agitator. Plus, you have to be a little pissed off that Percy Lacksman tried to play you. Focus on a suspicion that Senator Baxter might have wanted to justify some new pork barrel spending program that your memo was never designed to support," counseled John. "That gives you all the right intentions and justifies your actions but keeps you far enough away from what will actually transpire that no one can point a finger at you," John suggested.

"And Jill, don't forget, witch hunts are real, even though everyone insists that witches don't exist," intoned John. He knew he was being a bit melodramatic, but the situation could put Jill in peril, and he wanted to be clear with her.

"John, I understand that, and thanks for buttressing it for me. That helps," she said. After they hung up, she drafted an email memo to Vernon Cutcher, outlining her suspicions about the "coincidence" of Percy Lacksman's request to her for a research memo, and the classified briefing item she had seen a few days later referencing her memo as being the strongest backgrounder on the issue, and her strong suspicion that the timing was not a coincidence. Her memo to Cutcher speculated that Percy might be laying the groundwork for some form of pork barrel appropriation on Baxter's behalf. Its tone seemed very earnest. Jill emailed it off to Vernon Cutcher, with a cover message to him:

"I need ten minutes to discuss the attached draft. I don't want to 'cry wolf' so early in my tenure, so I'd like your comments on this. Also, will I need to send this to the inspector general, or will you do that?" It was a serious, 'I'm-not-fucking-around' email, not to be ignored.

Majedah Simon routed her document files with all of the communications and payments among Percy Lacksman, Yoko Senstra and Taras Shimko to a friendly agent John had arranged, located near Wayne Palmer's office at General Space. An hour later, the go-between agent had printed the files to hard copy, and they were then delivered by an untraceable cash-only messenger service to Wayne Palmer at his receptionist's desk. The documents, as such, were largely untraceable. Tipped off by John Gabriel, Wayne Palmer's office received the file and Wayne personally reviewed the materials, and as promised he redacted a few items to sanitize any potential trace-back to the source.

Wayne then gave the incriminating dossier to one of his key operatives, who reviewed it to devise a strategy with respect to Senator Baxter. Within a few hours, Wayne was reviewing the plan, and by the end of the day he had approved the strategy for how it would be used to swing the vote of Senator Baxter to the repeal of the Transparency Act amendment and the related executive orders.

Taras Shimko hung up the telephone. Abdullah confirmed that his client had received the DHS memorandum verifying that there was no American satellite killer in operation and was satisfied with it. The buyer was ready to pay and take control of Firebird. They chose a date in the coming week, with a gathering at the Doha hotel as the meeting point. They confirmed some final details of the flow-of-funds for the sale, agreeing the payment details of clearing $500 million dollars outside of the Bank of International Settlements, its SWIFT system and the prying eyes of the Patriot Act and related banking security measures.

Now that the Mossad knew of Taras and part of his plan, it was able to wiretap the call between Taras and Abdullah and had learned some of the funding details. It was the true smoking gun.

Majedah conferred with the head of anti-terror financing within the Mossad, and he suggested that the Mossad put a temporary watch notation on the accounts involved, which automatically caused a 24-hour delay on clearing of funds through those accounts. A colorable concern about unrelated heroin trafficking was the stated reason for the account hold. The delay would help mitigate the risk that the police might be an hour too late when they tried to seize the jihadist's $500 million transfer.

Together with the dossier delivered to Wayne Palmer, all of the dots were now connected.

T-MINUS UNTIL LAUNCH

At an assembled meeting, John told the entire group what some members already knew: That the target was a rogue Soviet nuclear satellite array about to be highjacked by a jihadist group. John asked that each team member summon every ounce of ability, focus and energy possible over the coming few days.

That evening, John Gabriel's team agreed on a launch date three days hence. It was T-minus three days, instead of six months. And in the 48 hours that followed, there was more frenetic activity inside their warehouse headquarters as well as at the Redondo Beach control room provided by General Space. Over a dozen people, each in his own zone, advanced things tag —team style while people grabbed 20-minute power naps. Group meet-ups happened like huddles during a football game.

John had Luke Mandeville acting as the de facto supply sergeant, arranging for various sourcing, supplies and otherwise managing logistics for the items needed to launch the vehicle. Luke had undergone a sort-of boot camp training during their operation in Nicosia along with Majedah's team. His learning curve was steep. In some ways it was unheralded work, but John knew that the only way to truly learn to run an operation was to practice. And Luke had been thrust into one hell of a learning experience.

The sun came up, the sun set; no one inside the

compound really paid attention to the time of day or night. And then, it was time: Launch date, and more particularly launch hour, loomed. John went to the launch site with his teams and the initial set of trucks. The selected launch site was a flat two-acre highway service yard about a quarter mile off the Angeles Crest Highway in the Angeles National Forest. It was remote, and the afternoon cumulus cloud cover would be massive. The cloud column typically rose to over twenty-five thousand feet by lunchtime.

John had picked the site for the natural cloaking that the cloud columns provided. One could launch a dozen Saturn-V[27] rockets into those clouds, and no one would notice. A group of 100 weather balloons, roughly the size of a large house, tethered together with a huge boom hanging below, would easily be obscured. In short, there would be no panicked calls by locals complaining of UFOs. And no FAA inquiries; at best the FAA might issue a "notice to airmen" advisory advising pilots to be on the lookout for some radar anomalies indicating possible wind shear conditions inside those clouds.

The balloon and centrifuge array were to work much like a big ceiling fan. The centrifuge, which looked like a two-bladed propeller, was attached below that beam and directly beneath the servo motor. Rather than being anchored to the ceiling, the fan array was attached to two batches of helium weather balloons. Below the balloons, the housing of a ceiling fan was instead a long beam or rod. On top of that beam, centered in the middle, was the servo motor. Embedded among the balloons were dozens of small solar panels, not much thicker than aluminum foil.

At the launch site, it took two hours to inflate the weather balloons with helium. Two extra U-Haul trucks laden with a cargo of cement blocks on pallets served as the ground weights tethered to the balloon arrays. The team attached additional various dampening rods, counterweights and the like. Wiring between the servo motor, solar panels, rocket payload and radio telemetry antennae were attached. In less than four hours, the balloon arrays were fully assembled in the gravel assembly lot.

Then it came time to attach the rocket to the spinner arm. The rocket was just under seven feet tall, and weighed just under 300 lbs. Opposite the rocket, on the other end of the spinner arm, a battery and generator were attached, serving a dual purpose as a counterweight and energy source.

The rocket itself was fairly simple as far as rockets went. Its booster stage was a four-nozzle, liquid oxygen-fed engine. Once ignited, it would burn for about ten minutes with about 3500 ft. lbs. of thrust. The upper stage consisted of steering and retro rocket nozzles and one main thrust nozzle. The upper payload included guidance and radio telemetry, as well as the taser unit head and battery panels.

The team had spent a good deal of time fabricating the clamps and riggings for the rocket and the counterweight. They attached them to the centrifuge arm rather quickly.

All systems were go. At least, as "go" as they could be under such circumstances.

LAUNCH

John took a deep breath and gave the launch order. The tether lines were released, and the array floated upward. The winds were variable but relatively calm. Delaying the launch would have been too dangerous.

It took less than three minutes for the balloons to disappear completely into the foggy cloud bank above. Moments after the balloons disappeared into the fog, the array hanging below it disappeared.

As luck would have it – good luck, that is – a highway maintenance truck made its way into the service yard a few moments before the balloon array had completely disappeared into the clouds. The team was in the initial stages of cleaning the site, but it was still odd for six U-Haul trucks to be situated there.

Some fast talk about having gotten the wrong logistics for a television commercial shoot scheduled for the following morning mollified the maintenance truck driver, who was taking off early from work. If he had looked up and seen the huge balloon array 500 feet overhead, it could have been a disaster. But his attention was diverted until the array was hidden in the clouds, and in any event, he had no interest in calling in a report which would establish that he had quit a few hours early.

The balloon array was actually outfitted with less than the maximum number of balloons that could have been used. This was intentional, to cause the array to rise more slowly and to stop rising at an altitude just over 100,000 feet. If too many balloons were used, the array could keep rising, which eventually would cause the balloons to burst, on account of them simply expanding too much in the thin atmosphere at such high altitude. There was a delicate balance to be achieved, so that the balloons would cease rising at the correct altitude.

John left the launch site to go to the control room, where the team would re-assemble in a few hours. Several hours later, the balloon array had risen and cleared the top of a cloudbank at around 45,000 feet, and thirty solar panels attached to the balloons began processing the afternoon sunlight to augment the battery power of the various radio and telemetry instruments. Once the balloon had risen to about 75,000 feet, John had the team engage the servo motor to begin slowly spinning the centrifuge arm. Had time permitted, John would have given Wayne Palmer the honors of engaging the servo that spins the centrifuge, since Wayne now owned the intellectual property rights to the centrifuge design.

Two small booster engines on the end of each arm were engaged with an explosive three-second burn, and a jolt of battery power was used to overcome the inertia of turning the half-ton arm. The gearing and tuning of the servo motor were sophisticated and precise. At over 15 miles altitude there was no drag, and after several hours the modest serve motor with its solar-enhanced battery and variable gearing was sufficient to slowly accelerate the centrifuge arm to 2,500 revolutions per minute.

The balloon platform had risen to its intended altitude of 105,000 feet – about twenty miles high. The spinning of the centrifuge arm created energy. Wayne Palmer had provided a sensor chip to be added near the servo which measured static electricity. Wayne Palmer hoped to engineer an increase in the available energy that could be used by various elements of the array. General Science Ltd. would be the beneficiary – as would Wayne's patent application.

At its apogee twenty miles high, the centrifuge arm speed had reached almost 3,000 RPM, which meant that the rocket attached to the centrifuge was spinning at well over 1,000 miles per hour. With the various counterweights, dampening weights and riggings attached, the centrifuge was spinning as smoothly as a top.

The launch of the rocket off of the array was the most delicate and demanding part of the operation and required the most precise cooperation among the various teams. Several things had to happen simultaneously. First, the rocket would be released off of the centrifuge spinner arm, which would result in the rocket flying off at about 1,250 mph. Also, the rocket's booster stage would ignite the moment it was released from the centrifuge arm. Third, the rocket's radio and telemetry would connect to ICE-3, and the rocket would be piloted away from the Earth to increase its altitude, and then, critically, the rocket would turn 90 degrees into an orbital path circling the Earth.

THE DOHA MEETING DURING A ROCKET FLIGHT

Doha.

Taras Shimko had arrived at the Ritz Carlton hotel in Doha for the closing.

The meeting began in Mr. Abdullah's suite. They exchanged funding instructions and codes, verifying that the routing of the five-hundred million dollars was being dispatched and washed through difficult-to-trace sources. Gold bullion were being transferred at the vault at the Bank of England. Chinese renminbi was being paid to an account in Hong Kong, where it was then being converted into a basket of other currencies including dollars, euros and and sterling. And the rights to the cargo of a fully laden oil tanker was being transferred to a shell company owned by Taras.

Several laptop computers tracked the particular routing steps of these various payments. In addition, Taras had established a dark Internet Tor portal with Firebird's control dashboard pre-loaded. He had the Firebird control dashboard up on his screen, which had been studied and approved by Abdullah's technicians in the prior weeks.

Los Angeles.

Back at the Redondo Beach control room, there were no problems reported by any team member. John was happy to give the order to launch the rocket by releasing it from the spinning centrifuge arm. Its four-nozzle engine began to flare just milliseconds before the rocket was released from the spinner arm, and as the clamping mechanism disengaged, the rocket flew clear of the arm via centrifugal force. The rocket engine burned quickly and accelerated to about 3,000 mph, still travelling parallel to the Earth's surface. It looked like a missile fired from a jet.

Jimmy Bedford and Terry Sands had loaded piloting instructions which were relayed to the rocket though the ICE-3 satellite, and the rocket then turned heavenward and began its climb in altitude. Its targeted altitude was 300 miles, which would place it above the 235 miles-high orbital path of the 1983 satellite. The rocket was travelling at almost a mile per second, and it only took about six minutes to reach its apogee of 300 miles altitude.

As the rocket reached its apogee, Jimmy gradually readjusted its trajectory, turning it back 90 degrees, and the rocket began to arc and turn toward the North Pole, and its rate of climb began to decrease as more of the rocket's burn was being routed towards moving it laterally rather than vertically. The rocket accelerated to about 17,000 miles per hour, now running parallel to the Earth's surface in low Earth orbit. Then Jimmy began piloting the rocket towards its interception point with the 1983 satellite. About 10 minutes after the rocket was launched off the balloon array, its booster stage ran out of fuel and was jettisoned. The rocket was in orbit with only its steering nozzles, or retro rockets.

Jimmy then entered a new set of commands, testing the retro rockets. They responded as directed, albeit there was a delay of several seconds between Jimmy's input and the receipt of confirmation that the data had been received. This was because of the slow speed of the computer processors on board the ICE-3 craft.

Jimmy then piloted the rocket's nose downward below the horizon, like a plane dropping its nose, and applied thrust. Gradually, this caused the speed of the rocket to increase like an accelerating dive bomber. The diving rocket lost about 65 miles of altitude as it moved lower in orbit toward its target, but in doing so its speed increased to about 20,000 mph as it approached the 1983 satellite at a 30-degree angle.

The piloting of the rendezvous involved several maneuvers. First, the rocket needed to be turned to line up in the same path as the satellite, like a fighter pilot coming in behind another plane in a dogfight. Second, the rocket needed to decelerate to match the speed of the 1983 satellite. Finally, the rocket needed to be brought up next to the 1983 satellite, as if docking with it. Each of these maneuvers entailed some tricky inputs.

Jimmy began pinging the radio telemetry for the 1983 satellite to see where it was in relation to the planned rendezvous coordinates. He advised John that the rendezvous was about five minutes away. Jimmy engaged several keys and spoke with his team members.

In the vacuum of space, drag cannot be used to slow a satellite, so retro rockets are used. Thus, Jimmy engaged the rocket's thrusters directly against the direction it was travelling. It took several minutes for the rocket to decelerate to the 18,000-mph speed of the 1983 satellite. Jimmy also used the lateral retro engine to align the rocket onto the same trajectory line as the satellite.

Jimmy advised John that it was time to move from digital control to visual navigation. Commands were input and relayed through ICE-3, and moments later, a fuzzy video stream pulled up on Jimmy's monitor, showing the video transmitted from the high-def camera on the attack rocket

With a flicker on the screen, a slow-moving image of the Earth's horizon filled the lower half of the monitor. The upper half was the black field of space. As the Earth image gradually shifted, the image would go a bit fuzzy every five seconds or so.

"That fuzziness is because the rocket is vibrating when I fire the retro rocket," Jimmy said to John. "Once we get closer and I stop firing the deceleration retro, the image will clarify. I hope."

Another few minutes passed, as Jimmy kept firing the various retro rockets. John and the others watched the monitor anxiously.

Jimmy then said, "OK I think I've got it pretty well lined up. I've aligned our approach with the sun behind our rocket, so let's see what it shows us. With any luck the satellite should be appearing as a little speck here pretty soon." They all peered closely at the monitor.

Milo pointed to a spot on the monitor, just above the

horizon line. The sun illuminated the 1983 satellite against the deep blue/black of the background sky. It was a small speck of white, easy to miss. But it was moving ever so slightly and growing in size as the 1983 satellite came into clearer view on the video feed.

"Yep, I think that's it. Good news, gentlemen. I think we've got our bird in sight," said Jimmy.

There were immediate cheers and exhalations of relief among the assembled team. "Now the hard part starts," joked Jimmy.

"Jesus H, I hope we picked the right satellite," said John with some concern. Everyone felt the anxiety.

Jimmy couldn't help interrupting the tension in the room. "Ummm…Moscow, we have a problem," he joked in his best Beavis and Butthead voice.

The rendezvous of the rocket with the 1983 satellite proceeded cautiously because of the clumsiness of the delay of the video and telemetry feed from ICE-3. During almost half an hour of maneuvering the intercept rocket with its retro jets, the rocket had continued to move closer, and now the satellite appeared about 75 meters off the port side of the rocket. The high-definition feed continued, albeit with flickers and delay.

The monitor then revealed to John what he had hoped for. Ten large tubes, each the size of two garbage cans stacked together, were arrayed around one end of the satellite. They appeared to be warhead fuselages, each housing one nuclear missile.

"Folks, the Firebird isn't a myth. It's real and we found

it," announced John. Excited gasps filled the control room as everyone strained to examine the monitors more closely.

"They're like relics from a sci-fi movie," said Luke.

Using this visual flight feed, Jimmy Bedford began a final sequence of retro firing and positioning to close the remaining gap with the satellite.

More minutes passed as Jimmy nudged the taser rocket closer to the 1983 satellite. It was oddly like parallel parking a car. When the rocket looked like it was only a few meters from the target, Nick asked Jimmy to engage the sensor rod, which would confirm the distance. The video feed seemed to be working reasonably well and the visual image seemed accurate, so the sensor rod was a backup tool.

From the video image, the taser tip appeared to be just one meter off the surface of the Firebird satellite. The satellite was rotating very slowing, allowing John and Jimmy to survey the satellite's outer skin. John gave Jimmy the OK to switch the high-def camera to a close-up mode, and the high-def camera recalibrated to show details of the surface of the Soviet bird.

There was no plan as to what particular part of the satellite to target with the taser, but an exterior panel came into view. It looked to be a port for external telemetry and servicing access. Three small green, red and white lights surrounded the panel. John and Jimmy agreed it appeared to be the best target for their lightening shock as they would likely see.

Doha.

With the payments having been dispatched, all that Taras needed to do now was to confirm his receipt of the various payments. Once received, Taras would give the password control code for the Firebird portal to Abdullah and his buyer. As they waited in the Doha hotel suite for confirmation of the payments, one of Abdullah's technicians whispered to him. Abdullah nodded and then asked Taras, "Mr. Shimko, can you please execute a 45-degree azimuth roll of the Firebird. As we've discussed, with the payments now in process, my colleague would like to verify that this control panel still operates as it did yesterday."

"Yes, of course, Mr. Abdullah, let me do that now," said Taras, who proceeded to make a series of keystrokes on his laptop.

Los Angeles.

As John's team watched their monitors showing the video feed of Jimmy piloting the attack rocket, without warning a disruption occurred. The retro rockets on the 1983 satellite suddenly emitted a few short bursts and the satellite began to slowly roll.

"What the fuck was that?" asked John in his most diplomatic voice.

"I think the technical term is, 'I have no fucking idea,'" said Jimmy. "This is an active satellite, that's all I'm saying."

After the satellite had rolled about 45 degrees, the retro rockets fired in reverse, and the satellite stopped rolling.

"Jesus Jimmy, zap this damned thing before it starts rolling again," said John.

"Yes, and before it moves to a different orbit," warned Jimmy.

Jimmy began a series of small bursts of the retro rockets to move the taser array closer to the service port panel. As Jimmy Bedford finalized his maneuvers of the rocket, John turned to Luke. "Do you have your phone or iPod close by?"

"Of course, said Luke. "Right here."

"Okay. If Robert Duvall got music, then dammit we're entitled to some. Audibilize this at will," ordered John.

Luke smiled, punched a few buttons, and plugged a cord into the desktop. In a few seconds, Richard Wagner's *"Ride of the Valkyries"* started to waft through the room.

"I'm not gonna second guess Robert Duvall," said Luke. The smile on his exhausted face was infectious.

John reached into his pocket and pulled out the copper coin he had lifted from Majedah Simon's desk in Cyprus. Almost unconsciously, his thumb rubbed it while he concentrated on the screen.

"What's that?" asked Luke.

"A little good luck token. We don't need to run into any submarine lurking on the other side of this bird," said John.

Doha.

Back in Doha, Mr. Abdullah's technician advised him that he was satisfied with the roll procedure. The various payments had been authorized a few minutes earlier, and payment confirmation would be coming in on Taras Shimko's text reader.

A few minutes later, Taras had verified that the payment confirmations were in order, and he announced to Mr. Abdullah that he was ready to deliver the algorithm password keys which would enable Abdullah to take control of Firebird.

"Let me authorize my people to text you those encryption keys," said Taras. "You'll have them shortly and we can verify them here."

There was excitement in the hotel suite. The transfer was being consummated. The jihadist Nadim Rachid would have his nuclear weapon satellite in short order. And Taras Shimko would have the means to live the gilded life of a global oligarch.

KIRK AND SULU

Los Angeles.
The service port panel reappeared on the screen.

"There it is," said Jimmy.

"Stay still this time," said John, as if commanding it.

Tired, excited, nervous, proud, worried and many other things, John couldn't repress his inner *Star Trek* geek. Everyone in the control room was glued to the monitors. "Mr. Sulu, fire at will," John said.

"Aye aye, Captain," replied Jimmy, as he punched a keystroke on his terminal.

As they watched, nothing happened for five seconds – was it merely a communications delay through ICE-3, or a failure of their untested rig? The delay seemed like an eternity. Then the screen revealed the answer. The monitor screen went white for fifteen seconds.

"What happened?" asked John.

"Well, either we blew up our own rocket, or the bright zap burnt the video feed, which will take some time to reset," said Jimmy with a Zen-like calm.

"How long?" asked John.

"Maybe ten seconds to reset, plus another five seconds on the upload and then another download though ICE," said Jimmy.

As Jimmy finished speaking, the monitor image began to change. A grainy image began to appear as the HD camera onboard the rocket regained its processing. As the white field faded and the image slowly came back into focus, the Firebird panel filled the screen. The green, red and white lights around the Firebird's access panel were dark, and there appeared to be burn marks around the panel's exterior edges, as if a small explosion had occurred within. The monitor refreshed itself with a better image every few seconds.

"I think we got it!" exclaimed Jimmy.

Every member of the team exclaimed their relief in their own words, from the profane to the religious. Luke's soundtrack continued playing.

"Hit it again," John said excitedly. "We didn't come this far to save battery power."

Jimmy keyed in another fire command. The screen image remained static for just over five seconds, and then the white-out on the screen occurred again. As the image gradually came back, no one had quite expected to see what the screen now revealed. The panel had actually been dislodged by half a meter, and was no longer squarely aligned with the port hole, as if it were now dangling in space by a wire like a gas cap dangling from a car. A few sparks emanated from behind the dislodged panel.

No one had expected such visual confirmation of a kill. But everyone was convinced that the Firebird had been dealt two crippling jolts. The group broke out into more gasps, then cheers. They appeared to have done it!

After some high-fiving, John turned back to Jimmy. "It looks like we hit it with an explosive! How could an electrical charge have done that?"

"Who knows what the Soviets were using in their capacitors and condensers back then. Ever seen a transformer box up on a telephone pole explode?" asked Jimmy. "Especially one that gets hit by lightning?"

Good point," said John. "Jimmy, if there is any juice still left in that taser battery, perhaps you should maneuver it around and take some surgical shots at any communications arrays. Be sure to attach our rocket somehow, so ICE can continue to track the dead bird.

"Oh, and Jimmy," John added with a little lightheartedness, "maybe you could share the trigger button with your colleagues, here," goading Jimmy to reward the team members with a little "stick time" to finish the kill.

Jimmy got a funny look on his face, first worrying that he had committed some faux pas, and then realizing this was just to let everyone get to play a little whack-a-mole with the satellite. Everyone wanted one swing at the piñata.

"Absolutely, John. Let's go in reverse alphabetical order, like in school," he offered.

The 1983 satellite was indeed the Firebird, and it was now successfully decommissioned.

John used an encrypted phone app to text a message to Majedah, Jill and Wayne. It simply said, "Confirmed, mission success. Firebird is now dead space junk."

The next hour was spent with each team member taking a swat at the Firebird piñata. They used the retro rocket to maneuver the attack rocket's nose over to Firebird's antennae array, and then took turns administering taser shots. Although the discharging battery reduced the strength of the taser jolts, each team member got the satisfaction of getting in a hit.

When the last taser shots had been fired, Jimmy used the remaining retro rocket to forcibly dock the rocket into Firebird by entangling the rocket with the Firebird antennae array. That way, the rocket's communications system would now effectively track the location of the dead Firebird.

As Jimmy completed the forced docking, John remarked, "Pity to whomever has to take charge of cleaning up this Chernobyl-in-orbit. That's tomorrow's problem — who the hell do we tell about this?"

Milo chimed in, "I think that is a good topic for an appropriate after-action meet-up. Paris?"

ALL HELL BREAKS LOOSE

Doha.

Taras watched, trying not to give away his anxiety, as Mr. Abdullah's associate tried for five minutes to input the satellite control code. The code successfully logged them in to the Firebird command dashboard, but any command given after the log-in resulted in the message "System failure, could not connect to the indicated gateway."

"Let me try that," Shimko said. The next hour became increasingly uncomfortable, as Shimko began to lose his cool as he tried to connect with the Firebird satellite.

Finally, the realization took hold with all the people in the Doha hotel room that they could not communicate with Firebird. No one in the room knew it yet, but the inability to contact Firebird was permanent – Firebird was a dead and lost satellite. John Gabriel's mission had successfully delivered several 55,000-volt charges to Firebird and electrocuted its telemetry and electrical systems.

Elsewhere.

Once Jill received John's "Firebird is dead" message, she hit "send" on a follow-up email to Vernon Cutcher, copying the DHS inspector general. "Could we all please meet on this matter?" her email asked.

Majedah received John's text and placed a call. "This is Majedah. Go ahead and post the first initiative, the Osiris 2 messaging." Moments later, a cryptic message was placed by a Mossad operative on a hacker bulletin board. It included a link originating from a Russian blog stating that China had successfully scammed ISIS out of $500 million by selling them a dead Soviet-era satellite. According to the site, the money was to be used by China to fund the costs of razing mosques in China's "Silk Road" territories. These wild claims were intended to ensure wide circulation of the rumor.

It took less than a day for the rumors to percolate up to the mainstream media and diplomatic corps, as well as into the Islamic mainstream media. The damage and setback could last years.

A few days later, one enraged ISIS-connected imam declared a fatwa on Putin as well as Xi. A few angry jihadist demonstrations sprang up at various Russian and Chinese embassies in the Middle East.

Michael W. Barnes

A VISIT WITH A SENATOR

Palmer had flown into Washington, DC, and after receiving John's text, he called for an immediate meeting with Senator Baxter. An hour later, Wayne Palmer and Senator Baxter sat together. It was a curt meeting. Palmer showed Senator Baxter the highlights from the Percy Lacksman dossier. Percy, as the senator's chief of staff who had a fair amount of influence on the senator's powerful aerospace oversight committee, was known as Baxter's right-hand man.

As Baxter looked at the dossier, Wayne Palmer advised Senator Baxter that Kyle Duke of the Wall Street Journal had just been called and was on his way to Palmer's office in New York City. The reporter was going to be handed two files. The first file was the one sitting in front of Senator Baxter, outing Lacksman as a traitor. It detailed precisely how Senator Baxter's Chief of Staff had been doing paid espionage work for Russian interests.

Palmer explained that Senator Baxter was being given a choice as to which second file would be provided to the reporters. The first alternative file consisted of reams of opposition research, strongly hinting that Senator Baxter had an unsound close relationship with Lacksman, and that Baxter had refused to fire Lacksman several weeks ago when first presented with the evidence that Lacksman was a traitor. It appeared that Baxter had attempted a cover-up of Lacksman's treason and payoffs.

The second alternative file would contain the transcript of a recorded statement, which Senator Baxter would record in a few moments on Wayne Palmer's HD cell camera, and which would be released just a few minutes later. Baxter's statement would denounce the Transparency Act and its amendment as having facilitated Percy Lacksman's spying, and announce that Baxter was joining as a co-sponsor of the pending repeal bill of the executive orders and the Transparency Act amendment. Baxter's statement would also include that Senator Baxter was sending the bill to the floor with the recommendation of his committee. This would result in the repeal bill having the veto-proof support of 67 members of the Senate. Seymour Gacy's Transparency Act would effectively be dead.

Wayne Palmer told Baxter that if he complied and recorded the statement, Wayne would give him the dossier on Lacksman, and would let Baxter himself alert the FBI as to Lacksman's espionage, thus allowing Baxter to take credit for busting his aide. Baxter would look like a hero. If not, the career-ending scandal for Baxter would be in full media swing within an hour. Career-ending, and potentially criminal.

Wayne told the senator he had five minutes to make up his mind, and that one minute had already passed.

Baxter was no fool. He immediately agreed to record the video statement and to call the FBI to take credit for exposing Lacksman. Wayne Palmer pulled a one-page talking points memo from his bag and handed it to Baxter. He then pulled out his high-def phone camera and attached it to a small tripod.

"Camera rolls in thirty seconds, are you ready, Senator?" asked Wayne.

Four minutes later – it took several takes to get it right – Senator Baxter had announced his position on the Transparency Act. Wayne Palmer uploaded the video to his press director right from Baxter's living room, and then he packed up his things to leave.

"There's one other thing, Senator. Kyle Duke at the Wall Street Journal was also advised that you'd be making a public statement in sixty minutes, and I believe the Journal's DC office has a camera crew on their way to your house right now. Good luck with this, and congratulations on unmasking this traitor," said Palmer.

He handed Baxter the thick file on Lacksman, shook Baxter's hand, and walked out.

Moments later, Senator Baxter was on the phone with his chief counsel, arranging for a call with the FBI regarding an urgent issue of national importance.

ACCELERATING TOWARDS HELL

Because of the intricacies of the flow of funds from the Doha closing of the Firebird sale, some of the intermediaries involved had already been wired their monies. This included Percy Lacksman, whose payment had already been wired to his offshore account. The particulars of Percy's offshore account were in the dossier provided to Wayne

Palmer, which in turn was given to Senator Baxter, who in turn provided it to the FBI as well as The Wall Street Journal. All of the details of the $500 million of transfers were there, too.

A few hours after Wayne Palmer's visit to Baxter, Percy Lacksman was on the phone with his credit card company, angry that he had received two notices that his card charges had been denied. Percy demanded to speak with a supervisor, and after a few minutes a representative told him all they could reveal at this time was that Percy's accounts had a "hold" placed on them. The Treasury Department and the DHS had ordered the account freeze. In reality, the freeze had been initiated by Vernon Cutcher, general counsel of the DHS, a few minutes after he had received Jill Serrano's email.

As Lacksman angrily argued with the banker on the phone, the cable news show on Percy's television screen was interrupted with a breaking story. "A spy ring inside a powerful congressional committee has been exposed by Senator Baxter." The screen then cut to a picture of Lacksman, including a screen shot of the amount that had been wired to his offshore account. Lacksman watched in disbelief as he slowly hung up the phone. He broke into a profuse sweat and began to bounce from wall to wall in his living room. Then he began to wail uncontrollably.

Moments later, there was a loud knock on his door, which became a pounding. "FBI – please open the door now," came the booming voice. Seconds later, his front door violently swung open, with the lock smashing out of the door jamb. Six FBI agents flooded into Percy's apartment, adorned in blue jackets with bright yellow "FBI" lettering and with their guns drawn.

HELL CAN'T GET MORE LOOSE

After almost two hours spent in an increasingly frantic effort to re-establish contact with the Firebird satellite, Mohammed Abdullah finished a phone call with his principal, Nadim Badr Rachid. Mr. Abdullah told Taras Shimko that Taras needed to meet immediately with the buyer to straighten things out. In the same manner as before, Taras was escorted from the Doha hotel room by Abdullah's security patrol, with a black-out bag placed on his head before leaving the room. Minutes later, with the bag still on his head, Taras was placed in the back seat of an SUV, which then exited the hotel garage. After a 15-minute drive, the SUV pulled over. A heavy iron baton cracked Taras' skull, and a bright flash was the final impulse his brain ever processed. His naked body was dumped in the city landfill an hour later.

Ilene Meinhoff called Seymour Gacy, alarmed.

"One of our guys just got busted. Lacksman, Percy Lacksman, chief of staff on Senator Baxter's aerospace committee," she said.

"He was a passive placement, wasn't he?" asked Seymour Gacy.

"Yes, he's a patsy," said Ilene. "There is no connection to us, but it's already all over the news. Apparently, he's being charged with espionage."

"Was there any advance notice of this?" Seymour asked.

"No, I had no idea. And that's what worries me. I don't know where this came from, and I don't like it. There will be reporters and scrutiny all over this," said Ilene.

Seymour thought for a moment, and said, "Baxter is one of our key guys in holding on to the Senate vote. I need you to do two things. First, get to Baxter and make sure he remains with us. Exert our maximum leverage. And second, you need to commence complete damage control, immediately. Scrub everything related to this Lacksman," directed Gacy.

"Will do. I already cued an Orange Fire protocol. I'll activate it now. It will be clean within thirty minutes," said Ilene, referring to the file cleansing procedures that Gacy's organization had in place to avoid detection of Gacy's syndicate of informers and agents.

"And Ilene, it goes without saying, but I'll say it. Find out who did this. Who is behind this? I want answers," commanded Gacy.

After he hung up, Seymour contemplated the situation. Then he began speaking as if he was talking to the caged birds in his study, but in reality he was speaking only to himself. "Whoever is behind this, they have no idea who they have fucked with," he said with a curing fury. "They are not going to just disappear. That's too kind. They are going to become very famous. Their lives will become the definition of hell, played out in public, presented for all to see. Their punishment will be my message - Do not oppose me. Ever," he finished.

Yoko Senstra was seated at a Georgetown restaurant surrounded by non-descript foreigners. Without warning, two clean-cut men in business suits, classic FBI, approached her table. They showed their badges and asked her to accompany them. Senstra began to make a scene and scolded them with, "How dare you? Do you know who I am?" and finally, "Get the hell away from me!" Two additional agents approached her table. She was lifted from her chair by both arms, arrested, handcuffed, read her rights and led away. It was all done very publicly.

Even though it was a tony restaurant, several diners pulled out their cellphone cameras and recorded the scene. Pictures and video were uploaded to social media within minutes, and the Washington DC bureaus of the cable news channels began playing the videos in endless repetition later that day. Analysts and opposition researchers were paraded in as guests speculating as to the mysterious arrestee Yoko Senstra, listing what nefarious crimes may be involved and asking "How high could this go?" Later, one cable channel, on the strength of a confidential tip from Senator Baxter's office, began to report that "reliable sources" confirmed that the arrest of Yoka Senstra was connected to the Percy Lacksman spy ring.

The chase and capture were just beginning.

When Senator Baxter's video denouncing the Transparency Act hit the media later that day, the smart money knew that the political winds had just changed. The House and Senate leaderships raced with each other to see which house of Congress could move faster and more forcefully against the Transparency Act. The House of Representatives had already voted four times to repeal President Jackson's executive orders under the Transparency Act, but the Speaker of the House wasn't about to let this publicity opportunity go to waste. The next morning, full debate commenced on over ten bills, each repealing various sections of the Transparency Act. By the end of the day, eight of the ten Bills had been passed by the House by veto-proof majorities, gutting the Transparency Act. Now it was up to the Senate.

Knowing that the Senate vote could over-ride any presidential veto, the Senate Majority Leader convened a session to vote on one of the old House bills, which cleanly repealed Jackson's executive orders. It passed the Senate, 77-13, with ten abstentions. It was a rout. Once it was clear that the bill would pass with enough votes to override any veto, an additional ten senators had flipped their votes.

The senators then began a day and a half of additional amendments and speeches, jumping on the legislative bandwagon. By the end of the next day, the Senate had also passed the same bills as the House. Ordinarily a conference committee would then convene to iron out any differences between the two versions, but the House and Senate leaders were not going to miss the publicity opportunities of this event.

A conforming bill was agreed upon by the leaders that

evening and put to vote on both floors the next morning. The sporadic procedural objections by a few loyalists to Seymour Gacy were steamrolled. By noon the next day, the omnibus Transparency Act Amendments were passed by both houses of Congress and delivered to President Jackson. Whether Jackson would actually veto it, or just let it sit for ten days unsigned to accomplish a Constitutional pocket veto, didn't matter. In eleven days, the Congress would overrule any such Presidential veto with the two-thirds majority vote now easily achievable. The Transparency Act was soon to be repealed.

Ilene Meinhoff called various senators non-stop to make threats to try to stave off the defeat. But few would even take her calls. One junior senator from South Dakota, Senator Quintin Whitley, actually did answer. Meinhoff threatened Senator Whitley regarding past campaign contributions and threatened to fund $2 million against Whitley in both a primary and general election opposition campaigns if Whitley did not comply with Ilene's demands regarding the vote.

Senator Whitley listened, and then said simply, "Ms. Meinhoff, I should advise you and your boss, Seymour Gacy, that under the federal Wiretap Act of 1968, as well as several laws enacted by the great state of South Dakota, this conversation has been recorded. And I have every intention not only of providing a copy of this recording to the FBI, but also using it in my own reelection campaign ads, showing that Senator Quintin Whitley cannot be bought by dirty money. Quintin Whitley is transparent and clean.

I can only hope my opponents don't take Gacy's money, either. Gacy is a foreigner, after all, so accepting his bribes would be a felony."

And then Senator Whitley hung up.

No politician had ever spoken to Ilene Meinhoff like that. Their fear of Meinhoff was gone.

This revolution was in full swing, and it was destined to be televised. Such was the nature of these things.

Ilene Meinhoff had called President Jackson demanding that he figure out a way to stop the repeal of the Transparency Act. Ilene's call was routed to Helen West, a long-time staffer of President Howard Jackson.

President Jackson had asked Helen for advice on how to handle Ilene Meinhoff and her boss Seymour Gacy. Helen loathed Seymour Gacy. She remembered Seymour Gacy well, from his meeting with Howard Jackson so long ago when Gacy became an early big-money Jackson donor, with the quid pro quo that Jackson would support Gacy's Transparency Act power schemes in exchange for Gacy's funding. Helen gave Jackson her recommendation, and after discussing it with the First Lady and other advisors, Jackson told Helen that her idea was brilliant and that she should put it into motion.

After a few key meetings, including the drafting of various documents, Helen returned Ilene's call. As Ilene began to speak heatedly to Helen, Helen interrupted. "Ms. Meinhoff, please let Seymour Gacy know that President Jackson will be issuing an executive order next week, in fact on the day before the President signs Congress' repeal of the Transparency Act. The President's executive order will grant clemency to anyone currently under investigation under the Transparency Act. Everyone - except for you and Seymour Gacy.

"Your machinations and extortion constitute felonies under the Transparency Act. Its repeal only applies going forward. You and Seymour Gacy are the only people whose actions are still criminal under the Transparency Act. And know this: If you ever try again to extort President Jackson, or me, or anyone associated with us, you and Gacy will be criminally prosecuted under the Transparency Act. You and Gacy will be destroyed, and Gacy's assets will be frozen immediately. You will go down in history as being the most famous indictments and convictions under the Transparency Act.

"And Ilene, one more thing. Go fuck yourself."

And with that, Helen West hung up.

TREASURE LOST TO THE HELL STORM

Mohammed Abdullah was sweating. It was a mild anxiety attack, but it was getting worse. He was not used to feeling out of control, and he had not anticipated that the satellite dashboard would be dead. His technical advisors had run through several demonstrations conducted by Taras Shimko. How could it have been a hoax? How could Shimko have thought he could steal from them? It must have been a set-up, he concluded. Nadim Badr Rachid was not going to be pleased.

But because of the covert payment methods involved, the dispatch of the $500 million purchase price had already occurred. Nadim Badr Rachid would not only be unhappy, he would be livid. Blood livid. Livid at Abdullah.

One-hundred-twenty-five million dollars had been paid late that morning, concurrently with the announcement of that day's London Gold Fix. It had been paid by one of Nadim Badr Rachid's front companies putting in a transfer order for $125 million of its gold bullion, to be disbursed from its bullion on deposit with the Bank of London to the numbered account for a shell company owned by Taras Shimko. A vault employee at the Bank of London had dutifully removed 275 gold ingots, each weighing 33 lbs., from Rachid's gold locker and placed the gold ingots into an account cage marked "Allocated Transfer Pending." Once those bars had been removed from Rashid's locker, they were no longer his property. Each gold bar bore an engraved certification, "London Good Delivery."

But this transaction was not going to be a good delivery. A few minutes later, the Bank of London vault manager appeared along with four detectives from Scotland Yard, and placed a "Do Not Transfer – Impound Order" label on each of the 275 ingots, with each label bearing a serial number. The chance that Nadim Badr Rachid would ever recover those 275 gold ingots was zero.

An additional $250 million was captured via a freeze order as the funds passed through a SWIFT intermediary bank in Switzerland. Rachid's front company had caused a Cyprus bank to post a letter of credit, drawable against a Lichtenstein bank's branch in Basel, Switzerland, payable to Taras Shimko's bank in Panama. As the transaction accounting attempted to clear through the Bank of International Settlements' bureau in London, the red flag had been inserted just hours earlier. $250 million had left Rachid's bank account never to be returned.

The final $125 million was deliverable in the form of a tanker full of oil. That trade came to an abrupt halt, as a US Coast Guard cutter pulled alongside the oil tanker as it was docking at the Louisiana Offshore Oil Port in the Gulf of Mexico. Coast Guard Admiral Louis Sully and two local functionaries bearing writs of seizure from four different courts – one in Lafourche Parish, Louisiana, one in Orleans Parish, Louisiana, another in New York City and another in London, England — presented seizure papers to the tanker's captain. Admiral Sully also had eight armed Guardsmen, two US Marshalls and a Coast Guard helicopter hovering nearby. It was a show of force. Both the Guardsmens' and Marshalls' publicists dutifully recorded the intercession on video. It was recruiting video-quality stuff in the making.

Admiral Sully directed the captain of the tanker to surrender command of the tanker, which he did without incident. Within a day, the oil would be offloaded, not for the account of Taras Shimko's shell company, but to the impound account of the United States Marshall for the Eastern District of Louisiana. Minor courtroom spats would ensue among Texas, Mississippi, Alabama, and Florida as to which states had colorable jurisdiction over the impounded oil and its proceeds, given that the capture had occurred at a deep-water port in the Gulf of Mexico.

Mere quibbles, though, in the larger scheme.

Nadim Badr Rachid's money was gone.

A STAR RISES AT DHS

Jill Serrano and Vernon Cutcher sat in a joint meeting with the Secretary of the Department of Homeland Security and a deputy US Attorney General.

"Before we go through these details, Ms. Serrano, I just want to say to you that I guess I initially underestimated you. It is reassuring and invigorating to see someone as capable as you working in the public interest. I might add a personal note, that I enjoy working with you, and if in any way I misstepped by underestimating you, let me start again. I'm old enough to admit my mistakes, but young enough to change when needed," Vernon Cutcher said.

"Thank you, Mr. Cutcher. I look forward to a long working relationship with you. And please... call me Jill," she said.

"Okay, Jill. Great work. You're a hero. And frankly, we need your kind of know-how. We need our people to be more like you. So please walk us through how you figured out there was something wrong with this Lacksman guy," Vernon said.

It was a great start of a great meeting.

A PRIVATE AFFAIR IN TEL AVIV

John Gabriel entered the nondescript office building and gave his name to the security guard sitting outside the interior security perimeter. There were armed security guards about. He was jetlagged but energized. A strong coffee at a Tel Aviv café had helped. A few moments later, Rebecca Biton emerged from the elevator and joined John at the security reception desk.

"I'm glad you made it, Mr. Gabriel. You are right on time. I hope this turns out to be okay," she said a bit nervously.

Rebecca had called John two days ago. Being privy to her boss' personal life – or lack thereof – Rebecca had decided to take things into her own hands. For the good of her boss. She had obtained approval from internal affairs to the extent that there really was any approval process for these sorts of things. Surprises were not really part of the *modus operandus* at an IDF/Mossad office building.

After a screening with two armed security guards including an x-ray exam, a thorough pat-down, and with his visitor badge in place, John was escorted by Rebecca to the elevator and up to the third floor. An armed IDF soldier was stationed in the elevator. As they exited, Rebecca led John to a set of double doors, again with a soldier at guard. The guard nodded, and Rebecca opened one door, and then entered the vestibule of a paneled conference room. About

20 people were assembled there, facing a riser at the other end of the room.

John and Rebecca squeezed in among the small crowd, and shortly thereafter two men emerged and took to the dais. One spoke briefly, and then Majedah Simon emerged from the holding room and joined them. From the other holding room, the Prime Minister of Israel entered. Brief words of commendation were spoken, and the Prime Minister then presented Majedah with a medal for her meritorious action in both the ISIS false-flag operation and the recent Firebird satellite operation. The small crowd of coworkers applauded. A few pictures were taken, and then the ceremony was all but over.

Some members of the audience lingered and gave personal congratulations to Colonel Simon. As the remaining people dispersed, Majedah looked over at Rebecca and saw John standing with her. A momentary look of confusion came to her face, but it quickly resolved itself into a bit of a blush and a smile, as she saw both Rebecca and John break into smiles.

"Get over there. Now!" Rebecca said to John.

John walked over to Majedah, and as he was about to extend his hand in a professional manner, Majedah somewhat clumsily pulled him forward to give him a hug and put her cheek to his, and said quietly, "What are you doing here? I mean… I… Did you come all the way here for this?" It was unrehearsed, but the surprise and smile on her face revealed all. As did John's.

"Congratulations, Colonel Simon," said John, as if one of Majedah's colleagues was still within earshot.

And then John dropped his voice a few decibels, as if some sort of discretion was required. "Do you think you might be able to find time in your busy schedule to make good on that dinner promise?" asked John.

Majedah looked over at Rebecca, who was hovering just a few yards away. "Were you in on this?" Majedah asked, with a mock rebuke of her assistant. Rebecca just smiled and gave an innocent shrug as she turned and walked away.

Majedah looked at John, not really doing a very good job at containing a happy smile. "I would be delighted if we could have dinner tonight, Mr. Gabriel."

After a beat, John said, "Will we need to include additional chairs for security detail in that reservation?"

Majedah's training could not conceal the slight blush that appeared on her face as she enjoyed the implied compliment. "I think Rebecca can arrange for an appropriate place. For just the two of us."

"Perfect," said John.

BOTH SIDES OF A GARDEN

The next morning, John rose before sunrise. He sat in a lounge chair covered by a warm blanket nursing a cup of coffee. He gazed through a set of glass French doors which opened out to a path through a walled garden. It was dead calm and only the faint sound of a few chirping birds could be heard. Tranquility governed the room.

Majedah quietly emerged from her bedroom, clad only in a short nightshirt. She gently picked up her wool shawl from the past evening and wrapped it around herself. She approached John from behind his chair and slowly and silently slid her arms around his shoulders. After a moment, John said softly, "Hi."

"Hi," replied Majedah.

Majedah let her head rest against John's. They remained that way for a minute. Neither wanted to interfere with the serenity of the moment. The first rays of the sun were moments from their debut.

Almost in a whisper, Majedah said, "I like this."

Minutes passed as the sun began to break, illuminating parts of the garden.

Still wrapped around John, Majedah spoke again. "There's something I like to play when I watch it." She gently unwound her arms and moved across the room. She cued the music, and half a minute later she was right back where she had been, with her arms around John's shoulders and her head again resting against his.

"Pachelbel," she said. "Magic."

Very softly, the sounds of Canon in D began to fill the room. After a minute or two, John turned slightly towards her and asked, "Which side of the garden are you in right now?"

Majedah thought in silence for a moment. "Both," she said.

Weeks Later

CELL RECEPTION IN THE HIGH DESERT

JIMMY BEDFORD AND his ICE-3 team watched as the final preparations were made in the bright winter sun of the high desert. It was launch day for another balloon array, and this one looked suspiciously like the balloon array they had used a few months earlier to disable the Firebird satellite, including with a rocket attached to a centrifuge arm.

Wayne Palmer had indeed paid John Gabriel the promised "bonus" for getting Senator Baxter's vote switched – a second General Science rocket had been delivered to John's CKS team. As a thank you, John had presented the rocket to Jimmy Bedford and his ICE-3 geek squad along with the suggestion that their decrepit ICE-3 satellite could use a little upgrading, delivered right to it in orbit like a pepperoni pizza.

Jimmy and several of his satellite chasers were now about to send aloft a long overdue care package to the aging ICE-3 satellite. Jimmy's rocket would not be delivering a taser shock to Firebird, but rather a series of bolt-on payload pods to the ICE-3 craft which would upgrade the decades-old ICE-3 satellite into a modern operational communications satellite.

John Gabriel, Wayne Palmer, Milo Patton, Nick de Stijl, Mike Shepard, Brian Dietz, Scott Canto and Luke Mandeville and a few other Firebird team members sat in folding picnic chairs under several sun canopies, enjoying the spectacle. Wayne Palmer had brought along his engineer Terry Sands and several key technicians who were intensely focused on the workings of the spinner arm and some adjustments they had already engineered to John's original design.

What a difference it made when there was no international world war emergency as the backdrop of a launch party.

As the team completed their launch preparations and the balloons were filling with helium, a small plume of dust arose on the horizon as a lone pickup truck approached on the high desert dirt road. Perhaps it was a local rancher. John kept an eye on the truck for several minutes, at times noticing an occasional dust devil kicked up by the truck as it approached his group's camp.

The truck finally pulled up about 20 yards from John's chair. The engine shut off, and the driver's window lowered.

With her sunglasses still in place, Jill Serrano stuck her head out.

"Is this the drone convention? I heard there's some kinda wine event that's meeting out here," Jill said, with a wry smile on her face. "I heard there's a couple of rules, but that I'm not supposed to talk about the rules."

John had stood up, and he looked at the group and took off his cap. He glanced at Wayne Palmer and mockingly asked, "Did you invite her?" Then he wiped a bit of dusty sweat off of his forehead, brushed back his hair with one hand and replaced his cap.

"It's invitation only," John replied, play-acting a bit.

"Oh yeah? Well…how might somebody get an invitation?" asked Jill.

John looked at his wine glass and replied, "It's kind of a Bring-Your-Own-Bottle sort of thing. Kinda."

"Well, I brought some cold Sonoma chardonnay and rosé," replied Jill, "but I might need a glass and a corkscrew."

"You're not with the fire marshal, are you?" John asked.

Jill slipped out of the truck door, holding a cooler bag with a couple of bottles of wine. Her clothing was straight out of a high-end beer ad, except she looked natural in it. Worn jeans, a sun hat and well-worn cowboy boots that looked like they'd been in use for a decade or more.

"Not today I'm not," Jill joked back.

Other than Luke, John had not told any of the group that Jill would be joining them. John stepped up and greeted her with a hug. "Glad you made it," he said.

"Me too," said Jill. She gazed around the small makeshift viewing stand. "I think."

Luke grabbed Jill's bag and handed her a glass. As the group watched, not quite sure if Jill's unexpected appearance was a good thing or not, and before John could make introductions, she walked straight over to Wayne Palmer, who rose from his chair as she approached.

"Hi Wayne," Jill said without missing a beat. "May I sit here? I'm kinda thirsty."

It took a second for Wayne to regain his grounding. He now fully recognized Jill and jumped right in.

"Do you know the password? I mean, we don't just let anybody into this club," Wayne said with a slight laugh.

Jill sat down in the chair as John approached with a bottle of wine. As he poured it for Jill, he said, "Mermaid."

Jill turned to Wayne and repeated, "Mermaid," as if saying the password through the door of a speakeasy.

"Mermaid," repeated Wayne as he sat back down next to Jill, glass in hand. "So the password is 'mermaid'?" After a beat he said, "Christ, Gabriel, you and your dang mermaids!"

Jill caught John's eye and she raised her glass slightly. He raised his glass almost imperceptibly, and they sipped a private toast.

THE SOVIET FIREBIRD SATELLITE PROGRAM

The Clash of Cold War Warriors – 1980's

The 1980s were the depth and endgame of the 40-year war known as the "Cold War" between the United States and the Soviet Union. The United States and its allies – the so-called First World – were squared off against the totalitarian Soviet empire – the Second World – for world domination.[28] The Cold War was the term for this decades-long clash of Soviet military expansionism against the United States' policy of stopping any such expansionism without there being a direct war between the two superpowers. Soviet political theory mandated totalitarian control over markets and people; otherwise, the Soviet empire would implode on account of the natural proclivity of people to want to organize their own lives. Like a mammal's need for oxygen, expansionism was an existential part of Soviet policy.[29]

The United States countered the Soviet's Cold War expansionist aggression with a patchwork policy of "containment," whereby the attempts by the Soviets to take over Third World [30] developing countries was be countered by direct American economic and military support of those countries.[31]

Along with expansionism, the Soviets maintained a massive nuclear arsenal with which they could threaten nuclear devastation on America or any other country. The American counterstrategy to the Soviet nuclear threat was for American to maintain its own large nuclear arsenal. The sheer number of nuclear weapons rendered the Soviet nuclear threat insufficient to guarantee the Soviets that they could survive any nuclear confrontation. The strategic balance became one of "MAD," or mutually assured destruction. This strategic stalemate was based upon the theory that neither the U.S. nor the U.S.S.R. would use its nuclear arsenal upon the other in a first strike, because no one side could destroy enough of the other side's thousands of nuclear weapons to ensure that the initial attack would not automatically be met with one (or many) nuclear counterstrikes against it in a retaliatory, tit-for-tat counterstrike.[32] So if one side launched its own nuclear missiles first – the so-called "first strike" - it nonetheless gained nothing, other than a guarantee that it would be destroyed by hundreds of nuclear weapons an hour later.

The Extraordinary Month of March 1983

March of 1983 was an extraordinary month. Ronald Reagan was midway through his first term as United States President, and remained an anomaly in American politics. A former actor turned California governor, he was also an ardent anti-communist, having witnessed the methods and effectiveness of the communist movement in Hollywood labor unions after WWII.[33]

Reagan took office in early 1981, and barely survived an assassin's bullet less than two months thereafter. His administration inherited a nation in military and economic decline that was losing the Cold War. This decline was masked by a number of fancy words and doublespeak.[34] One common doublespeak of the era was the term "détente,"[35] which was a rebranding of the 1930's foreign policy of appeasement. Détente was marketed to Americans as a positive thing. Another doublespeak was the late 1970's reference to there being a national "malaise"[36] in the attitudes of Americans, meant to imply that the Americans had come to have too high of expectations.[37] This malaise was not blamed upon poor policy choices by American leaders, but rather was blamed on a hostile Arab oil cartel manipulating worldwide prices to a level which crippled the Western economies.[38] In other words, outsiders were to blame, and the policy leaders of the most powerful economy and military in the world were blameless.

Reagan undertook policies to battle stagflation. Scores of notable economists signed letters and paid for full page newspaper advertisements criticizing him and his lunatic policies, which consisted of tax cuts, deregulating oil and gas production, and supporting the Federal Reserve's monetary policy of high interest rates to bleed out the inflationary expectations from industry and consumer sectors. In short, the policies worked brilliantly, albeit the country endured a year and a half of economic pain.

By 1983, Reagan was well on his way to having successfully tackled stagflation, and so the Reagan administration pivoted to foreign policy, which meant addressing the constant threat of nuclear annihilation that hung over the world as a feature of MAD and the Cold War. Where many continued to make the intellectual mistake of supporting some form of negotiated truce with the Soviet Union – i.e., détente - or even unilateral disarmament (as was popular on certain college campuses), President Reagan would have none of it.

The month of March 1983 featured American President Ronald Reagan delivering his famous "evil empire" speech, wherein Reagan warned against the fallacy of assigning moral equivalency to the competing U.S. and Soviet systems.

This was an extraordinary and unthinkable turn of events, equivalent to farting in a room of elites. Here stood Reagan stating publicly that it was wrong to think that the U.S. and the Soviets were somehow equally at fault for the Cold War, or that each was equally pressing legitimate objectives. To do so – to equivocate the two - would be to ignore that the Soviet Union was an "evil empire." To the diplomatic corps, this was an astonishing statement by a

U.S. President. It was so extraordinary, it was claimed that surely Reagan could not have meant it - it must have been a gaffe, and if not, it was hard evidence that Reagan was senile or simple-minded.

But it was not a gaffe; Reagan was just warming up. Because March of 1983 was like no other month. After his evil empire speech, in a televised address to the American people - which is what leaders did in those days - Ronald Reagan made an announcement that shocked the world:

> "I am directing a comprehensive and intensive effort to define a long-term research and development program to …eliminat[e] the threat posed by strategic nuclear missiles… Tonight we are launching an effort which holds the promise of changing the course of human history. There will be risks, and results take time. But I believe we can do it."

And with that, Reagan announced his Strategic Defense Initiative, which was an aggressive program to leverage the massive economic and technical superiority of the West to design and build a laser shield capable of shooting down Soviet nuclear weapons, thereby rendering them useless. The initiative's objective was that the nuclear threat of the Cold War would abate. Americans would someday no longer live under MAD; there would soon come a time when there would be no credible Soviet nuclear threat.[39]

At the same time, Reagan authorized a far more aggressive prosecution of the proxy wars in various Third World countries. Thus, Reagan directly countered the two key pillars of the Soviet expansionist policy – proxy wars and a nuclear threat.

To hardliners in the Soviet Union, Reagan's strategies were worrisome if not belligerent. They were the exact moves against which the Soviet Union had no long-term defense. No defense, in that the Soviets did not have an economy that was capable of paying for a new technological arms race and pouring unlimited men and materiel into proxy wars. To the Soviet hardliners, Reagan had just put the Cold War into its end-game phase. And, history would prove those hard-liners to have been spot-on correct, and the American intellectual class to have been flat wrong.

Soviet KGB chief Yuri Andropov was a ruthless and colorless man, having survived and thrived as head of the Soviet's secret police since the 1960s. Shortly after becoming head of state, Andropov suffered a kidney failure and began regular dialysis to stave-off his fast-approaching demise. Now with his kidney failure making him the e ultimate lame duck in the ruthless world of KGB intrigue and Politburo[40] maneuvering, Andropov knew his grip on power, and on life, would be short. This fueled his paranoia, honed by three decades as a Cold Warrior against the U.S.

Prior to Reagan becoming President, Andropov had played on a winning Soviet team. Andropov had co-engineered and enforced the victorious Soviet strategy of expansionism, which had prevailed in the 1960s and 1970s over the West's attempts at containment of Soviet expansionism and public expression of appeasement or détente. Andropov privately fretted that he would be denied the opportunity to battle against this newcomer cowboy,

Ronald Reagan, in a new chapter in the clash of Cold War empires.[41] But with only a few months to live, Yuri Andropov was figuratively powerless to take up the fight with Reagan. That would be for others in the Politburo.

How a Cold Warrior Launched a Soviet Nuclear Satellite

His body was dying, but the obsessive Andropov would still play his masterful coda in seeking a victory of the Soviets over the derelict West and its clarion, the United States.

Following the Evil Empire and SDI shocks of March 1983, Soviet Premier Andropov and his core Politburo team activated an emergency plan which had been in various stages since the late 1960s. It had originally been named the "Firebird Plan" after an old Slavic fable of a magical glowing bird. Andropov dusted off the Firebird Plan just weeks after Reagan's SDI announcement and secretly ordered it into full preparatory phase. Andropov, as head of both the KGB and the Politburo, understood the need for abject secrecy. Only a handful of persons knew of Firebird.

The Soviet Firebird Plan was reborn in reaction to Reagan's SDI "Star Wars" plan, and the Soviet fear of losing the nuclear arms race and a consequent rendering the Soviet nuclear arsenal to be ineffective. Andropov and his Politburo leaders were now faced with the possibility that Reagan's SDI would in fact render the Soviet intercontinental ballistic missiles to be ineffective. The Soviet Union had a nuclear missile threat against which the West had no defense, other than "mutually assured destruction."

The Soviet's threat helped them to project an aura of invincibility versus the U.S. in their conduct of proxy wars in the Third World. After all, rebels wanted to ally themselves with a predestined winner, not a loser. When Reagan's "Star Wars" program promised to neutralize the arsenal of Soviet nuclear missiles, the perception that the Soviets were invincible began to crack. Soon after came the realization that the Soviet Union was collapsing into the scrapheap of history. Those wars would become too expensive to fight if the almost inevitable Soviet victories were not so easily attained.[42]

By August of 1983, Andropov's cancerous kidneys had completely failed, and he checked into a state hospital, where he would remain on a dialysis machine. But he continued to direct his Firebird Plan.

Andropov used a standard play from the customary Soviet playbook: Propaganda by the State media to be rebroadcast by a network of knowing agents as well as dupes in the West. Andropov's propaganda was bold. He brazenly announced that the Soviets were "unilaterally abandoning all development of space-based weapons."

Andropov launched this propaganda program by memorandum to the Soviet Politburo members, and shortly thereafter by announcement through state media outlets Pravda and Izvestia, to activate the "useful idiot"[43] network worldwide. Per the Soviet propaganda playbook, following Andropov's announcement, there soon followed editorial support from the worldwide nuclear freeze movement,[44] and favorable coverage from key sympathetic media in the Western world.

It was the phraseology of the Soviet announcement that was important. The press releases stressed that the Soviets were "unilaterally abandoning all development of space-based weapons." This press was targeted at the Western media.

Decades later, it is impossible for a modern audience to understand the potency of the phrase, "unilaterally abandoning all development of space-based weapons," coming from the mouthpiece of the Soviet boss and falling on the ears of the détente adherents who defined the club of Western elites in the early 1980s. Similarly, a modern teenager would not understand the phenomenon of the appeal of a 1970s Farah Fawcett or Cheryl Tiegs swimsuit poster. But the sale of tens of millions of those posters ubiquitously displayed on every wall of every male between ages 13 and 22 at the time, proves the strength of the meme.

And likewise popular was the wholesale adoption by the early 1980s collegiate, media and political classes of the combined words "unilateral", "abandonment" and "weapons." It became a veritable religious belief. Those words were tony parlor porn for many in academia and government, as well as with the aspirants thereto, in the early 1980s. In colleges, millions memorized it, repeated it, and reaped the rewards of good grades from echo-chamber grad student teaching assistants. It was also helpful when trying for some late-night action from college coeds whose inhibitions dropped when confronted with a young man's earnest pledge of allegiance to "unilateral…abandonment… of weapons."

Exactly as Andropov intended, his "unilateral

abandonment" propaganda caused a furor in the West. How dare the Americans - and this stupid Reagan cowboy - unilaterally pursue a space-based Star Wars laser program? Had not the Soviets shown the proper way of civilized nations, by unilaterally abandoning such weaponization of space? Were not the Americans the ones at fault here? Wasn't America now the evil empire? Wasn't this evidence that perhaps Andropov, the KGB chief, really did just want a Nobel Peace Prize before he died? The pop culture bitingly reminded fans that even the Russians loved their children.

Successful propaganda, yes, but there was no "unilateral" Soviet abandonment. It was part of Andropov's cover for his actions – the execution of the Firebird Plan.

Since April, Andropov and a small team that included his defense minister, Dmitry Ustinov, armed a Soviet intercontinental missile with nuclear warheads. In October 1983, months after his unilateral disarmament pledge, Andropov and Ustinov presided over a secret orbital launch of a Soviet Proton-K rocket with 10 nuclear warheads. The launch had been delayed by a month because of the international press scrutiny regarding the Soviet Union's missile attack upon a civilian airliner, the Korean Airlines flight 007, the month before.[45]

KGB chief Victor Chebrikov was also tangentially involved in the Firebird launch, as it was in all affairs of state. But the KGBs role with the Firebird launch was largely to keep it confidential, given the intense international scrutiny of the KAL 007 shoot down just a month earlier. Other than Andropov, Defense Chief Ustinov and the KGB Chief Chebrikov, only a handful of technical and military personnel understood what was contained in the October 1983 launch payload aboard the Proton-K rocket.[46] Firebird was a bona fide Soviet state secret. Even the Politburo members themselves were not apprised by Andropov or Ustinov of its existence or details.

Pavel Gurin was a key Soviet missile scientist with the highest level of clearance, one of a few bona fide stewards of the Soviet missile and rocket fleet. Pavel acted as the technical point person for Firebird, and he was one of a very small group who knew the details of Firebird. Pavel Gurin himself selected and oversaw the key technicians who retrofitted the Proton-K with the payload of ten nuclear warheads.

International scrutiny of the KAL 007 attack began to dissipate, partly because Andropov, Ustinov and Chebrikov continued to pretend that the KAL 007 wreckage and flight recorder could not be found. (In fact, they had the black box in their possession, and Victor Chebrikov had reported that it convincingly revealed that Soviet's cover story about how the civilian jet was shot down was a complete fabrication). The hundreds of Western journalists who had been asking inconvenient questions about the location of eastern Soviet launch bases and other missile facilities, finally moved on to other stories. And so, the Firebird satellite was launched in October 1983 from a missile site less than a day's drive from the KAL 007 missile site. The Firebird launch was a success, with the 10 nuclear multiple independently targeted reentry vehicles (or "MIRVs") making it into orbit, and its details being "eyes only" with Andropov, Ustinov and Chebrikov.

The successful orbiting of the Firebird nuclear-armed

satellite could not reverse the inevitable for Andropov, who died a few months later on account of his failing kidneys. And without Andropov's support and protection, a few months later Defense Secretary Ustinov was eliminated from the Politburo inner circle by a shot to the head, reported by Pravda as "death by pneumonia."

The Firebird had managed to rise, but it was at best a bastard if not an orphan.

How The Soviets Forgot Ten Nuclear Bombs In Orbit

With both Andropov and Ustinov dead, and their close assistants dead or exiled to Siberia, the internal power struggle at the Kremlin resulted in a short-term appointment of Konstantin Chernenko as the Soviet leader. Terminally ill when appointed, Chernenko was dead a year after taking office, and in 1985 the reformer Mikhail Gorbachev became the General Secretary of the Soviet Union.

During this1984-1985 period of Kremlin chaos, only the non-political Pavel Gurin, the KGB chief Chebrikov, and a few of their key technicians retained any knowledge of the Firebird satellite and its secret nuclear payload. Chebrikov, overwhelmed with potential coups and palace intrigue at the Kremlin, paid scant attention to Andropov's secret Firebird nuclear array.

Gorbachev began a radical reorganization of Soviet policy beginning in 1985 with new policies of *"glasnost"* and *"perestroika,"*[47] and Chebrikov similarly was thus consumed with managing the stress of reorganizing the crumbling Soviet empire. Information was highly compartmentalized in the Soviet system, even more so during the crises periods that began in 1984. Chebrikov never did report to the Politburo any details of Andropov's Firebird satellite, in part out of fear that Gorbachev might attempt to bargain it away to Ronald Reagan in their various disarmament summits.[48]

Gorbachev's struggles against Soviet hard-liners resulted in his firing of Victor Chebrikov in 1988, and a year later the Berlin Wall fell. With the fall of the wall, known simply as "mauerfall" in Berlin, the Soviet Bloc was no longer overtly preventing people from leaving East Berlin. A mass exodus and brain drain by those trapped behind the Iron Curtain threatened the very existence of the Soviet Union, and over the next two years that ending played out.

But the Soviet walls, once breached, were not put back up. Instead, throughout 1990, the Soviet Bloc of states in eastern Europe and Asia broke away from Soviet control. By 1991, the constituent Soviet republics declared their independence from the USSR – similar to the Confederate States, one by one, seceding from the United States when Abraham Lincoln was elected in 1860.

As the Soviet empire disintegrated, by the summer of 1991 Gorbachev had lost the support of almost every key faction in the Kremlin. In a prior time – as recently as 1983, for example - Gorbachev would have been "disappeared" by the Politburo, with a bullet to the head and a subsequent announcement of his untimely death only after the new faction had taken control. Instead, in August 1991 an actual military coup d'état by the top echelon of Kremlin members was staged concurrently with an announcement that Gorbachev was "on vacation."

The coup was backed by almost the entire senior political and military leadership of the USSR — Gorbachev's
vice president, the Prime Minister, the Defense Minister,
the head of the KGB and many others. But for reasons
still debated, the short-lived coup failed, as key military
detachments refused to fire upon Soviet citizens who were
manning the defensive barricades in Moscow. As the coup
failed, the demise of the Soviet Union accelerated into
barely controlled chaos.

ENDNOTES

1   See the Annex at the end of this book, entitled "The Soviet Firebird Satellite Program".

2   "Siberia" was slang for a Soviet Gulag, which was a series of Soviet concentration camps for political prisoners and criminals from the 1920's until the early 1960's. Nobel Laureate Aleksandr Solzhenitsyn gave international exposure to the Gulags with his first-hand account in his 1973 book, *The Gulag Archipelago*. Twenty million Soviet people are estimated to have perished in the Gulags.

3   The small ruling elite of the totalitarian Soviet Union were often referred to as the "Kremlin," which was the building in which the offices of the Communist Party and the affiliated government bureaus were situated. It would be similar to referring to "Congress" or "The White House" to mean the United States government, except there were no effective separate branches of power in the Soviet Union. The terms "Kremlin" and "Politburo" respecting the ruling clique of the Soviet Union were interchangeable.

4   The Central Committee was a formalist body that administered the decisions of the Politburo.

5   The Al Jazeera broadcast network operating in Qatar was strongly criticized as being a mouthpiece of fundamentalist Islamists and as a propaganda media for jihad against the West. Later launched in the American market as Al Jazeera America, it folded less than three years later on account of low ratings.

6   Doha is a modern city and the capital of the oil-rich micro-state of Qatar. It sits on the Persian Gulf.

7   *So What?* is the first cut from the first side of Miles Davis' 1959 jazz album, *Kind of Blue*, which included saxophonist John Coltrane. It is a consistent top candidate for best jazz album of all time.

8   *Elevator to the Gallows* (in its original French, "*Ascenseur*

pour l'échafaud"), is a 1958 French crime thriller film directed by Louis Malle. Miles Davis scored its soundtrack in a single night.

9   A "rain-man" refers to a socially inept person who harbors some secret technical skill, typically math or computer programming.

10   Bermuda sits to the east of the Hatteras Abyssal Plain in the middle of nowhere in the Atlantic Ocean, but it was only a two-hour flight from most airports on the eastern seaboard, which makes it a favorite winter-time location for corporate retreats for doctors, lawyers and accountants.

11   This is the opposite of mere "malum prohibitum," or an act which happens to be prohibited by an authority, but which is not inherently wrongful (e.g., parking a car 5 feet into a red curb zone).

12   Blackwater was a high-profile mercenary and private security firm during the time of the Iraq War. The "Company" is slang for the Central Intelligence Agency.

13   Japan also entered a recession, which dried up some of the frenzied buying by Tokyo and its thirsty denizens, who had enjoyed their first real decade of good times since WW II. Amidst this, the 1989 Bordeaux vintage was exceptional and copious in quantity. Whether the 1989 was, ipso facto, the Black Tulip vintage - i.e., the signal of the top of a bubble market - is debatable.

14   Thousands of individuals had invested as "names" in Lloyd's business and become general guarantors of Lloyd's worldwide liabilities. Personal bankruptcy and court supervised administration resulted. Many of these now-bankrupted "names" faced months or longer of complete uncertainty as their life savings and funds were cut off.

15   The Druze is an ancient sect which incorporates elements of many religions, including Christianity and Islam. It is a tolerant religion which nonetheless was branded as heretical to Islam.

16   "Night of the Gliders" was a 1987 Palestinian guerilla attack into Israel staged from the south of Lebanon. Two Palestinians used hang gliders to launch a surprise attack

against an Israeli military camp. Six Israelis were killed and eight wounded. The attack was heralded as the beginning of the First Intifada, an ongoing military action by Palestinians against Israel. The attack exposed errors and lack of preparedness of the Israeli camp which caused a scandal in Israeli political and military circles.

17   In 1981, during the height of the Cold War, Israel successfully carried out a surprise air strike on an Iraqi nuclear reactor under construction just outside Baghdad. The preventative strike was by an elite team of Israeli airmen flying specially-fitted American F-16s, and the IDF mission was not cleared or coordinated with the U.S. Many world bodies decried the Israeli attack. However, upon being informed that Israel had carried out the attack using American jets, President Reagan commented to his senior aide, "Well, boys will be boys."

18   A slave collar, or punishment collar, was an unwieldy contraption of wrought iron that was fixed around a slave's neck, with three to six protruding arms that were one to three feet in length. Slave collars were used on slaves who had tried to escape their captivity. In addition to its great discomfort, the protruding arms made it extremely difficult to move through brush. Sometimes the arms had small bells attached as an escape alarm.

19   Brettanomyces, known colloquially to the wine trade as "brett," is a wild yeast which lives on grape skins, and when present in large amounts produces acetic acid, the taste of which can spoil an otherwise good wine. Most vintners generally try to control or eliminate 'brett in their wines.

20   TCA is short for tri-cloro-anisole, or "cork taint." It is a volatile chemical formed when chorine reacts with certain natural cork fungus, as is common in winery environments. Over time, TCA turns the aroma of a wine into wet cardboard, effectively destroying it.

21   In the 1971 Clint Eastwood film, *Play Misty for Me*, Clint plays a radio DJ who was a regular at a Carmel bar. When an attractive woman sat at the bar, Clint's bartender, played by real life Eastwood friend Don Siegel, pulled out a

saltshaker and shot glasses. Eastwood and the bartender arranged them on the bar, and began moving them around in turns, as if it were a game. There was no game. It was a nonsense arrangement, called "Cry Bastion" intended only to attract the pretty woman to come over and see what was going on. It worked in the film, except the woman was a bunny boiler. Bunny Boiler is slang for the Glenn Close stalker character in the 1987 film, *Fatal Attraction*.

22   In the past century, airborne weaponry and platforms represented a classic disruption of strategic military balance. At the start of WW II, Japan's Pacific carrier fleet and air squadrons were the equivalent of intercontinental ballistic missiles, able to make surprise attacks against unseen targets from far beyond the horizon. The US Pacific Fleet at Pearl Harbor was obliterated on account thereof. Just a few years later, the powerful WWII Japanese carrier-based air force had been destroyed, which enabled American bombers to evaporate half of Japan's cities by aerial fire-bombing, leading to Japan's unconditional surrender in 1945. In the 1944 Allied invasion of France, the once-powerful German Luftwaffe had functionally ceased to exist due largely to nightly bombing raids by Allied bombers. The lack of any German air cover greatly facilitated the historic success of the Allies' D-Day Invasion.

23   The Fractional Orbital Bombardment System (FOBS) was a Soviet missile program in the 1960s that could put a nuclear weapon into low earth orbit. The missile system was initially deployed in 1968, although it was reported that no nuclear missile was ever put into space. The missile program was banned by the 1967 Outer Space Treaty.

24   From the 1999 film, *Fight Club*: 1st rule: You do not talk about Fight Club. 2nd rule: You do not talk about Fight Club.

25   The New Castle Protocol was a confidentiality device that Tom Gallier had invented and described to John at their Paris meeting. It was a manner of sending a shipment of wine so that it could not be traced back to the sender, even

if a police agency with massive resources attempted the tracing. Because the value of some Bordeaux was so high, many senders needed to ship bottles in an untraceable manner to avoid triggering the threshold amounts on bribery laws, such as the Foreign Corrupt Practices Act. In other words, sending a couple bottles of wine might constitute a $10,000 bribe, so the New Castle Protocol cloaked the exchange. Its name was in reference to the Great Schism in the Catholic Church in the 14th Century, when a renegade papal faction set up a competing head-of-church papacy in Avignon, France, dubbed Chateauneuf du Pape (which translates to 'the Pope's new castle' in English.) Assassins and intrigue were abundant during the Great Schism, and basic supply lines between Rome and Avignon could be traced by assassins in order to locate and to kill competing factions vying for control over the papacy. Cloaking became the norm for any shipments between the two.

26   Spock and Captain Kirk were the fictional lead characters in the original late-1960's *Star Trek* television series. Spock was part alien, and generally exhibited logical personality traits without emotion. Kirk was human, and his emotions definitely guided his intellect and logic.

27   The Saturn-V rocket was the massive rocket used to launch the American Apollo astronauts to the moon.

28   The Cold War was an undeclared war from 1947 and 1991 between the United States and its Western European allies of the North Atlantic Treaty Organization (NATO), and the Soviet Union and its Warsaw Pact allies and puppet states. The term "Iron Curtain" was popularized by Winston Churchill to reference the Soviet's bloc of totalitarian states.

29   The Soviet Union's controlled economic governing system could only work if the entire world economy came under Soviet control. The Soviet policy of expansion was therefore deemed to be a state necessity, intended to eliminate the free markets which undermined the Soviet centrally planned economy. Its policies included the goal of termi-

nating the open Western democracies to which people (and business enterprises) would naturally flee to escape the totalitarian structure necessary to impose a controlled economy.

30 "Third World" referred to a developing country that was neither of the First World (the US and its allies) or the Second World (the Soviet Union and its Warsaw Pact allies).

31 Regional armed conflicts existed during the Cold War – constant, yet contained mini-wars confined to the Third World. They often were borne of run-of-the-mill civil wars, but the warring factions in these small wars were typically backed by the Soviets or the U.S., and thus they were referred to as "proxy wars."

32 This MAD scenario was ridiculed and denounced by many as being insane. Despite that, for 40 years it was successful, in that no nuclear weapons were deployed in any conflict.

33 Reagan was loathed by the international Left, including communists and socialists, because he had been a direct witness to their organizing activities in post-WW II Hollywood. Reagan forcefully exposed their organizations, and in response he was ridiculed by many as being delusional about the "red threat", and of being simplistic and naively patriotic. Regardless, history has since proven him to have been the most effective peace strategist in U.S. history, if actual results are the yardstick used.

34 "Doublespeak" refers to the intentional use of euphemisms and ambiguity in language to disguise, avoid or distort the meaning thereof.

35 "Détente" was the diplomatic term for a supposed easing of superpower tensions during the 1970s. Viewed from another perspective, it was a mere re-branding of the policy of appeasement. Upon taking office, Reagan confirmed that his hardline policy was replacing détente, announcing that détente had been a "one-way street that the Soviet Union has used to pursue its aims."

36 In July of 1979, President Carter spoke to the American people and exhorted them to abandon the expectations of

material prosperity under which the West had lived for 35 years. Instead, Carter urged Americans to adopt the trappings of faltered economies behind the Iron Curtain – specifically, to give up most air conditioning in the summer, to adapt to cold rooms in the winter and to forego driving cars and instead to use buses and carpools. The speech became known as the "malaise speech," which some argued was an implicit concession that Americans needed to accept that they were being defeated by Soviet aggression and the Middle East "OPEC" oil cartel. Candidate Reagan rejected such defeatist rhetoric, and in 1980 Carter lost his reelection bid to Reagan in a landslide.

37 The decade of the 1970's was marked by pervasive economic turmoil, most notably that inflation was eroding the standard of living for average Americans, and unemployment remained high. This persistent dual crisis was called "stagflation," i.e. stagnation + inflation. American political and economic policy failed to mitigate stagflation throughout the 1970's. By the time of Reagan's 1981 inauguration, inflation was above 10%, unemployment was at 7% (and rapidly rising towards 11%), and oil prices were at historic highs, crippling domestic output.

38 Reagan commenced a reversal of détente by allowing massive US natural gas and oil reserves to be tapped, which dropped the price of energy to the great benefit of the American economy, but also to the severe detriment of the Soviet Union. This price collapse denied the Soviets their main source of hard cash upon which its totalitarian command economy was built – selling energy to Europe. With these cheap energy programs and his active support of the Federal Reserve Chairman's massive hikes in interest rates to choke off inflationist mentalities, the American economy's long-cold fires turned red hot by early 1983, although Reagan's popularity temporarily plummeted prior to such rebound. He was re-elected in 1984 in an historic landslide.

39 Reagan's SDI announcement was viciously attacked in many circles, and it was derisively dubbed the "Star Wars"

defense after the popular motion picture series of the time. Being anti-Reagan was quite popular among policy wonks, professors, journalists and others who worked in hierarchical institutions that traded in thought policy. This antagonism arose in part because Reagan had no institutional intellectual credentials, and also because his center-right policies were in most cases directly inapposite of the left-leaning political and economic theories that had become accepted (if not dogmatic) during the prior 20 years. However, in the waning months of Reagan's second term, it became clear that his Cold War strategy was working, as the Soviet Union promised the UN that it would withdraw troops from occupied Eastern Europe. A few months after Reagan's last term ended (with Reagan's Vice President assuming the presidency), in the summer of 1989 various Soviet puppet states began to declare independence from the Soviet Union's control. By late 1989 the Berlin Wall fell and the "Second World" of the Soviet-aligned nations fell into full disintegration. Many on the political left harbor fervent negative opinions of Reagan, blaming him for crashing the "Second World" global collectivist state mechanism of the Soviet Union.

40   The Politburo was the ruling committee of the Communist Party in the Soviet Union. Because the Soviet Union government was controlled by a one-party system, party rule meant government rule. Soviet political subdivisions and governmental posts were mere functionaries of the Politburo.

41   By the 1970's, the disastrous outcome of the 1930s "peace in our time" appeasement policy of Neville Chamberlain (the British Prime Minister at the start of World War II) was two generations past and largely ignored by the new generation of policy makers. With the lessons of appeasement lost, an ill-fated pacifism and appeasement in response to Soviet aggression arose in the 1970s in a rebranded package as being part of an enlightened "détente" or "live and let live" strategy. It was exactly that slowly-creeping Soviet victory – thought by many, and

hoped for by others, to be an unstoppable expansion by the Soviets – that fueled a desire in many circles in the West for a negotiated peace with the Soviets. Others – like Reagan – argued that such was just a different name for appeasement and surrender to the Soviets. The existential question of the time was, "Better Red than Dead? Or Better Dead than Red?" Notably, both alternatives assumed a Soviet victory was inevitable.

42   In its proxy wars, the Soviets had two key advantages. First, the wars did not present an imminent threat to the daily lives of American citizens, so it was difficult for Western leaders to goad their citizens to rise up to the Soviet challenge. Second, the totalitarian Soviets had no meaningful anti-war pressure from their domestic home front. Accordingly, in a Soviet proxy war fought far from home, the Soviets and their "client states" were well-positioned to win a war of attrition – so long as these two key advantages were not disturbed. In practice, Soviet dogma and Third World communist guerillas all shared that tactic – to draw out a conflict and wait out the West, because eventually, it was thought that the West would always tire of the proxy war and leave. And territory by territory, over a generation the Soviets were victorious in the proxy wars. By the early 1980s, the Soviets were on a 15-year -long winning streak, having successfully expanded their client state system.

43   The term "useful idiot" has been attributed to Soviet founder Vladimir Lenin, and gained use in right-leaning groups in the West as a pejorative for communist and socialist sympathizers. The target of such epithet typically had a self-image as someone agitating for or promoting some honorable socialist cause that was in sympathy with the ideals of the Soviet Union, and therefore the person's motives were deemed to be unquestionably honorable. The Soviet mind generally viewed such a Western sympathizer as a lightweight disloyal patsy – that is, a useful idiot who naively and stupidly allowed themselves to advance the interests of the Soviet Union.

44   The international Left focused on fomenting dissent on

college campuses and large cities in America, and anti-nuclear protests were a daily occurrence at US campuses in the 1970s and 1980s. Most student participants did not realize that their organizing bodies were backed by the Soviet Communist Party and its operatives.

45   The Soviet Union's Air Force shot down a civilian airliner, Korean Air Lines Flight 007, in September 1983 over the Sea of Japan, near the Soviet Union's western Sakhalin Island area. The flight originated in New York City, connected through Anchorage Alaska, and was en route to its destination in Seoul, South Korea. 269 persons aboard died, including a US Congressman. The Soviets claimed that KAL 007 was a spy plane, a proposition for which no credible evidence was ever advanced. With the ailing Andropov clinging to power, the event elevated Cold War tensions - as well as internal Politburo strife and coup maneuvering - to a level that had not existed since the Cuban Missile Crisis of 1962.

46   The Proton K was a three-stage workhorse rocket for the Soviet military and space programs. It was used for over four decades, from the late 1960s until retirement around 2012. The Soviets used the Proton K in their failed attempts to beat the United States to the moon.

47   With respect to Soviet policy under Gorbachev, "*glasnost*" meant "publicity" or "government transparency," and "*perestroika*" meant "restructuring." Generally, these were posited as reflecting a reform-minded Soviet government, which was the opposite of Soviet hardliners' policy. These Gorbachev policies were strongly welcomed by the West. For political reasons, including the press loathing of Reagan, the American and Western European press generally did not credit Reagan's détente-ending policies for causing such Soviet policy changes. Following the fall of the Soviet Union in 1990 and the temporary opening of many Soviet state archives to Western researchers, such causal linkage between Reagan's policies and the Soviet collapse began to be widely documented. Reagan's policies – including his energy policies which ended the West's

subsidizing of the Soviet economy, and his SDI strategic missile initiative which the Soviet Union could not afford to keep pace with - did in fact collapse the Soviet Union in a bloodless end of the Cold War.

48   Gorbachev soberly realized that Reagan's strategy of using American economic power and advanced technology could not be countered by the Soviets. Gorbachev acted to prepare the calcified Soviet institutions for the coming changes which he understood were inevitable and which were quickly playing out due to Reagan's policies. He viewed those changes as vastly preferable to the Soviet hardliners' desire for war with America. Gorbachev thought that a nuclear arms treaty with the US was the Soviet Union's best path to manage the process. Both the Soviet space program and its intercontinental ballistic missile programs were put on hiatus by Gorbachev, although political feints and strategic pronouncements accompanied the various nuclear arms limitation summits between Reagan and Gorbachev during 1985-1988. Gorbachev knew that the Soviet Union could not afford the programs, nor could it afford to continue to conduct the proxy wars which had defined the Cold War.

AUTHOR'S NOTE

My father, Dr. Wayne Barnes, was a man of reserved judgment and easy friendships and alliances, and he possessed a spirit of forging ahead. Consciously or not, there's a lot of him - and what he might have been had circumstances tilted a bit differently - in the character John Gabriel. Thank you, Dad. Thank you Mom (Joyce Needham Barnes) for somehow maintaining creativity in the mix while raising seven unruly gangsters. That creativity is the foundation upon which this novel depends. Thank you Nathalie Chandler for enthusiastically approving my blueprint on a flight from New Orleans to Los Angeles and for putting up with me while I did this. (And for encouraging me to delete over a hundred footnotes). Thank you to Tracey, Jeffrey, Maggie and Kelly for your support and observations.

There are many others - you know who you are. A character in the film *Bladerunner* said, "There's some of me in you." I say, "There's some of you in this novel." Where do your pieces appear? I look forward to glasses of wine attempting to unpack that with each of you.

Thank you to the reader for indulging the book's rabbit holing into the world of wine as an improbable lattice undergirding the story. And thanks to the inspiration provided by those who shoehorned themselves into nosecones and cockpits aimed at the clouds and the moon. And thank you to Ronald Reagan for the advice he gave me in the Rose Garden back in 1981.

Some have asked me, "How did you do it?" as in, how did I start and finish a novel despite no formal training. Truth is, I did everything wrong, and my path is a model for how not to write a novel. Nonetheless, here it is, and I'm stoked. Now, write yours. I'll read it.

-MB